featured in
fIREBIRDS RISING

firebird
where fantasy takes flight™
where science fiction soars™

firebirds rising

an
anthology
of
original
science
fiction
and
fantasy

edited by Sharyn November

FIREBIRD

AN IMPRINT OF PENGUIN GROUP (USA) INC.

FIREBIRD
Published by the Penguin Group
Penguin Group (USA) Inc., 345 Hudson Street, New York, New York 10014, U.S.A.
Penguin Group (Canada), 90 Eglinton Avenue East, Suite 700,
Toronto, Ontario, Canada M4P 2Y3 (a division of Pearson Penguin Canada Inc.)
Penguin Books Ltd, 80 Strand, London WC2R 0RL, England
Penguin Ireland, 25 St Stephen's Green, Dublin 2, Ireland
(a division of Penguin Books Ltd)
Penguin Group (Australia), 250 Camberwell Road, Camberwell, Victoria 3124, Australia
(a division of Pearson Australia Group Pty Ltd)
Penguin Books India Pvt Ltd, 11 Community Centre,
Panchsheel Park, New Delhi - 110 017, India
Penguin Group (NZ), 67 Apollo Drive, Rosedale, North Shore 0745, Auckland, New Zealand
(a division of Pearson New Zealand Ltd.)
Penguin Books (South Africa) (Pty) Ltd, 24 Sturdee Avenue,
Rosebank, Johannesburg 2196, South Africa

Registered Offices: Penguin Books Ltd, 80 Strand, London WC2R ORL, England

First published in hardcover by Firebird,
an imprint of Penguin Group (USA) Inc., 2006
Published in paperback by Firebird, an imprint of Penguin Group (USA) Inc., 2008

1 3 5 7 9 10 8 6 4 2

Introduction copyright © Sharyn November, 2006
"Blood Roses" copyright © Francesca Lia Block, 2006
"What Used to Be Good Still Is" copyright © Emma Bull, 2006
"Hives" copyright © Kara Dalkey, 2006
"Cousins" copyright © Pamela Dean Dyer-Bennet, 2006
"Little (Grrl) Lost" copyright © Charles de Lint, 2006
"Quill" copyright © Carol Emshwiller, 2006
"Perception" copyright © Alan Dean Foster, 2006
"The Real Thing" copyright © Alison Goodman, 2006
"Unwrapping" copyright © Nina Kiriki Hoffman, 2006
"I'll Give You My Word" copyright © Diana Wynne Jones, 2006
"In the House of the Seven Librarians" copyright © Ellen Klages, 2006
"The House on the Planet" copyright © Tanith Lee, 2006
"The Wizards of Perfil" copyright © Kelly Link, 2006
"Jack O'Lantern" copyright © Patricia A. McKillip, 2006
"Huntress" copyright © Tamora Pierce, 2006
"Wintermoon Wish" copyright © Sharon Shinn, 2006

CIP DATA IS AVAILABLE.

ISBN 978-0-14-240936-7

Printed in the United States of America

† 130675

To you, the reader

contents

fIReBIRDS RISING

Introduction

Welcome to *Firebirds Rising*, also known as "the second Firebird anthology." I tend to skip introductions, myself—they are usually too pedantic or give too much away—so this one will be brief, and I will not say anything about the stories themselves. No spoilers!

But every book has a backstory.

The *Firebirds* anthology was an experiment: *Can I do a representative anthology for this imprint? Is there an audience out there?* There was. The success of the first book meant that I was able to do a second one, and for that, I thank you. Firebird, more than most imprints, is driven by its readers. If you're interested in something, I'll do my best to find out more about it; if there's an author you think I should check out, I do. I got a lot of e-mail about *Firebirds*, and I'm still getting it.

One of the things people pointed out was the first book's lack of science fiction. It wasn't for want of trying; the sf authors I queried didn't have stories for me. But I didn't have as many to ask then as I do now—the pool of available writers has grown with the Firebird list itself. Close to one-third of *Firebirds Rising* is sf. I'd love to shoot for 50 percent next time around.

Before I edited *Firebirds*, I wondered how one put together an anthology. Now I know. You start by just asking. I contacted all of the writers I'd published in Firebird and on the Viking list (where the original science fiction and fantasy I edit initially appears, in hardcover), as well as other people I *wanted* to publish.

I was shocked; everyone said yes. And the stories started coming in.

Some were practically perfect just as they were; others needed some editing. Still others weren't right for the collection, which killed me; I hate turning things down when they're good, but they didn't fit. I got so many stories for *Firebirds Rising* that a third collection is in the works.

Once all of the stories were in and edited, and I had bios and notes from the authors, I needed to sequence the book. It reminded me of doing set lists, when I was in a band; what do you start with? what goes in the middle? what should be last? It is not easy, and every editor has a different method. I never expect anyone to read an anthology from beginning to end in one shot—I know I don't!—but I want it to be possible.

I can't wait to hear what you think of *Firebirds Rising*. My e-mail is **firebird@us.penguingroup.com**, and I really do read everything everyone sends.

Sharyn November
August 2005

HUNTRESS

My dad left for good when I was ten. My mom kicked him out. "Fine!" he yelled. "I've had it with you, your family, and all that screwy New Age goddess crap! I should have left years ago! Now watch—you'll turn my own daughter against me!" He grabbed his bag and walked out. He didn't notice I was standing right there.

I should have said something. Instead I stared at my whatever-many-great-grandmother's portrait. It hung in front of where my dad had been standing. There was Whatevergrandma in Victorian clothes, laced in tight, with that crescent moon tiara on her head. He was so clueless he didn't even see Mom's family was into the goddess stuff back then, before anyone ever said "New Age" with capital letters. But that was my dad.

After the divorce, he found a girlfriend. They got married and had a kid. Kevin was sweet, but I stopped visiting. They were always joking, asking if Mom and my aunts had sacrificed any cats lately, or did I brew up some potion to get a boyfriend. I told Dad it wasn't funny, and then that he was boring my socks off. Finally I just told him I couldn't come to visit because I had practice. He bought it. Clueless, like I said.

But when it came to Mom's family portraits, and her religion, he wasn't the only one who thought it was just too weird. By the time I was in sixth grade, the friends I brought home were noticing the crescent tiaras and full moon pendants. They'd notice, and they'd ask, and I'd try to explain. I'd make them nervous. Then the jokes and whispers began. In seventh grade, the witch stuff blended in with whispers that I was too weird, even stuck-up, maybe a slut. I didn't even know where that had come from, but sixth grade had taught me I couldn't fight any of it. I acted like I couldn't hear. I would read for lunch and recess, by myself in a corner of some room. I kept my head down. I didn't even try to make friends. I didn't see the point. Sooner or later I would have to take them home. There they'd see the portraits, and the jewelry. They'd ask their questions. Back to square one.

The only good thing about school was track. I'd found out I was good at it in grade school. With a summer of practice and middle-school coaches, no one on our team could catch me by the time the seventh-grade spring meets rolled around. I came in second in the district in all my events but one, and that one I won. Winning was like a taste in my mouth. Everyone I raced against was a possible source of whispers, but I couldn't hear them if they ran behind me. They'd have to catch me to make their words hurt.

In eighth grade I won all of my middle-school events at the All-District meet. A bunch of the high-school coaches wanted me to come to their schools, but Mom had other plans. At the last meet of the year, she introduced me to the head coach from Christopher Academy. Christopher was offering a full scholarship, if I wanted it.

Wanted it? Christopher was one of the top private schools in the city, with one of the top track teams in the country. If I did well there, I could write my college track ticket. Better: nobody in my school could afford it. Nobody. And nobody else was getting a scholarship. My teammates didn't talk to me, but I heard everything. They would have told the world if they had gotten into the Christopher Academy. It was out of their reach. Christopher kids were like Beverly Hills kids on television, clean and expensive gods and goddesses. Nobody at my school would dare to talk to them. There wouldn't be any whispers in those expensive hallways.

When she saw I wanted this school and this chance, Mom went a little nuts. Over the summer, we moved from the old family apartment in the Village—and wasn't my Aunt Cynthia happy to take it when we left—to a squinched-up little place on the Upper East Side. Mom took a second job, tending bar at night, to cover the new expenses. Our apartment was near the school and near Central Park, where the Christopher runners trained. I could practice with the team and not have to worry about taking the subway home after dark, Mom said, putting her altar up in a corner of her tiny bedroom. I felt guilty. Mom and her sisters were true believers in the family religion. She wasn't happy with just a medallion, not even a proper hunt-goddess figure, instead of the shrine in our old place, but this was only for four years, I told myself. Maybe the apartment wasn't so much, but I could have friends, and bring them over, and only have to explain horseshoes over the doorways.

Anyway, I wasn't a believer in the family goddess after middle school. If their goddess was so wonderful, why didn't she fix my life? She protected maidens, right? Wasn't I a maiden? My dad was right about that much—the worship was screwy.

After all that, ninth grade still wasn't exactly a popularity explosion. It was made clear to me that while I had a track scholarship, ninth graders did not show up the upperclassmen. They trained and they waited for their turn, their chance. They ran with the team. If I heard it once during those first weeks, I heard it a dozen times: I belonged to the Christopher *team*, the Christopher tradition, the Christopher way of doing things. I warmed a bench and kept my mouth shut.

And there was another problem. Things had changed. I had changed. It wasn't easy for me to make friends since I'd stopped trying years ago. I still waited for whispers to begin, though months passed without them. It was like I thought the gossip was a weed that would sprout when my back was turned.

I did make two ninth-grade friends from the track team. We had lunch together, walked home together, sat together on the way to meets. We ran when Coach told us to. We cheered the upperclassmen and held down a leg on the relay team. We raced other ninth graders from other private schools, and we envied the older runners. The seniors weren't that interesting. Their eyes were locked on the Ivy Leagues.

They didn't draw our attention the way a certain junior did.

Felix soaked up light in the halls and gave it off again, from his bronze-and-gold gelled hair to his tanned calves. He was so right, so perfect, that no one ever gave him a hard time for the long, single braid he wore just behind one ear. People gave him tokens to wear in it—beads, ribbons, chains—but he didn't take everything. Just because he wore someone's token one day didn't mean he wouldn't give it back to them the next. He wrote his own rules for the school, too. The staff let him do it most of the time, maybe because the auditorium had his last name over the doorway. It was listed five times on the brass plaque that announced the past headmasters of the school. Felix was what Christopher Academy was about, and his crowd was Christopher Academy, just like track was Christopher Academy.

He ran, but he didn't care about it. He'd slide out of boys' warm-up laps to come over and flirt with his sophomore and junior girls, or his "lionesses," he called them. The first time I heard him say it, in April of my ninth-grade year, he called it to our coach as we circled the baseball diamond in our section of the park, our feet thudding on wet dirt.

"What do you think of my lionesses, Coach?" he called, keeping pace with his girlfriends in the middle of the pack. "Let's take them to the Serengeti, get some blood on them, show them how to hunt." He fiddled with a strip of camouflage cloth that was wound into his braid, running a finger over a dark spot on it.

"Ewww, Felix," cried Han, a Chinese girl who'd been lip-locked with him before practice. "Blood? No, thanks!"

"Can't break oaths sworn in blood, sweetness," he told her, falling back as we ran by. "Isn't that right, Corey?" he asked, slapping me on the arm.

He knew who I was. He called me by my last name, like I was any other member of the team, any other rich Christopher kid.

I forgot to be careful. I forgot that I was new, that I had to be one of the team and earn my place. Trying to outrun the blush that burned my cheeks, I sped up. I cut through his precious lionesses as they jeered at him, telling him he scared me. I stretched my legs until I caught up to the senior girls. They glanced back, saw me and glared. "Back of the pack, *freshman*," one of them grumbled.

So I stopped being sensible. It was only practice. "Afraid you'll have to work for it?" I asked, and picked up my pace. They weren't really trying: it was a warm-up. My cheeks burning now because they thought they could get first place handed to them, I trailed the seniors, looking for a way through their bunched-up group. When they closed in tighter, I powered around them in the turn. By the time it dawned on them that they ought to show me who was boss, they couldn't catch me.

Stupid, I told myself, slowing after I thudded past the finish, my temper burned off. Stupid when you want friends, stupid when you don't want to stand out. Stupid when you're "with the team."

Across the field the boys were hooting at the runners. I turned around to see the lionesses, juniors and sophomores together, cut through and around the red-faced seniors. One of them, redheaded Reed, looked back at the seniors and yelled, "You snooze, you lose."

Coach glared at me, then walked toward the seniors, clapping her hands. "You thought it was going to be easy, these final meets of the year?" she yelled to the seniors as the lionesses caught up with me. "You'd catch a break because it's your last year in the high-school leagues? Nobody cares! Younger girls are waiting to make their names, and they'll kick your asses. Two more laps before you quit for the day!"

"Showin' them, Corey." Reed tugged my braid.

"You rock," another one said quietly.

The lionesses collected me after practice. I looked at my two ninth-grade friends, but they shook their heads and grinned. They wanted me to go so I could tell them what it was like the next morning.

The way the lionesses acted it was no big deal, drinks and french fries at a diner on Madison Avenue, a sour-faced waitress watching as six of us jammed into a corner booth.

"Why don't you split up?" she wanted to know. "Make it easier on everybody?"

The older girls fell silent, staring at her. The air went funny. The waitress looked at them, then threw down the menus and left. The minute her back was turned, they began to laugh and nudge one another. "Shut *her* up," Reed said.

"Like that dealer," another muttered.

"Only he *ran,*" Beauvais, a platinum blonde, whispered. Reed elbowed Beauvais hard. She elbowed back but didn't say anything more as the waitress—a different waitress—came for our order.

I don't even remember if I talked very much, but I was there, with the kids everyone looked at. And the guys showed up, even Felix. I learned then that the guys were lions, to match the lionesses. Felix called them "my Pride," and said casually, "You should see them hunt."

Half of me wanted to stay, but half knew I was supposed to be home fifteen minutes ago. I had to run to be there when Aunt Lucy, who watched me while Mom worked, put dinner on the table. I expected a reaming, but my aunt was so happy I'd been with kids my age she didn't even yell. I pretended I didn't see her light a moon candle in thanks while I cleared the table. I guess I wasn't the only one who'd thought I was going to be a hermit all through high school.

After supper, we went for a walk. We talked with the neighbors for a while outside the building. I was playing with the baby of the couple downstairs, so I don't know how it started, but I heard the old guy who lived across the street say, ". . . just a dealer, so excuse me if I don't cry."

"Was it an overdose?" asked the baby's mom.

The old guy shook his head. "The cops say people were chasing him last night after dark, and he grabbed his chest and fell into the lake near the Ramble. Heart attack. A drug dealer, having a heart attack."

"Good riddance," said the baby's father. "But how could anybody see to chase him?"

"It was a full moon," Aunt Lucy and I said at the same time. She smiled at me and said, "Jinx," because we had echoed each other. She looked at the other grown-ups. "Plenty of light for a chase."

I shivered. The baby's mom saw and collected her from

me. "It's getting cold," she said. I didn't argue, though I don't think I had shivered because I was cold.

When I got to school in the morning, my life had definitely improved. Suddenly my two friends and I had more company at lunch. They liked that. I did, too.

I didn't exactly like it when, at the next meet, Coach pulled me out to run with the juniors and seniors. "You started this, you finish it, Corey," she muttered as she changed my place in the lineup. So I ran the way I did alone, and made the two best runners sweat to beat me. The Pride thought it was cool. They cheered for me at meets. At the All-District competitions, when I had the hundred-meter and the three-hundred-meter events, Felix gave me an ornament from his braid to wear, a little golden sun. I came in second in the hundred, first in the three hundred. He wouldn't take his sun back. He kissed me and told me to wear it instead.

I told myself he kissed all the girls. Then I went out and got a top-of-the-ear piercing done just for that earring. Once it was there, I looked at myself in the mirror and let myself dream about him.

The night after the last practice, I was on my way home when I saw one of the Neighborhood Watch people taking down the sketch of a rapist who had been working the Upper East Side. This one, with his spiky eyebrow piercing, had given me the shivers for weeks. "What happened?" I asked her. I was going home to an empty apartment—Aunt Lucy had finally convinced Mom a girl who was almost sixteen didn't need a babysitter—so I was being lazy about getting there. "They caught him?"

"They caught him," the woman said with a grim smile,

like she had been there. "The cops got an anonymous tip. He was at the bottom of Bethesda Terrace with a broken leg and a broken arm." I winced. That was a long, hard marble stair around the big fountain in Central Park. She told me, "Bastard said he was out for a run and he tripped. They found his rape kit under him, complete with souvenirs. He said a gang chased him. Good for them, that's what I say." She waved the flyers she'd already collected at me. "One down, plenty more to go."

I went on home, shaking my head. Whoever heard of a gang that chased somebody until they fell, then ran away? And who tipped off the cops? How did they know who he was?

I told the Pride about the rapist at lunch the next day.

"Cool gang," said Felix, laughing. He had a new addition to his braid that day, a spiky bar that could have been for an eyebrow piercing. "It captures criminals. A superhero gang. Maybe I can join. Do they wear cool jackets?"

We all cracked up. Maybe they called themselves a Pride, but I thought of bandannas and leather jackets and box cutters and low-rider cars when I thought "gang." These were trust fund babies. They were a world away from the ugly street and the gangs in the projects like the ones I knew. They were strong young animals dressed in light and fresh air, not dirt and blood.

"Hey, maybe it was us. We hang in the park when school's out," black-haired Jeffries said, tossing a rolled-up napkin from hand to hand. "Sure, it coulda been us. Except I'd probably just give a rapist my dad's card. He's always telling me even slime deserves a defense, right?"

Beauvais shoved him. "Like your dad would defend a *rapist*."

"One with money," Han said with a laugh. She sounded as Chinese as I did.

I smelled mint as Felix leaned back and whispered in my ear, "Sometimes we hang out after dark."

I reached down for my backpack, hiding my chest so he wouldn't see his effect on me. "Isn't it dangerous?" When I sat up, I cradled my pack, just in case he looked at my too-perky tits.

"We go as a group," Jeffries said. "Our gang, remember?"

"Have to be safe," Reed told us, sprawled over her section of the table. "Parental units throw a fit if they find out you're out in the scary old park."

Felix ran a hand down my arm. Of course the bell rang and monitors came out to move us along to class. Felix grabbed my wrist and tugged me down till his lips brushed the little sun in the top of my ear. "The next full moon, come out with us," he whispered. "We meet at the East Ninety-seventh Street entrance and go for a run to the Loch, just the Pride. You want to really be one of us, be one of my lionesses, right? You'd maybe even replace Reed one day as queen of the hunt. So come. Not a word to anybody, Corey. Pride business. Nine o'clock, the night of the full moon."

I had laughed at the Pride as a gang. But as a way to erase the misery of the last few years? It was pure gold. The presidents of the new senior and junior classes for next year belonged to the Pride, as well as the captains of both track teams and both soccer teams. Okay, so Felix seemed to be the boyfriend of almost all the girls off and on. The guys didn't seem to mind. Rich kids were different. A little of Felix was better than none, maybe. Or maybe he'd settle for only me.

I wouldn't be alone anymore. I wouldn't be weird, or strange. I'd belong, not as a happy outsider, like Mom and her family, but as a happy insider, smooth and tan and laughing, like my dad and his new family. As choices went, this one was easy.

So I was there, the night of the full moon, dressed to run, but dressed for Felix, too, in a black tank top and running shorts that hugged what I had. I thought about leaving my crescent pendant at home, but left it on. How many people knew what it was anymore? A lot of girls wore them as jewelry without knowing they had a religious meaning, or caring if they knew. I added a snake earring and a couple of gem studs, fixed a gold chain in my braid, and I was ready to go. No bracelets, no ankle bracelets, not when I ran. I carried my phone, my water, a towel, and other things I hoped I might need in my backpack.

Felix and some of the other guys of the Pride looked me over and made happy noises. Felix backed a couple of them off with slaps on the chest that could have been serious. The lionesses wore shorts like me, or cropped cargo pants, short blouses, running shoes. The guys wore shorts and T-shirts, summer wear. When Reed finally showed, wearing cargos, we set out across the park, a group of about seven girls and eight guys. Other people were out; it was still early enough and the moon was starting to rise. We passed dog walkers and other runners, bicyclists, skateboarders, Rollerbladers, men sitting alone on benches with paper bags beside them, men seated alone on benches waiting, arms stretched out on the backs of the benches, legs spread wide, a warning in flesh not to come too close. The girls of the group moved inside, the guys outside, though no one seemed nervous or even like they paid attention. I wondered what Mom was doing now.

There were peepers chirping all around us from the trees that circled the meadows. We moved out onto the grass and toward the rocks that led to the oldest part of Central Park, where trees from the old island had been left to grow beside Olmstead's carefully chosen plantings. I could hear an owl somewhere close by. There were bugs everywhere, big ones, some of them. A moth fluttered past. A rippling shadow darted after it and surrounded it. The bat moved on, but not the moth. Central Park, that seemed so people-friendly when we did our practices there during the day, was showing its real face now. I touched my snake earring, thinking about the hidden world, the one my family recognized.

We moved into a smaller meadow near the rocks and trees. "Our hunting ground," Felix said, looping an arm around my neck. "One of them, anyway. This one was our first ground. This is where we became a Pride. A person could get lost back in those trees."

"A person could get found," said one of the guys. The boys laughed.

The girls didn't. They put their stuff in a heap and began to stretch, getting ready to run. "Put your gear down," Felix said. "We'll keep an eye on it. Used to be around here we couldn't do that, but things have changed late—"

"You." A big guy, ragged and swaying, lurched over to us.

"You stinking kids. You play games with my friend and leave him in the street like *garbage*—"

Felix let me go and faced the homeless guy, fiddling with his long braid and its ornaments. "Which one was he?" Felix asked, sounding bored. "I guess you're talking about one of our hunts, loser."

"You made him run onto Fifth Avenue," the man accused. His eyes glittered in the moonlight as he watched the Pride fan out around him. Everywhere I saw shadowy figures moving, but none came to help or stop whatever was happening. This was a harder end of the park, closer to Spanish Harlem. I would never have come here alone.

"That one?" asked Jeffries with a yawn. "He wagged his dick at Han."

"My feelings were hurt," Han said with a pout. "It wasn't even a *good* dick."

"You chased him and got him killed," the big guy snarled. "I'm gonna fuck you up." He had knives, one in either hand. "Little rich bastards think you can run people to death."

My head spun as Felix put his arm around my neck again. "Okay, Corey, here's how it works," he explained, keeping his eyes on the big guy. "The lionesses have their claws. Right, girls?"

They held up their hands. They had slim knives I had never seen before, tucked between their fingers so a couple of blades jutted out of each fist, like claws. They were busily tying the blades to their palms with leather thongs so they wouldn't fall from their hands.

"We lions keep him from leaving the grass. The lionesses

drive him to you. You have to mark his face without him killing you. Then you girls drive him into the rocks"—Felix pointed—"and the lions chase him down and finish him. You get
the trophy to mark your initiation." Felix smiled down at me.
"Here. Your first claw." He handed me a long, slender knife.
"The trick is to run him till he's too exhausted to see straight.
One of these scumbags, it's not hard. They don't have any
lungs left because they're eaten up by crack, and their muscles
suck because they're too lazy to work. Don't worry about
cops. We have watchers, and they don't investigate this kind
of thing very hard. They have a saying for it." He looked at the
homeless man. "No Humans Involved."

My mouth felt stuffed with cotton. I wondered if I'd been
drugged, except I'd been drinking from my own water bottle
all the way here. "That's not funny."

"Sure it is," Felix told me. "One strong, healthy runner
against a degenerate bum. It's hilarious."

"You killed his friend?" I asked. I could hear my voice
shake.

"No," Felix said patiently. "The stupid mope ran out in
traffic and got killed. Another useless mouth who isn't getting
state aid. Corey, you're either a lion or a mouse."

My brain clattered into gear. "The drug dealer that got
chased. The rapist that got chased."

"Scum. Scum," Felix said patiently. His eyes sparkled oddly
in the growing moonlight. "Girls, get this hump moving."

The lionesses surged forward, running out to circle around
the homeless man. They looked small and slight against his
shadowy bulk, but they surrounded him. He flailed with his

knives. One girl darted in, then another. The man bellowed.

"No!" I cried, and dropped my knife. "This isn't an initiation. It's murder." I looked at him, wanting him to be gold again, not this white marble boy with eyes like ice. "Felix, are you crazy? I swear I won't tell, but I can't do this."

He made a cutting motion. The lionesses fell back, except for Reed. She pulled something from a pocket in her cargo pants and showed it to the homeless man. He put up his hands, letting his own knives drop. She had a gun. So that was how they made sure things always went their way. She motioned with it. The homeless guy ran, stumbling. He fell once and lurched to his feet.

"Don't hope he'll bring the cops, Corey," Felix said. "His kind knows better. And since you ruined our hunt with him, you'll take his place. Which is fine with us."

I stared at him.

"See, the cops will listen to you," Felix explained. "And frankly, most of us would rather have you for prey."

"You don't belong," Han said. "Not at the Academy. You don't understand how to wait your turn, making us eat your shit at the meets this spring. Sure, we laughed. We knew you'd be coming out here with us." She smiled and drew her knives gently down my chest. They didn't cut—this time.

My choices were clear. Argue or move, fast. I broke left, out of Felix's hold, away from Han. Three lionesses blocked my escape on that side. I whirled and darted in the opposite direction, jinking around Reed, then Jeffries, feeling my knees groan as my shoes bit into turf. I dashed for the rocks, but the lionesses swept out and around me, long-limbed and beautiful, moonlight gleaming on their muscled arms and legs. I'd lost surprise, and I knew all of them were good enough to give me a good run. I set out for the longer meadow to see if I could outlast them.

Bad luck: two of the lions joined them. I couldn't outrun or outlast lions. I kept running, looking for a way out. All I found was an audience. People had come to line the meadow's edge, homeless people, kids our age and older in gang colors—real gang colors. Hard-faced women and men, and men on their own, smoking, drinking, watching. There for a show. They knew. They knew this went on, and they came to see.

Still, I had to run. I searched for an opening not covered by a watcher or a member of the Pride. I don't remember how the first lioness crept up on me, but I felt that sharp sting on my back. I stumbled, swerved, clapped my hand behind me, and brought it up before my face. It glittered with blood. I spun and fell, tripping a lioness whose dad was president of some investment bank. She had been trying to be the second to cut me. I scrambled to my feet and bolted forward again, weaving between two more of the lionesses. Now the fear was filling my legs, turning my knees to jelly.

The next to rake my arm was Reed, who I liked. I got out of her reach and stayed away to ask, "Why are you doing this?"

Her eyes were wide and dark and hot. Her teeth shone in a moonlight grin. "Because I can," she said, and faked left, trying to drag my attention from Beauvais. I turned and dashed, tripped on a wrinkle in the ground, hit and rolled to my feet, flailing with my arms and legs for balance. I felt a blade catch in my shoe. It almost yanked me off my feet.

"Because you don't stay the best without *practice.*" Someone scored a long shallow cut across my head and ear and forehead, coming out of my blind spot.

I bolted and came up against one of the huge boulders that marked the edge of the broken ground leading up into the trees. I scrabbled and crawled onto it, panting, as the Pride moved in, forming a half circle around the base of the stone. Felix was there, toying with his braid. The lionesses stood with him, panting, some of them leaning on their knees. They were tired. I'd shown them some moves.

But my muscles were burning. I felt a bad shiver in my calves and hamstrings, a sign I was overworked. I ripped off my tank top, not caring if every creep in the park saw me in my sports bra. I tore the cloth into strips with hands that quaked. That shallow cut on the side of my head was the worst, dripping blood into the corner of my eye. I needed to get that covered up if I had to run again.

"Too bad you blew it, Corey," Felix said, his voice almost like sex. "Nobody's ever given the lionesses a run like this. The prey is usually blood sushi by now." He was getting off on this, maybe like he'd been getting off on the whole game of luring me in.

With my head and my arm bandaged, I grabbed my crescent pendant with one hand, squeezing it so hard the pointed ends bit into my palm, letting the pain clear my head. I wouldn't answer. I needed my breath for running. Screaming was useless. Screaming in Central Park at night was so useless. Here, away from the park's roads, the only way I'd get lucky would be if horse cops or undercover cops were somewhere near, and I had a feeling that ring of creeps would warn Felix about them. They wouldn't want anyone to spoil the fun.

There was leaf and earth litter between my boulder and the one behind it. I carefully felt around at my side for what rocks or glass pieces might be there. I'd need them for weapons.

"Now, you can come down here and race the lionesses some more," Felix said. He threw a bottle of water up to me. "Or we can play the next level."

"Shit," I heard one panting lioness say.

"Pick door number two, Corey," another of them advised, her voice hoarse.

I stared at him, then at the bottle. For a minute a black haze fizzed over my vision. My life, my *blood,* was a *game*? I reached for the bottle, ready to throw it straight back at his head and say "Fuck you"—but there was the gun. Reed had a gun.

I should drink the water. I'd lost so much fluid. But that was a bad idea, too. I wouldn't put it past Felix to drug the water to slow me down. He couldn't gamble on the cops being somewhere else all night. He'd want to end this.

So I threw it at him after all. He dodged, but I struck Han in the shoulder. She swore at me. Felix only shook his head. "A waste. I didn't think you were a hothead, Corey."

I ignored him. I'd exhausted the mess of leaves beside me. All I had to show for it was a handful of small stones. It wasn't good enough. I blinked tears away so they wouldn't see me wipe them off.

"Here's the deal. You come down here, or you can go up there." He pointed past me, into the rocks and trees of the wilder end of the park. "The lions will take over the hunt." They were already stepping back from the girls. Moonlight slid along the knives in their hands. "Hey, you might even find your way out up there. Or you might find a friend. Someone who's not with the Pride. Of course, they play kinda rough up here." He grinned as he unsheathed his knife. "And if the lions take you, we'll be wanting a little something extra for our trouble. Before we collect our trophy."

My stomach turned. They would rape me, he meant. "I'll get out, and you will be so dead," I croaked.

"When they find the drugs in your backpack? And Reed's family says we were at their place tonight? Our word against yours, Corey. Those very disturbing things you told my lionesses during all those after-practice get-togethers . . ." He shook his head. "Sad. You scholarship kids can be so troubled. So out of your element."

And I had wanted to be one of them? "At least if I don't get out of this I'll die clean," I mumbled to myself.

I looked at the meadow, and at the creeps. I looked at the lionesses. They were drinking water and adjusting their blades. I'd tried to break free out there. I wasn't sure I had the speed to do it now. The thought of letting any of that "audience" get their hands on me made my skin crawl. Turning my head, I looked back and up at the towering trees. Mom's family called these old parts of the park "godwoods." They said the old gods of the land still lived here.

Why was I thinking of their crap now? Look at me, trapped! Look at what their gods had done for me! Even the goddess that was supposed to look after me had done nothing. There she rode in the sky, or so they'd always told me, just a flat white disk. I could count on nothing from her except scratches from the stupid pendant I wore! I began to cry in silent anger. Furious, I shook my blood-streaked fists at the moon.

That's when I saw the broken bottle at the edge of the litter on my boulder. I sat casually, dangling my legs over, hiding my side as I grabbed its long neck. It was warm in my hand. Finally, a weapon I could use to do some damage before the Pride cut me down. "Do I get a head start?" I demanded, wiping my eyes with my free arm. "You guys are fresh. I want it. I get into the trees before you so much as take the trail into the rocks."

Felix stared at me. "Damn, I wish you didn't have to die," he said finally. "You're a *real* lioness. A real—"

"What would you know of lionesses, you perfumed and gelded whelp?"

A moment ago, when I had looked at the open meadow, she had not been there. Now she strode across it like a queen, a tall, ice-blonde woman in a white tank top and jogging shorts. Her long limbs were so pale they almost seemed to glow. Her ponytail picked up the moon's gleam as it bounced behind her. Even the woman's eyes were silver, colorless and icy as she looked the Pride over.

I don't know how she got there or what she thought she was doing, but I couldn't have her stepping into my shitstorm. "Lady, get out of here!" I screamed, or tried to. My throat was too dry for more than a croak, and I coughed as I spoke. "Go on, get out of here, call the cops—do you have a cell phone on you? Run—get—"

She held up a long-fingered hand as she came to a halt ten feet from the nearest lioness. It was as if she had laid her hand on my mouth. "Hush, maiden. Your courtesy is well intended, but needless. Under the circumstances, it is gallant. I will not forget." She looked at the Pride, which swung out to encircle her. "You seek a hunt," she said. "I fear you will not give me a hunt that will satisfy, but times are corrupt. Tonight you shall be *my* prey."

Jeffries laughed. "Wait your turn, bitch."

She stooped and picked up a quiver, which she slung over her back, then an unstrung bow—a big one. I knew damned well they hadn't been on that grass before.

"Once, you would have known to whom you spoke, and understood your death was before you," the woman told Jeffries. She took a bowstring from the pocket of her shorts. Everyone watched her. They had to. It wasn't possible to look anywhere else as she gracefully fitted one end of the string to the end of the bow she had placed between her running shoes. With hardly any effort she bent the heavy bow and slipped the string over the free end. "For your foulness, I shall not soil an arrow on you. I have better things for those of mongrel breeding."

Jeffries gasped. He always bragged on his family going back to European nobility in the 1600s and did not like her comment about his breeding. Ignoring him, she put two fingers to her lips and blew a whistle that had everyone clutching their ears. As its echoes faded, I heard sounds in the brush behind me and around me. Dogs trotted down from the rocks and trees. It was then, I think, that a few creeps decided life was better somewhere else. Some of those dogs were really big. They looked like they had rottweiler or wolfhound in them, but it was all part of a mix. Whatever the full mix was, it was dangerous. These were lean, hard-looking animals, cautious as they came out onto open ground.

The closer they got to Her—by now I understood the truth of Her being—the lighter they were on their feet, until they frisked around Her like puppies, tails wagging. They were glad to see Her. They were strays, their coats tangled, some ribs showing, but they weren't stray-cautious once they could smell Her.

"Fuck this." Reed broke the spell. She had her gun out and had pointed it at Her. "I don't know who—"

Up came the bow. I didn't even see the hand that took an arrow from the quiver. I glimpsed the arrow on the string, the ripple of muscle as She drew the string to her ear, and loosed. The arrow went through one of Reed's beautiful eyes. She fell, the gun still in her hand.

The goddess looked at Felix and the Pride. "I said, *you are my prey now.* You thought to hunt one who is under my protection. Now meet my price. I give you the chance you gave to her—the trees. Linger but a moment more, and I shall lose my patience." She looked at the dogs. "My children, see that one?" She pointed to Jeffries. "Tear him to pieces."

That set the Pride free of Her spell, if she had cast one. All of them, including Jeffries, bolted for the trees of the old forest. She let them go. Despite Her words, the dogs waited around Her feet, panting, scratching, rolling on the grass. She walked over, collected Reed's gun, and handed it up to me, along with the bottle of water Reed had carried in a holder at her waist. I took both with shaking hands and would not meet Her eyes. The goddess did a few runner's stretches for her legs, then chirped to the dogs. Running easily, the bow in one hand and an arrow in the other, She headed up into the rocks. The dogs fanned out around Her and caught up, all business now.

It was a long time before I found the nerve to come down and check Reed. She was dead, her skin as cold as marble. The arrow that had killed her had vanished. There wasn't even a mark where it had struck her.

I looked around. All of the creeps were gone. That was probably a good idea. The goddess might decide they were worth hunting next. There was no telling what might offend Her.

For a long time the only sounds I heard were the dogs' baying, and an occasional shriek, up among those old dark trees. I drank Reed's water, then made myself collect my knapsack and everything I had brought. I kept the gun for now, in case anyone decided that I looked like easy prey. I wiped it clean with tissues as I waited. On my way home, I could toss it into a storm drain, into the sewers. At some point there would be cops. I didn't want them finding anything of mine and tracking me to my door like they did on television. I knew they wouldn't believe me, but I didn't want the psychiatrists, or the medication, or the attention. I just wanted to curl up on my bed and think of ways to apologize to my mother's family for past disrespect.

Thinking of them, I checked my cell phone. There were no

calls, though it was long past midnight. I wondered if Mom knew who I was running around with so late. The thought made me giggle. The giggle sounded a little strange, so I made myself quit. Instead I sat down and waited. It never occurred to me to just go home. I hadn't been dismissed.

Sometime before dawn the dogs returned one by one. They were tired. After a look around, and a pee at the base of the rocks, they decided I was harmless. They lay down close to me and got to work licking the dark stains from their fur. Last to appear was their mistress, carrying a small terrier I had missed in all the confusion. His muzzle, too, was dark. He was more interested in trying to kiss Her face than in cleaning himself up.

I scrambled to my feet, though my legs were jelly from all my running. She would not catch *me* showing Her disrespect. She stopped in front of me and nodded.

"As I thought. They were better prey than hunters," She said in that chill and distant voice. "Here is my sign, to safeguard you on your way home." She pressed a blood-smeared thumb to my forehead and drew a crescent there. It felt as cold as her voice. I swayed and tried not to faint, either from Her touch or from the thought that I now had Pride blood on me. "Tell your family they have served Me well. I am pleased." She dropped something on the ground between us.

I looked down at Felix's braid. "I didn't ask for this," I whispered. "Or for them to die."

She smiled. "I answer prayers as I will, maiden. Only remember the others who perished at their hands. They would have taken more, in time." She yawned, and pulled the tie out of her ponytail. Ivory hair cascaded down over her shoulders. "Good night to you, maiden. Or rather, good day."

I watched as she strolled across the meadow, still carrying her terrier. A quick whistle called the rest of her pack. They followed her, panting, tails wagging. Somewhere in the middle of that long expanse of grass, with no trees or rocks to hide them, they all vanished.

TAMORA PIERCE is the *New York Times* best-selling author of twenty-three fantasy novels for teenagers, which are published worldwide in English and in translation in more than six languages. Her most recent book is *Beka Cooper: Terrier*, which is set in her invented city of Tortall. She lives in Syracuse, New York, with her husband, Tim Liebe, a Web designer and administrator, as well as their four cats and two parakeets.

Her Web site is **www.tamora-pierce.com**, and she periodically drops in at **www.sheroescentral.com**, a message board she founded with author Meg Cabot.

AUTHOR'S NOTE

The idea for "Huntress" came to me in 1990, when the case of the Central Park jogger and stories of teenagers "wilding," or playing criminal games in New York City's Central Park, were in the news. They came together in an unpleasant stew with images from the Robert Chambers 1988 assault on Jennifer Levin in that same park, and the story bubbled out of that. Originally my narrator was a bag lady, a schizophrenic former professor of mythology and folklore now known as Crayfish, who simply told what she observed. When Sharyn November asked me for a story for *Firebirds Rising*, I knew I would have to rewrite "Huntress" from the point of view of a teenage outsider. Writing it from a lioness's point of view was too alienating—not everyone wants to swim through the thoughts of a

sociopath. I would have written it, but if my husband refused to read it, I knew everyone else would hate it, too.

The thing is, I still wish I could do that. I still wish I could call the merciless Huntress down to deal with some of the girl-killers we have out there. I bet the number of murders of girls and young women would fall off sharply if word got out that their killers were showing up dead, and the killer was untraceable. I suppose that makes me a bad person. What do you suppose it makes the people who prey on those who can't fight back?

Nina Kiriki Hoffman

Unwrapping

Brenna, her arms around a black garbage bag stuffed with all the ingredients of her mummy costume, followed her best friend Nadia upstairs to Nadia's bedroom.

"Why won't you tell me what you're going to wear to the Halloween dance?" Brenna asked. "I get that you don't want Adam to know, and that's why you wouldn't talk about it at lunch." Adam and Jason had sat with them in the middle-school cafeteria, and not for the first time. It was the first time Jason had spoken directly to Brenna, though. "But we're alone now," she continued. "You can tell me."

Nadia smiled over her shoulder. "You'll see."

"Did you make your costume or buy it?" Brenna asked.

"You'll see."

Most of Nadia's house smelled like steamed broccoli, which Brenna hated. But Nadia's room smelled like incense and cinnamon. It looked like something out of the *Arabian Nights*. The bed was swathed in a rose satin coverlet. A pile of plump pillows in shades of pink and red overlapped one another at the head of the bed. The red carpet was thick; when you walked on it, you felt like you were walking on bubble wrap without the pops, bouncy, never quite touching the ground. The curtains were dark red, and the walls were hung with quilted silk squares in red, gold, and purple scattered with small round mirrors.

Brenna dumped her garbage bag on the floor and sank into one of the puffy, red chairs by the wooden dresser. She'd been coming to Nadia's house for three years now, since they were both eleven, and she was still pleased and delighted every time she saw this room.

Nadia's mom, Emily, was an antiques dealer, so the house was full of interesting furniture, but no other room was the color of Nadia's. Nadia's room didn't belong to the house the same way Nadia didn't seem to belong to her family. Mr. and Mrs. Wood were pleasant and friendly and normal, brown-haired, brown-eyed, not too plump and not too thin. Her older brother, Lewis, also brown-haired and brown-eyed, was the sort of boy you noticed the second or third time you looked at a group of boys.

If Nadia was anywhere in a room, you knew it, not just because of her red hair and amber eyes, but because of her electric spirit. Brenna suspected that Nadia was adopted, but she'd never asked. Sometimes it was nice to let a mystery alone.

Brenna had brown-gold hair and hazel eyes. Whenever she and Nadia shared a bathroom mirror, Brenna felt like Nadia's shadow. It was a role she liked. She got invited everywhere

Nadia did because everyone knew Nadia didn't go anywhere without Brenna, but no one paid attention to Brenna, so she could enjoy herself watching other people. Even before she met Nadia, sitting in the shadows and watching was something Brenna had been good at: her older sister, Amy, was a genius and an artist. Being someone's shadow felt natural to Brenna.

Unlike Amy, Nadia actually listened to Brenna and liked her.

Nadia squatted and opened Brenna's bag, pulled out the rolls of white medical gauze Brenna's mother had brought home from the hospital. "All right, Bren. Take off your clothes."

"Nadia!"

"What, you think mummies wore clothes before they got wrapped? Not hardly. Just an amulet here and there inside the wrappings. I've got a nice green scarab to place over your heart."

"I'm not going to strip."

"I knew you'd say that." Nadia straightened. "So I got out my body stocking. You *will* wear it." She picked up a wad of stretchy beige cloth from the other puffy chair and handed it to Brenna.

Brenna shook it out. It was leotard material that covered the entire body except the hands and head; it had snaps at the back and at the crotch. "Eww," she said, examining the crotch and wondering how to get it to work.

"Right, that part isn't fun, so don't drink anything."

"I'm wearing my underwear and bra."

"Sure, sure."

"I'm going to the bathroom first."

"Good idea."

Brenna took the body stocking into Nadia's bathroom. The dance started in an hour, and it was supposed to last until midnight, maybe longer. Could she really go seven hours without peeing? Why hadn't she thought of that when she came up with her costume?

She stripped, peed, and pulled on the body stocking over her underwear. From the neck down, she looked like a creepy Skipper doll. She came out of the bathroom with her arms straight in front of her, jerk-walking like Frankenstein's monster. "Night of the Living Doll," she said in her spookiest voice.

"Oh yeah? Just you wait. Hold that pose." Nadia grabbed the gauze and started wrapping Brenna. She overlapped each layer neatly and evenly, and fastened the gauze with small gold safety pins every time she got to the end of a roll or a body part. Brenna watched as her arms and then the rest of her was enveloped in a white pattern that looked like wickerwork. Nadia held a palm-sized green scarab against the center of Brenna's chest and wrapped it there, continuing the pattern. Brenna felt its weight. Trust Nadia to make even this beautiful: everything she did came out like art.

How had Brenna found such a great friend? Nadia had sat next to her in the cafeteria on her first day at school. "What's in your lunch?" Nadia had asked, and Brenna had showed Nadia one of the reasons she usually sat alone: she had a whole avocado from the organic market. She sliced it at the table to put on her cheese sandwich. Nadia had never seen an avocado before, or a satsuma mandarin orange. She loved them.

Brenna's first friend-capture method had been food.

Her second was listening, and answering weird questions without flinching. Nadia asked things nobody else did, like "What do you do when no one's looking that would embarrass you the most if anyone saw?" and "What do you think about just before you fall asleep?"

Brenna's third method was to be as honest as she could. Nadia trusted her judgment. No one else in her life ever had. Nadia listened to Brenna talk about TV shows, movies, books, and boys. She went off to check things out, and usually came back and said Brenna was right. They watched TV and movies together, read the same books at the same time, sat on the wall outside school and watched boys together—when boys weren't coming over to hit on Nadia. This led to many discussions, but very few arguments.

Actually, the trusting-Brenna's-judgment thing might have been how *Nadia* caught *Brenna*. Having Nadia listen and agree with her was better than food. At home, everything Big Sister Amy said was gold, and everything Brenna said was ignored. Nadia let Brenna be a shadow when Brenna wanted, but let her step into the light, too.

"Try bending," said Nadia. "I want to make sure you can move."

Brenna bent and touched her toes. "It's fine."

Still, she felt strange, as though she were losing herself under the bandages. She felt more naked than she had expected, even though every inch of her but hands and head was covered. The tight layers of gauze showed her real shape. She couldn't disguise the little bulge of her stomach, or hide her breasts the way she'd been doing since they appeared suddenly last summer. What would Jason think now that he could see what she really looked like?

She'd be in costume. Maybe he wouldn't recognize her. Maybe that was best: she'd just be the mummy and forget she was Brenna. But Jason had told her he'd meet her tonight, that she was supposed to save him a dance. He'd never said anything remotely like that before: she'd always thought he was another guy who just talked to her because she was with Nadia.

Well, wait and see what he thought of the costume, and if he seemed to like it, *then* let him know she was the one inside.

"Ta-da," said Nadia as she pinned the last end of gauze. "You have gloves and a mask, right? You can put them on before we leave. Just let me pin your hair." Nadia led Brenna to the vanity and seated her. Brenna stared at her white-gauze self as Nadia brushed her hair into a ponytail and bobby-pinned it to the top of her head. Nadia could do that and the pins would stay. When Brenna tried it, the pins always slipped out.

"Wow. Thanks, Nadia. I never could have done it so neat. So come on and tell me. What's your costume?"

Nadia smiled. "Close your eyes, Bren."

Brenna closed her eyes. She wanted to peek, but she wouldn't. Her ears sharpened: she listened to rustling, the slide of fabric on fabric, and then other sounds, fainter and harder to identify: ripping? A little slurpy noise? A sizzle, a hiss.

"You can look now," Nadia said.

Brenna opened her eyes.

Nadia's body glowed with ripples of red and orange. Her face looked like shaped glass with flame inside it. Her hair was a fiery halo, and her hands dripped flame that spiraled upward into smoke and vanished.

"Nadia," Brenna whispered.

"Yes? What do you think?"

"Nadia."

"I had this dream about Halloween. I was thinking I could finally be myself."

"Nadia."

"Bren, you're repeating yourself."

"But, Nadia—"

The flaming face leaned near to stare into Brenna's eyes. Or maybe not; since the firething's eyes were plain yellow-white, Brenna couldn't really tell where it was looking. Brenna blinked. Heat poured off the face. Was this really her best friend?

"Nadia?"

"Brenna?"

"Are you really there?"

"More than I've ever been. Too much?" Nadia paced, leaving black footprints on the red carpet. The smell of burning rose on the air. She glanced at the trail she had left. "Oh. I guess so."

Nadia strode to the bed and picked up some flat pink things. She sat on the bed and slid them onto her feet. Afterward, she had normal feet again, narrow and long-toed, the same feet Brenna had seen when they walked barefoot on the beach or dressed for gym together. Brenna held her nose against the scent of singeing silk. Nadia got up and looked at the smoking quilt. "There are some things about this dimension I really hate." She pulled more flattened pink things up over her legs to her belly. The bottom half of her looked normal again. She pulled on pink gloves. "Everything burns so easily."

This dimension, Brenna thought. *Everything burns.* She gulped a large, smoke-tinted breath and held it for a long moment.

Nadia had chosen Brenna for a friend, whatever she was. Something that could burn with a touch.

Something that watched movies with Brenna, let Brenna help her with her homework, watched boys, laughed at Brenna's jokes, grabbed her hand and dragged her along to places Brenna would never have gone by herself, made her talk to people she was afraid would ignore her. How many times had Brenna slept over in Nadia's big puffy bed? How many times had they talked long after they turned out the light? Too many to count. Nadia knew most of Brenna's secret fears and longings. Brenna knew what Nadia had said about her own desires.

Had Nadia ever told her the truth?

Nadia looked eerie, naked from the waist down, her normal-looking hands floating at the ends of flaming red arms, upper torso and her features aglow with fire, her eyes too bright to look into. Brenna crossed her wickerwork white arms over her chest and hugged her mummified self. A touch from Nadia could set her on fire.

"What are you?" Brenna whispered.

"A visitor. A student."

"The Woods—"

"My host family. They're lovely to me. I was lucky to find them."

"Do they know what you are?"

"They know I'm from somewhere else," Nadia said. "They don't know what I really look like, but now you do."

"What you really look like," Brenna whispered.

Nadia's normal-looking hand scratched her fiery nose, came away unburned. Nadia sighed, an exhalation of flame. "It isn't going to work, Bren," she said at last. "I can't be myself here." Tiny flames leaked from the inner corners of her eyes.

"Oh, Nadia. I'm sorry," Brenna said.

Nadia picked up the rest of the flat pink things on the bed. She pulled them on until she had covered herself. The last thing she pulled on was the head, with hair attached. The hair looked dull and brown until she tugged the head down to connect with her neck. Then the hair took on a red glow. She opened her eyes. Amber again, with only a hint of flame behind. She sat slumped on the bed, head hanging.

"Oh, Nadia." Brenna hugged her.

Nadia rubbed her eyes. "Well, I was stupid," she said. "I should have known that wouldn't work. What am I going to wear now?"

She stood, flung open the closet door. "Help me, Bren. I can't decide."

Is this what we do next, now that she's told me she's a creature from another dimension? Pick a costume? *Don't I scream and run away now, or something?* Brenna wondered.

Questions could wait.

Feeling strange and ghostly in her white wrappings, Brenna went into the closet and slid clothes hangers sideways. She loved Nadia's clothes. Sometimes Nadia let Brenna borrow something, but Brenna was too shy to wear the really wild outfits. Brenna pulled out a midnight-blue floor-length evening dress in shiny satin, sprinkled with rhinestones like tiny stars. "What about this one?" She handed it to Nadia and shifted clothes until she found something else she remembered: a fringed silvery shawl, crocheted spiderwebs. "And this. And—could you, uh, just take off your head? Maybe with that part showing, you won't burn anything, and everybody will think it's some kind of costume."

Nadia smiled.

NINA KIRIKI HOFFMAN is the author of a number of acclaimed novels, most recently *Spirits That Walk in Shadow*, which was named a finalist for both the *Locus* and Mythopoeic Awards and was a *Locus* Recommended Reading Selection. She is also known for *A Stir of Bones* (a *Locus* Recommended Reading Selection, a Bram Stoker Award Finalist, and an Endeavour Award Finalist) and its two sequels: *A Red Heart of Memories* (a World Fantasy Award Finalist) and *Past the Size of Dreaming*. Her first book, *The Thread That Binds the Bones*, won the Bram Stoker Award for First Novel. She has also written and sold over two hundred short stories, which have appeared in both anthologies and magazines.

Nina Kiriki Hoffman lives in Eugene, Oregon, with cats, friends, and many creepy toys.

AUTHOR'S NOTE

"Unwrapping" started out as a Halloween story for my Tuesday-night writers' workshop, the Eugene Wordos. We have a practice of writing theme stories for Halloween and Christmas/winter holidays, and then getting together to read them aloud and share holiday treats. I wrote "Unwrapping"on the theme of costumes.

I have a wall of masks in my office where I write, and when I'm stalled, I look at those strangers' faces. I love thinking about the masks we wear, both around holidays and in every-day life. I wonder who's hiding behind your mask. Sometimes I wonder about my own.

Alison Goodman

---

tHe ReaL tHiNɕ

The mind experiment had seemed like a good idea an hour ago. Now I wasn't so sure; Mavkel and I barely had the basics of telepathy covered, let alone this kind of thing.

"Are you prepared, Joss-partner?" Mav sang, the tips of his double-jointed ears quivering with excitement. He was Chorian, a mainly telepathic race, but when he did speak he used his two mouths to harmonise the words.

He flicked back his second eyelids. I stared into the dark, pupilless eyes of my time-jumping partner and nodded. Maybe this time the mind connection wouldn't hurt so much.

"Then execute the experiment," he sang.

A fiery spike stabbed through my temple. I grabbed the edge of the table and held my breath, exhaling as the pain eased into the soft warm weight of Mav in my mind. Concentrating on the fragile connection, I slowly lifted the real-bacon sandwich and took a bite.

"Well?" I said through the mouthful.

THE REAL THING

Salt? Lipids? Smoke? the pale green of his mind-voice said. *Chew more.*

I chewed. His primary mouth grimaced.

"You enjoy this food?" he sang out loud.

I winced as our connection broke and his pale green presence vanished from my mind. It had only been a few months since Mav and I first joined during a *Rastun,* a Chorian mind-weapon, and we weren't too slick in the connecting and disconnecting department. I still couldn't initiate proper contact with him—Mav had to set up the link—but considering everyone kept telling us that humans and Chorians aren't meant to join minds, we were doing okay. It was getting a bit easier each time we tried. According to Mav, my mind-voice was developing into a nice shade of orange, which apparently is about the level of a Chorian toddler.

"A girl needs a bit of real-meat now and again," I said, taking another bite and rolling the rich bacon and mayo juices around my mouth. "So, you could really taste it?"

"Not for long, but taste some, yes," he sang, holding up his two-thumbed hand. I slapped it in victory, my palm stinging as it met his squat, immoveable strength.

"Wait till you try a curry," I said.

"If this can be done with food, then it can be done with other things," he sang excitedly. "I am interested in experiencing your sex."

I stared at him, the sandwich halfway to my mouth. "*What?*"

"Your reproductive act. It involves much sensory input, yes?"

"No way, Mav," I said, shaking my head. "Forget it. It's not going to happen." I dropped the sandwich onto my plate. "You Chorians may like an audience, but I don't. And anyway, a human needs a partner and I don't have one."

I couldn't help sneaking a look at Kyle Sandrall. He'd just bought a couple of coffee cans at one of the machines and was heading towards the large table of cadets at the far end of the busy mess hall. It was the unwritten code of the University of Australia Centre for Neo-Historical Studies that the back table in the mess was reserved for the comp-kids, the genetically engineered students. A few weeks ago, Kyle had asked me to join them, but I'd said no. Not because I didn't want to, but because I knew I wasn't a real comp-kid. My mother had only used one gene donor with minimal engineering. She didn't want to risk too many donors or gene manips in case I developed CGD—Cascading Gene Defect Syndrome, a nasty collapse of pleiotropic genes. So, I wasn't a comp-kid, but I wasn't a real-kid either. And a few months ago I'd discovered I also had a bit of Chorian DNA in my mix, too. I didn't feel like trying to explain all that to Kyle, the poster boy for tailor-made kids. He'd probably only asked me to sit with him because he thought I was a real comp.

I watched him slide the coffees onto the table and sit down, hooking his long legs under the stool. He passed a can to the girl beside him, a blonde with her hair twisted into a flawless pleat and her chest in the tightest red halter top this side of an X-vid. Tarrah something-or-other; she was in sixth year with Kyle. I touched my own dark scraggly ponytail. It needed a cut again. And I could probably do with a few new tops, something a bit more feminine than my usual black T-shirts. I brushed sandwich crumbs off my chest, chancing another look at Kyle.

He was looking at me.

He smiled.

He nodded.

I smiled back . . . then realised my hand was still resting on my boob.

"What is wrong, Joss-partner?" Mav sang. "Why do you redden? Are you ill?"

I snatched my hand away. Terrific. Kyle probably thought I was so hot for him I couldn't control myself in public. Out of the corner of my eye, I saw him stand up.

"I'm okay," I said to Mav. "Want to get out of here?"

"No." Mav flattened the tops of his ears and leaned across the table. "Something is wrong. What is wrong?"

"Nothing," I said, waving him back to his seat.

Kyle was definitely heading towards us. I wiped the corners of my mouth with the back of my hand and pushed my hair out of my eyes.

"Have I got mayo on my face?" I whispered.

"No," Mav whispered back. "Should you?"

Then Kyle was standing beside the table.

"Hey, Joss," he said. "Hey, Mavkel."

Mav bowed, his ears lifting. "Kyle Sandrell, this pair greets you most cordially."

Kyle grinned. "Good to see you, too, Mavkel." He turned to me. "How are you, Joss?"

"Terrific," I said. "Fantastic. Brilliant. You know, really good."

I smiled widely, trying to cover my sudden morph from eighteen-year-old college student into babbling idiot.

"Are you two taking Chenowyth's time dynamics class this semester?" Kyle asked.

I nodded, puzzled. All first years had to take Professor Chenowyth's class—Kyle would know that. He licked his lips. They were great lips, kind of full, but not pouty. I dragged my eyes off them.

"Yeah, it's a tough class," Kyle said. "If you and Mavkel ever need any help, just let me know."

"Thanks," I said.

Mav beamed a double-barrelled smile. "You are very kind, Kyle Sandrell."

There was an awkward silence. Mav looked from me to Kyle, his ears hovering uncertainly.

"Why do you stare at one another?" he sang. "Is this a game?" He started jumping up and down in his chair, attracting stares from nearby tables. "This is a courting ritual, is it not?"

I glared at him. His ears collapsed like windless flags.

"I'm sprung," Kyle said, laughing. He rubbed the back of his head, scruffing up his dark hair. "I really came over to see if you'd like to go out Friday night."

"Friday night?" I echoed. Kyle Sandrell—sixth-year demi-god and all-round nice guy—was asking me out on a date? I suddenly had an image of kissing him, and ducked my head.

"I thought we could grab something to eat," he said. "And

a friend of mine is throwing a party. We could drop in on that, too."

"Sure," I said, trying to sound casual. "Sounds good." Underneath the table, I dug my fingernails into my palms.

"Great." He grinned again. "Can you infra me your screen code?" He held out his wrist, a sleek armscreen wrapped around it.

"Sorry, I don't wear a screen," I said. "My stand against constant surveillance."

He laughed. "Not a prob. You're quartered in P3, aren't you? How about I come round sevenish?"

"Seven's good. You'll have to wait in the security office, though. Just get them to comm me."

Instead of the usual student housing, Mav and I had a suite in P3, the state-of-the-art security building. Mav was the first Chorian to study on Earth and he was getting the red-carpet treatment. As his time-travel study partner, I got to go along for the first-class ride.

"See you then." Kyle gave me one last lingering smile. I watched him walk back to the comp-kid table; his rear view was as fine as his front view. When he sat down next to Tarrah, I saw her say something, an impeccable eyebrow lifted. Was she asking about me? I grinned to myself. Who cared about Tarrah tight-top? Kyle Sandrell had asked me out!

"I have read about this," Mav sang. "This is a date, is it not? A first date. I read that it is very important that you do not 'put out' yet."

"'Put out'? Where did you get that from?"

"It is from a late 1900s text. A magazine for young females.

It says you must wait until you know it is 'the real thing.'"

"Wasn't that an old advertisement for some kind of drink?" I said.

I was sure I'd heard our professor mention it in our Beginnings of Pop Culture class. I was taking it because I wanted to specialise in music history, mainly twentieth-century blues and jazz. I couldn't wait to time-jump back to the mid-1900s and see some of the big gigs of the golden age.

Mav's ears flicked. "No, that is not correct. *Sparkle* says that 'the real thing' is a pairing that is fated."

"*Sparkle?*" I rolled my eyes. "You can't take something called *Sparkle* as an authority on human relationships."

"It is on the recommended reading list," Mav sang, crossing his arms.

I looked over at Kyle. He was stretching, the movement hitching his T-shirt up over a flat stomach and cut abs. I didn't know much about fate, but I wouldn't mind testing out the idea that Kyle was the real thing.

"Still sticking to your own kind, Aaronson?" a slimy voice asked behind me. "Comp freaks?"

I turned around. Chaney Horain-Donleavy was sitting at the table behind me with his usual posse of losers. He jerked his head toward Kyle. "I heard they made that model sterile."

His gang sniggered.

I knew that some of the girls in our course thought Chaney was good-looking. He had a whole Renaissance-archangel thing going on: dark red curly hair, high cheekbones, golden tan. But I knew that inside, he was a total snake. He'd made it clear that if you weren't from one of the big-money hyphen families, you might as well not exist. Unless he felt like tormenting you.

"Don't you ever get tired of being a snorkwit?" I said.

His pale blue eyes were unblinking. "Someone's got to make sure you freaks don't get too up yourselves."

"Up yourselves?" Mav sang uncertainly. "What does this mean?"

"It means, flap-head, that comps are trying to stop us from getting into the time-jumping course," Chaney said. He turned to his friends. "They reckon they're better than us, so they should be the first and only choice."

There was a murmur of disgust.

"What a load of screte," I said. "The Centre has strict comp *and* noncomp quotas. It's law."

"Well, you should know," Chaney said slyly. "Aren't you and your mother major shareholders in the Centre?"

I stared at him. How did he know I'd inherited a controlling interest in the Centre? My donor father had left it to me, and I'd had to choose between sitting on the board and studying. It was a no-brainer; who wanted to worry about budgets when they could travel through time? But I thought the whole situation had been kept hush-hush by the Centre bigwigs.

Chaney glanced back at his friends. "That would explain why she got a place. There's no other reason why she's here."

They all laughed.

"I didn't get in because of that," I said.

"No, of course not," he said mockingly. "Come on, Aaronson. Quit zooming. You may be a comp, but you've been kicked out of nearly every school you've ever been in."

He shook his head. "No, you're here because you've got a rich, famous shareholder mother who donated a little admin building. Just like I'm here because my family name is on the library." So he didn't know the whole story. He picked up a veggie fry from his plate and jabbed it into a puddle of tomato sauce. "In the end, it's always who you know and how much you've got that's more important in this world."

"Only in your twisted mind, Chaney," I said.

He pointed his fry at the comp table. "Their parents scrimped and saved and risked CGD to make their kids prettier and smarter than Joe Average. And what for? Just to give them a shot at getting where we already are—at the top. Our families have done it all without any enhancements. Now, you tell me who's better?" He stuffed the fry in his mouth.

Jorel, Chaney's right-hand lout and jump-partner, leaned forward. "My dad says the comp lobby group is getting really strong. He reckons before you know it, the comps will be trying to take over."

Jorel's dad was in government; obviously not a liberal.

"I've heard there's an extremist comp group on campus," Pino said. As usual, he was trying to outdo Jorel. He nodded towards the comps. "Probably them."

Chaney's gang all turned to look at the table at the far end of the hall.

"You should be more careful," I said. "Someone will have you up on a civ charge."

Chaney snorted. "Not if it's true."

"Yeah, not if it's true," Pino echoed. "What about the graffiti painted on the Time Admin building wall: NOT COMP, NOT

GOOD ENOUGH. Bet that was done by comp extremists."

"Haven't seen it," I said, shrugging, but a little coil of unease tightened in my gut.

"Graffiti?" Mav sang. "Is this an artwork?"

"It's like a protest painted on a wall," I said.

"Maybe we should paint one ourselves," Chaney said. "DELETE THE COMP SCRETE."

His gang laughed, loudly repeating the slogan to one another.

Chaney leaned over to me. "I know you're not a real comp, Joss," he said under the cover of their noise. "One donor, enhancements kept to a minimum. You're almost pure. Why do you want go out with someone like Kyle Sandrell?"

I stiffened. Where was he getting all this info about me?

A sudden sharp pain in my head made me wince, but it was gone in a nanosecond. Mav's mind presence washed over me like warm water.

I am here. His mind voice was dark green, strident.

I shot a greasy look at him. I'd told him over and over again he couldn't just barge into my head whenever he felt like it. Especially since I couldn't barge into his head.

But you are alarmed, his mind presence said. *Of course I am here. Contact seemed easier this time, yes?*

It had been easier, but I was too annoyed to agree.

I turned back to Chaney. "I am comp," I said, keeping my voice low. "I may not have ten donors, but I'm still comp."

Why does Chaney alarm you? Mav rocked up in his chair towards the oblivious Chaney, his ears angled back aggressively.

No! No alarm!

Mav stopped and looked at me, then nodded reluctantly. I felt his mind warmth slip away.

"Are you sure the comps will think you're one of them?" Chaney asked. "For a bunch of freaks, they're getting real picky about who makes the grade." He raised his pale red eyebrows. "You should think carefully about who you want to be associated with, Aaronson."

I gritted my teeth, wanting to slap the smug smile off his real-kid-old-money face. He thought he had it all pinned.

"You're absolutely right," I said, standing up. "Come on, Mav, I don't want to associate with these scretes any more. Let's get out of here."

Mav stood up, his ears straight and tense.

"We do not leave you with any cordiality," he said to Chaney.

I couldn't have said it better myself.

"You've got to stop gate-crashing my head like that," I said, waving my security wristband across the lighted door panel. It flashed to green and the door to our quarters slid open.

Beside me, Mav hummed disconsolately with his ears at half-mast, but I wasn't going to fall for his "poor little alien" act.

"It's kind of like walking in on me when I'm getting dressed, except a lot worse."

"But you were alarmed, Joss-partner. I wished to be of assistance."

"I wasn't alarmed," I said brusquely, stepping into our lounge room. "Chaney doesn't alarm me."

"Chorian pairs are always mind-joined," Mav sang plaintively. "We should always be joined, not this sometimes joined. It is a not a real pairing."

I knew why Mav wanted us to be joined all the time—all Chorians had a constant telepathic link to their birth pair as well as to the rest of their race, and Mav's birth pair, Kelmav, had died in an accident. But something in me balked at trying to maintain a constant link. The last thing I wanted was Mav in my head full-time. I didn't want anyone eavesdropping on that constant murmuring stream of reality, fantasy, dream and emotion that flowed through my head. It was my own private narration of my life. And I had a feeling it was an important part of being human.

I headed for my bedroom, Mav trailing behind me. I had dragged him back to P3 as soon as we'd left the mess hall. He had wanted to stop and look at the graffiti, but I was a woman on a mission: to seek out and discover if I had anything to wear on a date with Kyle Sandrall. Poor Mav didn't have a chance—I practically put him in a headlock and marched him past the Time Admin building.

I threw my bag on the bed and slapped my hand against the v-robe sensor. The two virtual wardrobe doors disappeared with a soft pop. I stared at my sad collection of clothes. Apart from the regulation T-shirts and dress uniform, I had three black T-shirts, two red T-shirts, another pair of black jeans and a black jacket. Great for fast packing, not so great for a first date. I picked up an old black cashmere jumper lying on the wardrobe floor and shook the dust out of it.

"What do you think?" I asked.

Mav took the jumper between his two thumbs and held it up. "It will keep you warm and covered."

"Great. Just what I want on a hot date."

"Then that is settled," Mav sang happily. "I would like to see the graffiti now."

I snatched back the jumper. "No, it's not settled. I can't wear that on Friday. I need something . . . sexy."

Mav's ears flattened at the top. "Sexy? The 2-D images in *Sparkle* indicate that human sexy is achieved with much skin and little cloth."

"That's not really me." I couldn't see myself in one of Tarrah's little red halter tops, or a skintight cling dress. "I need something that is . . . well, at least not totally sexless."

"Lisa," Mav said.

"What?"

"Lisa will help you. I heard Jorel tell Pino that Lisa was sexy."

I frowned, conjuring up a mental picture of our friend Lisa. Long brown hair, savvy grey eyes, nice teeth. Was she sexy? I had never really thought about it. When someone gets shot on your behalf, you never really think of anything but their courage and spirit. A few months ago, she'd helped Mav and me jump back in time to save Mav's life and had got a laser through her shoulder for her trouble. I suppose she always wore makeup, but not much, and her hair was always shiny. Her clothes weren't anything special, although they did kind of skim her body. In all the right places. Damn, Mav was right; Lisa was sexy. And classy.

"Good idea," I told him. "Maybe she'll be able to lend me something."

His ears lifted. "We will visit the graffiti now. If we leave now, we will have six minutes to view it and two minutes to travel to our next class."

Sure enough, by the time we were standing in front of the graffiti on the south wall of the Time Admin building, the clock tower showed we had exactly eight minutes before the start of class. Who needed an armscreen with Mav around?

I stared up at the large slogan. Someone had gone to a lot of trouble; the outline of each letter was sprayed in red and filled in with yellow. The colours of the Genetic Enhancement Lobby Group. The big, beautifully drawn letters boldly declared war: NOT COMP, NOT GOOD ENOUGH. My gut tightened again.

Mav rocked back on his hind claws. "It is very neat," he sang. "And the lettering is aesthetically pleasing. Is this not art?"

"No, it's trouble."

"Why?"

"There's a lot of comps who are wondering why they should apologise for being better."

Mav looked back at the wall. "Comps consider themselves superior to nonenhanced humans?"

"I suppose some do," I said reluctantly.

"Is this not the aim of their genesis. To create superiority?"

"Superior attributes, but not superiority."

"Ah"—Mav nodded—"a semantics problem."

"Sometimes," I said drily, thinking of all the times I had been called a freak or unnatural. "It's just that a lot of humans like to think we're all equal, or that we at least start off equal. Some people think comps have an unfair advantage. Like it's cheating."

"Cheating?" Mav wrinkled his noses. "But if an attribute is created by the fortuitous combination of two unknowns, then it is considered not cheating?"

"Then it's good luck."

Mav's ears flattened. "Luck is acceptable, but design is not?"

"Luck is better because it doesn't need tons of money. Anyone can have luck," I said. "Not everyone can afford to take the chance out of luck."

"I do not understand," Mav sang dolefully.

I turned away from the wall. I wasn't sure I understood either. I just knew that sometimes I felt guilty for being alive.

"Come on," I said, wanting to get away from the graffiti. "We've only got one and half minutes to get to class."

Mav took the bait. "Incorrect, Joss-partner," he shrilled behind me. "We have two minutes, six seconds and four one-hundredths."

"I brought a whole load of stuff," Lisa said, dumping a pile of clothes and shoes on my bed. "Didn't know where you and Kyle were going, so I figured I'd cover all possibilities." She absently adjusted her tank strap over her bandaged shoulder. "You should have commed me sooner. We could have gone shopping."

It was D-Day—Date Day—and Lisa had jumped at the chance to make me over.

I poked at the clothes. "It's not a big deal," I said. Maybe if I said it enough times I'd believe it. "It's only going to be some dinner somewhere and then maybe a party." I pulled a

bright blue slip of silky material out of the stack. "What's this?
A scarf?"

Lisa snatched it out of my hand. "Very funny. It's a top.
Looks great with blue jeans."

"I can still wear jeans?" I'd been imagining microshorts and
cling tops.

"Of course. I don't think you should make any drastic
changes. Just move away from wearing so much black and
smarten things up a bit."

She pulled back her fall of brown hair and deftly twisted it
into a loose bun, tying it into itself. Amazing. All I could ever
do with mine was whack a band around it and hope it held, or
stuff it under a beret.

I pushed the clothes aside and sat on the edge of the bed.
"So, you've been studying here for five years. What's the Kyle
story."

Lisa got down to business. "For the last year or so he's
been a bit of a serial dater," she said. "But before that, he and
Tarrah were a couple right through to fourth year." She made
a wry face. "The golden comp couple. They were probably
whipped up in the same laboratory." She realised what she'd
said. "Screte. I'm sorry, Joss, I didn't mean anything by that."
She touched my arm in apology. "I think I was channelling my
stepfather."

"Not a comp fan, huh?" I said tightly.

"You could say that. Both Mum and Leo are old-line religious. You know, 'Love thy neighbour as long as thy neighbour isn't a comp.' They're always saying that the scientists
are playing God and that we shouldn't be messing with the

Lord's creations." She met my eyes. "Look, I'm a big girl now. I don't buy into their beliefs. I say live and let live. Okay?"

I nodded. "Okay." I stood up, wanting to physically shake off the sudden awkwardness between us. "So what went wrong between Kyle and Tarrah."

"Not sure," Lisa said, obviously relieved to be talking about something else. "One rumour was that he found her in a clinch with another guy. Another one said Tarrah started getting a bit too intense about the Comp Lobby and Kyle wasn't so into it."

"They're still friends, though, aren't they? I saw them in the mess together."

"Absolutely. Kyle's a nice guy, he likes to be friends with everybody," Lisa said. She pulled out a top in a soft pink knit. "Try this on. We're about the same size, so it should fit you." She picked up a pair of jeans. "And these, too."

I took the clothes just as Mav loped through the doorway.

"Lisa," he sang. "This pair greets you with great pleasure." He gripped Lisa's hand and bowed, entwining her thumb in the complicated Chorian friendship grip.

Lisa bowed back. "Hi, Mav. You're looking good."

"Yes, I feel much equilibrium. Does your injury heal?" Mav asked, his hand hovering over her shoulder. He began to hum softly.

Before he became a time-jumping student on Earth, Mav had been studying to be a Chanter, the Chorian version of a doctor. He'd once tried to explain to me how he'd been learning to sense injuries and emotional states through sound vibrations, but I'd got lost about five minutes into it.

"It's a lot better," Lisa said. "The doctors say I'll be a hundred per cent in a month or so."

Mav nodded. "They are correct." He dropped his hand and looked at the clothes on the bed. "You bring much cloth for Joss." His ears flattened. "She says I cannot accompany her on her first date to observe human sexual courting behaviour."

"Not on the first date or any date," I said firmly, ignoring Lisa's snort of laughter.

"She feels much apprehension about this first date with Kyle Sandrell," Mav sang. "It is good that you are assisting her to be at least not totally sexless."

I covered my face with my hands. "Think I'll go and drown myself in the bather now."

"While you're in there, try those on," Lisa said, still laughing. She pushed me towards my ensuite. "And don't forget the shoes." She handed me some sandals.

I stepped into the bathroom. "For the record, I am not nervous about this date," I said loftily. I hit the sensor pad, closing the door. My reflection stared at me from the far mirror. "Not one bit," I told it. It nodded.

Eight clothes changes later, we had a winner. I stepped out of the bathroom in a crisp fitted white shirt with thin stripes of blue and silver, a pair of mem-jeans that were already settling themselves around my shape, and silver sandals.

Lisa nodded. "Oh yeah, that's it." She stood up. "Just one thing." She reached over and undid my top two shirt buttons, creating a deep V.

Mav walked around me, considering. "It is pleasing," he

finally announced. "However, it needs a decorative metallic neckpiece."

Lisa and I stared at him.

"You know, he's right," Lisa said. "Have you got a silver necklace?"

I found a twisted silver chain and clasped it around my neck.

"So?" I asked. I changed the v-robe doors into mirror mode and looked at myself.

Lisa and Mav nodded. I smiled at them in the reflection of the mirror.

"You're gorgeous," Lisa said. "I've seen your mother reading the news tons of times, but I've never really noticed how much you look like her. Except she's blonde and you're dark, of course."

"That's what she ordered," I said. "The Eurasian version of herself—wouldn't want another blonde bombshell in the family, would we? And just enough multi-ethnicity to boost her audience numbers."

Even I heard the bitter edge in my voice.

"I'm sure your mother didn't want you just for that," Lisa said softly.

I turned to look at her. "My mother chose to manipulate the genes that create symmetrical facial structure, athletic body type and good teeth. Looks, looks and looks. I think that says it all."

Lisa and Mav looked at me solemnly.

"So all those brains you've got are natural?" Lisa finally said, smiling.

I reluctantly grinned back. "Must be."

Lisa stood up. "Well, it doesn't matter what way you got that face and body. I say, if you've got it, flaunt it." She zeroed in on me. "Come on, we've got to do something with your hair and makeup."

I turned to face the mirror as she smoothed back my fringe. Lisa was wrong. How you got it was important, and my gut told me that flaunting it might soon be very dangerous.

A few minutes before seven, the CommNet jingle sounded from the computer on the bedside table. Lisa was holding a pair of silver hoops against my ears and we both jumped as the screen moved smoothly around to face us.

"Joss, you've got a comm message from Sergeant Vaughn at the P3 Security Office," the computer said.

I met Lisa's eyes. This was it. She snatched away the earrings and stepped back, nodding encouragingly.

I took a deep breath. "Okay, connect."

Vaughn's fashionably altered face appeared on the screen. "Well now, don't we look purty." He leered. "Your little boyfriend is waiting for you."

I gave him a cool death glare, but my heart was already picking up pace.

"Thank you. Tell him I'll be out in five. Disconnect." The screen flicked back to the CommNet logo.

"Okay, he's here," I said, standing up. "Looks like I'm going now." I felt strangely reluctant to leave.

"Are you sure I cannot accompany you?" Mav asked, his ears hiking up hopefully.

"She's sure," Lisa said. She handed me a ridiculously small silver evening bag. "Good luck. And have a great time."

That was the plan.

⊠　⊠　⊠

Kyle tapped his spoon against the toffee crust of the crème brûlée that sat between us on the table. "Want to help me break it?" he asked.

I nodded and picked up my spoon.

He sat up straight, holding his hand over his heart. "I dedicate this crème brûlée to all those who believed in it and held the dream in their hearts of a better, happier dessert."

Laughing, we broke through the thin layer, exposing the smooth pale custard underneath.

"I think we've struck gold," he said softly, and I had a feeling he didn't just mean the dessert. "You go first."

I dug out a spoonful of toffee and custard and tasted it.

"Ohmigod," I breathed, letting the honey vanilla melt on my tongue. "That is fantastic."

"Told you," Kyle said, helping himself.

I looked around the crowded café. It had been quiet when we arrived and the headwaiter had seated us in the open double windows that looked out into Mall 11, the boutique area of the Melbourne central mall network. Now the restaurant was buzzing, and the energy in the place was pumping through me.

Kyle and I had talked nonstop about the Centre, discussing our majors (history of architecture for him, music for me), the tough fitness program, the best and worst teachers, and the first terrifying ten seconds of a time-jump. We'd even discussed Mav and the mind link, although I had moved the conversation on fairly quickly—it felt too much like talking behind Mav's back. The arrival of dessert had created a natural break in conversation, but I sensed that we were about to shift into more personal territory. And for once, I didn't mind. I spooned out some more of the crème brûlée, concentrating on scooping up as much toffee as possible.

"That Horain-Donleavy kid from your class cornered me yesterday," Kyle said.

That made me look up—Chaney had never been high on my list of romantic dinner topics.

Kyle shook his head. "One of these days someone's going to buck the civ laws and lay into that kid. And with that mouth on him, he'll deserve it. He wanted to have a 'little chat' about you."

I hurriedly swallowed my mouthful of dessert. "What did he say?"

Kyle shrugged. "That you weren't really comp."

The lingering sweetness in my mouth turned sour. The next time I saw Chaney, he'd better start running.

"I am comp," I said. "I may only have one donor, but I'm enhanced. I'm still comp." It came out more vehemently than I expected.

Kyle held up his hands. "Hey, I'm with you—if someone's enhanced, then they can call themselves comp. I know some comps wouldn't agree with that, but they're a bit hard-line." He picked up his glass and drained it. "You know Tarrah, don't you?"

"I've seen her around, but we haven't met," I said, trying not to sound too happy about it.

"She's well in with the Comp Lobby, and she told me they're trying to get some kind of criteria set for comp status.

A certain number of donors and things like that."

I looked at Kyle's beautiful face, a horrible thought hitting me like a hammer between the eyes. "Would it matter to you if I wasn't a comp?"

It was like everything in the café ground to a halt while I waited for his answer. Was this gorgeous, funny guy the flip side of Chaney? I had very specific ideas about where this evening was heading, and they would all disappear in a flick of a clean sheet if he said yes.

He shook his head. "Of course not."

The magic words. My evening was still intact.

"But I've kind of stopped dating noncomps now," he continued. "Not that there's anything wrong with them—it's just that they don't really understand what it's like. You know what I mean."

"Sure, but . . ." I had been about to say that anyone with an ounce of empathy would be able to work it out, and that went both ways. But earlier, Lisa had delicately suggested I tone down my attitude, especially on the first date. *Leave it to the second date*, she'd said. So, I swallowed the comment, although it kind of stuck in my throat.

Kyle looked at me expectantly. "But what?"

"But do you want coffee?" I said lamely.

"How about we skip coffee and head to the party?" Kyle said. "I promised we'd drop in, but we don't have to stay long."

I caught the lilt in his voice. My thoughts exactly.

We took the Venturi Loop back to campus. I've never been keen on the underground trans system—being sucked through a tube in a metal capsule without windows always creeps me out—but it seemed like a good idea to get to the party as quickly as possible. The sooner we got there, the sooner we could leave.

It was being held in Trinity College, the sixth-year-student quarters. Kyle and I took the most direct route through campus, along the wide tree-lined central boulevard. The huge oaks had formed a canopy over the walkway and the University had installed old-fashioned streetlamps that created pools of buttery light and soft shadows. Although it was officially autumn, the night air was still warm, courtesy of the ever-expanding ozone hole, and a number of other couples were strolling hand in hand. It seemed like a good idea. I glanced across at Kyle. He met my eyes and smiled, both of us moving at the same time. I yelped as my finger mashed against his palm. We jumped apart then started laughing.

"I think we got our timing wrong," he said. "Let's try that again."

Our hands slid together. Something inside me lurched as I felt his long fingers curl around mine.

We walked up the steps to the arched entrance of Trinity College.

"What do you say we only stay for half an hour," I said, tightening my grip.

The door to the party dorm was opened by a sixth-year girl with short black hair intricately twisted back into beaded sections. She kissed Kyle on the cheek then pointed in the direction of the eating area.

"Drinks down there," she yelled over the pounding music.

I followed Kyle through a crowded living room and into the eating area. James, a cheerful fifth-year I'd met through Lisa, was manning the food dispenser.

"Hey Joss, how are you doing? I didn't know you belonged."

Belonged? To what? I opened my mouth to ask, but James had turned to Kyle.

"So what do you want to drink?" he asked.

"Beer?" Kyle said, turning to me for confirmation.

"Sure."

I took the cold glass and studied the group of people. Something was bugging me, but I couldn't work out what.

"Kyle!" a girl's voice yelled. We both turned around. Tarrah was heading towards us in a pale green cling dress, her blonde hair falling in VR star waves. She kissed Kyle on both cheeks, her bright hazel eyes on me.

"So glad you decided to come. And you, too, Joss," she said, smiling widely. "It's always good to have a new member."

Member? And then it clicked. Everyone in the room was a comp. I shot a look at Kyle.

"Member of what?" I asked.

"The Comp Lobby," Tarrah said. "Didn't Kyle tell you this is a meeting?"

"Me and Joss are just here for the beer," Kyle said.

"Come on, Ky, you're going to have to get off your fence one day." Tarrah turned around to face the crowd. "Hey, turn the music off," she called. "It's time to start."

There was immediate silence. I scanned the room; everyone had turned expectantly towards Tarrah.

"I'm not going to rave on for very long," she said. "This is just a prelim to see who is interested in the march on the Director's offices next week."

Four heavyset guys with rugby player necks raised their beers and cheered.

"Let's storm the place," one of them yelled. A few girls near them giggled.

"Thanks for your enthusiasm, Liam," Tarrah said. "But for the moment we're just marching. And that reminds me, although we all appreciate the sentiments of the graffiti on the admin building, it would be better if the artists played it cool for a while. Until the march is over."

"What are you marching against?" I asked.

Tarrah looked back at me and smiled. "Everyone, say hello to Joss. She's in first year, so all you old hands can give her some pointers about surviving the course," she said.

A friendly buzz of *hellos* rippled around the room. I caught a thumbs-up from the black-haired bead girl and a wink from James. I smiled, the warmth of the crowd surprising me.

Tarrah brushed back her hair. "We're marching against the quotas," she said, a strident note entering her voice. "It's just institutionalised prejudice against us. We're supposed to be living in a meritocracy, but potential comp students are being turned away, even though they're outstripping the noncomps in all areas."

"Don't the quotas work both ways?" I asked, curious.

Tarrah nodded. "It used to work both ways. But we're not just oddities any more. At the moment, five per cent of births are comps and that's rising. More and more comps are coming through the school system. Why should they give way to the mediocre?" She turned back to the room of people and raised her voice into a rallying cry. "I say that if you're better, then you should get into the course. And I've seen the statistics—comps are better! Let's face it, that's why our parents took the chance."

The room erupted into a frenzy of whoops and cheers and clapping. Liam and his mates started chanting "Not comp, not good enough!"

"If you want to march, go see Birri over there," Tarrah yelled, pointing to a tall black woman at the back of the room. "Put your name down. Let's show them we mean business."

People started to move towards the sign-up. Beside me, Kyle drained his glass and put it on a nearby table.

"Want to get going?" he asked.

I nodded. "You don't seem very impressed with all this," I said, taking a last swig of beer.

"Are *you* impressed?"

I looked around the room. "I don't know. I suppose I'm impressed by the solidarity."

Kyle raised his eyebrows. "Yeah, Tarrah's good at that."

"Did I hear my name?" Tarrah said, moving away from the four rugby players.

"We're taking off now," Kyle said smoothly.

"Already?" Tarrah looked put out. "I hope you'll come again, Joss," she said. "We comps have to stick together, right?"

"Sure," I said.

She gave me an appraising look. "Think about it, Joss. I know you've had your fair share of screte from noncomps. Do something about it." She quickly kissed Kyle on the cheek. "Don't be like Ky, here. He doesn't like to get involved. Do you, darling?"

"Only with the right person," he said lightly. And although he didn't look at me, I felt a rush of heat through my body.

Tarrah's laugh was brittle. "Always sidestepping the issue. See you tomorrow." Then she was gone, surrounded by her disciples, her voice urging and caressing towards the sign-up table.

Kyle took my hand and we made our way towards the door. I looked back at the milling group waiting to sign their names; arms draped over friends' shoulders, bursts of laughter, loud teasing, and underneath it all a real sense of camaraderie. Of belonging. James was standing at the back of the room and caught my eye. He motioned towards the sign-up table, his eyebrows raised. I shrugged. He nodded and smiled, mouthing "Next time." Perhaps I would, next time. I waved as Kyle gently tugged at my other hand.

Outside, in the warm night air, we paused at the top of the steps.

"Sorry about that," Kyle said. "I didn't know she was going to turn it into a rally."

"It's okay. I can sort of see where she's coming from. And I really liked the vibe."

"Yeah, it's nice to relax with your own kind," he said as we walked side by side down the steps. I felt a fleeting twitch of unease at his phrasing. "That's why I go," he continued. "To hang with other comps. I'm not so keen when Tarrah starts politicising."

"I wouldn't mind hanging with them again," I said.

As if we could read each other's mind, we both turned towards one of the smaller paths that branched off from the main boulevard. A more secluded path. The lamps were farther apart, creating soft-edged spotlights in the darkness. Kyle caught up my hand again and we walked in silence, the energy between us building. Every centimetre of my skin was aware of the warmth of his body, the flat smooth planes of his muscles, the soft curve of his lips. As we moved into the glow of one of the lights, I glanced up at him and saw him staring at me. The flare of his dark pupils pulled me towards him. I stopped and draped my arms over his shoulders. He leaned into me, his body firm against mine. As I rose to meet him, our bodies pressed closer together and I thought I could feel his heartbeat, as quick as mine. The kiss was gentle, a soft taste of each other, but I wanted more. I opened my mouth, feeling him move with me, all my focus on the shivering sensation running though my body.

I feel your desire, Joss-partner! It is beautiful!

I jerked back, the intrusion like the slash of a cold knife.

"What's wrong?" Kyle asked anxiously, his arms still around me.

My mind flamed into burnt orange fury.

No! Get out!

The link snapped, a whisper of lime green remorse colouring my consciousness.

I slammed my wristband across the security panel of our front door. Barely waiting for it to slide open, I stalked into the hexagonal living room. Behind me, Kyle paused in the doorway.

"Mav, get out here," I yelled.

There was no answer. His bedroom door was closed, the lock panel glowing red. I slapped it anyway.

"Mav, don't you try and hide."

"I will come when you no longer shout," he sang.

I glared at the door. That was going to be a long time coming.

"Maybe I should go," Kyle said.

I turned back to him.

"Screte! I'm sorry, Kyle." I ran my hand through my hair, messing up Lisa's careful styling.

"Look, don't worry. You've got stuff to work out here. How about we catch up tomorrow night?" He hesitated. "That is, if you'd like to."

"I'd love to," I said. I walked over to him. "Thanks. And I'm sorry."

We kissed, brief but full of promise. I watched the door close behind him.

Damn it. I marched across to Mav's door again.

"You wrecked my date. You can at least come out and face me," I said, trying to modulate my voice.

The door slid open. Mav stood in front of me, his ears flat against his head.

"This is the correct time to say sorry, yes?" he sang meekly.

"'Sorry' doesn't cut it," I snapped. "I was having a fantastic time until you barged in!"

"I know," Mav sang.

"Do you know how creepy that is?" I said tightly. "To have someone in your mind when you're . . . " I stopped, not really wanting to describe what Kyle and I were doing.

Mav's ears raised placatingly. "On Choria, it is always an honour to be joined at such times."

"I don't give a damn if it's an honour on Choria," I yelled. "I don't want to share my love life with you. Do you understand?"

"Yes," Mav sang contritely. His ears flattened again. "But tell me why you still want Kyle when you do not trust him? I do not understand."

"What?" I stared at him, crossing my arms.

"You do not trust Kyle. I felt it through your desire."

"I don't know what you're talking about. You're just trying to change the subject."

"No, Joss-partner. Deep in you there is not-trust. Why do you fail to acknowledge this instinct?"

"Deep in me is pissed off. With you." I stamped across to my bedroom. "Don't even think about coming near me for a few days. I don't want to see you."

I didn't look back as my bedroom door slid shut. I slapped the lock panel then dived, full-length, onto my bed. I trusted Kyle, just fine. And anyway, what did Mav know about trust? I'd trusted him to stay out of my head for one night, and he couldn't even do that. Maybe this partnership wasn't going to work, after all.

The next day was Saturday, rest day, and Mav took me at my word; whenever I came out of my bedroom, he ducked back

into his room. I heard him leave the suite about midday.

As soon as I heard the front door slide shut, I commed Kyle and organised to meet him at the University basketball game at eight. Then I hotfooted it over to Lisa's quarters to borrow more clothes. She lent me a soft, sexy red jumper and red heels, then made me promise I'd go clothes shopping with her later in the week. I didn't mention my fight with Mav—he was wrong, but Lisa had a bad habit of looking at both sides of a situation.

At about a quarter to eight, I left our quarters. Mav was still out. We usually spent Saturday nights together at the Buzz Bar, catching up with our friend Lenny Porchino, the bar owner. Was that where Mav was now? In Lenny's private booth, listening to the house blues band? Sometimes I'd jam with the band on my blues harp and Mav would harmonise my line with intricate humming. We always got encores. It felt strange not being there with him.

I hurried over to the huge, central gym. The basketball game was between the University team and their old adversaries from Monash Uni. It was already crowded when I made it into the stadium. I scanned the seats for Kyle, but couldn't see him. This was one of the times when not wearing an armscreen backfired. Maybe I'd have to get one, now that I *wanted* someone to contact me. I saw Chaney and Jorel in the top row, throwing chips down at four big guys crammed together in the small seats: Liam and his friends from Tarrah's party. They already looked wasted. And now they also looked pissed off—Chaney liked to live dangerously.

I still couldn't see Kyle. Had he decided not to come? I

pushed down a hollow feeling and studied the rows, one by one. Finally I saw him guarding a spare seat in the far corner. A few girls were looking back at him, trying to catch his eye, but he was obviously on the lookout for me—bad luck, girls. I couldn't help grinning as I made my way across the bleachers.

"Hey, just in time," he called when he saw me climbing over legs and bags. He stood up to let me pass. As I brushed past him, I smelled hot man and citrusy cologne. It made me want to drag him out of the stadium.

I'm sure I cheered our team in the right spots and yelled at the refs' decisions, but I can't really remember. All I noticed was the energy between me and Kyle. He held my hand the whole time, softly stroking my palm, sometimes my arm. I pressed my thigh against his, and then my hip, until the whole of our sides were touching, the heat from our bodies only partly due to the crowd around us. By the end of the game, I felt like my whole body was vibrating against his and I knew, from the dark intent of his eyes, that we weren't going to be hanging around for the victory party.

By the time we made it out of the stadium, most of the crowd had cleared.

"It's still early," Kyle said. "Did you want to get a drink or something?"

I stared him in the eyes and shook my head slowly.

"No," I said, and smiled.

He grinned back. "My roomie has gone to stay with a mate," he said. "Want to come back to my place?"

"Why, thank you, Mr Sandrell. Don't mind if I do."

He laughed and squeezed my hand. "Let's cut through the science buildings. It's faster."

We started running, hand in hand, across the stadium quadrangle, leaving behind the last stragglers of the basketball crowd. Kyle led me in between the tall, dark science buildings, through a deserted arched walkway, and down a steep set of steps.

"Wait," I panted, laughing. "I can't run in these silly shoes."

I dragged on his hand. He stopped and we stood for a moment in a dark alleyway. I pulled him closer, angling my face to kiss.

The small space suddenly echoed with a sharp cry and the scraping sound of struggle.

I pulled back. "What's that?"

"Dunno, but it's from over there," Kyle said, turning towards the far end of the alley.

We started towards it, the sounds of heavy breathing and pain-filled gasps more insistent. I rounded the corner into a shadowy courtyard. For a second all I saw was a dark mass on the far edge. Then it became four heavy guys kicking two hunched forms on the concrete. Liam and his mates belting the screte out of two kids. Even before I saw the night-bleached flash of red curly hair, I knew it was Chaney. And Jorel.

Chaney covered his head with his arms as Liam savagely kicked him.

"Don't ever call me a freak again, you little bastard," Liam said.

I started forward, but Kyle's hand dug painfully into my arm, pulling me back.

"Don't," he whispered.

"What do you mean? We've got to stop it!" I jerked my arm away.

"It's not our fight."

"What's that got to do with it?"

Kyle's face was set. "You know Chaney and his friend were asking for it."

I stared at him. "You can't just walk away from people getting hurt."

"It's the only thing those type understand," he said harshly, stepping into the shadows of the alley. "Leave it, Joss. Don't get involved." He went to grab my arm again, but I jumped back.

"No, we have to do something. They're getting creamed."

"Look, I'll call Security," he said.

"They'll be too late."

He took a step back, shaking his head. "I'll call Security."

"Don't knock yourself out," I said as he disappeared down the alley.

I turned towards the fight, suddenly feeling very alone. One of the rugby thugs was down, writhing on the ground. Nearby, Jorel was lying very still on the concrete. Chaney was curled into a ball with the other three thugs on top of him.

"Oi," I yelled, running towards them. "Get off him."

Liam looked up. "Get lost."

He turned back to Chaney. His mistake. I punched him in the side of the head. My mistake. I should have gone for his gools.

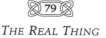

"Bloody hell," he roared. And swung. I jumped back. He only grazed my shoulder, but it felt like a sledgehammer.

"Didn't I see you last night?" he demanded.

All three of his mates turned their attention to me. Not so good. On the ground, Chaney groaned, one side of his head covered in blood.

"So?" I said, slipping off my shoes. I couldn't fight in them and they had handy heels. Two of the guys had got up and were circling around me.

"You're comp," Liam said.

"So what?"

"So, these guys are lousy bigots. We're just teaching them a little lesson."

"No, you're not. You're bashing the screte out of them. Leave them alone."

"You're going to stop us, are you?" the thug on my right asked. He swung another kick into Chaney.

"Too right," I said. At least my voice was steady.

I felt the warmth of a body behind me just as Liam rushed me. I should have kept an eye on Left Thug. I zeroed in on Liam's crotch and kicked. Liam buckled as pain burst through my toes. Then I felt Left Thug's arms tighten around my chest.

"Silly bitch," Right Thug yelled.

The rush of adrenaline masked the pain of his first punch to my stomach, but it didn't soften the ground or the kick into my side. I heard Liam moaning near me, and saw Chaney try to get up and pull one of the thugs off me. Mav! I needed Mav! I strained every fibre of my being towards his mind, screaming as the burning pain in my body matched the orange fire in my head. *Hear me! Mav, hear me!* The edges of my sight faded into grey haze as I gasped for breath. Something heavy on my chest. Can't breathe. *Mav!* I pushed against the human weight. Pushed against the confines of my mind. Screaming inside. Outside. Until there was no more breath.

Joss? His mind voice was startled, jubilant, darkening into anxiety. *I come.*

And then I knew why Mav wanted to be joined all the time. Waves of Mav, of everything that was Mav, broke over me, filling me with the certainty that I was not alone, would never be alone. A swirling, dizzying closeness, understanding, acceptance. Joss melding into Mav into Joss, a merging of minds and spirits. A joining of stories, thoughts, emotions, dreams. We flowed together; pasts, presents, futures fused into a rolling, endless stream. We were Pair.

We will be there soon. We will stop the pain. We will be together. We are Pair.

No!

Deep down, part of me struggled for separateness. A bolt hole of isolation. Nothing but the bare essence of Joss. Alone. Human. *One.*

I don't know if it was that, or the punch in the face that suddenly blacked out the world.

I heard humming. Insistent, annoying humming. I licked my lips. Dry. I tried opening my eyes. Bright, painful light. Antiseptic. White walls.

Hospital.

I focused on a hand hovering over my face. Two thumbs.

"Mav?"

The humming stopped.

"Joss-partner. I am here."

Mav's double-barrelled smile appeared in front of me.

"We've got to stop meeting like this," I croaked.

"You are bruised on your face and body and have one rib broken," Mav sang. "All will be well."

"Can't feel anything," I said. Must have been full of Alphcine. "How are Chaney and Jorel?"

"They both live," Mav sang somberly. "Jorel is still unconscious. He is injured inside and is now in the place of special care. Chaney is cut and swollen on his face and also has ribs that are broken. He is much grateful to you."

"What about Liam and his friends?"

"Those who attacked you? They are with your law enforcers. There is loud shouting and anger about comps and noncomps."

I tried to nod, but the effort was too great. The comp trouble had finally come.

"Kyle Sandrall wishes to see you," Mav sang. "He waits outside, asking about your health."

I closed my eyes. How did I feel about that? An image of Kyle disappearing down the alleyway flashed through my mind.

"All right, let him in."

Mav touched the wall panel and the door slid open. He motioned Kyle inside.

"Hi, Joss," Kyle said hesitantly.

He was holding a posy of flowers.

"Hey," I said, trying to summon up a smile. I shifted in the bed as my body remembered his arm across my shoulder, the warmth of his lips against mine.

Kyle looked across at Mav then back at me. "Could we have a moment alone?"

Mav's opaque eyelids flicked shut, shielding his eyes.

"I'd like Mav to stay," I said.

Kyle's face tightened. "Okay." He looked down at the flowers. "I just wanted to say I'm sorry."

"Why'd you take off like that? You left me there."

"I know. I'm sorry. I did call Security, though."

What had Tarrah said about him? Always sidestepping the issue?

Mav crossed his arms. "It was not proper courting behaviour," he sang stiffly.

Kyle nodded. "Joss has got a lot of guts," he said.

"It is not only guts," Mav sang, his ears high. "Joss has much generosity."

Kyle frowned. He didn't understand. He probably never would.

"Well, thanks for coming by," I said, suddenly feeling very tired.

He held out the posy. "Still friends?"

I took the flowers and laid them on the bed beside me. "Sure, Kyle. Maybe I'll see you round."

He smiled—he was still gorgeous, but something was missing. Honour, perhaps, or maybe empathy. Mav had been right about my instincts, after all. Not that I'd ever tell him that—I'd never hear the end of it.

Kyle walked out, the door sliding shut behind him.

Mav flicked back his second eyelids. "There is still much to like in Kyle Sandrell," he sang gently.

I blinked, trying to clear my eyes.

Mav peered at me. "You are weary. Shall I go?"

"No, stay." I swallowed against a dry ache. "Got any water there?"

Mav picked up a glass and held it to my lips. I took a small sip, the coolness slipping down my scratchy throat.

"Thanks."

He put the glass down.

I squinted with effort, trying to focus my mind. *And thanks for help.*

You called me. I came. His mind voice was bright green, pulsating with joy. *You called me!*

"I know. It was amazing," I said, picking up his hand and closing it around my fist. The closest I could come to the Chorian friendship clasp right now. "I feel honoured to know you in that way."

"It is my honour."

"But, Mav, I can't have you in my mind all the time," I said slowly. "I'm sorry, I just can't. Humans are separate. I have to think my own thoughts, narrate my own life."

Mav sighed. "I know, Joss-partner." He sat forward, his thumbs tightening around my hand. "But now you call me. We will make our own joining. And sometimes we will make a paired story. Is this good?"

Yes, it is good.

ALISON GOODMAN is the author of *Singing the Dogstar Blues*, a science-fiction comedy thriller, which won the 1998 Aurealis Award for Best Young Adult Novel and was listed as a 1999 C.B.C. Notable Book. It was also published in the United States in hardback by Viking and in paperback by Firebird, and was named an ALA Best Book for Young Adults.

Alison lives in Queensland, Australia, with her husband, Ron, and their two exuberant Parson Russell terriers, Xander and Spike. She is currently working on *Eon/Eona*, a fantasy duology based upon Chinese astrology; the first volume will be published by Viking in 2008.

Visit her Web site at **www.bssound.com.au/goodman**.

AUTHOR'S NOTE

When Sharyn invited me to write a short story for *Firebirds Rising*, I jumped at the chance to continue the Joss and Mav story that I started in my novel *Singing the Dogstar Blues*. In the process of writing a novel, there are always interesting tangents that an author can't follow due to the necessities of plot streamlining or character development. One of the tangents I had to leave in *Singing the Dogstar Blues* was a short scene where Joss first meets Kyle Sandrall and decides not to accept his invitation to a "comp kid" party. "The Real Thing" grabs that small interplay between Joss and Kyle and runs with it, taking Joss into a minefield of love, lust and prejudice. I was also keen to write about Mav's interest in human courting rituals—I loved writing his puzzled study of the strange processes that we humans go through when we fancy each other. Sometimes they puzzle me too! "The Real Thing" also expands on some of the questions raised in *Singing the Dogstar Blues*, such as what might happen to a society where some members have been engineered to be "better"? Would engineered people feel entitled? Would nonengineered people feel threatened? Science fiction specialises in asking "what if?" which is why I enjoy writing it. I believe that when we start thinking about the future, we are on our way toward understanding our present.

Little (Grrl) Lost

Scritch, *scritch, scritch.*

There it was again.

T.J. had first realised that something was living in the walls when she'd see the cat staring at the baseboards in her bedroom. It was as though Oscar could see right through the wood, and the plaster behind it.

Back when she still thought it was mice, she kept him out of her bedroom and didn't tell anybody. She liked the idea of mice sharing this new house in a new subdivision with her family. If she mentioned it, the traps would come out, just as they had in the old farmhouse where she'd grown up, and her brother, Derek, would be waving little dead mice under her nose again. Ugh. They were so cute with those big eyes of theirs. But they were also dead and gross.

So, no. Telling anyone that the new house had mice was right out.

Instead, she listened to the *scritch*ing at night, while lying in her bed. She'd flick on her bedside light, but of course

the sound immediately stopped when she did that. It started up again shortly after the light was turned off, but it was impossible to see anything in her shadowy room—even with the curtains open and light coming in her window from the streetlight outside.

So tonight, after Mom and Dad had come in to say their good nights, she pulled her sleeping bag from under her bed and rolled it out beside the part of the wall where she heard the sound most often. Grabbing her pillow, she'd snuggled into the sleeping bag and waited, almost falling asleep before the now-familiar sound brought her wide awake again.

Scritch, scritch.

Except it wasn't really like the sound of mouse claws running around inside the walls. This close . . . she leaned her ear right up against the baseboard . . . it sounded an awful lot like voices. Which was stupid. But then she remembered a story her uncle had told her once about how sometimes, when you heard crows in the forest, they could almost sound like human voices. Like real voices, but distant enough that you just couldn't quite make out what they were saying.

That's what the *scritch*ing sounded like.

Oh, right. Like there were crows living inside the walls.

There were a lot of things she didn't like about this new house in the suburbs, but she didn't think she could logically add wall-dwelling crows to the list.

Distracted, she rolled onto her back and stared at the ceiling. She could obsess for hours on the unfairness of having had to move from their farmhouse outside of Tyson to this stupid subdivision, where everything looked pretty much the same from one street to the next. From one *house* to the next. The first time she'd gone out riding her bike, she'd actually found herself pedalling up the wrong driveway when she was coming back home. Could you feel more stupid?

So that was a big reason to hate being here.

Nobody was very friendly either. All the kids pretty much ignored her—when they weren't making fun of her accent. But she could live with that. The friends part wasn't totally bad. Sure, she'd had to leave hers behind, but she and Julie could instant-message and e-mail all day long, and Tyson was close enough that they could theoretically take the bus to stay with each other on the weekend, though they hadn't yet.

She didn't need a new best friend because she already had one, thank you very much.

But that wasn't totally good either, because talking by phone and computer couldn't begin to be the same. Not when they used to be able to simply cut across the cornfield and just *be* at each other's house.

She missed that. She missed the farm. But most of all, she missed Red. Her handsome, sweet-tempered, mischievous Red. He—okay, technically, it—had been the perfect horse, but she'd had to give him up.

That was what was so *totally* unfair.

So, maybe it wasn't her parents' fault. She didn't understand much about the stock market, except that if you had your money in the wrong kind of investment, you could end up losing it all if the market crashed. Which was what had happened to them.

But shouldn't you be able to see that coming?

Apparently not.

Apparently, you could lose all your savings, and your family home, and have to start over fresh again, where you were supposed to put on a good face, your best foot forward, soldier on. Even when it meant you'd lost the most important thing in your life.

When you hadn't lost so much, dealing with it wasn't so hard. Mom was happy with her new job at the hospital. Dad didn't seem to mind going to an office every day instead of working out of the spare room the way he'd done pretty much forever. Even stupid Derek was happy, because now he was in a place where he could start up a real band and there were clubs where he could play. He already had a new bunch of friends, though obviously no loyalty to old ones the way she did.

Red mattered to her. Julie mattered to her.

Did anyone ever consider *her* feelings? Of course not. She was only fourteen. No one cared about what *she* thought.

It was all, "You'll make new friends."

Like her old ones weren't important.

Or, "We can't afford to board Red, T.J. Maybe in a couple of years we can get you a new horse."

But a new horse wouldn't be Red.

It was all Dad's fault for losing their money.

And Mom's for taking this stupid job—which had brought them to the city in the first place—and then acting like the change would be good for the whole family.

And Derek's for being so happy to live here.

She could feel the tears welling up behind her eyes like

they always did when she thought of her beautiful Red. Like they did when she was "just feeling sorry for herself instead of embracing life's challenges," as Mom would say. Well, she had every reason to feel sorry for herself.

Scritch, scritch.

The sound brought her back. She wiped her sleeve against her eyes, and turned to stare at the wall. She wished she had Oscar's apparent X-ray vision, because it really did sound like voices. But now, instead of being curious, she was kind of bored and irritated. She raised her fist to bang on the wall, then froze.

Because the impossible happened.

A small section of the baseboard opened as though it was a tiny door, spilling out a square of light. A girl appeared in the doorway, looking back inside. She held a duffel bag in one hand and was wearing a jean jacket over a T-shirt, a short red-and-black plaid skirt, and black clunky shoes. Her hair was a neon blue. She looked to be about sixteen or seventeen.

And stood about six inches high.

"I'm not that person," she called back to someone inside, her voice hard and angry. "I don't want to be that person. I'm *never* going to be that person and you can't stop me!"

"Tetty Wood. You come back inside this instant!" a voice called from within.

"And my name's not Tetty!" the miniature girl shouted back.

She stepped outside and slammed the baseboard door shut.

The sudden loss of light made T.J. blink in the darkness.

I've fallen asleep, she thought. Fallen asleep and started to dream that action figures can come to life. Because that was what the girl appeared to be. The size of one of Derek's old action figures, complete with duffel-bag accessory.

But her eyes had now adjusted to the low light and there the miniature girl was. She stared back at T.J., her eyes apparently adjusting at the same time, and suddenly realising that she wasn't alone.

"Oh, crap," she said. "Don't swat me."

T.J. realized that she still had her fist in the air from when she was going to bang it against the wall.

"I thought you were mice," she said, lowering her hand.

"Do I look like a mouse?"

"No, but when I could only hear you . . . "

T.J.'s voice trailed off. She felt stupid, like she did too much of the time since they'd left the farm. And why should she? People supposedly got that way when they were nervous or scared—according to her father—but she was a hundred times bigger than this uninvited guest glaring up at her. What did she have to be scared about?

And it was *her* bedroom.

"So what *is* your name?" she asked.

It seemed the most polite question. Better than what *are* you and why are you living inside my bedroom walls?

"Elizabeth."

"But whoever was inside—"

"My uptight parents."

"—called you Tetty."

"It's a stupid nickname. *Their* stupid nickname. My name's Elizabeth."

"I'm Tara Jane, but most people call me T.J." She waited a moment, then added, "I like having a nickname."

"Whatever works for you," Elizabeth said.

She'd dropped her duffel bag to the floor and stood looking up at T.J. with her hands on her hips, a challenge in her eyes.

"So what's your damage?" she asked.

"I'm sorry?"

"For what?"

"I meant, what do you mean?" T.J. said.

Elizabeth gave a wave of her tiny hand. "Why are you sleeping on the floor when you've got a perfectly good bed?"

"I was curious about the noises I was hearing . . . "

Elizabeth laughed. "See, they've got this huge worry thing going on. 'Don't be seen.' 'Always stay hidden.' But it turns out that all their yelling was just *attracting* attention."

"You mean your parents?"

"Oh yeah. There's, like, a hundred rules and regs, and they've been drilling them into us since the day we were born."

T.J. nodded. She knew all about parents. Like the kind who just gave away your horse and moved you to some ugly subdivision, and then expected you to be happy about it.

She peered more closely at Elizabeth.

"So do you have wings?" she asked.

"Do you see wings?"

"No. I just thought they might be folded up under your jacket."

"Why would I have wings?"

"Well, aren't you a fairy?"

"Oh, please. I'm a Little."

"I can see that."

"No, it's like you saying you're a human being. A Little's what I am."

"I don't think I'd ever say that. Who goes around saying they're a human being, except maybe the Elephant Man?"

"Whatever." Elizabeth cocked her head, reminding T.J. of a bird. "So you're okay with a little person just showing up in your bedroom like this?"

"I suppose I shouldn't be—I mean, it's totally unreal, isn't it?—but I don't feel surprised at all and I don't know why."

Elizabeth nodded. "And the 'rents get all in a twist about anyone even guessing that we exist. I knew it would be no big deal."

"Well, it *could* be a big deal," T.J. said.

"How do you figure?"

"Think about it. If the world found out someone like you is real, it'd be all over the news."

"Cool. I'm so ready for my fifteen minutes of fame. Look out, world, 'cause here I come."

"I don't think it would be like that. I think it'd be more like they'd put you in a terrarium in a laboratory to study you. And everybody'd be tearing up their baseboards looking for more of you." She paused for a moment, before adding, "Do you have, like, a house back there?"

"Oh, sure. It's just all small and secret, you know, and it stretches out through the walls. But we've got all the amenities. We only moved here a few years ago, when they first built these houses, but it's totally comfortable now. My brothers and I even dragged in an old miniature TV that we found in the garage and hooked it up to the cable. It's like big screen for us."

"So why do you want to leave?" T.J. asked. "I mean, that's what you're doing right? Running away?"

"I'm not running. I'm old enough to make my own decisions about my life."

"You don't look much older than me."

"I'm sixteen."

"That's not old enough to live on your own."

"My mother was already married and had her first kid when she was my age."

"Gross."

Elizabeth shrugged. "It's no biggie." She looked around the room. "So do you mind if I crash here with you tonight? I'd kind of like to avoid going outside until it starts to get light."

She might be two years older than me, T.J. thought, but at least I'm not afraid of the dark.

"I like it outside at night," she said. "Sometimes I sneak out and just sit and look at the sky for a while, but it's not the same here as it was back home. The sky's way duller."

"That's because of the light pollution from the city. And I'm not scared of the dark."

"Then why won't you go out at night?"

"I didn't say I couldn't. It's just not safe with cats and owls and foxes and all."

"Oh, right."

"So are you staying here on the floor? Because I want to

bed down somewhere that you won't roll over on me in the middle of the night."

"No, of course not."

T.J. threw her pillow onto the bed and got up, being careful not to drop the flap of her sleeping bag on the Little or step in her direction.

"I'm going to put on the light for a minute," she said. "Is that okay?"

"It's your room. Knock yourself out."

The bright glare blinded both of them. Blinking, T.J. went over to her dresser and took her old teddy bear out of the little stuffed chair it was sitting in. She put the chair on her night table then turned to Elizabeth.

"You can use this," she said. "I guess it's big enough to be a couch for you."

"Thanks."

"Do you want a hand up?"

Elizabeth gave her withering look. "Do I look like a cripple?"

"No, it's just . . . "

T.J.'s voice trailed off as Elizabeth opened her duffel bag and took out a length of rope with a hook on the end. The hook folded out into three prongs so that it looked like an anchor. After a couple of swings over her head, up it went, catching in the cloth of the comforter at the top of the bed. She gave the rope an experimental tug. When she was satisfied it would hold her weight, she slung her duffel onto her back, using its handles as straps, and shimmied up the rope.

"Wow," T.J. said. "You're strong. I am so useless trying to do ropes in gym."

Elizabeth grinned, pleased. "We learn how to get around at an early age."

She worked the hook out of the comforter and coiled the rope, then walked across the top of the bed and jumped over to the night table. It was only a few inches, but when T.J. worked out the proportions, she realised it would be like her jumping over a gap as wide as her own height.

Elizabeth acted like it was no big deal. Dumping her duffel and the rope on the top of the night table, she stretched out on the chair. It wasn't quite a couch for her, but easily big enough that she could lounge comfortably in it.

T.J. got into bed and lay down with her head facing her guest.

"I still can't believe you're real," she said.

"Get used to it. The world's a big and strange place, my dad says, and just because you haven't seen a thing doesn't mean it doesn't exist."

"Obviously."

It was funny. Elizabeth said she hated her parents, but when she'd mentioned her dad just now, she seemed kind of proud of him.

"Will they come looking for you?" she asked. "Your parents?"

"I doubt it. They'll be totally freaking right now that you've seen me. They're probably packing up and moving the whole family out as we speak."

"They don't have to do that. I won't tell anyone."

"That doesn't mean anything to them. You could promise on

whatever you care for the most and they figure you'll tell anyway. 'Don't trust a Big.' That's, like, one of the major rules."

T.J. was insulted.

"Hey, don't look so bummed. It's not personal. That's just what they believe. And it's worse 'cause you're a kid, and in the world of my parents, kids only do what they're supposed to when you keep them under your thumb. God forbid you should have a thought of your own."

"Yeah, I know that feeling."

"So that's your horse?" Elizabeth asked, hooking a thumb in the direction of the picture of Red, which shared the night table with her chair and a small lamp.

"Was my horse."

"Yeah, I've heard you arguing with your parents about it. That sucks." She shook her head. "You know, it's funny, you thinking we were mice, because I had a pet mouse once. His name was Reggie."

A sweet-sad look came into her eyes and T.J. realized that this was the first time Elizabeth's features had softened. Up until that moment, she'd worn a look of steady confrontation, as though everything in the world was her enemy and she had to stand up against all of it.

"What happened to him?" she asked.

"Same as what happened to you. My parents made me get rid of him."

"But why?"

"Well, you know mice. They just poop and pee whenever they have to, no matter where they are. You can't train them. I'd take him out with me when we were foraging—for his exercise and the company. The 'rents said that his pellets would make the Bigs think their house was infested with mice and they'd call in an exterminator or something, and then where would we be?"

"I like mice," T.J. said, feeling a little guilty for all the ones that had been trapped and killed back on the farm.

"What's not to like? Besides the pooping and peeing, I mean. I promised to clean up after him—like they cared or believed me. But I would have."

She sighed, then added, "I loved that old fellow. I really did. I think that's when I started to hate my parents."

"You don't really hate them."

"Don't I?" She had that hard look in her face again. "I'm surprised you don't hate yours—considering what they did."

T.J. thought about that. Her parents exasperated her, and she was still upset for what they'd done, but she didn't hate them. How could you hate your own parents?

"I just don't," she said.

"Whatever."

"So are you really going to go out into the world and let everyone know you exist?"

"No, I'm not crazy. I know it would be a horror show. When you're my size, being secret and sneaking around is about all you've got going for you. A Big could just smash me like a bug and there wouldn't be anything I could do about it."

"So what are you going to do?"

She shrugged. "I don't know. Get away from here and find someplace to live, I guess. Someplace snug, where I can have a mouse if I want one."

"You could stay here," T.J. said. "I don't know if having a mouse is the greatest idea, but I could get you a bunch of little furniture and sneak you food and stuff."

"Oh, so I could be your pet?"

"No, nothing like that. I just thought it would be fun and, you know, safe for you."

Elizabeth shook her head. "Not going to happen. Don't take this personally, but you're a little too Goody Two-shoes for my tastes and anyway, the whole purpose of going out on my own is to prove that I can do it."

T.J. would have felt insulted about being called Goody Two-shoes, except she knew she was. She did what she was told and tried to do well in school. She kept her blonde hair cut to her shoulders and she would never have worn a skirt as short as Elizabeth's.

"But who are you going to be proving it to if your family moves away?" she asked.

"That's a dumb question," Elizabeth told her.

But she had a funny look in her eyes as she said it—there for a moment, then quickly gone.

"You should turn out the light," she said. "I'd like to get some sleep before I take off in the morning."

"Okay."

T.J. reached for the light switch, then paused before turning the light off.

"I probably won't be awake when you go," she said. "I'm not much of a morning person. So, good luck, and you know, everything. I hope you find a way to be happy."

"Soon as I'm out of here, I'll be happy."

"And if you want to leave your family a note or something—to let them know that I really won't tell, I mean—you should, so that they won't move."

"Like they'd ever listen."

"Um, right. Well, good night."

"Sure. Can you get that light?"

T.J. flicked the switch and the room plunged into darkness.

Just before she fell asleep, she thought she heard Elizabeth say softly, "But just because you're a Goody Two-shoes doesn't mean I don't think you're okay."

But maybe that was only because it was something she wanted to hear.

T.J. awoke to find that Saturday had started much earlier without her; the sun was already well above the horizon. She looked at her night table. There was no Little sleeping in her teddy's stuffed armchair. There was no Little anywhere to be seen, nor any sign that there'd ever been one.

That's because you were dreaming, she told herself.

But it certainly felt as though it had been real.

She lay in bed for a while, remembering the punky six-inch-tall Elizabeth with her neon blue hair and enough attitude for a half-dozen full-size girls.

It would have been cool if she had been real.

After a while T.J. got up and turned on her computer. While she waited for it to boot up, she knelt on the floor where, in her dream, a door had opened in the baseboard. She couldn't see any sign of it now—except for maybe *there*. But that was probably only where one board had ended and another had been laid in.

When she returned to her computer, she went online and Googled the word "Little." Her screen cleared and then the first ten entries of two hundred and fifteen million appeared on her screen.

Well, that hadn't been a particularly good idea.

She tried refining the search by adding "people" and got links to toy lines, the Little People of America site, an archaeological news report on the finding of the remains of a miniature woman on an island in Indonesia—except since her head was the size of a grapefruit, she wasn't exactly tiny. T.J. scrolled through a few more pages, but nothing was useful, even if there were only some forty-seven million hits this time.

"Little magical people" got her thirty-seven hits that were closer to what she was looking for, but nothing that resembled Elizabeth.

What? she asked herself. You were expecting something from a dream to show up on the Net?

She tried "Littles" and that was no help either.

Finally, she tried "little people living behind the baseboards" and was surprised when something came up—a site called "Fairies, Ghosts and Monsters." It sounded pretty Game Boy-useless, but she clicked through anyway. It turned out to be run by a professor who used to teach at one of the local universities and contained an odd mix of stories and scholarly essays.

She found the Littles a few pages in, under "miniature secret people." The article cited literary references like *Gulliver's Travels* and *Mistress Masham's Repose*, the Borrowers of Mary Norton's books, the Brownies from a Sunday comic strip that was long gone, and the Smalls from a book written by some old English guy named William Dunthorn.

There were two anecdotal entries, both about little people who lived behind the baseboards. One talked about "penny-men," who turned into pennies when people looked their way. And then there were the Littles. The way they were described seemed very close to what Elizabeth had told her. There was even a children's picture book about them: *The Travelling Littles*, written and illustrated by someone named Sheri Piper, who, like the professor whose Web site this was, also lived in town.

According to Piper's book, Littles had originally been birds who got too lazy to fly on after they'd found a particularly good feed. Eventually, they lost their wings and became these little people who had to live by their wits, taking up residence in people's houses, where they foraged for food and whatever else they needed.

She Googled the author, but the only links that came up were to eBay and used-book stores. Apparently, the book was long out of print, although she had written a number of others. None of those seemed to be about Littles. At least, she couldn't tell from the few links she clicked on to get more information.

She made a note of the author's name and the title of the one relevant book so that she could look them up at the library, then went to have a shower and some breakfast.

When she came into the kitchen her mother was just about to let Oscar out the back door.

"Don't let him out!" T.J. cried.

What if he came upon Elizabeth's scent and tracked her down to where she was hiding?

Her imaginary scent, the logical part of her corrected.

"Why ever not?" her mother asked.

"Because . . . I . . . I want to brush him first."

Her mother gave her a look that said, "When have you *ever* willingly brushed the cat?"

"Can you just leave him in?" T.J. asked. "Just until I've had breakfast and can brush him."

"Stop you from taking on a responsibility?" her mother said. "Not this mom."

"Ha ha."

But her mother left the cat inside. Oscar complained at the door, then shot T.J. a dirty look as though he was well aware of who was responsible for his lack of freedom before he stalked off down the hall.

T.J. poured herself some orange juice and took a box of cereal from the cupboard before joining her mother at the kitchen table.

"We're almost out of milk," her mother said. "Better use it before your dad gets up and takes it for his coffee."

"I will."

"So what has you up so early? Surely not just to brush the cat."

Saturday morning everyone in the house slept in except for T.J.'s mother. Back on the farm, T.J. had gotten up early, too, but she didn't have Red to look after anymore, and so had gotten into the habit of staying up late at night and sleeping in as long as possible.

T.J. shrugged. "Maybe I'm turning over a new leaf."

"Well, I'm happy for the company."

T.J. shook cereal into her bowl. She looked over at her mother as she reached for the milk.

"So, when you were a kid," she said, "did anyone ever take something away from you that you really, really cared about?"

Her mother sighed. "Please, T.J. I know you feel terrible about having to give up Red. Believe it or not, *I* feel terrible about it, too. But we have to move on."

"No, I didn't mean that. I was wondering about *you*. What did you do? How did you move on?"

Did you make up imaginary six-inch-high Littles to help you cope? she added to herself.

"Why are you asking me this?"

"I don't know. I . . . "

T.J. knew she couldn't talk about the Littles. For one thing, she'd promised not to. For another, her mom would think she was nuts. So she improvised.

"It's just there was this girl in the park yesterday," she said, "and we got to talking about . . . you know, stuff. And it turns out she was running away from home because she hates her parents, and the reason she hates them—or at least the main one, I guess—is that they made her get rid of her . . . um, pet dog that she'd had forever. So I was wondering—"

"What's her name?" her mother asked. "We need to tell her parents."

"*Mom*. We can't do that. It's not our business."

Her mother shook her head. "Sometimes we have to

involve ourselves in other people's lives, whether they want us to or not."

"Well, I don't know anything about her. I don't even know if she lives around here. I just met her in the park and she was already on her way."

"T.J., this is serious."

"I know. But it's something that's already done, and that wasn't the point of it anyway."

Her mother studied her for a moment.

"Do you hate us?" she asked.

T.J. shook her head. "I get mad whenever I think of how you made me lose Red, but . . . I don't know. It's not like it'd make me hate you."

"Thank God for that."

"Not like I hate living here."

"We've been through the why of it a hundred times."

"I know. I was just mentioning it, since you brought it up."

Her mother gave her a look.

"Okay," T.J. said. "So I did. But you still didn't answer my question."

"What exactly are you worried about?"

"That I'll end up hating you like this Elizabeth does her parents. So that's why I was wondering if something like this had ever happened to you."

"No," her mother said. "It never did. And don't think either your father or I are even remotely happy that things have turned out this way. We know how much you loved that horse."

"Red. His name's Red."

T.J. had to look down at her cereal and blink back the start of tears. Her mother's hand reached across the table and held hers.

"I know, sweetheart," she said. "I really am so sorry."

"I guess."

"And I don't think you'll start hating us—at least I hope to God you won't, because that would be just too much to bear. But if we can still have a talk like this, then I think we're okay."

Except they weren't, T.J. thought. At least she wasn't.

She didn't hate her parents. But that didn't help the big hole in her chest where Red used to be.

T.J. dutifully brushed Oscar after breakfast—a chore that neither of them appreciated very much—then reluctantly, she let him outside. Surely, Elizabeth would have taken cats into account and hidden herself away in some place where they wouldn't be able to find her. Assuming Elizabeth was even real.

And speaking of real . . . once she'd closed the door behind the cat, she went up to her room and knelt down by the wall where last night a little door had opened in the baseboard.

"I don't know if you're still in there," she said, "or if you can even trust me—but I just want you to know that no matter what happens, your secret's safe with me. I mean, it's not like someone hasn't already written a book about you, and you *can* be looked up on the Web. But I won't add my two cents—not even if someone asks me, point-blank. I already lied to my mother about you, and I hated having to do that. I've never done it before. But that's how seriously I take keeping my word."

There was no reply.

Well, she hadn't exactly been expecting one. It was just something she felt she'd needed to say.

A week went by, and then another. T.J. didn't hear any more noises behind the baseboards. She didn't see any little people, or even signs of them. She did find *The Travelling Littles* at the library and read it. The book didn't tell her any more than she'd already known from Elizabeth and the Web site. It was kind of a little kids' story, but she liked the artwork. The Littles in the pictures were old-fashioned, but old-fashioned in an interesting way.

Goody Two-shoes, she remembered Elizabeth saying.

Maybe she should get a new haircut—something cooler.

She laughed at the thought. Right. Get a makeover because of a put-down by an imaginary, miniature girl.

But that was the odd thing about it. Although she was about ninety-five percent sure she'd just dreamed the whole business, the memory of it didn't go away the way dreams usually did. She kept finding herself worrying about Elizabeth, out there in the big world on her own. And what about her family? What had happened to them? Had they moved? They must have moved, because it was so quiet behind the walls now. Even Oscar had stopped staring at the baseboards.

But maybe they were just being really, *really* careful now.

They had some of Sheri Piper's other books in the library,

and she was surprised to find a second book about the Littles. It was called *Mr. Pennyinch's Wings* and was about how the Littles regained their ability to turn into birds. She wondered if Elizabeth and her family knew about it.

Of course, it was just a book. That didn't mean the story was real.

It didn't even mean Littles were real. Just that someone was writing about them.

She was true to her word and never said anything to anyone. The only time she felt guilty was when she was talking on the phone to Julie. They'd never had secrets before and now she had a Big One.

Maybe this was what happened when best friends were separated by a distance. You started keeping things to yourself, then you started calling each other less. And then finally, you stopped being best friends. She hoped that wasn't going to happen, but there'd already been a day last week when she hadn't phoned or messaged Julie.

The thought made her feel sad and sent her into a whole blue mood that started with Julie, and took her all the way back to the memory of the day they'd had to walk Red into the horse trailer and take him to his new home.

The closest she came to telling Julie was a week after she'd had her encounter with Elizabeth, when they were on the phone.

"Have you ever seen a fairy?" T.J. found herself asking.

"Oh, sure. Duncan's father is supposed to be one."

"Really?"

"That's what Melissa told me. But you shouldn't call them that. Just say they're gay."

"No, I meant a real fairy."

Julie started to laugh. "What, with little wings and everything? God, what's that city doing to you? I thought only country bumpkins like me were supposed to believe in things like that."

"I still feel like a bumpkin."

"So does that mean *you* believe in fairies?" Julie asked.

Elizabeth hadn't had wings, T.J. thought, so technically, she couldn't be considered a fairy and there was no need to lie.

"Of course I don't," she said.

"So are there *any* cute guys there or what?"

"There's lots of cute guys. They just never think *I'm* cute."

"The dummies."

"Totally."

T.J. had taken to brushing Oscar on a regular basis.

It had started out as a continuation of her cover-up that first morning when Elizabeth had run away, but now they'd both come to enjoy it. T.J. would sit with Oscar out on the back porch, where the view of the one maple and three spruce in the yard let her pretend she was still back on the farm. At least, it worked if she looked up into their branches, instead of across at the neighbour's backyard.

She'd hold the cat on her lap and brush him with long gentle strokes, carefully working out the mats. Oscar would soon start purring and T.J. would slip into the same sort of contemplative mood that used to come over her when she was currying Red.

She was staring dreamily off into space one morning, hand on a sleeping Oscar, the brushing long finished, when her brother, Derek, interrupted her.

"Hey, doofus," he said. "Still playing with dolls?"

When she looked up, he tossed something at her. She caught it before she could see what it was, startling Oscar, who bolted across the lawn.

"You are such a moron," she started to tell him.

But then she looked at the small duffel bag she held in her hand and she could feel her face go pale. Luckily, Derek didn't appear to notice.

"Where did you get this?" she asked him, standing up.

"In the shed. Or should we start calling it the dolly house?"

"In the shed?"

"Yeah. I needed to replace the brake on my in-line skates and was looking for my spare. That thing fell off a shelf when I was moving some boxes around. What were *you* doing in there with your dollies?"

"Nothing."

He cocked his head, then asked, "So it's not yours?"

"Did you look inside it?"

"Sure. It's full of doll clothes."

Of course it would seem that way, T.J. thought. It belonged to Elizabeth. Who was real. How long had she been living in the shed? Was she even still there? Had Derek crushed her, moving around boxes?

Derek was still looking at her. To cover for Elizabeth, T.J. swallowed her pride.

"Of course it's mine. I was just . . . you know . . . "

Derek laughed. "Nope, I don't. And I don't want to either."

He grinned at her and walked off, shaking his head.

She waited until he'd gone around the side of the house and into the garage, then ran for the shed. It was hard to see in there, shadows deepening the farther she looked. It smelled icky, like machinery and the gas for the mower.

"Elizabeth?" she called softly. "Are you in here?"

There was no answer.

Oh God. She'd been eaten by a cat. Or a . . . a weasel or something.

"Elizabeth, please say something."

She looked everywhere, but there was nobody to be found. Especially not a six-inch Little with bright blue hair.

It was all T.J. could think about for the rest of the day.

She went back into the shed twice more with no better luck. That night, lying in bed, she couldn't stand it. She certainly couldn't sleep. So she got dressed, found a flashlight, and went back out to the shed once more, the little duffel bag stuck in the pocket of her jacket.

She'd never been afraid of the dark, but it was spookier than she liked at the back of the yard. The shed door made a loud creak when she opened it and she stood silent, holding her breath. But no lights came on in the house behind her. Allowing herself to breathe again, she flicked on the flashlight and stepped inside.

The first thing its beam found was a disheveled Elizabeth sitting on a spool of wire on the middle shelf. She blocked the light from her eyes with one hand and frowned.

T.J. aimed the light at the floor.

"Thank God you're okay," she said.

"Piss off."

"What?"

"I said, piss off. I don't need your stupid sympathy. I'm doing just fine, okay?"

"But why are you still here?"

"Maybe I like it here."

T.J. never liked to make trouble or impose where she obviously wasn't wanted. It was what was making it so hard for her to make new friends in the neighbourhood and at school. So her first inclination was to leave Elizabeth alone. But then she remembered what her mother had said.

Sometimes we have to involve ourselves in other people's lives, whether they want us to or not.

"I don't think you do," T.J. said. "God, what have you been living on out here?"

She didn't add that it was obvious Elizabeth could really use a bath and to wash her hair.

Elizabeth shrugged. "I found an old bag of birdseed and put out a container to catch rainwater."

"You have to come back to the house with me. I'll get you some real food."

"They're gone, aren't they?"

"You mean your family?"

"No, the zits on your butt. Of *course* I mean my family."

"I don't know," T.J. said. "Maybe they're just being really quiet."

"No, they're gone."

"I guess . . . "

"So what's the point of going back? It would have been horrible going back, having to admit they were right. I *can't* survive out here on my own. But now they're not even there."

"So what's the point of staying out here?" T.J. asked.

Elizabeth shrugged. "It's what I deserve for being such an idiot."

"Now you're just talking stupid."

Elizabeth looked up at her, eyes flashing.

"Remember what I said when you came in?" she asked. "Why don't you just do it? Piss off and leave me alone."

T.J. didn't move.

"Look," Elizabeth said. "You have no idea what it's like being me. Not having friends. Living somewhere you don't want, with people who don't understand you. Okay? So don't pretend *you* understand and can somehow make it better."

"You are so full of crap," T.J. said.

"What?"

"You act so brave, but here you still are, hiding out in my shed."

"You don't think I'd go if I could? But the night's full of owls and cats and the day's full of hawks and dogs and more cats. The few times I've tried to get away, I almost got eaten alive!"

"So what? You think you're the only person to feel scared or alone? Do you think I have all kinds of kids falling over me, wanting to be my friend? Do you think I don't miss the farm and Red?"

"At least you're a normal size."

"Oh yeah. That makes it really easy."

Elizabeth glared at her. "So what's your big point?"

"God, you are such a piece of work," T.J. snapped. "I should just wrap some tape around that big mouth of yours, stick you in a padded envelope and mail you somewhere."

Elizabeth's eyes widened a little. And then she actually smiled.

"Wow," she said.

"Wow what?'

"You do have some backbone."

T.J. wasn't sure if she should feel complimented or insulted. That old "Goody Two-shoes" comment still rankled.

"Sorry, I wasn't being snarky," Elizabeth added.

"Did I just hear you apologise?"

Elizabeth went on as though T.J. hadn't spoken. "It's just you go around and let everybody walk all over you."

"I don't. I just like to get along."

"Even if you don't get your way?"

T.J. sighed. "It's not like that. It's not all about getting your own way. Sometimes there's a bigger picture. Sure, I hate that we moved. And I really, really hated having to give up Red. But we're still a family and things had to change because . . . because they just did. It wasn't anybody's fault. It's just how it worked out."

"So you just go along with it?"

"Yes. No. I don't know. I'm trying to make the best of it, okay? Which is more than I can say for you. All you do is go around with a big chip on your shoulder. How does that make it better for you or anybody around you?"

"You're probably right."

T.J. blinked in surprise. "I am?"

Elizabeth shrugged. "Well, look where it's got me so far."

Neither of them said anything for a long moment.

"So do you want to come back to the house?" T.J. finally asked.

"I guess."

"We could try to find your family," T.J. went on. "Or some other Littles. I could carry you so that you don't have to worry about being attacked or anything."

"Like a pet."

T.J. rolled her eyes. "No, like a friend."

"I guess . . ."

"You know there's books about Littles."

Elizabeth nodded. "One, at least. None of us can figure out how she got the story so right."

"She's written a new one."

Elizabeth raised her eyebrows.

"It's about how the Littles have learned to turn back into birds. You know, like werewolves or something. They can just go back and forth and they don't even have to wait for a full moon."

"No way."

T.J. shrugged. "Well, it's just a book."

"Yeah, but her other one was dead-on."

"So maybe we could look her up. She lives here—or at least in the city."

Elizabeth got up and brushed the dust from her very short, very dirty skirt. It didn't do much good.

"I *am* kind of hungry," she said. "For real food, I mean."

"We've got plenty."

"And I'm dying to be clean again."

"We've got water, too."

Elizabeth nodded. "So . . . thanks, T.J. I guess I'll take you up on your hospitality."

"Do you . . . um, want to go under your own steam?"

"Instead of being carried like a pet?"

"It wouldn't be—"

Elizabeth smiled. "I know. I'm just pushing your buttons. Yeah, I'd appreciate the lift."

T.J. laid her hand palm-up on the shelf beside the Little. When Elizabeth climbed on, she carefully cupped her hand a little and stuck up a finger for Elizabeth to hang on to. Elizabeth didn't hesitate to use it.

"So where does this writer live again?" she asked as T.J. lifted her into the air.

"The librarian said somewhere downtown."

"I wonder how hard she'd be to find?"

"Shh," T.J. told her as she stepped out of the shed. "You're supposed to be a secret, remember?"

"Maybe you could mail me to her."

"Shh."

"But in a box. With padding and airholes . . . "

"Really, you need to shush."

"Can't you just imagine her face when she opens it and out I pop?"

"*Shh.*"

But they couldn't stop giggling softly as they made their way back into the house.

CHARLES DE LINT has been a seventeen-time finalist for the World Fantasy Award, winning in 2000 for the short story collection *Moonlight and Vines*, which is set in his popular fictional city of Newford. The novel based upon this story, also titled *Little (Grrl) Lost*, is soon to be published by Viking. His other recent works include *Widdershins*, *Promises to Keep* (both featuring Jilly Coppercorn), and *Dingo*. He is also the author of *A Circle of Cats*, a children's picture book illustrated by Charles Vess.

De Lint is a respected critic in his field, and is currently the primary book reviewer for *The Magazine of Fantasy and Science Fiction*.

A professional musician for over twenty-five years, specializing in traditional and contemporary Celtic and American roots music, he frequently performs with his wife, MaryAnn Harris—fellow musician, artist, and kindred spirit. They live in Ottawa, Ontario, Canada.

Visit Charles de Lint's Web site at **www.charlesdelint. com** and MaryAnn Harris's at **www.reclectica.com**.

AUTHOR'S NOTE

I've always had a fondness for little people living hidden on the periphery of our lives, from Gulliver's Lilliputians (both in Swift's book, and in T. H. White's *Mistress Masham's Repose*) to the Brownies from the old Sunday colour comics. I've explored the theme before in books such as *The Little Country*

(1991) and short stories like "The Pennymen" (which was reprinted in *Moonlight and Vines*, 1999) and "Big City Littles" (*Tapping the Dream Tree*, 2002), but this story is the first time I've done it with contemporary teenage characters, and I have to say, I had the best time visiting with them.

Diana Wynne Jones

I'll Give You My Word

P eople were always asking Jethro, "How do you *manage* with a brother like yours?"

Jethro mostly smiled and answered, "No problem. He makes me laugh."

This was not really a lie. Jethro used to laugh a lot in the days when he and Jeremy shared a bedroom and Jeremy used to kneel up in his bunk-bed every morning, rocking from side to side and singing—to a tune he had made up himself—"Computers, computers. Caramel custard computers." He sang until Dad banged on the wall and shouted that it was only *dawn,* for goodness' sake, and would Jeremy just *shut up!* At this Jeremy would turn his very knowing big blue eyes toward Jethro, a small smile would flit across his mouth, and he would sing in a whisper, "Collapsed cardinal caramel custard computers!" Jeremy had a way of making his face into a solemn egg-shape and staring crazily into the space between Jethro's head and the window while he uttered, "Sweet cervical béchamel with empirical gladiolus." This never failed to send Jethro off into squeals of laughter. And their father banged on the walls again.

But Jethro's problem was that he was a worrier. In those days he worried that he would stop breathing in the night or that he would prick himself in his sleep and lose all the blood in his body, so that it was always a relief to be woken by Jeremy's singing. When eventually their father, Graeme, got so sick of the singing that he cleared out the box room at the end of the passage and their mother, Annabelle, made it into a bedroom for Jeremy, Jethro started to worry about Jeremy too. Jeremy took to wandering round the house then, saying things. "Ponderous plenipotential cardomum," he would say. "In sacks." And after a bit, "Sententious purple coriander."

"Does that come in sacks too?" Jethro asked him.

"No," Jeremy said. "In suitcases."

"What does *plenipotential* mean?" Jethro asked. "Or *sententious*?"

Jeremy just made his face egg-shaped and stared crazily over Jethro's head. At first Jethro thought that Jeremy was simply inventing these words, and he worried that his brother was mad. But then it occurred to Jethro to look them up in one of the many dictionaries in their house, and he found they were real. *Plenipotential* meant *possessing full power and authority* and *sententious* meant *tending to indulge in pompous moralizing*. And it was the same with all the other words Jeremy kept coming up with: they were always in one dictionary or another, although Jethro was fairly sure Jeremy had no idea what any of the words meant. He began worrying about how they got into Jeremy's head.

Their house was full of dictionaries. Graeme and Annabelle's main work was running an agency called Occult Security, which protected clients of all kinds from magical dangers, exorcised haunts and cleansed evil from houses; but this agency did not pay very well and there were long intervals between commissions. So when they were not getting rid of malign spirits or clearing out gremlins from factories, they both did other things. Annabelle wrote little books called Hall's Guides to Witchcraft and Graeme feverishly composed crossword puzzles for several newspapers. There were three computers in the house, one devoted to Occult Security, one on which Annabelle pattered away, frowning and murmuring, "Now is that strictly shamanism, or should it go under folk magic?" and a third full of hundreds of black and white square patterns and lists of words. Graeme was usually to be found in front of this one, irritably tapping a very sharp pencil and muttering, "I want something Q something something K here and I'm not sure there *is* a word." Then he would reach for one of the wall of dictionaries behind his desk.

Jethro began to suspect that these dictionaries—or maybe the computers or the crosswords—were leaking into his brother's brain.

Meanwhile Jeremy was marching round the house chanting, "Borborygmata, borborygmata!"

Jethro looked this one up too and found that it meant *rumblings of the stomach*. "Mum," he said. "Dad, I think this is serious."

Graeme shook his head and laughed. "You'd think he had a direct line to a dictionary somewhere."

"Yes," said Jethro, "but *how*?"

"You worry too much, my love," Annabelle said. "He probably only wants his lunch. I'd better stop this and find him some food."

"But it's not *natural*!" Jethro said. "And he doesn't know what any of his words *mean*. *Ask* him!"

Graeme bent down to Jeremy and said, "Jeremy, old son, have you any idea what *borborygmata* means?"

Jeremy went egg-shaped and angelical and answered, "Avocado pears."

"That's just your favourite food, old son," Graeme explained. "It means tummy rumblings."

"I know," Jeremy said, looking crazily over Graeme's right shoulder. "With pendulous polyps."

"You see!" said Jethro. "He can't go on like this! What happens when he starts school?"

"I think school will cure him," Annabelle said. "You have to remember we're a rather special household here. When Jeremy discovers that none of the other children talk like he does, he'll stop doing it—you'll see."

Jethro had nothing like Mum's faith in this. The week before Jeremy started school, Jethro took his brother outside and tried to explain to him that school was very different from home. "You have to speak normally there," he said, "or everyone will laugh at you."

Jeremy nodded placidly. "You laugh at me."

"No, *not* like I laugh at you," Jethro said. "I mean they'll *jeer*. Some of them may hit you for being peculiar."

"Cacophonous incredulity," Jeremy retorted. "Turnip

fondue." And then went back indoors. Jethro sighed.

He worried a lot about Jeremy when school actually started. Jeremy was put in Miss Heathersay's class. Miss Heathersay was known to be a really nice, understanding teacher. If anyone could deal with Jeremy, Jethro hoped it was Miss Heathersay. He watched anxiously that afternoon as Jeremy came out with the rest of the class, ready to go home. Jeremy sauntered out, serene and angelic, as if nothing at all had happened to disturb him, and smiled blindingly when he saw Jethro. Jethro noticed that a crowd of other little kids followed after Jeremy, looking awed and maybe even respectful.

"What happened?" Jethro asked. "Did you talk normally?"

"Replenishment," Jeremy replied. "Hirsute haplography."

Whatever that meant, it was all Jeremy would say. Jethro never did manage to find out how his brother got on in Miss Heathersay's class, except that it seemed perfectly peaceful there. No one complained. Nobody seemed inclined to bully Jeremy. All that happened was that more and more people came up to Jethro and asked, "How do you *manage* with a brother like that?" Jethro got very used to answering, "No problem. He makes me laugh." Which was only half a lie, because Jethro *did* laugh at Jeremy even while he worried about him more than ever.

All through the summer holidays that followed Jeremy's first school year, Jethro laughed and worried. Annabelle and Graeme were very busy sitting over the Occult computer, trying to solve the problem of a lady Town Councillor who kept hearing voices, and whether it was because that computer was leaking or for some other reason, Jeremy came up with a new set of strange words every half hour or so.

"Impermanent epistemological urethra," he remarked to Jethro in exactly the same tone of voice ordinary people would say, "Nice day, isn't it?" At Jethro's worried stare, the knowing look came into Jeremy's round blue eyes and he added, "Febrile potlatch, don't you think?"

Jethro's worry turned to giggles as he looked these words up in several dictionaries. *Urethra* meant *the canal that in most mammals carries urine from the bladder out of the body.* He told Jeremy it did and Jeremy answered, "Obloquy," with a cheerful smile.

"Do go and laugh somewhere else, you two," Annabelle implored them. She and Graeme were leaning over a recording they had managed to make of the Town Councillor's voices. It was faint and far off and ghostly.

"These are real," Graeme said. "Mrs Callaghan is certainly not imagining them."

"And she's not going mad either," Annabelle agreed. "I'm so glad for her, Graeme."

"No, they're being broadcast to her somehow," said Graeme. "Someone's playing a very unkind psychic trick on the poor lady. Now, how do we make life bearable for her while we track down who's doing it?"

"Earplugs?" Jethro suggested, on his way to the dictionary to find out what *obloquy* meant.

"Now that's a very good idea," Graeme said. He pointed his beautifully sharpened pencil at Jethro in the way that meant "Congratulations!"—which was almost exactly the opposite of *obloquy*, Jethro discovered. "Occult earplugs," Graeme said.

"How do we go about making some, Annabelle?" He and Annabelle began tapping keys and bringing up diagrams.

"Scrutinizing congenial tinnitus," Jeremy remarked, coming in to look at the diagrams. "Pending conglomerate haruspication."

"Shut up, Jeremy! Go away!" both his parents commanded.

"Toads," Jeremy said disgustedly, "implicated in paradigms of exponential frogspawn."

He went away, and Jethro pulled down the dictionary again. But Jeremy kept coming back while his parents were doing delicate wiring on two deaf-aids and leaning between them to make remarks such as, "Subaverage nucleosis," or, "Tendentious bromoids."

At last Graeme said, "Jeremy, we are very busy with something very small and delicate that we have to get *right*. If you don't want your neck wrung, go *away!*"

"Halitosis," Jeremy said. "You never have time for *me*."

"Play with him, Jethro," Annabelle said, "and I'll double your pocket money."

"But he's so boring," Jethro objected. "He only knows Snap."

"So teach him a new game," Graeme said "Just get out, the pair of you."

Jethro gloomily took Jeremy away and tried to teach him to keep goal in football. It was no good. Jeremy always dived the wrong way like a goalkeeper missing a penalty and the football kept going over into the road. But Jethro had to keep playing with Jeremy, all that summer, because Graeme and Annabelle soon grew busier yet. While they were still trying to trace the person who was broadcasting Mrs Callaghan's voices, trekking out at night with earphones and backpacks of equipment, Mrs Callaghan was wearing the deaf-aids. These earplugs cut out the broadcast so effectively that Mrs Callaghan became convinced that Occult Security had already solved her problem. She recommended Graeme and Annabelle to everyone else on the Council. The consequence was that the Lord Mayor ordered psychic protection around the Council Building, several Councillors requested their homes made safe against occult invasion, and—while Annabelle began worrying that she was not going to meet her deadline with her latest Guide to Witchcraft—Jack Smith, the local Member of Parliament, came to visit them in person.

"Elephantiasis," Jeremy said. Jack Smith was indeed rather fat.

Jack Smith was convinced that he was being persecuted by a coven of witches. "It's hard to explain—it's so nebulous," he said, rubbing his fat hands nervously together. "Most nights I wake up with a jump, thinking I've been hearing horrible strident laughter, and then I can't get to sleep again. Or I become quite sure someone is walking softly about in the house, when I *know* I'm the only person there. And if I have an important speech, or an urgent journey to make, I'm sure to get ill in some way. It happens too often to be an accident. By now I feel quite awful, and I'm getting a name for being a shirker too. The Party Chairman has said hard words to me—and all the time I feel as if something malevolent is watching me and sniggering at my misfortunes."

"It sounds more like a curse," Annabelle said. "What makes you think it's witches?"

"Stridently nebulous," Jeremy explained to her. "Perforated herrings."

Jack Smith shot him an astonished look. Graeme sighed. "Jethro," he said, "take your brother away and teach him another game, or I won't answer for the consequences."

"I've taught him everything I can *think* of," Jethro said sulkily. "I've even invented—Oh, all *right*," he said hastily as his father started to get up. "But don't blame me if we break something."

So they played cricket and Jeremy somehow bowled a ball backwards and broke the kitchen window. Jethro protested that it was not *his* fault. "I was only acting under orders," he said.

"Follow your orders out in the park next time," Annabelle told him, "or I might be tempted to use an unkind spell on you. Look at this mess! My saucepans all full of glass!"

"With you two about, who needs witches?" Graeme grumbled, fetching the broom. "As if we haven't enough to do with Jack Smith's coven."

By the end of that summer, Graeme and Annabelle were still nowhere near discovering Jack Smith's witches. "They're coming in out of the astral plane, obviously," they kept telling each other anxiously. "We have to protect him *there,* as well as physically."

"I suspect they're the same lot as Mrs Callaghan's," the other would reply. "We have to locate that coven and close it down."

But the witches proved to be very well hidden indeed. Graeme filled and surrounded Jack Smith's house with every detection device he could think of, with tracers on each device to lead him to the coven. And no tracers led anywhere. Not one sniff or sound of a witch could be detected. In the end, he simply enfolded Jack Smith himself with a hundred different protections and went on looking. Jack Smith arrived, rubbing his hands and smiling, saying he felt much better now. "My dear fellow," he said to Graeme, "the two of you are like hounds. Never let go of a scent, do you?"

"We don't like to leave a thing like this unsolved," Graeme said. "Neither of us do. But you don't need to go on paying us. It's something we both feel we have to do."

"My dear fellow," Jack Smith said. "My dear lady."

Things were at this stage when the boys started school again. Jethro was now in the top class, the last one before he moved up into the senior school. Every lesson seemed to start with, "You'll be in trouble in Seniors if you don't learn this *now*," or, "Everyone in Seniors has to know this before they begin." To a worrier like Jethro this was seriously alarming. He lay awake at night worrying about the way he was going to arrive to Seniors knowing nothing and be punished for it. And as if this was not enough, Jeremy was put in Miss Blythe's class.

Miss Blythe was notoriously strict. People made rude drawings of her in her tight purple sweater and big round glasses. She had a beaky nose and thin black hair that frizzed out around her angry owl-face. All the best drawings did her as an owl with thick legs and clumpy shoes and these often looked very like Miss Blythe indeed. In Miss Blythe's class no one was allowed to talk or fool about, and they had to form up in lines before they did anything. Miss Blythe called the ones who never talked or played and who formed up in lines quickest her little flowers. The best ones were called her little daisies. You could always tell someone who had been in Miss Blythe's class by their subdued, frightened look and by the way they sat with their hands primly folded and their feet side by side. It was said they were trying to be daisies. Jethro could not imagine Jeremy being made into a daisy. He worried about that almost as much as he worried about Seniors.

For a fortnight nothing much seemed to happen. Then, one lunchtime, Jethro stood in the playground and watched Miss Blythe's class come outside, walking in a line as usual. As usual, Jeremy was about halfway along the line, looking more than usually egg-shaped and angelic. Jethro paused long enough to see that Jeremy was there and turned away to his friends, who were worrying about Seniors too.

The next moment, Jeremy came charging out of the line straight towards Jethro. He flung both arms round Jethro and butted his face into Jethro's chest.

"Hey!" Jethro said. "What's up with you?"

Jeremy said nothing. He just butted harder. People began gathering round to stare.

"Now, look—" Jethro was beginning, when Miss Blythe came shooting out of the school and advanced on Jethro and Jeremy with big strides.

"Jeremy Hall, "Miss Blythe said, "did I or did I not order you to stay behind and wash your mouth out with soap?"

Jeremy just clutched Jethro harder. Jethro realised he was supposed to protect Jeremy, although he was not sure how.

He looked up at Miss Blythe. She was even more like the rude drawings than he had known. She glared like an angry owl.

"Jeremy Hall," said Miss Blythe, "let go at once and look at me!"

Jethro, feeling distinctly brave, said, "What has my brother done wrong?"

"Disobeyed me," snapped Miss Blythe. "Went out with the others when I *told* him not to, and now he's behaving like a baby! After he said such things!"

Jeremy turned his head sideways. He said, "I only said words."

"Don't you contradict *me*!" Miss Blythe said. "Indoors at once! Now!"

"Shan't," said Jeremy, and he added, "Hendiadys."

Miss Blythe gasped. "*What* did you call me?"

Jeremy repeated it. "Hendiadys."

At this Miss Blythe made a noise somewhere between a growl and a scream and seized hold of Jeremy's arm. "For this," she said, "you are going to come with me to the Headmaster this instant, my boy. Come along." She pulled, irresistibly. Jeremy was forced to go where she pulled. But, since he refused to let go of Jethro, Jethro was forced to go too. Like this, watched by nearly the entire school, Jethro shuffled with Jeremy's head in his stomach, into the school, along a corridor and to the door of the Headmaster's study. MR GARDNER, said the notice on this door. HEADMASTER.

Miss Blythe gave the notice an angry bang, flung the door open and dragged both boys inside. Mr Gardner looked up with a jump from his egg sandwich. Jethro could see he did not like being disturbed in the middle of his lunch. "What is this about?" he said.

"Mr Gardner," said Miss Blythe, "I demand that you expel this boy from the school at *once!*"

"Which one?" Mr Gardner asked. "There are two of them, Miss Blythe."

Miss Blythe looked down and was clearly surprised to find she had brought Jethro along as well. "The small one of course," she said. "Jeremy Hall. He does nothing but make trouble."

Mr Gardner looked at Jeremy. Jeremy turned his face out of Jethro's stomach to give Mr Gardner an abnormally egg-shaped and angelic look. Mr Gardner gave the look a strong scrutiny and did not, to Jethro's alarm, seem to be convinced by it. "He's not a troublemaker, sir," Jethro said. "Honestly. He's just strange."

Mr Gardner looked at Jethro then. "And why are *you* here?" he said.

Jethro began to feel rather like a lawyer called in when the police have just arrested a criminal. "He's my brother, sir," he said.

"Can't he speak for himself, then?" Mr Gardner asked.

"Speak? I should just think he can speak," Miss Blythe burst out. "Do you know what this child has just called me, Mr Gardner? Hendiadys, Mr. Gardner. He said it twice too! Hendiadys."

A strange look came over Mr Gardner's face. "And what, exactly, Miss Blythe," he asked, "do you take 'hendiadys' to mean?"

"Some sort of bird, I imagine," Miss Blythe said. "It was an obvious insult anyway."

Jethro, feeling more like a lawyer than ever, cut in hastily, "My cli—er—brother—er, Jeremy never knows what any of his words mean, sir."

"Really?" said Mr Gardner. "Well, Jeremy, what *does* 'hendiadys' mean?"

Jeremy's eyes went round and gazed over Mr Gardner's shoulder. He contrived to look sweetly baffled. "Mouse eggs?" he suggested.

"Jethro," said Mr. Gardner. "Your turn to guess now."

"I—er—think it could be a kind of crocodile," Jethro guessed. He tried to ignore the venomous glare he got from Miss Blythe.

"Do you indeed?" Mr Gardner turned and picked up the dictionary lying beside his lunch. "Let's see what the truth of the matter is," he said, turning pages with an expert whip-whip-whip. "Oh yes. Here we are. 'Hendiadys, *noun*, a rhetorical device by which two nouns joined by a conjunction, usually *and,* are used instead of a noun and a modifier, as in *to run with fear and haste* instead of *to run with fearful haste.*' Did you know that?" he asked Jeremy.

Jeremy looked stunned and shook his head.

"Neither did I," admitted Mr Gardner. "But it isn't a kind of crocodile, is it? Miss Blythe, I fail to see that a rhetorical device by which two nouns et cetera can possibly be any form of insult, quite honestly. I suspect we have a personality clash here. Jethro, take your brother home. You can have the afternoon off. Jeremy, you are suspended from school for half a day while Miss Blythe and I talk this matter over. Off you go."

They went, thankfully scooting under Miss Blythe's purple arm. Before they reached the door, Miss Blythe was slapping her hand down on Mr Gardner's desk and saying, "I don't care what that word means, it was *intended* as an insult! That child is nothing but trouble. I ask them all to say what flower they're going to be, and what does he say?"

"I said I'd be *Rhus radicans*," Jeremy said when they were outside. "That's a flower. She made me stand out in front all morning. I don't like her."

"I don't blame you. She's a hag," said Jethro. "What do we tell Mum and Dad?"

As it happened, they did not have to tell their parents anything. They arrived home to a scene of excitement. A lady called Pippa from Annabelle's publisher was there with a briefcase stuffed with letters, contracts, forms and maps. It seemed that Hall's Guides to Witchcraft had become so popular that Pippa was arranging for Annabelle to go on a world tour to covens and magic circles as far away as Australia to promote the latest Guide. She was to go in three weeks' time, in order to be in New York for a Hallowe'en book-signing, and Pippa was to go with her. Such was the excitement that Jethro nearly forgot to look up *Rhus radicans*. When he did, he found it was poison ivy. Hm, he thought. Perhaps Jeremy *does* know what his words mean, after all. He thought it was lucky he had not discovered this before they were hauled in front of Mr Gardner.

Altogether he felt a fierce mixture of relief and worry: relief that neither of his parents had asked why he and Jeremy were home so early, worry that Jeremy was in bad trouble; relief that something nice had happened for a change, worry because Mum had never been away so far or for so long before; relief that his father was taking the plan on the whole quite well—

"Of course I can manage," Graeme was saying, a touch irritably. "I've no wish to stand in your way, and Jethro is pretty sensible these days." This brought on Jethro's worry again as he realised he would have to look after Dad and Jeremy while Annabelle was away. "But," Graeme continued, "if we haven't located this coven before you leave, I can always go on looking by myself. You go and enjoy yourself. Don't mind me."

While Jethro was trying to decide whether this meant he could feel relieved, Annabelle said to him, "Don't look so worried, love. I'll be back by Christmas."

"Hirsute intropic ampoules," Jeremy said gloomily.

Did Jeremy know what this meant? Jethro wondered. Worry came out on top. And there was always Seniors to worry about as well.

They went back to school next day to discover that Jeremy had been transferred from Miss Blythe's to the parallel class taught by Mr Anderson. Mr. Anderson was young and jolly. When Jethro had been in Mr Anderson's class, he remembered, Mr Anderson's favourite saying had been "Let's have fun looking this up together, shall we?" He wondered if this would suit Jeremy. Or not.

Anyway, Jeremy did not complain. Nor, more importantly, did Mr Anderson. Life rolled on quite peacefully for three weeks, until Annabelle departed for the airport in a flurry of schedules, maps and lecture notes. The house felt amazingly quiet and rather sombre almost at once. Jeremy went round saying "Calisthenic ketchup" in a small dire voice and sighing deeply. Both of them missed Annabelle badly.

Graeme tried to make it up to them. He put in a real effort for a while. He took them to the cinema and the zoo and he provided pizza and ice-cream for every meal until, after a week or so, even Jeremy began to get tired of pizza. "Dad," Jethro said, worrying about it, "this kind of diet is bad for you. We'll all be overweight."

"Yes, but you know I can't cook," Graeme said. "I'm much too busy with this witch hunt to spend time in the kitchen. Bear with me. It's only till Christmas."

"That's *two months*, Dad," Jethro said.

"Proverbial bouillabaisse," Jeremy said, and sighed deeply.

The next day they had a cook. She was a large quiet lady called Mrs Gladd who came silently in while the boys were having breakfast. Graeme seemed as surprised as they were to see her. "I don't do dishes," she said, putting on an overall covered with sunflowers. "Or," she added, tying the belt, "beds or cleaning. You might want to get someone else for that."

Mrs Gladd was still there when the two of them came home from school, cooking something at the stove which smelt almost heavenly. The kitchen table was spread with cakes, jam tarts and sticky buns.

"Herbacious anthracite," Jeremy said, sniffing deeply. "Hagiography," he added, nodding appreciatively at the table.

Mrs Gladd just shrugged. "Eat up," she said.

They did so. Everything was superb. It almost made up for

the fact that Mrs Gladd was living in and had to have Jethro's room, while Jethro moved in with Jeremy in the little room down the corridor. Graeme had to break off his witch hunt in order to heave beds about—Jethro spent several uncomfortable nights because his father had somehow twisted Jethro's duvet inside its cover. It was like sleeping under a knotted sheep. And Jethro didn't do beds any more than Mrs Gladd did. Even with Jeremy trying to help him he only succeeded in giving the duvet a second twist, so that he now seemed to be sleeping under a rather large python.

But this was straightened out by the end of that week when Rosie, Josephine and Kate arrived, Rosie to wash up the stacks of plates and pans in the kitchen, and Josephine and Kate to make beds and clean the house. Consequently, when Annabelle phoned from Los Angeles that Sunday, Jethro and Graeme were able to assure her that they were doing splendidly. Jeremy said, "Curdled phlogiston," which may or may not have meant the same thing.

On the Monday, however, Josephine and Kate said the work was too heavy for just the two of them and were joined by Gertie, Iris, Delphine, and Doreen. As Jethro and Jeremy left for school, all six ladies were hard at work mopping floors from steaming buckets. Graeme had turned all the computers off and was composing crosswords instead. Jethro spared a worry about how Graeme was going to tell which lady was which. Nearly all of them had blonde hairdos and smart jeans. Iris, Doreen, and Josephine wore pink sweaters and two of the others had glasses, but they were otherwise hard to tell apart. All were slim and very talkative. The house rang with happy chatter, the clanking of buckets and the drone of vacuum cleaners.

Jethro could only spare a few seconds for Graeme's problems, however. This week there were going to be Tests on All Subjects, and if you had bad results, your life was going to be not worth living in Seniors. He was far too nervous to think much about anything else.

On Tuesday, three terrifying tests later, Jethro came home trying to forget the tests by wondering what cakes and fat buns Mrs Gladd had made today for tea. He found their car out on the drive in a puddle of water, surrounded by three ladies with cloths tied round their heads. Two had large sponges and the third had a hose. They were shrieking with laughter because one of them had just had her shoes hosed by mistake. Jethro thought at first this one was Rosie and that the others were probably Katie and Iris, but when he looked closely, he saw they were three quite new ladies.

"Perspicuous colonization," Jeremy remarked to him.

Jethro took him along to find Graeme. Graeme's study was knee-deep in sleeping bags. Graeme himself, already noticeably plumper from Mrs Gladd's cooking, was sitting at a new table in the corner of the kitchen. Crossword patterns and dictionaries were heaped on the table, but Graeme was busy eating a large sticky bun. Someone had provided him with new, wider jeans and a wide bland sweater. He hardly looked like Dad any more.

"Dad, who are the new ones washing the car?" Jethro asked.

Graeme smiled, again quite unlike himself. "Two Kylies

and a Tracy," he said. "They do the outside work, garden, wash the windows, all that. Aren't we lucky?"

"Troglodytic contralto," Jeremy said.

"Yes, but," Jethro said, eyeing the sheets of half-made crosswords, "can you get on with your witch hunt with all these people about?"

"Not at the moment," Graeme admitted. "But it's only temporary—only till Christmas—after all."

But *was* it only temporary? If Jethro had had any worry to spare from the tests, he thought he would have been quite worried about this. There were ten new chairs round the kitchen table—which seemed much bigger than it ought to be, somehow—and here Mrs Gladd served succulent meals for fourteen. Jethro ate with his head down, avoiding elbows, and his hearing filled with screams of laughter at jokes he didn't understand. All eleven ladies seemed to be living here now, not only Mrs Gladd. There were sleeping bags everywhere, in the airing cupboard, behind the sofa and bundled to the sides of the upstairs corridor. On Friday, when Jethro had done a test on everything possible from spelling to cookery, the ladies turned the living room and Graeme's study into hairdressing salons and did one another's hair. The booming of vacuum cleaners was replaced by the roaring of hair dryers. The house filled with strong perfumes.

Almost the only place that was empty of ladies was Annabelle's deserted study. Jethro took to sitting there beside Mum's blank turned-off computer, worrying about the results of the tests and wishing he knew the password to get into that computer. He thought he might feel better if he could read some of the things Annabelle had been writing before she left. But when Annabelle rang that Sunday from Sydney in Australia, Jethro had not the heart to tell her about the tests or the ladies either. He was sure he had failed all the tests and there was nothing he could do about the ladies. Graeme, beaming all over his newly plump face, said they were getting along marvellously. Jeremy said, "Hypno-therapeutic distilled amnesia. In blue bottles." At which Mum laughed and said, "Oh *really*, Jeremy!"

Jethro came home from school the next day in a worse worry than ever. None of the results of the tests were ready. Every teacher he asked told him to be patient: it took time to mark them all, they said. He made for Annabelle's study, tripping over sleeping bags on the way, longing for some peace and quiet to worry in, only to find Jeremy in there. Jeremy was sitting at the computer, playing a computer game.

"How did you find the password?" Jethro demanded.

Jeremy turned to him, angelically egg-shaped. "Imperfect clandestine logistics," he said.

Jethro stumped away to consult a dictionary, which was not easy. Mrs Gladd pushed him aside when he tried to reach the one in the kitchen, and Delphine and Rosie said, "Not in here, please!" when he tried Dad's study. When he took down one of the dictionaries in the living room, Josephine moved the small table away in order to do her toenails on it and he was forced to spread the heavy book out on the floor. The sofa was filled with Tracy, one of the Kylies and Josephine, who were all laughing about something. Jethro had to push away a heap of sleeping bags to make room for the dictionary, from which he discovered that *logistics* meant *the science of moving, supplying and maintaining of military forces in the field*. It had nothing to do with logging on, as Jethro had supposed. He went back to Annabelle's study. "I want to use the computer after you," he told Jeremy. "Or it's not fair."

"Fulminating lohan," Jeremy said.

Jethro tried to do without a dictionary, this time by going and asking Graeme when *lohan* meant. But Graeme simply crouched at his corner table and tapped with his pencil. "Don't bother me now," he said. "I have to find a proper clue for *stethoscope*."

Sighing, Jethro collected all the dictionaries the ladies would let him get near and took them up to the little room he was forced to share with Jeremy. It was really annoying, he thought, turning pages, the way he and Jeremy and Graeme were getting pushed away into the corners of their own house. The ladies seemed to feel it belonged to them now. A *lohan*, he discovered, was a rather good Buddhist—something he himself would never be, Jethro knew. He was too worried about those tests. He sat on his bed and worried.

It was an awful week. None of the tests got marked and Jethro began to fear that he was not going to be allowed to go to Seniors. When he got home, the house was always full of vacuum cleaners and shrieks of laughter, and however early he arrived, Jeremy had somehow managed to get to Mum's computer before Jethro did. He tried complaining to Graeme, but Graeme simply tapped his pencil on his teeth and said, "I can't find a decent clue for *stethoscope*." After five days of this, Jethro said to Jeremy, "Dad isn't listening to a word I say."

Jeremy astonished him by saying, "Yes, I know," before turning back to his game.

"No long words?" Jethro asked.

"Not yet," Jeremy said, and killed a swathe of aliens with one burst of gunfire.

"Supper! Hurry up!" Mrs Gladd called from the kitchen.

Jeremy left the computer running, and as they both went down to the kitchen, Jethro was determined to get back to that computer before Jeremy did or die in the attempt.

Supper seemed to be over very quickly. Graeme went straight to his corner then. Jethro and Jeremy edged through the bustle of clearing up, each with an eye on the other, each ready to make a dash for the computer as soon as the other did. They had only just reached the door when someone rang the doorbell at the front door. Josephine and one of the Kylies pushed them aside, right up against Graeme's table, rushing to answer it.

Jeremy looked at Jethro. "Penultimate epiphany," he said. They stayed to see who it was.

It was Miss Blythe. She came striding in, all owl face and purple bosom, and rapped on the kitchen table. "Everybody gather round," she said. As Mrs Gladd turned from the fridge and Kate from the sink and the nine other ladies came back into the kitchen, most of them carrying hair dryers, Jethro had one of those horrible moments when you realise you have been worrying about quite the wrong thing. He had spent all the last fortnight worrying about tests at school, when he should have been looking at what was going on in his own house. He stared at Miss Blythe, feeling empty.

"Now, my flowers," Miss Blythe said, when everyone was gathered by the table, "most of you have been here a full two weeks. I want full reports on progress made and objectives achieved. Mrs Gladd?"

"The way to a man's heart is through his stomach," Mrs Gladd said. "I've cooked up three spells daily and four at weekends. All three of them should be well under by now."

"So I see," Miss Blythe said. Her glasses flashed towards Graeme sitting chewing his pencil in his corner, and then travelled quickly, with evident dislike, across Jethro and Jeremy. "Well done," she said. "Kylie, Kylie and Tracy?"

One of the car-cleaners, the one who wore glasses, said, "We've made absolutely sure that none of their neighbours even see us, Miss Blythe, and we've stopped all communication from outside."

"So have we," said Rosie, stroking her blond hairdo. "Not a soul has been able to consult Occult Security since we came here. The only phone calls we allow in are from Mrs Hall."

"We're working on making everyone forget the Halls exist," Josephine added. She giggled. "Mr Hall's forgotten already."

They all looked over at Graeme, who frowned at his crossword and did not seem to notice.

"Good," said Miss Blythe. "Occult Security isn't going to bother us any more then—none of them are going to bother us much longer. We'll be able to sell this house soon. Have you worked out how much we'll get for it?"

"We priced it up," Kate said. "A quarter of a million seems about right."

A very satisfied expression came across Miss Blythe's face

at this. "Then we're in business," she said, "except for one little matter." Her satisfaction faded rather. "Have any of you worked out what we do about getting rid of *Mrs* Hall? Coven Head will be here any minute, and he'll want to know what we're doing about her."

Mrs Gladd said, "She's leaving Australia later today and flying to Rome."

"Lots of nice deep ocean on the way," said Doreen.

Iris added, "What say we simply bring the plane down while it's over the water?"

Miss Blythe nodded. "Yes, that should do it. It sounds like the neatest way. You can start setting that spell up as soon as Coven Head gets here."

The doorbell rang again.

"Here he is now," Miss Blythe said. "One of you let him in."

As Josephine scudded away to the front door, Jethro stood next to Jeremy thinking, What are we going to do? They're behaving as if we don't exist. *Do* we exist any more?

Just as if thinking that was a signal, Miss Blythe's big owl spectacles turned Jethro's way. She pursed her lips irritably as if he were something offensive like a very dirty sock someone had dropped on the floor. Then she turned with an effusive smile as Josephine ushered Jack Smith into the kitchen. "Oh, Coven Head," she said. "Good to *see* you!"

Jack Smith was fatter and more tightly packed into his expensive suit than ever. He beamed round at the ladies and nodded happily at Graeme in his corner. "Good, good, all going to plan, I see," he said. Looking very humorous, he reached into his waistcoat and then into his pockets and fetched out hundreds of charms, protections and wires, which he threw into a heap on the table. "No need to carry these silly things about any more," he said, tossing a couple of batteries onto the heap. "I see the Hall family is pretty well obliterated."

"Not quite," Miss Blythe said, pointing at Jethro and Jeremy. "Those two don't seen to me to be quite under yet."

"Oh, we'll soon settle that." Jack Smith rubbed his hands together and came to stand over Jethro and Jeremy, smiling down at them, exuding such good cheer that he could have been Santa Claus in a dark suit. "Boys," he said, "this is very important. I need you both to give me your solemn word that you will never, ever say one thing about any of us here—about me, or Miss Blythe, or any of these charming ladies. You." He beamed at Jethro. "Give me your word. Now."

Jethro felt some sort of huge numbness spreading his brain out, squashing it flat, combing away all feelings until there was nearly nothing but a blank white space where all his thoughts usually were. Almost the only thing left was frantic worry. This is *awful*! he thought. If I give him my word I shall be like this for *ever*!

"*I'll* give you my word," Jeremy said from beside Jethro. He stared up towards Jack Smith, past Jack Smith and into empty space deep beyond Jack Smith, and his face was more egg-shaped and angelic than Jethro had ever seen it before. "I'll give you my word," Jeremy said, "and my word is FLOCCIPAUCINIHILIPILIFICATION!"

Jethro suddenly felt much better. Jack Smith said, *"What?"*

"Take no notice," said Miss Blythe. "He's a naughty little boy. He's always doing this."

"All right," Jack Smith agreed. "Forget the kids. Fill me in. What have we decided to do about dispensing with Annabelle Hall?"

"Bring down her plane between Australia and Italy," Miss Blythe told him. "Over the sea if we can. Does that seem good to you?"

Jack Smith said, "Perfect. Let's get on and set the spell then." He strode over to the table and sat himself in the chair next to the sink, rubbing his hands together gladly. Miss Blythe and the other ladies hurried to pull out chairs and sit round the table too. Amid the squawking of chair legs on floor, Jethro bent down to his brother and whispered, "What does floccipaucinihilipilification *mean?*"

Jeremy shrugged, egg-shaped and innocent. *"I don't know."*

Jethro snatched a look at everyone sitting at the table and staring respectfully at Jack Smith and whirled round to Graeme, smiling vaguely at his table just behind them. "Dad!" he said urgently. "Dad, what does floccipaucinihilipilification mean?"

"Eh?" Graeme said. "Floccipaucinihilipilification? Supposed to be the longest word in the language. It means—" Jethro held his breath and watched the smile drain from his father's face into the pinched, grumpy and attentive look he was much more used to. "It means, Jethro, *the act of regarding something as worthless,*" Graeme said. Now he looked almost his usual self. He seemed to have gone thinner, with lines where he had had smooth fat cheeks before. He stared silently at the twelve ladies seated at the table and at Jack Smith sitting by the sink, facing them. "My God!" he said. "A full coven! What are they doing?"

"Casting a spell to make Mum's plane crash," Jethro said.

"Right," said Graeme. None of the coven had even noticed him. He leapt up from his corner and went with long, noiseless steps, through the kitchen doorway and round into his study, where he kicked aside three sleeping bags and dived into the chair in front of his Occult Security computer. "Exorcism programme," he muttered as the machine hummed and flickered, "spell cancellation, expulsion of alien magics programmes, all of them I think, block and destroy magics . . . what else am I going to need?"

Jeremy's voice rose up from the kitchen. "Wanton aquamarine steroids. Epigrammatic yellow persiflage with semiotic substitution."

"Oh yes, personal protection for both you boys," Graeme said. "Go and get Jeremy *out* of there, Jethro!" The exorcism programme came up and he began stabbing at keys, furiously and at speed.

Hendiadys! Jethro thought. Instead of *with furious speed.* He sped back to the kitchen to find everyone sitting in a fixed, spell-making, concentrating silence, except for Jeremy. Jeremy was marching up and down beside the cooker, chanting. "Haloes and holograms, ubiquitous embargoes, zygotes and rhizomes in the diachronic ciabatta." Miss Blythe kept turning her spectacles towards him venomously, but she did not seem to be able to interrupt the spell-making in order to stop Jeremy.

Jethro seized his arm. "Come away. It's dangerous!"

"No, I've got to stay. *Gladiolus!*" Jeremy shrieked, bracing both feet. "Rosacea! Dahlias and debutante begonias.

Recycled stringent peonies. Pockmarked pineapples, torment-
ed turnips, artichokes with acne. Let *go*, Jethro! Cuneiform
cauliflowers. It's *working!*"

Right in front of Jethro, Mrs Gladd shrank to nothing in
her chair. Where she had been sitting there was now a fat clod
of earth with a small spiked shoot sticking out of it.

"*See!*" Jeremy shouted. Rosie winked out downwards as he
yelled, into a smaller clod with two green leaves glimmering
on top of it. "Monocotyledenous, dicotyledenous, myrtle and
twitch!"

Almost at once—blink, blink, blink—Kate, Doreen,
Josephine and both Kylies shrank likewise and became
clumps of earth with tiny seedlings growing in them. Though
Jethro had no doubt that Graeme's programmes were now
running, he was also equally sure that Jeremy was somehow
directing what these programmes did. Blink, blink, blink, all
round the table. Gertie, Iris, Delphine and Tracy shrank into
seedlings too, until only Jack Smith and Miss Blythe were
left. Jack Smith was staring around in bewilderment, but Miss
Blythe flopped forward with her face in her hands, looking
tired and defeated.

"It's Miss Blythe's magic, see," Jeremy explained out of the
corner of his mouth, and turned back to shriek at Jack Smith,
"*Defenestration!*"

Jack Smith sailed up out of his chair and hurtled backwards towards the window.

"*Oleaginous* defenestration, I meant," Jeremy said quickly,
just as Jack Smith's fat back met the glass.

Jethro watched, fascinated, as the glass went soft and

stretched like elastic to let Jack Smith shoot through into the flower bed outside. Then it snapped back into unbroken glass again. Through it, Jethro watched Jack Smith pick himself up and shamble off, looking puzzled, to the big car parked in their driveway.

"You appalling little boy!" Miss Blythe said faintly. "How did you know all my girls were flowers from my garden? And just look at what you've done to that poor dear man, Jack Smith! He was going to be Prime Minister with our coven for a Cabinet."

"Questionable offal," Jeremy retorted. *"You* were going to kill my mum."

"Well, we had to neutralise your parents," Miss Blythe said, in a tired, reasonable way, "or they would have spoilt all his plans, poor man. They are far too good at their job."

Jethro felt he had had enough of Miss Blythe. He went up to her and took hold of her by one purple arm. "The front door's this way," he said. "You'd better go now."

Graeme's programmes were obviously running sweetly by then. Miss Blythe stood up quite meekly and let Jethro lead her out of the kitchen and through the hall. "He was going to let me be his private secretary," she said sadly as they went.

Jethro felt the school could probably do without Miss Blythe too. "Why don't you give up teaching and be his secretary anyway?" he suggested, opening the front door and giving her a push.

"What a good idea!" Miss Blythe exclaimed. "I think I will." She turned round on the doorstep. "Jethro Hall, you're a very understanding boy."

Jethro shut the door on her, wondering if he really wanted to be called understanding by someone like Miss Blythe, and scooted to Graeme's study to check on his father.

Graeme, looking lean and irritable and entirely his usual self, was bending over the computer, where programme after programme was racing downwards on the screen. "I don't know which flight your mother's going to be on," he told Jethro. "I'm having to put protection round every plane that comes into Rome for the next twenty-four hours. Go and shut Jeremy up. He's distracting me."

In the kitchen, Jeremy was still chanting words, although they now seemed to have become a song of triumph. "Highly benevolent botulism," he howled as Jethro came in. "Crusading gumbo extirpated by chocolate pelmanism. Transcendent aureate thaumaturgy!" Jeremy's eyes blazed and his cheeks were flushed. He had worked himself into quite a state.

"Stop it!" Jethro told him. "It's over now."

"Creosote," Jeremy said, the way other people might use a swear word. "Ginseng. Garibaldi biscuits." His cheeks faded to a normal colour and he looked humorously up at Jethro. "I've never done real magic before," he said. "Has Dad made Mum's plane safe?"

"He's just fixing it now, " said Jethro. "What do we do with all these seedlings? Throw them away?"

"No, plant them of course," Jeremy said. "Tomorrow."

So, when Annabelle rang up from Rome the next day, after Graeme had said as usual that they were all fine, Jethro took the phone and told her that he and Jeremy had been gardening. Then Jeremy snatched the phone to say, "And we got rid of those witches for you. They weren't attacking Jack Smith because they didn't exist really."

"Oh good!" Annabelle said. "And *I* want to tell you that Pippa and I have had enough. There was no one at all at the signing this morning. We're going to cancel the rest of the tour and fly home tomorrow." She stopped in a surprised way. "What's this, Jeremy? No more of your big words?"

"No," said Jeremy. "I've used them all up."

Jethro let his breath out in a long, gentle sigh. There was nothing to worry about any more. He was not even worried about the tests, he found. What was done was done.

Graeme wrestled the phone from Jeremy's fist. "Give me your flight number," he said. "I'll put protection round it, just in case."

"If you feel you need to," Annabelle said. "It might make Pippa feel better. She turns out to be terrified of flying."

DIANA WYNNE JONES was born in London, England. At the age of eight, she suddenly *knew* she was going to be a writer, although she was too dyslexic to start until she reached age twelve. There were very few books in the house, so Diana wrote stories for herself and her two younger sisters. She received her B.A. at St. Anne's College in Oxford before she began to write full-time.

Her many remarkable novels include the award-winning *Archer's Goon*, *Howl's Moving Castle*, *Fire and Hemlock*, the Dalemark Quartet, *Dark Lord of Derkholm*, *Year of the Griffin*, *The Merlin Conspiracy*, and the Chrestomanci books (*Charmed Life*, *Witch Week*, *The Lives of Christopher Chant*, *The Magicians of Caprona*, *Conrad's Fate*, and *The Pinhoe Egg*). Firebird has reissued her classic *Tough Guide to Fantasyland* (a World Fantasy and Hugo Award Finalist), and published an original novella, *The Game*. Her most recent novel is *House of Many Ways*.

Diana Wynne Jones lives with her husband, the medievalist J. A. Burrow, in Bristol, England, the setting of many of her books. They have three grown sons and five grandchildren.

Her Web site is **www.leemac.freeserve.co.uk**.

AUTHOR'S NOTE
This story started with my love of dictionaries, not just for being full of words—and I love words—but because of the wildly different words that occur side by side in them. You

find *shire horse* next to *shoestring* and *cutwater* beside *cynical*. My grandson Thomas loves words too, the more preposterous the better. I was trying to teach him "borborygmata" when I got the idea. He was delighted with the word, particularly when he discovered it meant your tummy rumbling, but he couldn't say it. The nearest he got was "babagatama," which ought to be a word anyway. But the main character in the story is in fact another of my grandsons, Gabriel, who spends much of his time away in a distant part of his own head. Then he comes back and tells you something extraordinary. I suspect him of having uncanny powers. This worries his brother, who is Jethro in the story, and a worrier.

Ellen Klages

In the House of
the Seven Librarians

Once upon a time, the Carnegie Library sat on a wooded bluff on the east side of town: red brick and fieldstone, with turrets and broad windows facing the trees. Inside, green glass-shaded lamps cast warm yellow light onto oak tables ringed with spindle-backed chairs.

Books filled the dark shelves that stretched high up toward the pressed-tin ceiling. The floors were wood, except in the foyer, where they were pale beige marble. The loudest sounds were the ticking of the clock and the quiet, rhythmic *thwack* of a rubber stamp on a pasteboard card.

It was a cozy, orderly place.

Through twelve presidents and two world wars, the elms and maples grew tall outside the deep bay windows. Children leaped from *Peter Pan* to *Oliver Twist* and off to college, replaced at Story Hour by their younger brothers, cousins, daughters.

Then the library board—men in suits, serious men, men of money—met and cast their votes for progress. A new library, with fluorescent lights, much better for the children's eyes. Picture windows, automated systems, ergonomic plastic chairs. The town approved the levy, and the new library was built across town, convenient to the community center and the mall.

Some books were boxed and trundled down Broad Street, many others stamped DISCARD and left where they were, for a book sale in the fall. Interns from the university used the latest technology to transfer the cumbersome old card file and all the records onto floppy disks and microfiche. Progress, progress, progress.

The Ralph P. Mossberger Library (named after the local philanthropist and car dealer who had written the largest check) opened on a drizzly morning in late April. Everyone attended the ribbon-cutting ceremony and stayed for the speeches, because there would be cake after.

Everyone except the seven librarians from the Carnegie Library on the bluff across town.

Quietly, without a fuss (they were librarians, after all), while the town looked toward the future, they bought supplies: loose tea and English biscuits, packets of Bird's pudding and cans of beef barley soup. They rearranged some of the shelves, brought in a few comfortable armchairs, nice china and teapots, a couch, towels for the shower, and some small braided rugs.

Then they locked the door behind them.

Each morning they woke and went about their chores. They shelved and stamped and cataloged, and in the evenings, every night, they read by lamplight.

Perhaps, for a while, some citizens remembered the old library, with the warm nostalgia of a favorite childhood toy that had disappeared one summer, never seen again. Others assumed it had been torn down long ago.

And so a year went by, then two, or perhaps a great many more. Inside, time had ceased to matter. Grass and brambles grew thick and tall around the fieldstone steps, and trees arched overhead as the forest folded itself around them like a cloak.

Inside, the seven librarians lived, quiet and content.

Until the day they found the baby.

Librarians are guardians of books. They guide others along their paths, offering keys to help unlock the doors of knowledge. But these seven had become a closed circle, no one to guide, no new minds to open onto worlds of possibility. They kept themselves busy, tidying orderly shelves and mending barely frayed bindings with stiff netting and glue, and began to bicker.

Ruth and Edith had been up half the night, arguing about whether or not subway tokens (of which there were half a dozen in the Lost and Found box) could be used to cast the I Ching. And so Blythe was on the stepstool in the 299s, reshelving the volume of hexagrams, when she heard the knock.

Odd, she thought. It's been some time since we've had visitors.

She tugged futilely at her shapeless cardigan as she clambered off the stool and trotted to the front door, where she stopped abruptly, her hand to her mouth in surprise.

A wicker basket, its contents covered with a red-checked cloth, as if for a picnic, lay in the wooden box beneath the Book Return chute. A small, cream-colored envelope poked out from one side.

"How nice!" Blythe said aloud, clapping her hands. She thought of fried chicken and potato salad—of which she was awfully fond—a Mason jar of lemonade, perhaps even a cherry pie? She lifted the basket by its round-arched handle. Heavy, for a picnic. But then, there *were* seven of them. Although Olive just ate like a bird, these days.

She turned and set it on top of the Circulation Desk, pulling the envelope free.

"What's *that*?" Marian asked, her lips in their accustomed moue of displeasure, as if the basket were an agent of chaos, existing solely to disrupt the tidy array of rubber stamps and file boxes that were her domain.

"A present," said Blythe. "I think it might be lunch."

Marian frowned. "For you?"

"I don't know yet. There's a note . . ." Blythe held up the envelope and peered at it. "No," she said. "It's addressed to 'The Librarians. Overdue Books Department.' "

"Well, that would be me," Marian said curtly. She was the youngest, and wore trouser suits with silk T-shirts. She had once been blond. She reached across the counter, plucked the envelope from Blythe's plump fingers, and sliced it open it with a filigreed brass stiletto.

"Hmph," she said after she'd scanned the contents.

"It *is* lunch, isn't it?" asked Blythe.

"Hardly." Marian began to read aloud:

This is overdue. Quite a bit, I'm afraid. I apologize.
We moved to Topeka when I was very small, and
Mother accidentally packed it up with the linens.
I have traveled a long way to return it, and I know
the fine must be large, but I have no money. As
it is a book of fairy tales, I thought payment of a
first-born child would be acceptable. I always loved
the library. I'm sure she'll be happy there.

Blythe lifted the edge of the cloth. "Oh, my stars!"

A baby girl with a shock of wire-stiff black hair stared up at her, green eyes wide and curious. She was contentedly chewing on the corner of a blue book, half as big as she was. *Fairy Tales of the Brothers Grimm.*

"The Rackham illustrations," Blythe said as she eased the book away from the baby. "That's a lovely edition."

"But when was it checked out?" Marian demanded.

Blythe opened the cover and pulled the ruled card from the inside pocket. "October 17th, 1938," she said, shaking her head. "Goodness, at two cents a day, that's . . ." She shook her head again. Blythe had never been good with figures.

They made a crib for her in the bottom drawer of a file cabinet, displacing acquisition orders, zoning permits, and the instructions for the mimeograph, which they rarely used.

Ruth consulted Dr. Spock. Edith read Piaget. The two of them peered from text to infant and back again for a good long while before deciding that she was probably about nine months old. They sighed. Too young to read.

So they fed her cream and let her gum on biscuits, and each of the seven cooed and clucked and tickled her pink toes when they thought the others weren't looking. Harriet had been the oldest of nine girls, and knew more about babies than she really cared to. She washed and changed the diapers that had been tucked into the basket, and read *Goodnight Moon* and *Pat the Bunny* to the little girl, whom she called Polly—short for Polyhymnia, the muse of oratory and sacred song.

Blythe called her Bitsy, and Li'l Precious.

Marian called her "the foundling," or "That Child You Took In," but did her share of cooing and clucking, just the same.

When the child began to walk, Dorothy blocked the staircase with stacks of Comptons, which she felt was an inferior encyclopedia, and let her pull herself up on the bottom drawers of the card catalog. Anyone looking up Zithers or Zippers (*see "Slide Fasteners"*) soon found many of the cards fused together with grape jam. When she began to talk, they made a little bed nook next to the fireplace in the Children's Room.

It was high time for Olive to begin the child's education.

Olive had been the children's librarian since before recorded time, or so it seemed. No one knew how old she was, but she vaguely remembered waving to President Coolidge. She still had all of her marbles, though every one of them was a bit odd and rolled asymmetrically.

She slept on a daybed behind a reference shelf that held *My First Encyclopedia* and *The Wonder Book of Trees,* among others. Across the room, the child's first "big-girl bed" was yellow, with decals of a fairy and a horse on the headboard, and a rocket ship at the foot, because they weren't sure about her preferences.

At the beginning of her career, Olive had been an ordinary-sized librarian, but by the time she began the child's lessons, she was not much taller than her toddling charge. Not from osteoporosis or dowager's hump or other old-lady maladies, but because she had tired of stooping over tiny chairs and bending to knee-high shelves. She had been a grown-*up* for so long that when the library closed, she had decided it was time to grow *down* again, and was finding that much more comfortable.

She had a remarkably cozy lap for a woman her size.

The child quickly learned her alphabet, all the shapes and colors, the names of zoo animals, and fourteen different kinds of dinosaurs, all of whom were dead.

By the time she was four, or thereabouts, she could sound out the letters for simple words—*cup* and *lamp* and *stairs*. And that's how she came to name herself.

Olive had fallen asleep over *Make Way for Ducklings,* and all the other librarians were busy somewhere else. The child was bored. She tiptoed out of the Children's Room, hugging the shadows of the walls and shelves, crawling by the base of the Circulation Desk so that Marian wouldn't see her, and made her way to the alcove that held the Card Catalog. The heart of the library. Her favorite, most forbidden place to play.

Usually she crawled underneath and tucked herself into the corner formed of oak cabinet, marble floor, and plaster walls. It was a fine place to play Hide-and-Seek, even if it was mostly just Hide. The corner was a cave, a bunk on a pirate ship, a cupboard in a magic wardrobe.

But that afternoon she looked at the white cards on the fronts of the drawers, and her eyes widened in recognition. Letters! In her very own alphabet. Did they spell words? Maybe the drawers were all *full* of words, a huge wooden box of words. The idea almost made her dizzy.

She walked to the other end of the cabinet and looked up, tilting her neck back until it crackled. Four drawers from top to bottom. Five drawers across. She sighed. She was only tall enough to reach the bottom row of drawers. She traced a gentle finger around the little brass frames, then very carefully pulled out the white cards inside and laid them on the floor in a neat row:

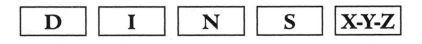

She squatted over them, her tongue sticking out of the corner of her mouth in concentration, and tried to read.

"Sound it out." She could almost hear Olive's voice, soft and patient. She took a deep breath.

"Duh-in-s—" and then she stopped, because the last card had too many letters, and she didn't know any words that had Xs in them. Well, xylophone. But the X was in the front, and that wasn't the same. She tried anyway. "Duh-ins-zzzigh," and frowned.

She squatted lower, so low she could feel cold marble under her cotton pants, and put her hand on top of the last

card. One finger covered the X and her pinkie covered the Z
(another letter that was useless for spelling ordinary things).
That left Y. Y at the end was good: funnY, happY.

"Duh-ins-see," she said slowly. "Dinsy."

That felt very good to say, hard and soft sounds and hiss-
ing Ss mixing in her mouth, so she said it again, louder, which
made her laugh, so she said it again, very loud: "DINSY!"

There is nothing quite like a loud voice in a library to get
a lot of attention very fast. Within a minute, all seven of the
librarians stood in the doorway of the alcove.

"What on earth?" said Harriet.

"Now what have you . . . " said Marian.

"What have you spelled, dear?" asked Olive in her soft little
voice.

"I made it myself," the girl replied.

"Just gibberish," murmured Edith, though not unkindly. "It
doesn't mean a thing."

The child shook her head. "Does so. Olive," she said,
pointing to Olive. "Do'thy, Edith, Harwiet, Bithe, Ruth." She
paused and rolled her eyes. "Mawian," she added, a little less
cheerfully. Then she pointed to herself. "And Dinsy."

"Oh, now, Polly," said Harriet.

"Dinsy," said Dinsy.

"Bitsy?" Blythe tried hopefully.

"Dinsy," said Dinsy.

And that was that.

At three every afternoon, Dinsy and Olive made a two-person
circle on the braided rug in front of the bay window, and had

Story Time. Sometimes Olive read aloud from *Beezus and Ramona* and *Half Magic*, and sometimes Dinsy read to Olive, *The King's Stilts*, and *In the Night Kitchen*, and *Winnie-the-Pooh*. Dinsy liked that one especially, and took it to bed with her so many times that Edith had to repair the binding. Twice.

That was when Dinsy first wished upon the Library.

A note about the Library:

Knowledge is not static; information must flow in order to live. Every so often one of the librarians would discover a new addition. *Harry Potter and the Sorcerer's Stone* appeared one rainy afternoon, Rowling shelved neatly between Rodgers and Saint-Exupéry, as if it had always been there. Blythe found a book of Thich Nhat Hanh's writings in the 294s one day while she was dusting, and Feynman's lectures on physics showed up on Dorothy's shelving cart after she'd gone to make a cup of tea.

It didn't happen often; the Library was selective about what it chose to add, rejecting flash-in-the-pan best-sellers, sifting for the long haul, looking for those voices that would stand the test of time next to Dickens and Tolkien, Woolf and Gould.

The librarians took care of the books, and the Library watched over them in return. It occasionally left treats: a bowl of ripe tangerines on the Formica counter of the Common Room; a gold foil box of chocolate creams; seven small, stemmed glasses of sherry on the table one teatime. Their biscuit tin remained full, the cream in the Wedgwood jug stayed fresh, and the ink pad didn't dry out. Even the little pencils stayed needle sharp, never whittling down to finger-cramping nubs.

Some days the Library even hid Dinsy, when she had made a mess and didn't want to be found, or when one of the librarians was in a dark mood. It rearranged itself, just a bit, so that in her wanderings she would find a new alcove or cubbyhole, and once a secret passage that led to a previously unknown balcony overlooking the Reading Room. When she went back a week later, she found only blank wall.

And so it was, one night when she was sixish, that Dinsy first asked the Library for a boon. Lying in her tiny yellow bed, the fraying *Pooh* under her pillow, she wished for a bear to cuddle. Books were small comfort once the lights were out, and their hard, sharp corners made them awkward companions under the covers. She lay with one arm crooked around a soft, imaginary bear, and wished and wished until her eyelids fluttered into sleep.

The next morning, while they were all having tea and toast with jam, Blythe came into the Common Room with a quizzical look on her face and her hands behind her back.

"The strangest thing," she said. "On my way up here I glanced over at the Lost and Found. Couldn't tell you why. Nothing lost in ages. But this must have caught my eye."

She held out a small brown bear, one shoebutton eye missing, bits of fur gone from its belly, as if it had been loved almost to pieces.

"It seems to be yours," she said with a smile, turning up one padded foot, where DINSY was written in faded laundry-marker black.

Dinsy wrapped her whole self around the cotton-stuffed body and skipped for the rest of the morning. Later, after Olive gave her a snack—cocoa and a Lorna Doone—Dinsy cupped her hand and blew a kiss to the oak woodwork.

"Thank you," she whispered, and put half her cookie in a crack between two tiles on the Children's Room fireplace when Olive wasn't looking.

Dinsy and Olive had a lovely time. One week they were pirates, raiding the Common Room for booty (and raisins). The next they were princesses, trapped in the turret with *At the Back of the North Wind,* and the week after that they were knights in shining armor, rescuing damsels in distress, a game Dinsy especially savored because it annoyed Marian to be rescued.

But the year she turned seven-and-a-half, Dinsy stopped reading stories. Quite abruptly, on an afternoon that Olive said later had really *felt* like a Thursday.

"Stories are for babies," Dinsy said. "I want to read about *real* people." Olive smiled a sad smile and pointed toward the far wall, because Dinsy was not the first child to make that same pronouncement, and she had known this phase would come.

After that, Dinsy devoured biographies, starting with the orange ones, the Childhoods of Famous Americans: *Thomas Edison, Young Inventor.* She worked her way from Abigail Adams to John Peter Zenger, all along the west side of the Children's Room, until one day she went around the corner, where Science and History began.

She stood in the doorway, looking at the rows of grown-up books, when she felt Olive's hand on her shoulder.

"Do you think maybe it's time you moved across the hall?" Olive asked softly.

Dinsy bit her lip, then nodded. "I can come back to visit, can't I? When I want to read stories again?"

"For as long as you like, dear. Anytime at all."

So Dorothy came and gathered up the bear and the pillow and the yellow toothbrush. Dinsy kissed Olive on her papery cheek and, holding Blythe's hand, moved across the hall, to the room where all the books had numbers.

Blythe was plump and freckled and frizzled. She always looked a little flushed, as if she had just that moment dropped what she was doing to rush over and greet you. She wore rumpled tweed skirts and a shapeless cardigan whose original color was impossible to guess. She had bright, dark eyes like a spaniel's, which Dinsy thought was appropriate, because Blythe *lived* to fetch books. She wore a locket with a small rotogravure picture of Melvil Dewey and kept a variety of sweets—sour balls and mints and Necco wafers—in her desk drawer.

Dinsy had always liked her.

She was not as sure about Dorothy.

Over *her* desk, Dorothy had a small framed medal on a royal-blue ribbon, won for "Excellence in Classification Studies." She could operate the ancient black Remington typewriter with brisk efficiency, and even, on occasion, coax chalky gray prints out of the wheezing old copy machine.

She was a tall, rawboned woman with steely blue eyes, good posture, and even better penmanship. Dinsy was a little frightened of her, at first, because she seemed so stern, and because she looked like magazine pictures of the Wicked Witch of the West, or at least Margaret Hamilton.

But that didn't last long.

"You should be very careful not to slip on the floor in here,"

Dorothy said on their first morning. "Do you know why?"

Dinsy shook her head.

"Because now you're in the nonfriction room!" Dorothy's angular face cracked into a wide grin.

Dinsy groaned. "Okay," she said after a minute. "How do you file marshmallows?"

Dorothy cocked her head. "Shoot."

"By the *Gooey* Decimal System!"

Dinsy heard Blythe tsk-tsk, but Dorothy laughed out loud, and from then on they were fast friends.

The three of them used the large, sunny room as an arena for endless games of I Spy and Twenty Questions as Dinsy learned her way around the shelves. In the evenings, after supper, they played Authors and Scrabble, and (once) tried to keep a running rummy score in Base Eight.

Dinsy sat at the court of Napoleon, roamed the jungles near Timbuktu, and was a frequent guest at the Round Table. She knew all the kings of England and the difference between a pergola and a folly. She knew the names of 112 breeds of sheep, and loved to say "Barbados Blackbelly" over and over, although it was difficult to work into conversations. When she affectionately, if misguidedly, referred to Blythe as a "Persian Fat-Rumped," she was sent to bed without supper.

A note about time:

Time had become quite flexible inside the library. (This is true of most places with interesting books. Sit down to read for twenty minutes, and suddenly it's dark, with no clue as to where the hours have gone.)

As a consequence, no one was really sure about the day of the week, and there was frequent disagreement about the month and year. As the keeper of the date stamp at the front desk, Marian was the arbiter of such things. But she often had a cocktail after dinner, and many mornings she couldn't recall if she'd already turned the little wheel, or how often it had slipped her mind, so she frequently set it a day or two ahead—or back three—just to make up.

One afternoon, on a visit to Olive and the Children's Room, Dinsy looked up from *Little Town on the Prairie* and said, "When's my birthday?"

Olive thought for a moment. Because of the irregularities of time, holidays were celebrated a bit haphazardly. "I'm not sure, dear. Why do you ask?"

"Laura's going to a birthday party, in this book," she said, holding it up. "And it's fun. So I thought maybe I could have one."

"I think that would be lovely," Olive agreed. "We'll talk to the others at supper."

"Your birthday?" said Harriet as she set the table a few hours later. "Let me see." She began to count on her fingers. "You arrived in April, according to Marian's stamp, and you were about nine months old, so—" She pursed her lips as she ticked off the months. "You must have been born in July!"

"But when's my birth*day*?" Dinsy asked impatiently.

"Not sure," said Edith as she ladled out the soup.

"No way to tell," Olive agreed.

"How does July fifth sound?" offered Blythe, as if it were a point of order to be voted on. Blythe counted best by fives.

"Fourth," said Dorothy. "Independence Day. Easy to remember?"

Dinsy shrugged. "Okay." It hadn't seemed so complicated in the Little House book. "When is that? Is it soon?"

"Probably." Ruth nodded.

A few weeks later, the librarians threw her a birthday party.

Harriet baked a spice cake with pink frosting, and wrote DINSY on top in red licorice laces, dotting the *I* with a lemon drop (which was rather stale). The others gave her gifts that were thoughtful and mostly handmade:

A set of Dewey Decimal flash cards from Blythe.

A book of logic puzzles (stamped DISCARD more than a dozen times, so Dinsy could write in it) from Dorothy.

A lumpy orange-and-green cardigan Ruth knitted for her.

A snow globe from the 1939 World's Fair from Olive.

A flashlight from Edith, so that Dinsy could find her way around at night and not knock over the wastebasket again.

A set of paper finger puppets, made from blank card pockets, hand-painted by Marian. (They were literary figures, of course, all of them necessarily stout and squarish—Nero Wolfe and Friar Tuck, Santa Claus and Gertrude Stein.)

But her favorite gift was the second boon she'd wished upon the Library: a box of crayons. (She had grown very tired of drawing gray pictures with the little pencils.) It had produced Crayola crayons, in the familiar yellow-and-green box, labeled LIBRARY PACK. Inside were the colors of Dinsy's world: Reference Maroon, Brown Leather, Peplum Beige, Reader's Guide Green, World Book Red, Card Catalog Cream, Date Stamp Purple, and Palatino Black.

It was a very special birthday, that fourth of July. Although Dinsy wondered about Marian's calculations. As Harriet cut the first piece of cake that evening, she remarked that it was snowing rather heavily outside, which everyone agreed was lovely, but quite unusual for that time of year.

Dinsy soon learned all the planets, and many of their moons. (She referred to herself as Umbriel for an entire month.) She puffed up her cheeks and blew onto stacks of scrap paper. "Sirocco," she'd whisper. "Chinook. Mistral. Willy-Willy," and rated her attempts on the Beaufort scale. Dorothy put a halt to it after Hurricane Dinsy reshuffled a rather elaborate game of Patience.

She dipped into fractals here, double dactyls there. When she tired of a subject—or found it just didn't suit her—Blythe or Dorothy would smile and proffer the hat. It was a deep green felt that held slips of paper numbered 001 to 999. Dinsy'd scrunch her eyes closed, pick one, and, like a scavenger hunt, spend the morning (or the next three weeks) at the shelves indicated.

Pangolins lived at 599 (point 31), and Pancakes at 641. Pencils were at 674 but Pens were a shelf away at 681, and

Ink was across the aisle at 667. (Dinsy thought that was stupid, because you had to *use* them together.) Pluto the planet was at 523, but Pluto the Disney dog was at 791 (point 453), near Rock and Roll and Kazoos.

It was all very useful information. But in Dinsy's opinion, things could be a little *too* organized.

The first time she straightened up the Common Room without anyone asking, she was very pleased with herself. She had lined up everyone's teacup in a neat row on the shelf, with all the handles curving the same way, and arranged the spices in the little wooden rack: ANISE, BAY LEAVES, CHIVES, DILL WEED, PEPPERCORNS, SALT, SESAME SEEDS, SUGAR.

"Look," she said when Blythe came in to refresh her tea. "Order out of chaos." It was one of Blythe's favorite mottoes.

Blythe smiled and looked over at the spice rack. Then her smile faded and she shook her head.

"Is something wrong?" Dinsy asked. She had hoped for a compliment.

"Well, you used the alphabet," said Blythe, sighing. "I suppose it's not your fault. You were with Olive for a good many years. But you're a big girl now. You should learn the *proper* order." She picked up the salt container. "We'll start with Salt." She wrote the word on the little chalkboard hanging by the icebox, followed by the number 553.632. "Five-five-three-point-six-three-two. Because—?"

Dinsy thought for a moment. "Earth Sciences."

"Ex-actly." Blythe beamed. "Because salt is a mineral. But, now, chives. Chives are a garden crop, so they're . . ."

Dinsy bit her lip in concentration. "Six-thirty-something."

"Very good." Blythe smiled again and chalked CHIVES

635.26 on the board. "So you see, Chives should always be shelved *after* Salt, dear."

Blythe turned and began to rearrange the eight ceramic jars. Behind her back, Dinsy silently rolled her eyes.

Edith appeared in the doorway.

"Oh, not again," she said. "No wonder I can't find a thing in this kitchen. Blythe, I've *told* you. Bay Leaf comes first. QK-four-nine—" She had worked at the university when she was younger.

"Library of Congress, my fanny," said Blythe, not quite under her breath. "We're not *that* kind of library."

"It's no excuse for imprecision," Edith replied. They each grabbed a jar and stared at each other.

Dinsy tiptoed away and hid in the 814s, where she read "Jabberwocky" until the coast was clear.

But the kitchen remained a taxonomic battleground. At least once a week, Dinsy was amused by the indignant sputtering of someone who had just spooned dill weed, not sugar, into a cup of Earl Grey tea.

Once she knew her way around, Dinsy was free to roam the library as she chose.

"Anywhere?" she asked Blythe.

"Anywhere you like, my sweet. Except the Stacks. You're not quite old enough for the Stacks."

Dinsy frowned. "I am *so*," she muttered. But the Stacks were locked, and there wasn't much she could do.

Some days she sat with Olive in the Children's Room, revisiting old friends, or explored the maze of the Main Room. Other days she spent in the Reference Room, where Ruth and Harriet

guarded the big important books that no one could ever, ever check out—not even when the library had been open.

Ruth and Harriet were like a set of salt-and-pepper shakers from two different yard sales. Harriet had faded orange hair and a sharp, kind face. Small and pinched and pointed, a decade or two away from wizened. She had violet eyes and a mischievous, conspiratorial smile and wore rimless octagonal glasses, like stop signs. Dinsy had never seen an actual stop sign, but she'd looked at pictures.

Ruth was Chinese. She wore wool jumpers in neon plaids and had cat's-eye glasses on a beaded chain around her neck. She never put them all the way on, just lifted them to her eyes and peered through them without opening the bows.

"Life is a treasure hunt," said Harriet.

"Knowledge is power," said Ruth. "Knowing where to look is half the battle."

"Half the fun," added Harriet. Ruth almost never got the last word.

They introduced Dinsy to dictionaries and almanacs, encyclopedias and compendiums. They had been native guides through the country of the Dry Tomes for many years, but they agreed that Dinsy delved unusually deep.

"Would you like to take a break, love?" Ruth asked one afternoon. "It's nearly time for tea."

"I *am* fatigued," Dinsy replied, looking up from *Roget*. "Fagged out, weary, a bit spent. Tea would be pleasant, agreeable—"

"I'll put the kettle on," sighed Ruth.

Dinsy read *Bartlett's* as if it were a catalog of conversations, spouting lines from Tennyson, Mark Twain, and Dale

Carnegie until even Harriet put her hands over her ears and began to hum "Stairway to Heaven."

One or two evenings a month, usually after Blythe had remarked "Well, she's a spirited girl," for the third time, they all took the night off, "for Library business." Olive or Dorothy would tuck Dinsy in early and read from one of her favorites while Ruth made her a bedtime treat—a cup of spiced tea that tasted a little like cherries and a little like varnish, and which Dinsy somehow never remembered finishing.

A list (written in diverse hands), tacked to the wall of the Common Room.

10 Things to Remember When You Live in a Library

1. We do not play shuffleboard on the Reading Room table.
2. Books should not have "dog's ears." Bookmarks make lovely presents.
3. Do not write in books. Even in pencil. Puzzle collections and connect-the-dots are books.
4. The shelving cart is not a scooter.
5. Library paste is not food.
   [Marginal note in a child's hand: True. It tastes like Cream of Wrong soup.]
6. Do not use the date stamp to mark your banana.
7. Shelves are not monkey bars.
8. Do not play 982-pickup with the P-Q drawer (or any other).

9. The dumbwaiter is only for books. It is not a carnival ride.
10. Do not drop volumes of the Britannica off the stairs to hear the echo.

They were an odd, but contented family. There were rules, to be sure, but Dinsy never lacked for attention. With seven mothers, there was always someone to talk with, a hankie for tears, a lap or a shoulder to share a story.

Most evenings, when Dorothy had made a fire in the Reading Room and the wooden shelves gleamed in the flickering light, they would all sit in companionable silence. Ruth knitted, Harriet muttered over an acrostic, Edith stirred the cocoa so it wouldn't get a skin. Dinsy sat on the rug, her back against the knees of whomever was her favorite that week, and felt safe and warm and loved. "God's in his heaven, all's right with the world," as Blythe would say.

But as she watched the moon peep in and out of the clouds through the leaded-glass panes of the tall windows, Dinsy often wondered what it would be like to see the whole sky, all around her.

First Olive and then Dorothy had been in charge of Dinsy's thick dark hair, trimming it with the mending shears every few weeks when it began to obscure her eyes. But a few years into her second decade at the library, Dinsy began cutting it herself, leaving it as wild and spiky as the brambles outside the front door.

That was not the only change.

"We haven't seen her at breakfast in weeks," Harriet said as she buttered a scone one morning.

"Months. And all she reads is Salinger. Or Sylvia Plath," complained Dorothy. "I wouldn't mind that so much, but she just leaves them on the table for *me* to reshelve."

"It's not as bad as what she did to Olive," Marian said. "*The Golden Compass* appeared last week, and she thought Dinsy would enjoy it. But not only did she turn up her nose, she had the gall to say to Olive, 'Leave me alone. I can find my own books.' Imagine. Poor Olive was beside herself."

"She used to be such a sweet child." Blythe sighed. "What are we going to do?"

"Now, now. She's just at that age," Edith said calmly. "She's not really a child anymore. She needs some privacy, and some responsibility. I have an idea."

And so it was that Dinsy got her own room—with a door that *shut*—in a corner of the second floor. It had been a tiny cubbyhole of an office, but it had a set of slender curved stairs, wrought iron worked with lilies and twigs, which led up to the turret between the red-tiled eaves.

The round tower was just wide enough for Dinsy's bed, with windows all around. There had once been a view of the town, but now trees and ivy allowed only jigsaw puzzle–shaped puddles of light to dapple the wooden floor. At night the puddles were luminous blue splotches of moonlight that hinted of magic beyond her reach.

On the desk in the room below, centered in a pool of yellow lamplight, Edith had left a note: "Come visit me. There's mending to be done," and a worn brass key on a wooden paddle, stenciled with the single word: STACKS.

The Stacks were in the basement, behind a locked gate at the foot of the metal spiral staircase that descended from the 600s. They had always reminded Dinsy of the steps down to the dungeon in *The King's Stilts*. Darkness below hinted at danger, but adventure. Terra Incognita.

Dinsy didn't use her key the first day, or the second. Mending? Boring. But the afternoon of the third day, she ventured down the spiral stairs. She had been as far as the gate before, many times, because it was forbidden, to peer through the metal mesh at the dimly lighted shelves and imagine what treasures might be hidden there.

She had thought that the Stacks would be damp and cold, strewn with odd bits of discarded library flotsam. Instead they were cool and dry, and smelled very different from upstairs. Dustier, with hints of mold and the tang of vintage leather, an undertone of vinegar stored in an old shoe.

Unlike the main floor, with its polished wood and airy high ceilings, the Stacks were a low, cramped warren of gunmetal gray shelves that ran floor to ceiling in narrow aisles. Seven levels twisted behind the west wall of the library like a secret labyrinth that stretched from below the ground to up under the eaves of the roof. The floor and steps were translucent glass brick, and the six-foot ceilings strung with pipes and ducts were lit by single caged bulbs, two to an aisle.

It was a windowless fortress of books. Upstairs the shelves were mosaics of all colors and sizes, but the Stacks were filled with geometric monochrome blocks of subdued colors: eight dozen forest-green bound volumes of *Ladies' Home Journal* filled five rows of shelves, followed by an equally large block of identical dark red *LIFEs*.

Dinsy felt like she was in another world. She was not lost, but for one of the few times in her life, she was not easily found, and that suited her. She could sit, invisible, and listen to the sounds of library life going on around her. From Level Three she could hear Ruth humming in the Reference Room on the other side of the wall. Four feet away, and it felt like miles. She wandered and browsed for a month before she presented herself at Edith's office.

A frosted glass pane in the dark wood door said MENDING ROOM in chipping gold letters. The door was open a few inches, and Dinsy could see a long workbench strewn with sewn folios and bits of leather bindings, spools of thread and bottles of thick beige glue.

"I gather you're finding your way around," Edith said, without turning in her chair. "I haven't had to send out a search party."

"Pretty much," Dinsy replied. "I've been reading old magazines." She flopped into a chair to the left of the door.

"One of my favorite things," Edith agreed. "It's like time travel." Edith was a tall, solid woman with long graying hair that she wove into elaborate buns and twisted braids, secured with number-two pencils and a single tortoiseshell comb. She wore blue jeans and and vests in brightly muted colors—pale teal and lavender and dusky rose—with a strand of lapis lazuli beads cut in rough ovals.

Edith repaired damaged books, a job that was less demanding now that nothing left the building. But some of the bound volumes of journals and abstracts and magazines went back as far as 1870, and their leather bindings were crumbling into dust. The first year, Dinsy's job was to go through the aisles, level by level, and find the volumes that needed the most help. Edith gave her a clipboard and told her to check in now and then.

Dinsy learned how to take apart old books and put them back together again. Her first mending project was the tattered 1877 volume of *American Naturalist*, with its articles on "Educated Fleas" and "Barnacles" and "The Cricket as Thermometer." She sewed pages into signatures, trimmed leather, and marbleized paper. Edith let her make whatever she wanted out of the scraps, and that year Dinsy gave everyone miniature replicas of their favorite volumes for Christmas.

She liked the craft, liked doing something with her hands. It took patience and concentration, and that was oddly soothing. After supper, she and Edith often sat and talked for hours, late into the night, mugs of cocoa on their workbenches, the rest of the library dark and silent above them.

"What's it like outside?" Dinsy asked one night while she was waiting for some glue to dry.

Edith was silent for a long time, long enough that Dinsy wondered if she'd spoken too softly, and was about to repeat the question, when Edith replied.

"Chaos."

That was not anything Dinsy had expected. "What do you mean?"

"It's noisy. It's crowded. Everything's always changing, and not in any way you can predict."

"That sounds kind of exciting," Dinsy said.

"Hmm." Edith thought for a moment. "Yes, I suppose it could be."

Dinsy mulled that over and fiddled with a scrap of leather, twisting it in her fingers before she spoke again. "Do you ever miss it?"

Edith turned on her stool and looked at Dinsy. "Not often," she said slowly. "Not as often as I'd thought. But then I'm awfully fond of order. Fonder than most, I suppose. This is a better fit."

Dinsy nodded and took a sip of her cocoa.

A few months later, she asked the Library for a third and final boon.

The evening that everything changed, Dinsy sat in the armchair in her room, reading Trollope's *Can You Forgive Her?* (for the third time), imagining what it would be like to talk to Glencora, when a tentative knock sounded at the door.

"Dinsy? Dinsy?" said a tiny familiar voice. "It's Olive, dear."

Dinsy slid her READ! bookmark into chapter 14 and closed the book. "It's open," she called.

Olive padded in wearing a red flannel robe, her feet in worn carpet slippers. Dinsy expected her to proffer a book, but instead Olive said, "I'd like you to come with me, dear." Her blue eyes shone with excitement.

"What for?" They had all done a nice reading of *As You*

Like It a few days before, but Dinsy didn't remember any plans for that night. Maybe Olive just wanted company. Dinsy had been meaning to spend an evening in the Children's Room, but hadn't made it down there in months.

But Olive surprised her. "It's Library business," she said, waggling her finger, and smiling.

Now, that was intriguing. For years, whenever the Librarians wanted an evening to themselves, they'd disappear down into the Stacks after supper, and would never tell her why. "It's Library business," was all they ever said. When she was younger, Dinsy had tried to follow them, but it's hard to sneak in a quiet place. She was always caught and given that awful cherry tea. The next thing she knew it was morning.

"Library business?" Dinsy said slowly. "And I'm invited?"

"Yes, dear. You're practically all grown up now. It's high time you joined us."

"Great." Dinsy shrugged, as if it were no big deal, trying to hide her excitement. And maybe it wasn't a big deal. Maybe it was a meeting of the rules committee, or plans for moving the 340s to the other side of the window again. But what if it *was* something special . . . ? That was both exciting and a little scary.

She wiggled her feet into her own slippers and stood up. Olive barely came to her knees. Dinsy touched the old woman's white hair affectionately, remembering when she used to snuggle into that soft lap. Such a long time ago.

A library at night is a still but resonant place. The only lights were the sconces along the walls, and Dinsy could hear the faint echo of each footfall on the stairs down to the foyer.

They walked through the shadows of the shelves in the Main Room, back to the 600s, and down the metal stairs to the Stacks, footsteps ringing hollowly.

The lower level was dark except for a single caged bulb above the rows of *National Geographics*, their yellow bindings pale against the gloom. Olive turned to the left.

"Where are we going?" Dinsy asked. It was so odd to be down there with Olive.

"You'll see," Olive said. Dinsy could practically feel her smiling in the dark. "You'll see."

She led Dinsy down an aisle of boring municipal reports and stopped at the far end, in front of the door to the janitorial closet set into the stone wall. She pulled a long, old-fashioned brass key from the pocket of her robe and handed it to Dinsy.

"You open it, dear. The keyhole's a bit high for me."

Dinsy stared at the key, at the door, back at the key. She'd been fantasizing about "Library Business" since she was little, imagining all sorts of scenarios, none of them involving cleaning supplies. A monthly poker game. A secret tunnel into town, where they all went dancing, like the twelve princesses. Or a book group, reading forbidden texts. And now they were inviting her in? What a letdown if it was just maintenance.

She put the key in the lock. "Funny," she said as she turned it. "I've always wondered what went on when you—" Her voice caught in her throat. The door opened, not onto the closet of mops and pails and bottles of Pine-Sol she expected, but onto a small room paneled in wood the color of ancient honey. An Oriental rug in rich, deep reds lay on the parquet floor, and the room shone with the light of dozens of candles. There were no shelves, no books, just a small fireplace at one end where a log crackled in the hearth.

"Surprise," said Olive softly. She gently tugged Dinsy inside.

All the others were waiting, dressed in flowing robes of different colors. Each of them stood in front of a Craftsman rocker, dark wood covered in soft brown leather.

Edith stepped forward and took Dinsy's hand. She gave it a gentle squeeze and said, under her breath, "Don't worry." Then she winked and led Dinsy to an empty rocker. "Stand here," she said, and returned to her own seat.

Stunned, Dinsy stood, her mouth open, her feelings a kaleidoscope.

"Welcome, dear one," said Dorothy. "We'd like you to join us." Her face was serious, but her eyes were bright, as if she was about to tell a really awful riddle and couldn't wait for the reaction.

Dinsy started. That was almost word for word what Olive had said, and it made her nervous. She wasn't sure what was coming, and was even less sure that she was ready.

"Introductions first." Dorothy closed her eyes and intoned, "I am Lexica. I serve the Library." She bowed her head once and sat down.

Dinsy stared, her eyes wide and her mind reeling as each of the librarians repeated what was obviously a familiar rite.

"I am Juvenilia," said Olive with a twinkle. "I serve the Library."

"Incunabula," said Edith.

"Sapientia," said Harriet.

"Ephemera," said Marian.

"Marginalia," said Ruth.

"Melvilia," said Blythe, smiling at Dinsy. "And I, too, serve the Library."

And then they were all seated, and all looking up at Dinsy.

"How old are you now, my sweet?" asked Harriet.

Dinsy frowned. It wasn't as easy a question as it sounded. "Seventeen," she said after a few seconds. "Or close enough."

"No longer a child." Harriet nodded. There was a touch of sadness in her voice. "That is why we are here tonight. To ask you to join us."

There was something so solemn in Harriet's voice that it made Dinsy's stomach knot up. "I don't understand," she said slowly. "What do you mean? I've been here my whole life. Practically."

Dorothy shook her head. "You have been *in* the Library, but not *of* the Library. Think of it as an apprenticeship. We have nothing more to teach you. So we're asking if you'll take a Library name and truly become one of us. There have always been seven to serve the Library."

Dinsy looked around the room. "Won't I be the eighth?" she asked. She was curious, but she was also stalling for time.

"No, dear," said Olive. "You'll be taking my place. I'm retiring. I can barely reach the second shelves these days, and soon I'll be no bigger than the dictionary. I'm going to put my feet up and sit by the fire and take it easy. I've earned it," she said with a decisive nod.

"Here, here," said Blythe. "And well done, too."

There was a murmur of assent around the room.

Dinsy took a deep breath, and then another. She looked around the room at the eager faces of the seven librarians, the only mothers she had ever known. She loved them all, and was about to disappoint them, because she had a secret of her own. She closed her eyes so she wouldn't see their faces, not at first.

"I can't take your place, Olive," she said quietly, and heard the tremor in her own voice as she fought back tears.

All around her the librarians clucked in surprise. Ruth recovered first. "Well, of course not. No one's asking you to *replace* Olive, we're merely —"

"I can't join you," Dinsy repeated. Her voice was just as quiet, but it was stronger. "Not now."

"But why *not,* sweetie?" That was Blythe, who sounded as if she were about to cry herself.

"Fireworks," said Dinsy after a moment. She opened her eyes. "Six-sixty-two-point-one." She smiled at Blythe. "I know everything about them. But I've never *seen* any." She looked from face to face again.

"I've never petted a dog or ridden a bicycle or watched the sun rise over the ocean," she said, her voice gaining courage. "I want to feel the wind and eat an ice-cream cone at a carnival. I want to smell jasmine on a spring night and hear an orchestra. I want—" She faltered, and then continued, "I want the chance to dance with a boy."

She turned to Dorothy. "You said you have nothing left to teach me. Maybe that's true. I've learned from each of you that there's nothing in the world I can't discover and explore for myself in these books. Except the world," she added in a whisper. She felt her eyes fill with tears. "You chose the Library. I can't do that without knowing what else there might be."

"You're *leaving*?" Ruth asked in a choked voice.

Dinsy bit her lip and nodded. "I'm, well, I've—" She'd been practicing these words for days, but they were so much harder than she'd thought. She looked down at her hands.

And then Marian rescued her.

"Dinsy's going to college," she said. "Just like I did. And you, and you, and you." She pointed a finger at each of the women in the room. "We were girls before we were librarians, remember? It's her turn now."

"But how—?" asked Edith.

"Where did—?" stammered Harriet.

"I wished on the Library," said Dinsy. "And it left an application in the Unabridged. Marian helped me fill it out."

"I *am* in charge of circulation," said Marian. "What comes in, what goes out. We found her acceptance letter in the book return last week."

"But you had no transcripts," said Dorothy practically. "Where did you tell them you'd gone to school?"

Dinsy smiled. "That was Marian's idea. We told them I was home-schooled, raised by feral librarians."

And so it was that on a bright September morning, for the first time in ages, the heavy oak door of the Carnegie Library swung open. Everyone stood in the doorway, blinking in the sunlight.

"Promise you'll write," said Blythe, tucking a packet of sweets into the basket on Dinsy's arm.

The others nodded. "Yes, do."

"I'll try," she said. "But you never know how long *anything* will take around here." She tried to make a joke of it, but she was holding back tears and her heart was hammering a mile a minute.

"You will come back, won't you? I can't put off my retirement forever." Olive was perched on top of the Circulation Desk.

"To visit, yes." Dinsy leaned over and kissed her cheek. "I promise. But to serve? I don't know. I have no idea what I'm going to find out there." She looked out into the forest that surrounded the library. "I don't even know if I'll be able to get back in, through all that."

"Take this. It will always get you in," said Marian. She handed Dinsy a small stiff pasteboard card with a metal plate in one corner, embossed with her name: DINSY CARNEGIE.

"What is it?" asked Dinsy.

"Your library card."

There were hugs all around, and tears and good-byes. But in the end, the seven librarians stood back and watched her go.

Dinsy stepped out into the world as she had come—with a wicker basket and a book of fairy tales, full of hopes and dreams.

ELLEN KLAGES lives in San Francisco. Her story "Basement Magic" won the Nebula Award for Best Novelette in 2005. Her short fiction has appeared in *The Magazine of Fantasy and Science Fiction* and SCI FICTION, and has been on the final ballot for the Hugo and Spectrum Awards. She was also a finalist for the John W. Campbell Award, and is a graduate of the Clarion South writing workshop.

Her first novel, *The Green Glass Sea* (Viking), won the 2007 Scott O'Dell Award for Historical Fiction, and she is currently working on the sequel. Her first story collection, *Portable Childhoods*, was recently published by Tachyon.

Ellen also serves on the Motherboard of the James Tiptree, Jr. Award (www.tiptree.org), and is somewhat notorious as the auctioneer/entertainment for the Tiptree auctions. When she's not writing fiction, she sells old toys on eBay and collects lead civilians.

Visit her Web site at **www.ellenklages.com**.

AUTHOR'S NOTE
This story came bubbling up in the Well of Ideas from a couple of different sources.

During a psychic reading about four years ago (a birthday gift from my sister), I was told that my spirit guides were seven librarians, who would help me find the answers to the questions in my life. I'm not sure I believed that, but I liked the idea, because the library was always my favorite refuge, and there have been many significant librarians in my life.

I have always lived with and around books. There was a battered, blue buckram-bound copy of *Heidi* on the bookshelf in the upstairs hall of the house I grew up in. Old book, with nice color plates, dating back to my mother's childhood.

When I was about eight I discovered that *Heidi* had a library-card pocket inside the cover. Overdue library books were a capital crime in my family, and this one had been checked out in 1933, when my mother would have been eight herself. I asked her about it, and to my surprise, she looked very embarrassed and said, in a determined but apologetic voice, "I *am* going to return it."

She'd checked it out of the Bristow, Oklahoma, library and her family had moved out of the state two weeks later. It had gotten packed by mistake. She'd been carting it around, from house to house, to college, into her marriage, feeling guilty about it for thirty years.

Sometime in the mid-1970s, she and a friend were planning a road trip, and Mom looked at the map and realized that if they made a 150-mile detour (each way), they could stop in Bristow. So that summer, my mother marched up the steps of the Bristow Public Library, plunked *Heidi* down on the circulation desk, and said, "This is overdue." An understatement. It was more than *forty years* overdue.

The librarian looked at the book, looked at my mother.

"I'll pay the fine, whatever it is." Mom pulled out her checkbook.

"That won't be necessary," the librarian said. Then she got her DISCARD stamp, whacked *Heidi,* and handed the book back.

It's sitting on my desk as I type this.

When I started thinking about a story for *Firebirds Rising*, my guiding librarians picked up *Heidi* and wandered into my brain again. They puttered around in there for months before the story began to gel. I wrote most of the first draft in a little cottage in the desert outside Tucson, with downloaded photos of old libraries on my laptop. When I got home, the manuscript and I visited a dozen old Carnegie libraries in northern Ohio, where I sat and wrote and looked at old wooden wainscoting and Craftsman-tiled fireplaces and pebbled-glass office doors. I spent a week sitting on the floor of the Stacks in a Case Western University library, making notes about the smells and the textures so that I could give them to Dinsy.

Sharon Shinn

WINTERMOON WISH

All the way from Wodenderry to Merendon, I sat alone in the coach and scowled. I couldn't believe that no one, not even my cousin Renner, was willing to leave the royal city and miss the queen's ball.

But I had never spent a Wintermoon away from my grandparents' inn in Merendon, and I was not about to start now. Now that the whole world was bleak and my life nothing but a blighted promise.

My aunt tells me I am a fanciful girl with a flair for the dramatic. My mother says more plainly that I overreact to everything. In this instance, at any rate, I was sure I had a broken heart and nothing would mend it except a trip to Merendon, and even that didn't seem likely to do the trick. But who would want to stay in Wodenderry, when Trevor was in love with Corrinne and taking her to the Wintermoon ball?

The weather was bitterly cold and even my father's well-built carriage could not keep out the drafts. Our frequent stops for hot tea at little inns along the way were still not enough to warm me all the way through. By the time we arrived in Merendon, just around sunset, my feet were icicles in their fashionable fur-lined boots and I couldn't feel my fingers in my gloves. We pulled up in front of the Leaf & Berry Inn and my heart sank: there were no welcome lights pouring from the front door or the upper-story windows. The inn looked as dark and cold as the interior of the coach.

But when the driver carried my luggage around back to the kitchen door, my spirits rose again. I could see my grandmother through the window, working at the stove, her white hair piled on top of her head, her hands busy, her face serene. I could smell the baking bread and roasting chicken. The very shape and scent of the scene before me matched the picture of *home* I always carried in my heart.

I was almost in tears as I burst through the door, and my grandmother dropped her spoon with a clatter. "Lirril! You startled me. Oh, look at you, you're half-frozen. Come sit by the stove. Bob! Build up a fire in the parlor! Lirril's here and she's a little ice-child."

I felt better than I had for days.

My grandfather bustled in, gathered me in a big hug, paid a handsome tip to the driver, and made sure the man had a place to spend the night. I sat at the kitchen table, sipping tea and inhaling the smells of the house. Dinner and wine and pie in here; wax and polish and soap drifting in from the other rooms. Overlaying it all, a sharper, sweeter odor, the very scent of Wintermoon.

"You've started the wreath already, haven't you?" I said, my voice just a touch accusatory. "You knew I was coming, and you couldn't wait until I got here?"

My grandmother looked amused. "We've gathered some

spruce and some rowan, and I've put some greens over the banister, but we haven't finished braiding the wreath," she said. "Don't worry, you'll have plenty to do."

"A mighty cold Wintermoon it's going to be," my grandfather observed, stepping out the door to fetch another pile of wood. "Glad you made it here before the snow. Supposed to start falling tomorrow afternoon."

In a few moments, the three of us were gathered cozily around the kitchen table, eating my grandmother's excellent meal and catching up on events. Well, mostly *I* told *them* everything that had been happening to me lately. Their lives tended not to hold much excitement or variation. *Oh, we had three guests come through last week, and a family of five stopped here the week before. Things were slow over the summer, but that gave us time to sew new curtains and finish the floors in the back bedroom on the second floor.* I had far more to relate.

I hadn't planned to bring up Trevor's name, but my grandmother had an uncannily good memory, which sometimes came in handy and sometimes did not. "What about that boy?" she asked as she served the pie. "The one you were so keen on this summer? Trevor? Was that his name?"

"Oh, I'm not interested in him anymore," I said, my voice quite airy. "He's—well, he's—anyway, Corrinne has been flirting with him most shamelessly. So of course he's practically infatuated with her. He even wrote her a poem a couple of weeks ago. A poem! Did you ever hear of such a silly thing?"

I had been shockingly jealous when Corrinne showed it to us—to me, and the other girls from my school who had formed a circle of friends. It wasn't a very good poem, it didn't even rhyme, but you could tell by its extravagant praise how much Trevor adored her. I had been in love with Trevor all my life—or, at least, since he had danced with me two years ago when I was fourteen and allowed to go to my first Summermoon ball at the palace. But he had never so much as written my name on a calling card to be left at my parents' house.

My grandparents looked amused. "Never was much of one for poems myself," my grandfather said. "Still, that seems like a powerful sign of attraction. Man who'd write a poem for a girl would do anything for her, I suppose."

"I wonder if your father ever wrote a poem for your mother," my grandmother said to me.

"He would have if she'd asked him to," my grandfather spoke up. "That man would have done anything she wanted. He courted her for months. He's still courting her, all these years later."

Revolted, I put up my hands. "Please. Stop."

"I'm going to ask him about that poem," my grandfather said, teasing me.

My grandmother stood. "I'm going to clear the dishes. You two get started on the wreath."

The best part of Wintermoon: braiding the wreath. I happily settled on the floor beside my grandfather and helped him plait the long, whippy branches together, tying them at intervals with red and gold cords. My fingers were soon sticky with sap and I had sharp little needles all over my dress. My grandmother joined us about thirty minutes later, carrying a basket of odds and ends.

"Oh, here's a few pearls from that necklace that broke . . . let's tie those on. Those will be for—well, what do you think? A wedding? Yes, pearls for a wedding. And some of that blue silk from the back bedroom. How about serenity? Now don't forget the dried fruit—that's for prosperity, Lirril, never make a wreath without it."

My grandfather had his own contributions—dried cedar chips and a bird's wing and a scrap of fabric from a ship's ripped sail—though sometimes his connections between object and the magic they could confer seemed tenuous at best. I had only one extra bit to bind into the wreath, a long ribbon embroidered with alternating hearts and birds.

"That's for love," I said, knotting it around the woven branches.

"That's something everyone needs every year," my grandmother said.

When we were done, my grandfather hung the great wreath over the fireplace and it made a dense shape of promise over the mantel. Tomorrow night we would build a bonfire in the back, between the chatterleaf and kirrenberry trees that gave the inn its name, and we would throw the wreath into the blaze. All our hopes for the new year written in flame. Guaranteed to come true.

I slept deeply and well—for the first time in days—in the small bedroom on the third floor. It was the room that had belonged to my mother and her twin when they were growing up. Even once I woke, I didn't realize how far advanced the morning was, because so little light was coming in the double windows. When I finally rose and dressed and peeked outside, I understood why: snow was falling so heavily that the sky was leaden and gray. The clouds were piled so deeply overhead that I couldn't imagine the sun would ever shine.

I skipped downstairs, calling, "Look at the snow! Look at it! There must be two feet on the ground already!" I didn't care much for snow on the crowded streets of Wodenderry, but here in Merendon, where I didn't need to leave the inn for a single necessity, snow was a delight.

"No one will be traveling far this day," my grandmother observed. "So anyone who has somewhere to get on Wintermoon had better be there by now."

I danced around the kitchen. "No one's here—we've got the inn all to ourselves," I exclaimed. "We can eat all the pie—and drink all the cider—and stay up as late as we want. No guests! No chores!"

My grandmother laughed. My grandfather said, "I'll just go chop some more wood."

Half an hour later, the stage from Oakton arrived.

It came feeling its way through the blizzard like a blind child down a tunnel and arrived at the front door like an omen of doom. My grandfather ran out to exchange a few words with the coachman. I watched as the door to the coach pushed open—a maneuver that took some effort against the wind—and a single figure stepped out, landing knee-deep in the drift of snow. He was tall and reedy, wearing an inadequate coat against the searing chill of the weather, and his head was uncovered. I could see his face, angular and thin, and his eyes, dark and devoid of hope. He couldn't have been more than a year or two older than I was, but he looked weighed down by cares or disappointments. A more pitiful, dispirited, unwelcome visitor you could not imagine having arrive on your doorstep on Wintermoon.

"Oh no," I breathed as he fought his way up the walk toward the front door. "Oh *no*."

My grandmother had materialized beside me and was looking out the front door, serene as always. She said, "Looks like we've got company for Wintermoon."

His name was Jake. That was about all we learned about him during dinner that night, and I wasn't even interested in that much information. The four of us sat around the bigger table in the dining room and passed around food while we made labored conversation. His name was Jake, he was headed toward Thrush Hollow. He was sorry to be caught in the storm, yes, ma'am, so glad there was a place that could take him in, he was sorry if he was any trouble. He had the money to pay. He was polite and, once he'd warmed up a little, not unattractive in an intense and moping fashion. But who wanted strangers around on Wintermoon? Wintermoon was a time for family! For being with the people you loved most in the world! There was almost never anyone at the inn for Wintermoon. Why hadn't he started his journey a day or two earlier if he was so eager to join up with his parents or siblings or cousins or whomever he was off to visit? Why was he *here, now,* with *my* family, spoiling *my* Wintermoon? I could not have been unhappier if I had still been in Wodenderry.

Well, yes, I could have. But not much.

"So, Jake, would you like to help me build the bonfire?" my grandfather asked in his genial way as we finished the pie. I had to admit, even though we'd had to share it, there was plenty of pie for everyone. "It's dark enough now."

Jake came to his feet, looking uncertain. "You build a bonfire? Do you burn a wreath, too?"

"Well, goodness, doesn't everybody?" my grandmother exclaimed.

Jake gave her a crooked grin and looked, for the first time, boyish. "I haven't. Not for years."

"You don't have to help," my grandfather said.

"He wants to," my grandmother replied briskly. "Go on out there, you two. Lirril and I will clear the dishes. We'll come out when the fire's good and hot."

Jake put on his threadbare coat and followed my grandfather out the kitchen door to where most of the fire had already been laid. I watched from the window as they brushed away the accumulated snow and searched for dry kindling. Jake moved slowly, like a man at an unfamiliar task, but willingly, as if learning something he would like to know. Twice I saw him smile at something my grandfather said. He had only smiled once throughout the entire meal.

"He seems like a nice boy," my grandmother said, scrubbing at the dishes.

I sniffed. "How can you tell? He hardly said a word."

"Looks like he's had a hard life, though."

"He's so wretched he's pathetic."

My grandmother gave me one of her rare looks of disapproval. Her eyes were an odd blue, pale but pretty; my own eyes were exactly the same color. "Better to be pathetic than to be cruel," she said.

My eyes widened. "I wasn't mean to him!"

"See that you aren't," she said.

I had just wiped down the table when Jake came back inside. "Bob says I should get the wreath down," he said in an apologetic voice, as if he thought it was something that would upset us. My grandmother just nodded, but I was instantly antagonized.

"It's not *time* to burn the wreath yet," I said. "We *never* burn it till midnight."

Jake nodded somberly. "No. That's what he said. He thought maybe I'd have something to bind to the branches."

I was frowning, but my grandmother was nodding. "That's a good idea. What would you like to add in?"

Jake looked despondent. "I don't know. Nothing I can think of."

"Nonsense. Everyone has a wish at Wintermoon," my grandmother said. "Come help me take it down, and Lirril and I will tell you all the wishes we've tied on to it so far. Then you can tell us what it's missing."

We put this plan into action, although—as I could have foretold—none of our blue silk and bird feathers and cedar chips inspired Jake to articulate his own desires. He did finger my embroidered ribbon and look wistful when my grandmother told him it represented love.

"Man-and-woman love or home-and-family love?" he asked.

"Either. Both," my grandmother said firmly.

"And these dried apricots—these mean a happy home?"

"A prosperous one," my grandmother corrected. "But, now, I like that. Let's find something to stand for a warm house, filled with joy. Jake, what did you bring that we can tie to the wreath?"

His expression was a little bitter. "Nothing you can use for that, I'm afraid."

"No, I'll pull a splinter from the front sign and tie that on with some ribbon. No place happier than the Leaf & Berry! Though that sign is a disgrace. More than twenty years old now, so weathered you almost can't read the lettering. There's paint in the barn, but Bob hasn't had a minute to sit down and put on a fresh coat." She paused, remembered why she had started her sentence, and continued. "But that's not what I meant. We need something of yours to wrap around the wreath. So you're part of the celebration. So your own wishes will catch on fire. Then, you know, they're more likely to come true."

Smiling a little, Jake investigated his pockets to reveal them almost empty. It didn't take much imagination to picture his single duffel bag to be the same. I couldn't imagine that he would have a thing worth contributing to our wreath, but I knew my grandmother well enough to know she would not be satisfied until we had *something* of Jake's to throw in the flames tonight.

"What about the top button on your shirt?" I asked. "It's about to fall off, anyway." My grandmother gave me a look that I couldn't interpret, so I added, "Or I could get a needle and thread and sew it back on for you."

Jake lifted a hand and yanked the button off with one quick pull. "No, I'll be happy to donate it to the wreath," he said. "It's metal, though—I don't know if it will burn."

"Then you can rescue it tomorrow morning and sew it on then," my grandmother said. "Something that survives the fire is always luck."

Soon enough we had attached our last contributions and leaned the wreath against the wall. My grandfather came stamping in, alternately rubbing his ears and blowing on his fingers. "*Mighty* cold out," he observed. "Believe I'll come in for a spell and warm up. Lirril, do you and Jake want to go out and watch the fire for a while?"

Jake looked surprised at the invitation, but I was already on my feet; I'd known it was coming. That was the tradition at the Leaf & Berry. My grandfather always started the fire, then he let someone else tend it till midnight, when the wreath was thrown on. Then he and my grandmother stayed up till dawn, watching the flames, shooing everyone else back inside so they could be alone before the dying fire. I had always wondered what made Wintermoon such a special holiday for the two of them. Neither my mother nor my aunt knew the answer.

"Go on. You two young ones keep the fire going," my grandmother said, waving us toward the door. "We'll come out later."

So I pulled on my gloves and my winter coat and my fur-lined boots and followed Jake out the kitchen door. The snow had stopped falling but lay thick on the ground like acres of profligate diamonds. The bonfire was a brilliant living jewel against the sere dark. The air was so cold that for a minute I lost the ability to breathe. I ran through the snowdrifts and hovered as close to the fire as I could bear. Jake followed more slowly but came just as close. For a while we stood in silence, stretching our hands out to the flames, inhaling the scents of cedar and spruce and snow.

It occurred to me that Jake was not the most talkative of people, and that the night was going to be extremely dull and extremely long if we passed it in silence, and that if I wanted conversation, I was going to have to initiate it myself. I glared resentfully into the dark, and then sighed and glanced over at him.

"So, Jake," I said. "I take it your family lives in Thrush Hollow?"

He eyed me uncertainly. "Some of them. An uncle and some cousins."

"Do you always spend Wintermoon with them?"

"No."

I waited, but he had no more to add. "Where do you come from? Did you ride the stage all the way from Oakton?"

He nodded.

I found myself starting to wish I was keeping the Wintermoon vigil by myself. "What do you do there? I'm guessing you have a job?"

He nodded again. "Had one. Worked in a carpenter's shop. I did a lot of the staining and painting. I wasn't that good with the lathe and tools."

I could hardly miss his use of the past tense. "But you don't work there now?"

"Now I'm moving to Thrush Hollow."

"To be with your uncle?" That elicited another nod. "That'll be nice." He shrugged.

I let the silence run out for a good long while. Long enough for the flames to die down and for Jake to carefully pile on a few more logs. Long enough for him to glance at me, glance away, look back at the house, cut his eyes in my direction again. I was feeling anything but kindly, but I gave him a nod meant to be encouraging. *Go ahead. Your turn to ask questions.*

"Um," he said. "So they call you Lirril?" I nodded. He said, "I never came across that name before."

"It's a mirror name," I said. He looked blank. "It's the same forward and backward. My grandmother's and grandfather's names, too. Hannah and Bob. It's something our family does."

"And you live here with your grandparents?"

"No. I live in Wodenderry with my mother and father. But we always come to Merendon for Wintermoon and I didn't want to miss it this year just because—" I shut my mouth with a snap.

"Because?"

I shrugged. "Oh, there's a ball there, and everyone wanted to attend, but *I* didn't want to go, I wanted to be *here,* and so I came to the inn while they stayed behind. They'll be here tomorrow, though, with my aunt and my uncle and my cousin Renner." I shot a look up at the sky. "If it's stopped snowing. If the roads are clear."

"Why didn't you want to go to the ball?" he asked.

Why would he think to ask that? And his voice was so soft, so serious, as if he really cared to know the answer. I shrugged again, not quite so pettishly. "Because my feelings were hurt. Because I was afraid it would make me sad. There's a man I know and he—" I hunched my shoulders. "And I'd rather be here. I love it here."

"I would, too," he agreed. "If I had a place like this to go to? I wouldn't wait till Wintermoon. I'd stay here all the time."

I was starting to think I could guess the answer for myself, and I didn't even want to *know* it, but I asked anyway. "So where are your parents?"

"Dead," he said flatly.

He added nothing to the single word. "I'm—that's—I'm sorry," I stammered. "When did—what happened?"

Now he was the one to give a shrug. "My mother died a long time ago. My father last year."

I could scarcely imagine such a thing. "What did you do without them?"

A ghost of a smile. "Worked. Found a place to stay. I did all right."

"But what about your family? Your aunts and uncles and grandparents? Why didn't you go to them?"

"I'm going now. To my uncle."

I had a sudden dreadful premonition. "Does he know you're coming?"

Jake almost laughed. "No."

"Will he be happy to see you?"

Jake looked lost for a moment, young. My age or even younger. "I don't know. He and my father hadn't spoken for years. He doesn't even know my father's dead. I just thought— it was worth a try. I don't have anywhere else to go."

"Why couldn't you stay in Oakton?"

"I could. I'll go back, I guess, if things don't work out in Thrush Hollow. But the carpenter I worked for sold his shop and the new owner had sons of his own to do the work and I—there wasn't a place for me there. I was always curious about my uncle. Seemed like as good a time as any to find out what he was like."

I felt so sorry for him that I almost despised him. Who could be so wretched and alone? Who could be so adrift in the world? I didn't want to wonder what his life might be like, so different from my own. I closed my heart and glanced away.

"I'm sure you'll like Thrush Hollow," I said, my voice indifferent. "Everyone says it's very pretty." He caught my tone, rebuffed as I meant him to be. He merely nodded and did not answer. He watched the fire a little longer, then added a few more logs. The old ones collapsed in a shower of sparks, which flung themselves into the snow and hissed out. Neither of us so much as winced away.

Now a determined silence held us both. My feet were numb inside my plush boots, and my cheeks ached with cold. Overhead, the sky was impossibly clear; the hard stars looked merciless. The full moon was so white and so brilliant it could have been sculpted from fresh snow. I wondered how much longer we had till midnight.

Jake added more fuel to the fire, then stood a moment with his back to the flames, as if to warm the other half of his body. I noted crossly that his coat was too thin. He must be even colder than I was.

"You should be wearing something heavier than that," I said.

He just looked at me for a moment. "This will do," he said.

I shrugged. Fine. If he didn't want to go in and put on a sweater, I didn't care.

We were quiet for another long stretch. The fire shifted again and the flames contracted, licking their small orange tongues around the charred embers of the bottom logs. Jake knelt to poke at the templed branches, teasing the fire back out. I accidentally glanced down at the bottoms of his feet.

"You have *holes* in your *shoes!*" I exclaimed. "What are you—you could get *frostbite* out here on a night like this!"

He gave me a dark look but didn't answer, merely continued prodding at the fire till the blaze caught again. He knelt there awhile longer to make sure the fire was really going, then he stood up. "I'm fine," he said. "I rarely feel the cold."

I stared at him. "*Everybody* feels the cold on a night like this! Why don't you—I'll watch the fire. You go put on another pair of shoes."

"This is the only pair I have," he said quietly.

I stared at him a moment, hating him more than I had ever hated anyone in my life. "Very well," I said, through gritted teeth. "You watch the fire." And I stomped back into the house, so angry that I almost slammed the door behind me, so furious that I was almost blinded by the emotion. Or blinded by something. I bumped into the kitchen door and stumbled a little as I turned into the hallway. I wasn't crying, though. No, I certainly wasn't. I brought a candle with me and set it on the hall table, then peered into the closet and began to root around.

Ten minutes later I was back outside, and I practically

flung a few items to the ground at Jake's feet. "Here. Put that on. It's my father's coat." No surprise that Jake didn't answer. I continued in a hard, fast voice. "He never wears it unless he's here and the weather's so cold he can't endure it. He says it's the most unfashionable cut imaginable and no man with any taste would ever wear it." I nudged the other pieces over with my toe. "Same thing about the boots. He won't put them on. He keeps trying to give them away, but no one will take them. They're ugly, but they're warm. I brought you some socks, too."

Jake didn't make a move. "I can't take those things."

"Well, you can wear them for a night, can't you? No one else needs them this very minute. It's stupid not to put them on and then freeze to death because you were proud and stubborn."

His eyes dropped; he looked longingly at the warm wool coat. "I could pay you something," he said.

"No, you couldn't! You could just be reasonable and put this coat on. *And* these boots. Here. Give me your coat. Give it to me right now."

And I stepped up to him and started unbuttoning his own garment, tattered and miserable as it was. Two of the buttons came off in my hands; something else to tie to the wreath if we had a little time and some extra ribbon. He resisted a moment, his face creased with doubt, but I started yanking at the sleeves, and he gave in. A few moments later, wearing his new coat, he was sitting on his old one and tugging off his shoes and his thin socks.

"Socks first," I said, handing him a thick, scratchy roll.

He hesitated. His bare feet looked so white and so cold that my own toes curled in sympathy. "No man wants to lend his socks to someone else," he said. "He'd never want them back."

"Fine. Don't give them back. My father won't mind." My father wouldn't mind because he didn't even know he owned this particular pair. I'd bought them as a rather uninspired Wintermoon gift. "Jake. *Put them on.*"

Either my tone convinced him or he was too cold and tired to argue. He pulled on the socks, then laced up the boots, then rose to his feet. Unfashionable it may have been, and too big for him it definitely was, but the long dark coat gave Jake some needed weight and a certain air of grace. He looked taller, broader, older, and very, very serious.

"I wish you would let me pay you something," he said.

I stamped my foot, almost bruising it against the iron-hard earth. "It's just a stupid extra coat!" I exclaimed. "You don't owe me anything!"

"Still, I should—"

"Shovel the walk, then! Chop some firewood. My grandparents will be delighted."

"Yes, but you're the one who—"

I was so *furious.* He was so *stupid.* I gave him impossible tasks. "Make me a necklace of icicles."

"I meant something I could actually—"

"Find roses in the snow. Write me a poem." Why had I said that? I rushed on. "Bring a bluebird to breakfast."

He was silent, merely watching me with those earnest eyes. I couldn't tell if he thought I was cruel or ridiculous. "Or just say thank you," I said. "That's all that's required."

He made a stiff little motion that could have been a bow. "Thank you," he said. "Lirril. You are—thank you. This was truly kind."

Now I really did want to weep. "It wasn't kind. It was mean," I said in a muffled voice. "I just didn't want to have to feel sorry for you. So there."

Now he smiled a little. "A generous impulse born of an ungenerous thought," he said. "But I'm still warm."

"It's so unfair," I burst out.

"What is?"

"That I have—it shouldn't be that way! I have so many people who love me, and you don't have any."

"That's the way the world goes," he said.

I stared at him. If I cried, I thought my tears might freeze to my face. "But don't you want more than what you have?" I whispered.

"Of course I do," he replied. "I want a place where I fit in, people who love me, friends who come when I cry for help. I want to do work that matters, make a home that's full of happiness. I want to be the friend who goes to others when they call out. I want all those things. Who doesn't? Maybe I'll find them in Thrush Hollow. I haven't given up. I'm going to keep looking."

My mouth had formed a little O, and I stared at him by ragged firelight. Who would have expected such a passionate speech from him? He must have realized how much he astonished me, for his face softened as he looked down at me.

"And what do you want, Lirril? What wishes did you tie to the Wintermoon wreath?"

Everything I had ever wanted in my life now seemed trivial and trite. Trevor to notice me. My friends to envy me. My parents to buy me explicit and expensive presents. "I wished— just—for little things," I stammered.

"That man," he said. "The one you didn't want to see at the ball. Did you wish for him to fall in love with you?"

Nothing so specific, though it had been Trevor's face I envisioned when I wrapped the ribbon around the wreath. "Even if I did, he never will," I said. "He's very fond of another girl."

"You don't need to worry," Jake said. "You probably have no idea how many others are just standing ready, waiting for you to notice them."

It was so untrue that I had to laugh. "When I'm back in Wodenderry, I'll look around," I said.

After that, strangely, it was easy to talk to Jake. He told me a little about his father, a somewhat feckless man who had painted lovely landscapes and sold them for pennies. I told him about my own father, filled with such laughter, and my mother, whose standards of honesty I had always found it hard to live up to. He liked music but did not know how to dance; I was an excellent dancer but could not play an instrument if it would save me from hanging. We had nothing in common and yet, somehow, much to discuss. I was a little shocked when my grandfather pushed through the kitchen door, the wreath in his hands. Midnight already? My grandmother was right behind him, carrying mugs of hot tea.

"Gracious, it's cold out here!" she exclaimed, as if we might not have noticed. "Here, I brought something to warm you both up."

We gratefully gulped the steaming liquid, and then Jake set down his cup so he could help my grandfather hoist the greenery onto the fire. The flames shot up, greedy for a taste of our heartfelt desires. I saw my embroidered ribbon turn to red fire, to black cinder, to gray smoke. My dreams of romance drifted through the star-scattered sky and crossed the face of the wide-eyed moon.

"That was a good wreath," my grandfather said approvingly. "There'll be a lot of wishes come true next year."

"You two go on into the house," my grandmother said. "We'll watch the fire till dawn."

"Are you sure?" Jake asked. "It's so cold. I could come back out in a few hours and spell you."

"They always stay out from midnight till morning," I said, stepping up to my grandfather and kissing his cheek. "May all your Wintermoon wishes come true," I murmured in his ear. He replied in kind.

Then I kissed my grandmother's soft skin, and we exchanged wishes as well. I was so cold and so tired that I wasn't absolutely certain I could cross the lawn and find my way back inside the inn. I yawned and my grandmother gave me a little push toward the door.

"Go in, now," she repeated. "You're about to fall asleep on your feet. Oh, and show Jake to his room! He's on the second floor, in the green room."

I nodded and hurried for the house, Jake behind me. Candles awaited us in the kitchen, and we carried them upstairs, their flames wavering against the hands that we had lifted to shield them. The green room was right off the stairwell, a big and cheerful chamber with the most comfortable mattress in the house. Still yawning, I pointed out the amenities.

"If you need anything else, the rest of us all sleep on the top floor. No one gets up much before noon, but you can help yourself to food in the kitchen tomorrow morning. If there's a commotion anytime, don't worry—it'll probably be my family arriving from Wodenderry. My father has a loud voice. That's how you'll know it's him."

Jake had set his candle down on the dresser across the room, and now he was watching me with those grave, intent eyes. "Thank you so much for everything you've done," he said.

I shook my head, too tired to argue. "I didn't do anything."

I turned for the door, but he surprised me by catching my arm and turning me back to face him. Bending slightly, he blew out my candle, so that we were standing in nearly total darkness. I looked up, surprised, and he took the opportunity to kiss me. His mouth was warm. His hands, raised to cup my cheeks, were cold. Fire and moonlight.

I pulled back, too amazed to say anything, either to scold or flirt. Even in the darkness, I could tell he was laughing silently. "Good night, Lirril," he said. "May all your Wintermoon wishes come true."

The noonday sun came through my bedroom window the next day with such force that it seemed to be muscling its way into the house. I lay drowsing in my bed a few moments, allowing myself to slowly remember the evening before. Wintermoon. My grandmother's richly satisfying meal. The glacial vigil at the bonfire. With Jake. Who had kissed me at the door just before I ran out of his room—

Well, that might make for an awkward moment or two at the dining room table. I felt a small smile play around my mouth. Jake would be more embarrassed than I. He would expect me to be angry or distant or cool. Instead, I would treat him exactly as I had at dinner the night before, as if he were a not very interesting stranger. He would not know what to think by the time he left on the stage for Thrush Hollow.

That made my smile disappear. I had forgotten. Jake would be moving on as soon as the roads were clear. He wouldn't be staying in Merendon long enough for me to tease him.

Well, who cared, anyway? Stupid old Jake. Sad, stupid, misfit Jake. It wouldn't bother me if I never saw him again.

Sounds and smells from downstairs convinced me that my grandmother was up and cooking. My room was cold, so I rose, washed, and dressed in the fastest possible time. As I skipped down the steps, I glanced at the door to Jake's room, visible from the stairwell. His door was closed, and I gave a little sniff. Still sleeping, like a man with no responsibilities or appointments. No ties, no one depending on him, not even his uncle eager to see him. No wonder he had no incentives to get out of bed.

My foot had just touched the floor at the bottom of the

steps when my grandfather called to me. "Lirril, come see this! I'm so tickled."

I followed the sound of his voice to the parlor, where the Wintermoon gifts were stacked before the fireplace. I had put my own out the night before, and, as was tradition, my grandparents had added theirs to the pile while the rest of the house lay sleeping. There were dozens of presents laid out before the fire, and there would be dozens more by the time my parents, my aunt, and my uncle made their own contributions.

My grandfather was holding up a wide, flat board, and it took me a moment to recognize it. "Look at this," he said, and turned it so I could see the other side. It was the Leaf & Berry sign, lovingly repainted, the red words laid in crisply against a stark white background, small curlicues decorating the four corners.

I came closer to admire it. "When did you have time to do that?" I asked. The oily, pleasant smell of fresh paint drifted to my nose.

"I didn't! I'm guessing it was that young man. He must have stayed up all night to do this."

I felt my face suddenly heat with an unidentifiable emotion. "Jake? Did this? Last night after we were all in bed?" I remembered that he told me he had done painting and staining for the carpenter in Oakton. But I hadn't expected this.

"Must have," my grandfather said, turning the sign this way and that as if to detect hidden subtleties. "Or even while Hannah and I were watching the fire. He cleared the walks, too, front and back."

I felt a shiver go down my back. Which of the other tasks

that I had suggested to him had he also decided to accomplish? "That's—well. What a nice thing for him to do," I said.

My grandfather nodded toward the pile of gifts. "He left you something, too. I didn't open it, of course."

My eyes were pulled irresistibly to the bounty laid out on the hearth. In all that welter, I instantly spotted it—a scroll bound with what looked like a shoelace. My name had been carefully lettered on a scrap of paper. What would I find inside?

"I've got to go thank him again," my grandfather said, carrying the sign toward the kitchen.

"I think he's still asleep."

"No, he's out back, chopping firewood for your grandmother. I must say, I do like that boy," my grandfather said, and disappeared through the swinging door.

There was no way I could keep myself from dropping to the floor and untying the makeshift ribbon. I unrolled the single sheet of paper. In handwriting that I instantly knew was Jake's, I found a poem. I read it as if I were gulping it down.

Longest night, and coldest, of the year.
Lights beat back the blackness of the sky:
Bonfire blazes, jubilantly garish;
Full moon rises, perfect as a pearl.
I do not know what fortune brought me here—
Good or ill—and yet I know that I
Will not forget, until the day I perish,
Wintermoon, and the kindness of a girl.

I could not breathe. My cheeks were so hot I thought they

might scald my fingers if I touched my own skin. I read the poem again.

I heard voices and I leaped to my feet, not sure where to lay the poem so no one could see it, not sure how to hold my hands or what expression to summon to my face. But the voices stayed outside as my grandfather and Jake came around to the front of the inn and began to discuss the best way to hang the fresh sign. A minute after they decided the old hooks would work just fine, my grandfather was hailed by a new voice.

"Hullo there, Bob! Warm Wintermoon to you and yours!" It was Adam Granger, who owned a tannery a few streets over. He was getting a little frail with age, and there was some talk he might be hiring a younger man to take over his business soon. "Your grandson in town yet?"

"No, the girls are coming in a few days. Maybe longer, if the roads aren't clear."

"That's too bad. I had some work I needed done over at the house and I was hoping to hire Renner for a few hours."

"Jake, here, he's good with his hands," my grandfather said. "What do you want done?"

"Oh, I need a couple windows reframed and there's a table that's missing a leg. Small things, but I recall that your grandson helped me out last summer, so—"

"I can do all that," Jake spoke up. His voice was quiet and confident. He didn't sound like a man who had stayed up all night, thinking up ways to show people his appreciation.

Adam sounded pleased. "Really? I got two, three more things like that you could do if you had the time."

"Stage to Thrush Hollow probably won't be through till tomorrow or the day after," my grandfather said. "Good chance for you to earn a little extra money."

"When could you come over?" Adam asked.

"Soon as the sign's hung," Jake replied. "Give me a minute."

I felt myself start to breathe again. Adam could come up with a million tasks for a strong young man. Jake might not be taking the first stage out of Merendon after all, even if it came tomorrow.

I heard some clattering above the front door as the sign was put in place, and then the fading sound of voices as Jake and Adam walked down the street. I crossed to the front window to watch them go, but all I could see was Jake's back, slim but somehow sturdier in my father's rejected coat.

My grandmother stepped into the parlor just as my grandfather came in through the front door, bringing icy air with him. "Well, I was about to ask where everyone's gone off to," my grandmother said. "I've got a meal almost ready. Where's Jake?"

"Headed out with Adam Granger to do a few chores. Seemed mighty happy at the idea of earning a few coins, too," my grandfather said.

My grandmother looked pleased. "Now, that's good for both of them," she said. "I do like that young man. Did you see all that wood he split and set up against the door? You're not going to have to lift an ax all winter."

My grandfather grinned. "Fine by me. I've got a few chores of my own I can set Jake to when he's done at Adam's."

I looked up at that, feeling even more hopeful. My hand was behind my back, holding the poem so no one could see it, but I had a feeling that my grandfather knew what I was hiding, anyway. My grandmother almost certainly realized I was concealing something, and could guess that it was a token of someone's affection. She had probably even figured out whose. She was very good at sorting out secrets.

"Do you think Jake'll stay, then?" my grandmother asked. "Here in Merendon?"

My grandfather glanced at me and he almost laughed. "Oh, I think he might," he answered. "If we give him a little encouragement."

My grandmother nodded. "I'm going to set the table. Lirril, you can run out and check the ashes if you like. See if anything's survived the fire."

"Oh—yes—that is—I will," I said, and they both turned away to hide their smiles at my disjointed speech. I waited till they were out of the room, then carefully rolled up my poem and tied it with the shoelace. Grabbing my coat from the hall closet, I hurried through the kitchen and out into the cold air, which was not at all warmed by the cheerful sunshine. Shivering a little, I knelt beside the coals and began sorting through the remains of the bonfire.

I was really only looking for one thing, and I found it almost immediately—the small metal button from Jake's shirt. The heat of the fire had contorted it to a strange shape and darkened its shiny surface, but it was whole, recognizable, too stubborn to give way to neglect and misuse. I cleaned it in the snow and slipped it into my pocket. I would only give it back if Jake thought to ask for it, but I was sure he wouldn't.

The button had carried a wish that wasn't mine, but I could make it come true.

SHARON SHINN has won the William C. Crawford Award for Outstanding New Fantasy Writer, and was twice nominated for the John W. Campbell Award for Best New Writer. Her many books include three set in the world of this story: *The Safe-Keeper's Secret* (an ALA Best Book for Young Adults), *The Truth-Teller's Tale*, and *The Dream-Maker's Magic*. Her most recent novel is *General Winston's Daughter*.

A graduate of Northwestern University, Sharon Shinn now works as a journalist for a trade magazine. She has lived in the Midwest most of her life.

Visit her Web site at **www.sharonshinn.net**.

AUTHOR'S NOTE

I had been thinking for some time that I wanted to write a Christmas story—or at least the kind of Christmas story that would unfold in a fantasy setting. The world would be full of cold, snow, and darkness, but small, determined lights and acts of simple charity would provide moments of hope and luminous beauty.

I had already written three novels that featured the Wintermoon ceremony, my own amalgamation of solstice, the Yule log, and New Year's resolutions. So I decided to set my tale at Wintermoon, when a self-absorbed young woman comes to realize that a material gift given to a desperate stranger will be repaid a thousandfold.

Kelly Link

tHE WIZARDS of PERFIL

The woman who sold leech-grass baskets and pickled beets in the Perfil market took pity on Onion's aunt. "On your own, my love?"

Onion's aunt nodded. She was still holding out the earrings she'd hoped someone would buy. There was a train leaving in the morning for Qual, but the tickets were dear. Her daughter Halsa, Onion's cousin, was sulking. She'd wanted the earrings for herself. The twins held hands and stared about the market.

Onion thought the beets were more beautiful than the earrings, which had belonged to his mother. The beets were rich and velvety and mysterious as pickled stars in shining jars. Onion had had nothing to eat all day. His stomach was empty, and his head was full of the thoughts of the people in the market: Halsa thinking of the earrings, the market woman's disinterested kindness, his aunt's dull worry. There was a man at another stall whose wife was sick. She was coughing up blood. A girl went by. She was thinking about a man who had gone to the war. The man wouldn't come back. Onion went back to thinking about the beets.

"Just you to look after all these children," the market woman said. "These are bad times. Where's your lot from?"

"Come from Labbit, and Larch before that," Onion's aunt said. "We're trying to get to Qual. My husband had family there. I have these earrings and these candlesticks."

The woman shook her head. "No one will buy these," she said. "Not for any good price. The market is full of refugees selling off their bits and pieces."

Onion's aunt said, "Then what should I do?" She didn't seem to expect an answer, but the woman said, "There's a man who comes to the market today, who buys children for the wizards of Perfil. He pays good money and they say that the children are treated well."

All wizards are strange, but the wizards of Perfil are strangest of all. They build tall towers in the marshes of Perfil, and there they live like anchorites in lonely little rooms at the top of their towers. They rarely come down at all, and no one is sure what their magic is good for. There are balls of sickly green fire that dash around the marshes at night, hunting for who knows what, and sometimes a tower tumbles down and then the prickly reeds and marsh lilies that look like ghostly white hands grow up over the tumbled stones and the marsh mud sucks the rubble down.

Everyone knows that there are wizard bones under the marsh mud and that the fish and the birds that live in the marsh are strange creatures. They have got magic in them.

Children dare each other to go into the marsh and catch fish. Sometimes when a brave child catches a fish in the murky, muddy marsh pools, the fish will call the child by name and beg to be released. And if you don't let that fish go, it will tell you, gasping for air, when and how you will die. And if you cook the fish and eat it, you will dream wizard dreams. But if you let your fish go, it will tell you a secret.

This is what the people of Perfil say about the wizards of Perfil.

Everyone knows that the wizards of Perfil talk to demons and hate sunlight and have long twitching noses like rats. They never bathe.

Everyone knows that the wizards of Perfil are hundreds and hundreds of years old. They sit and dangle their fishing lines out of the windows of their towers and they use magic to bait their hooks. They eat their fish raw and they throw the fish bones out of the window the same way that they empty their chamber pots. The wizards of Perfil have filthy habits and no manners at all.

Everyone knows that the wizards of Perfil eat children when they grow tired of fish.

This is what Halsa told her brothers and Onion while Onion's aunt bargained in the Perfil markets with the wizard's secretary.

The wizard's secretary was a man named Tolcet and he wore a sword in his belt. He was a black man with white-pink spatters on his face and across the backs of his hands. Onion had never seen a man who was two colors.

Tolcet gave Onion and his cousins pieces of candy. He said to Onion's aunt, "Can any of them sing?"

Onion's aunt indicated that the children should sing. The twins, Mik and Bonti, had strong, clear soprano voices, and when Halsa sang, everyone in the market fell silent and listened. Halsa's voice was like honey and sunlight and sweet water.

Onion loved to sing, but no one loved to hear it. When it was his turn and he opened his mouth to sing, he thought of his mother and tears came to his eyes. The song that came out of his mouth wasn't one he knew. It wasn't even in a proper language and Halsa crossed her eyes and stuck out her tongue. Onion went on singing.

"Enough," Tolcet said. He pointed at Onion. "You sing like a toad, boy. Do you know when to be quiet?"

"He's quiet," Onion's aunt said. "His parents are dead. He doesn't eat much, and he's strong enough. We walked here from Larch. And he's not afraid of witchy folk, begging your pardon. There were no wizards in Larch, but his mother could find things when you lost them. She could charm your cows so that they always came home."

"How old is he?" Tolcet said.

"Eleven," Onion's aunt said, and Tolcet grunted.

"Small for his age." Tolcet looked at Onion. He looked at Halsa, who crossed her arms and scowled hard. "Will you come with me, boy?"

Onion's aunt nudged him. He nodded.

"I'm sorry for it," his aunt said to Onion, "but it can't be helped. I promised your mother I'd see you were taken care of. This is the best I can do."

Onion said nothing. He knew his aunt would have sold Halsa to the wizard's secretary and hoped it was a piece of luck for her daughter. But there was also a part of his aunt that was glad that Tolcet wanted Onion instead. Onion could see it in her mind.

Tolcet paid Onion's aunt twenty-four brass fish, which was slightly more than it had cost to bury Onion's parents, but slightly less than Onion's father had paid for their best milk cow, two years before. It was important to know how much things were worth. The cow was dead and so was Onion's father.

"Be *good*," Onion's aunt said. "Here. Take this." She gave Onion one of the earrings that had belonged to his mother. It was shaped like a snake. Its writhing tail hooked into its narrow mouth, and Onion had always wondered if the snake was surprised about that, to end up with a mouthful of itself like that, for all eternity. Or maybe it was eternally furious, like Halsa.

Halsa's mouth was screwed up like a button. When she hugged Onion good-bye, she said, "Brat. Give it to me." Halsa had already taken the wooden horse that Onion's father had carved, and Onion's knife, the one with the bone handle.

Onion tried to pull away, but she held him tightly, as if she couldn't bear to let him go. "He wants to eat you," she said. "The wizard will put you in an oven and roast you like a suckling pig. So give me the earring. Suckling pigs don't need earrings."

Onion wriggled away. The wizard's secretary was watching, and Onion wondered if he'd heard Halsa. Of course, anyone who wanted a child to eat would have taken Halsa, not Onion.

Halsa was older and bigger and plumper. Then again, anyone
who looked hard at Halsa would suspect she would taste sour
and unpleasant. The only sweetness in Halsa was in her singing. Even Onion loved to listen to Halsa when she sang.

Mik and Bonti gave Onion shy little kisses on his cheek.
He knew they wished the wizard's secretary had bought Halsa
instead. Now that Onion was gone, it would be the twins that
Halsa pinched and bullied and teased.

Tolcet swung a long leg over his horse. Then he leaned
down. "Come on, boy," he said, and held his speckled hand
out to Onion. Onion took it.

The horse was warm and its back was broad and high.
There was no saddle and no reins, only a kind of woven harness with a basket on either flank, filled with goods from the
market. Tolcet held the horse quiet with his knees, and Onion
held on tight to Tolcet's belt.

"That song you sang," Tolcet said. "Where did you learn it?"

"I don't know," Onion said. It came to him that the song
had been a song that Tolcet's mother had sung to her son,
when Tolcet was a child. Onion wasn't sure what the words
meant because Tolcet wasn't sure either. There was something
about a lake and a boat, something about a girl who had eaten
the moon.

The marketplace was full of people selling things. From his
vantage point Onion felt like a prince: as if he could afford to
buy anything he saw. He looked down at a stall selling apples
and potatoes and hot leek pies. His mouth watered. Over
here was an incense seller's stall, and there was a woman telling fortunes. At the train station, people were lining up to

buy tickets for Qual. In the morning a train would leave and Onion's aunt and Halsa and the twins would be on it. It was a dangerous passage. There were unfriendly armies between here and Qual. When Onion looked back at his aunt, he knew it would do no good, she would only think he was begging her not to leave him with the wizard's secretary, but he said it all the same: "Don't go to Qual."

But he knew even as he said it that she would go anyway. No one ever listened to Onion.

The horse tossed its head. The wizard's secretary made a *tch tch* sound and then leaned back in the saddle. He seemed undecided about something. Onion looked back one more time at his aunt. He had never seen her smile once in the two years he'd lived with her, and she did not smile now, even though twenty-four brass fish was not a small sum of money and even though she'd kept her promise to Onion's mother. Onion's mother had smiled often, despite the fact that her teeth were not particularly good.

"He'll eat you," Halsa called to Onion. "Or he'll drown you in the marsh! He'll cut you up into little pieces and bait his fishing line with your fingers!" She stamped her foot.

"Halsa!" her mother said.

"On second thought," Tolcet said, "I'll take the girl. Will you sell her to me instead?"

"What?" Halsa said.

"What?" Onion's aunt said.

"No!" Onion said, but Tolcet drew out his purse again. Halsa, it seemed, was worth more than a small boy with a bad voice. And Onion's aunt needed money badly. So Halsa got up on the horse behind Tolcet, and Onion watched as his bad-tempered cousin rode away with the wizard's servant.

There was a voice in Onion's head. It said, "Don't worry, boy. All will be well and all manner of things will be well." It sounded like Tolcet, a little amused, a little sad.

There is a story about the wizards of Perfil and how one fell in love with a church bell. First he tried to buy it with gold and then, when the church refused his money, he stole it by magic. As the wizard flew back across the marshes, carrying the bell in his arms, he flew too low and the devil reached up and grabbed his heel. The wizard dropped the church bell into the marshes and it sank and was lost forever. Its voice is clappered with mud and moss, and although the wizard never gave up searching for it and calling its name, the bell never answered and the wizard grew thin and died of grief. Fishermen say that the dead wizard still flies over the marsh, crying out for the lost bell.

Everyone knows that wizards are pigheaded and come to bad ends. No wizard has ever made himself useful by magic, or, if they've tried, they've only made matters worse. No wizard has ever stopped a war or mended a fence. It's better that they stay in their marshes, out of the way of worldly folk like farmers and soldiers and merchants and kings.

"Well," Onion's aunt said. She sagged. They could no longer see Tolcet or Halsa. "Come along, then."

They went back through the market and Onion's aunt bought cakes of sweetened rice for the three children. Onion ate his without knowing that he did so: since the wizard's servant had taken away Halsa instead, it felt as if there were two Onions, one Onion here in the market and one Onion riding along with Tolcet and Halsa. He stood and was carried along at the same time and it made him feel terribly dizzy. Market-Onion stumbled, his mouth full of rice, and his aunt caught him by the elbow.

"We don't eat children," Tolcet was saying. "There are plenty of fish and birds in the marshes."

"I know," Halsa said. She sounded sulky. "And the wizards live in houses with lots of stairs. Towers. Because they think they're so much better than anybody else. So above the rest of the world."

"And how do you know about the wizards of Perfil?" Tolcet said.

"The woman in the market," Halsa said. "And the other people in the market. Some are afraid of the wizards and some think that there are no wizards. That they're a story for children. That the marshes are full of runaway slaves and deserters. Nobody knows why wizards would come and build towers in the Perfil marsh, where the ground is like cheese and no one can find them. Why do the wizards live in the marshes?"

"Because the marsh is full of magic," Tolcet said.

"Then why do they build the towers so high?" Halsa said.

"Because wizards are curious," Tolcet said. "They like to be able to see things that are far off. They like to be as close as possible to the stars. And they don't like to be bothered by people who ask lots of questions."

"Why do the wizards buy children?" Halsa said.

"To run up and down the stairs," Tolcet said, "to fetch them water for bathing and to carry messages and to bring them breakfasts and dinners and lunches and suppers. Wizards are always hungry."

"So am I," Halsa said.

"Here," Tolcet said. He gave Halsa an apple. "You see things that are in people's heads. You can see things that are going to happen."

"Yes," Halsa said. "Sometimes." The apple was wrinkled but sweet.

"Your cousin has a gift, too," Tolcet said.

"Onion?" Halsa said scornfully. Onion saw that it had never felt like a gift to Halsa. No wonder she'd hidden it.

"Can you see what is in my head right now?" Tolcet said.

Halsa looked and Onion looked, too. There was no curiosity or fear about in Tolcet's head. There was nothing. There was no Tolcet, no wizard's servant. Only brackish water and lonely white birds flying above it.

"It's beautiful," Onion said.

"What?" his aunt said in the market. "Onion? Sit down, child."

"Some people find it so," Tolcet said, answering Onion. Halsa said nothing, but she frowned.

Tolcet and Halsa rode through the town and out of the town gates onto the road that led back toward Labbit and east, where there were more refugees coming and going, day and night. They were mostly women and children and they were afraid. There were rumors of armies behind them. There was a story that, in a fit of madness, the King had killed his youngest son. Onion saw a chess game, a thin-faced, anxious, yellow-haired boy Onion's age moving a black queen across the board, and then the chess pieces scattered across a stone floor. A woman was saying something. The boy bent down to pick up the scattered pieces. The king was laughing. He had a sword in his hand and he brought it down and then there was blood on it. Onion had never seen a king before, although he had seen men with swords. He had seen men with blood on their swords.

Tolcet and Halsa went away from the road, following a wide river, which was less a river than a series of wide, shallow pools. On the other side of the river, muddy paths disappeared into thick stands of rushes and bushes full of berries. There was a feeling of watchfulness, and the cunning, curious stillness of something alive, something half-asleep and half-waiting, a hidden, invisible humming, as if even the air were saturated with magic.

"Berries! Ripe and sweet!" a girl was singing out, over and over again in the market. Onion wished she would be quiet. His aunt bought bread and salt and hard cheese. She piled them into Onion's arms.

"It will be uncomfortable at first," Tolcet was saying. "The marshes of Perfil are so full of magic that they drink up all other kinds of magic. The only ones who work magic in the marshes of Perfil are the wizards of Perfil. And there are bugs."

"I don't want anything to do with magic," Halsa said primly.

Again Onion tried to look in Tolcet's mind, but again all

he saw were the marshes. Fat-petaled, waxy, white flowers and crouching trees that dangled their long brown fingers as if fishing. Tolcet laughed. "I can feel you looking," he said. "Don't look too long or you'll fall in and drown."

"I'm not looking!" Halsa said. But she *was* looking. Onion could feel her looking, as if she were turning a key in a door.

The marshes smelled salty and rich, like a bowl of broth. Tolcet's horse ambled along, its hooves sinking into the path. Behind them, water welled up and filled the depressions. Fat jeweled flies clung, vibrating, to the rushes, and once, in a clear pool of water, Onion saw a snake curling like a green ribbon through water weeds soft as a cloud of hair.

"Wait here and watch Bonti and Mik for me," Onion's aunt said. "I'll go to the train station. Onion, are you all right?"

Onion nodded dreamily.

Tolcet and Halsa rode farther into the marsh, away from the road and the Perfil market and Onion. It was very different from the journey to Perfil, which had been hurried and dusty and dry and on foot. Whenever Onion or one of the twins stumbled or lagged behind, Halsa had rounded them up like a dog chasing sheep, pinching and slapping. It was hard to imagine cruel, greedy, unhappy Halsa being able to pick things out of other people's minds, although she had always seemed to know when Mik or Bonti had found something edible; where there might be a soft piece of ground to sleep; when they should duck off the road because soldiers were coming.

Halsa was thinking of her mother and her brothers. She was thinking about the look on her father's face when the soldiers had shot him behind the barn; the earrings shaped like snakes; how the train to Qual would be blown up by saboteurs. She was supposed to be on that train, she knew it. She was furious at Tolcet for taking her away; at Onion, because Tolcet had changed his mind about Onion.

Every now and then, while he waited in the market for his aunt to come back, Onion could see the pointy roofs of the wizards' towers leaning against the sky as if they were waiting for him, just beyond the Perfil market, and then the towers would recede, and he would go with them, and find himself again with Tolcet and Halsa. Their path ran up along a canal of tarry water, angled off into thickets of bushes bent down with bright yellow berries, and then returned. It cut across other paths, these narrower and crookeder, overgrown and secret looking. At last they rode through a stand of sweet-smelling trees and came out into a grassy meadow that seemed not much larger than the Perfil market. Up close, the towers were not particularly splendid. They were tumbledown and lichen-covered and looked as if they might collapse at any moment. They were so close together one might have strung a line for laundry from tower to tower, if wizards had been concerned with such things as laundry. Efforts had been made to buttress the towers; some had long, eccentrically curving fins of strategically piled rocks. There were twelve standing towers that looked as if they might be occupied. Others were half in ruins or were only piles of rocks that had already been scavenged for useful building materials.

Around the meadow were more paths: worn, dirt paths and canals that sank into branchy, briary tangles, some so low that a boat would never have passed without catching. Even a swimmer would have to duck her head. Children sat on the half-ruined walls of toppled towers and watched Tolcet and Halsa ride up. There was a fire with a thin man stirring something in a pot. Two women were winding up a ball of rough-looking twine. They were dressed like Tolcet. More wizards' servants, Halsa and Onion thought. Clearly wizards were very lazy.

"Down you go," Tolcet said, and Halsa gladly slid off the horse's back. Then Tolcet got down and lifted off the harness and the horse suddenly became a naked, brown girl of about fourteen years. She straightened her back and wiped her muddy hands on her legs. She didn't seem to care that she was naked. Halsa gaped at her.

The girl frowned. She said, "You be good, now, or they'll turn you into something even worse."

"Who?" Halsa said.

"The wizards of Perfil," the girl said, and laughed. It was a neighing, horsey laugh. All of the other children began to giggle.

"Oooh, Essa gave Tolcet a ride."

"Essa, did you bring me back a present?"

"Essa makes a prettier horse than she does a girl."

"Oh, shut up," Essa said. She picked up a rock and threw it. Halsa admired her economy of motion, and her accuracy.

"Oi!" her target said, putting her hand up to her ear. "That hurt, Essa."

"Thank you, Essa," Tolcet said. She made a remarkably graceful curtsy, considering that until a moment ago she had

had four legs and no waist to speak of. There was a shirt and a pair of leggings folded and lying on a rock. Essa put them on. "This is Halsa," Tolcet said to the others. "I bought her in the market."

There was silence. Halsa's face was bright red. For once she was speechless. She looked at the ground and then up at the towers, and Onion looked, too, trying to catch a glimpse of a wizard. All the windows of the towers were empty, but he could feel the wizards of Perfil, feel the weight of their watching. The marshy ground under his feet was full of wizards' magic and the towers threw magic out like waves of heat from a stove. Magic clung even to the children and servants of the wizards of Perfil, as if they had been marinated in it.

"Come get something to eat," Tolcet said, and Halsa stumbled after him. There was a flat bread, and onions and fish. Halsa drank water that had the faint, slightly metallic taste of magic. Onion could taste it in his own mouth.

"Onion," someone said. "Bonti, Mik." Onion looked up. He was back in the market and his aunt stood there. "There's a church nearby where they'll let us sleep. The train leaves early tomorrow morning."

After she had eaten, Tolcet took Halsa into one of the towers, where there was a small cubby under the stairs. There was a pallet of reeds and a mothy wool blanket. The sun was still in the sky. Onion and his aunt and his cousins went to the church, where there was a yard where refugees might curl up and sleep a few hours. Halsa lay awake, thinking of the wizard in the room above the stairs where she was sleeping. The tower was so full of wizards' magic that she could hardly breathe. She imagined a wizard of Perfil creeping, creeping down the stairs above her cubby, and although the pallet was soft, she pinched her arms to stay awake. But Onion fell asleep immediately, as if drugged. He dreamed of wizards flying above the marshes like white lonely birds.

In the morning, Tolcet came and shook Halsa awake. "Go and fetch water for the wizard," he said. He was holding an empty bucket.

Halsa would have liked to say *go and fetch it yourself,* but she was not a stupid girl. She was a slave now. Onion was in her head again, telling her to be careful. "Oh, go away," Halsa said. She realized she had said this aloud, and flinched. But Tolcet only laughed.

Halsa rubbed her eyes and took the bucket and followed him. Outside, the air was full of biting bugs too small to see. They seemed to like the taste of Halsa. That seemed funny to Onion, for no reason that she could understand.

The other children were standing around the fire pit and eating porridge. "Are you hungry?" Tolcet said. Halsa nodded. "Bring the water up and then get yourself something to eat. It's not a good idea to keep a wizard waiting."

He led her along a well-trodden path that quickly sloped down into a small pool and disappeared. "The water is sweet here," he said. "Fill your bucket and bring it up to the top of the wizard's tower. I have an errand to run. I'll return before nightfall. Don't be afraid, Halsa."

"I'm not afraid," Halsa said. She knelt down and filled the bucket. She was almost back to the tower before she realized that the bucket was half empty again. There was a split in the wooden bottom. The other children were watching her and she straightened her back. *So it's a test,* she said in her head, to Onion.

You could ask them for a bucket without a hole in it, he said.

I don't need anyone's help, Halsa said. She went back down the path and scooped up a handful of clayey mud where the path ran into the pool. She packed this into the bottom of the bucket and then pressed moss down on top of the mud. This time the bucket held water.

There were three windows lined with red tiles on Halsa's wizard's tower, and a nest that some bird had built on an out-cropping of stone. The roof was round and red and shaped like a bishop's hat. The stairs inside were narrow. The steps had been worn down, smooth and slippery as wax. The higher she went, the heavier the pail of water became. Finally she set it down on a step and sat down beside it. *Four hundred and twenty-two steps,* Onion said. Halsa had counted five hundred and ninety-eight. There seemed to be many more steps on the inside than one would have thought, looking at the tower from outside. "Wizardly tricks," Halsa said in disgust, as if she'd expected nothing better. "You would think they'd make it fewer steps rather than more steps. What's the use of more steps?"

When she stood and picked up the bucket, the handle broke in her hand. The water spilled down the steps and Halsa threw the bucket after it as hard as she could. Then she marched down the stairs and went to mend the bucket and fetch more water. It didn't do to keep wizards waiting.

At the top of the steps in the wizard's tower there was a door. Halsa set the bucket down and knocked. No one answered and so she knocked again. She tried the latch: the door was locked. Up here, the smell of magic was so thick that Halsa's eyes watered. She tried to look *through* the door. This is what she saw: a room, a window, a bed, a mirror, a table. The mirror was full of rushes and light and water. A bright-eyed fox was curled up on the bed, sleeping. A white bird flew through the unshuttered window, and then another and another. They circled around and around the room and then they began to mass on the table. One flung itself at the door where Halsa stood, peering in. She recoiled. The door vibrated with pecks and blows.

She turned and ran down the stairs, leaving the bucket, leaving Onion behind her. There were even more steps on the way down. And there was no porridge left in the pot beside the fire.

Someone tapped her on the shoulder and she jumped. "Here," Essa said, handing her a piece of bread.

"Thanks," Halsa said. The bread was stale and hard. It was the most delicious thing she'd ever eaten.

"So your mother sold you," Essa said.

Halsa swallowed hard. It was strange, not being able to see inside Essa's head, but it was also restful. As if Essa might be anyone at all. "I didn't care," she said. "Who sold you?"

"No one," Essa said. "I ran away from home. I didn't want to be a soldier's whore like my sisters."

"Are the wizards better than soldiers?" Halsa said.

Essa gave her a strange look. "What do you think? Did you meet your wizard?"

"He was old and ugly, of course," Halsa said. "I didn't like the way he looked at me."

Essa put her hand over her mouth as if she were trying not to laugh. "Oh dear," she said.

"What must I do?" Halsa said. "I've never been a wizard's servant before."

"Didn't your wizard tell you?" Essa said. "What did he tell you to do?"

Halsa blew out an irritated breath. "I asked what he needed, but he said nothing. I think he was hard of hearing."

Essa laughed long and hard, exactly like a horse, Halsa thought. There were three or four other children, now, watching them. They were all laughing at Halsa. "Admit it," Essa said. "You didn't talk to the wizard."

"So?" Halsa said. "I knocked, but no one answered. So obviously he's hard of hearing."

"Of course," a boy said.

"Or maybe the wizard is shy," said another boy. He had green eyes like Bonti and Mik. "Or asleep. Wizards like to take naps."

Everyone was laughing again.

"Stop making fun of me," Halsa said. She tried to look fierce and dangerous. Onion and her brothers would have quailed. "Tell me what my duties are. What does a wizard's servant do?"

Someone said, "You carry things up the stairs. Food. Firewood. Kaffa, when Tolcet brings it back from the market. Wizards like unusual things. Old things. So you go out in the marsh and look for things."

"Things?" Halsa said.

"Glass bottles," Essa said. "Petrified imps. Strange things, things out of the ordinary. Or ordinary things like plants or stones or animals or anything that feels right. Do you know what I mean?"

"No," Halsa said, but she did know. Some things felt more magic-soaked than other things. Her father had found an arrowhead in his field. He'd put it aside to take to the schoolmaster, but that night while everyone was sleeping, Halsa had wrapped it in a rag and taken it back to the field and buried it. Bonti got the blame. Sometimes Halsa wondered if that was what had brought the soldiers to kill her father, the malicious, evil luck of that arrowhead. But you couldn't blame a whole war on one arrowhead.

"Here," a boy said. "Go and catch fish if you're too stupid to know magic when you see it. Have you ever caught fish?"

Halsa took the fishing pole. "Take that path," Essa said. "The muddiest one. And stay on it. There's a pier out that way where the fishing is good."

When Halsa looked back at the wizards' towers, she thought she saw Onion looking down at her, out of a high window. But that was ridiculous. It was only a bird.

The train was so crowded that some passengers gave up and went and sat on top of the cars. Vendors sold umbrellas to keep the sun off. Onion's aunt had found two seats, and she and Onion sat with one twin on each lap. Two rich women sat across from them. You could tell they were rich because their shoes were green leather. They held filmy pink handkerchiefs like embroidered rose petals up to their rabbity noses. Bonti looked at them from under his eyelashes. Bonti was a terrible flirt.

Onion had never been on a train before. He could smell the furnace room of the train, rich with coal and magic. Passengers stumbled up and down the aisles, drinking and laughing as if they were at a festival. Men and women stood beside the train windows, sticking their heads in. They shouted messages. A woman leaning against the seats fell against Onion and Mik when someone shoved past her. "Pardon, sweet," she said, and smiled brilliantly. Her teeth were studded with gemstones. She was wearing at least four silk dresses, one on top of the other. A man across the aisle coughed wetly. There was a bandage wrapped around his throat, stained with red. Babies were crying.

"I hear they'll reach Perfil in three days or less," a man in the next row said.

"The King's men won't sack Perfil," said his companion. "They're coming to defend it."

"The King is mad," the man said. "God has told him all men are his enemies. He hasn't paid his army in two years. When they rebel, he just conscripts another army and sends them off to fight the first one. We're safer leaving."

"Oooh," a woman said, somewhere behind Onion. "At last we're off. Isn't this fun! What a pleasant outing!"

Onion tried to think of the marshes of Perfil, of the wizards. But Halsa was suddenly there on the train, instead. *You have to tell them,* she said.

Tell them what? Onion asked her, although he knew. When the train was in the mountains, there would be an explosion. There would be soldiers, riding down at the train. No one would reach Qual. *Nobody will believe me,* he said.

You should tell them anyway, Halsa said.

Onion's legs were falling asleep. He shifted Mik. *Why do you care?* he said. *You hate everyone.*

I don't! Halsa said. But she did. She hated her mother. Her mother had watched her husband die, and done nothing. Halsa had been screaming and her mother slapped her across the face. She hated the twins because they weren't like her, they didn't *see* things the way Halsa had to. Because they were little and they got tired and it had been so much work keeping them safe. Halsa had hated Onion, too, because he *was* like her. Because he'd been afraid of Halsa, and because the day he'd come to live with her family, she'd known that one day she would be like him, alone and without a family. Magic was bad luck, people like Onion and Halsa were bad luck. The only person who'd ever looked at Halsa and really seen her, really known her, had been Onion's mother. Onion's mother was kind and good and she'd known she was going to die. *Take care of my son,* she'd said to Halsa's mother and father, but she'd been looking at Halsa when she said it. But Onion would have to take care of himself. Halsa would make him.

Tell them, Halsa said. There was a fish jerking on her line. She ignored it. *Tell them, tell them, tell them.* She and Onion were in the marsh and on the train at the same time. Everything smelled like coal and salt and ferment. Onion ignored her the way she was ignoring the fish. He sat and dangled his feet in the water, even though he wasn't really there.

Halsa caught five fish. She cleaned them and wrapped them in leaves and brought them back to the cooking fire. She also brought back the greeny-copper key that had caught on her fishing line. "I found this," she said to Tolcet.

"Ah," Tolcet said. "May I see it?" It looked even smaller and more ordinary in Tolcet's hand.

"Burd," Tolcet said. "Where is the box you found, the one we couldn't open?"

The boy with green eyes got up and disappeared into one of the towers. He came out after a few minutes and gave Tolcet a metal box no bigger than a pickle jar. The key fit. Tolcet unlocked it, although it seemed to Halsa that she ought to have been the one to unlock it, not Tolcet.

"A doll," Halsa said, disappointed. But it was a strange-looking doll. It was carved out of a greasy black wood, and when Tolcet turned it over, it had no back, only two fronts, so it was always looking backward and forward at the same time.

"What do you think, Burd?" Tolcet said.

Burd shrugged. "It's not mine."

"It's yours," Tolcet said to Halsa. "Take it up the stairs and give it to your wizard. And refill the bucket with fresh water and bring some dinner, too. Did you think to take up lunch?"

"No," Halsa said. She hadn't had any lunch herself. She cooked the fish along with some greens Tolcet gave her, and ate two. The other three fish and the rest of the greens she carried up to the top of the stairs in the tower. She had to stop to rest twice, there were so many stairs this time. The door was still closed and the bucket on the top step was empty. She thought that maybe all the water had leaked away, slowly. But she left the fish and she went and drew more water and carried the bucket back up.

"I've brought you dinner," Halsa said, when she'd caught her breath. "And something else. Something I found in the marsh. Tolcet said I should give it to you."

Silence.

She felt silly, talking to the wizard's door. "It's a doll," she said. "Perhaps it's a magic doll."

Silence again. Not even Onion was there. She hadn't noticed when he went away. She thought of the train. "If I give you the doll," she said, "will you do something for me? You're a wizard, so you ought to be able to do anything, right? Will you help the people on the train? They're going to Qual. Something bad is going to happen if you won't stop it. You know about the soldiers? Can you stop them?"

Halsa waited for a long time, but the wizard behind the door never said anything. She put the doll down on the steps and then she picked it up again and put it in her pocket. She was furious. "I think you're a coward," she said. "That's why you hide up here, isn't it? I would have got on that train and I know what's going to happen. Onion got on that train. And you could stop it, but you won't. Well, if you won't stop it, then I won't give you the doll."

She spat in the bucket of water and then immediately wished she hadn't. "You keep the train safe," she said, "and I'll give you the doll. I promise. I'll bring you other things, too. And I'm sorry I spit in your water. I'll go and get more."

She took the bucket and went back down the stairs. Her legs ached and there were welts where the little biting bugs had drawn blood.

"Mud," Essa said. She was standing in the meadow, smoking a pipe. "The flies are only bad in the morning and at twilight. If you put mud on your face and arms, they leave you alone."

"It smells," Halsa said.

"So do you," Essa said. She snapped her clay pipe in two, which seemed extravagant to Halsa, and wandered over to where some of the other children were playing a complicated-looking game of pickup sticks and dice. Under a night-flowering tree, Tolcet sat in a battered, oaken throne that looked as if it had been spat up by the marsh. He was smoking a pipe, too, with a clay stem even longer than Essa's had been. It was ridiculously long. "Did you give the poppet to the wizard?" he said.

"Oh yes," Halsa said.

"What did she say?"

"Well," Halsa said. "I'm not sure. She's young and quite lovely. But she had a horrible stutter. I could hardly understand her. I think she said something about the moon, how she wanted me to go cut her a slice of it. I'm to bake it into a pie."

"Wizards are very fond of pie," Tolcet said.

"Of course they are," Halsa said. "And I'm fond of my arse."

"Better watch your mouth," Burd, the boy with green eyes, said. He was standing on his head, for no good reason that Halsa could see. His legs waved in the air languidly, semaphoring. "Or the wizards will make you sorry."

"I'm already sorry," Halsa said. But she didn't say anything else. She carried the bucket of water up to the closed door. Then she ran back down the stairs to the cubbyhole and this time she fell straight asleep. She dreamed a fox came and looked at her. It stuck its muzzle in her face. Then it trotted up the stairs and ate the three fish Halsa had left there. *You'll be sorry,* Halsa thought. *The wizards will turn you into a one-legged crow.* But then she was chasing the fox up the aisle of a train to Qual, where her mother and her brothers and Onion were sleeping uncomfortably in their seats, their legs tucked under them, their arms hanging down as if they were dead—the stink of coal and magic was even stronger than it had been in the morning. The train was laboring hard. It panted like a fox with a pack of dogs after it, dragging itself along. There was no way it would reach all the way to the top of the wizard of Perfil's stairs. And if it did, the wizard wouldn't be there, anyway, just the moon, rising up over the mountains, round and fat as a lardy bone.

The wizards of Perfil don't write poetry, as a general rule. As far as anyone knows, they don't marry, or plow fields, or have much use for polite speech. It is said that the wizards of Perfil appreciate a good joke, but telling a joke to a wizard is dangerous business. What if the wizard doesn't find the joke funny? Wizards are sly, greedy, absentminded, obsessed with stars and bugs, parsimonious, frivolous, invisible, tyrannous, untrustworthy, secretive, inquisitive, meddlesome, long-lived, dangerous, useless, and have far too good an opinion of themselves. Kings go mad, the land is blighted, children starve or get sick or die spitted on the pointy end of a pike, and it's all beneath the notice of the wizards of Perfil. The wizards of Perfil don't fight wars.

It was like having a stone in his shoe. Halsa was always there, nagging. *Tell them, tell them. Tell them.* They had been on the train for a day and a night. Halsa was in the swamp, getting farther and farther away. Why wouldn't she leave him alone? Mik and Bonti had seduced the two rich women who sat across from them. There were no more frowns or handkerchiefs, only smiles and tidbits of food and love, love, love all around. On went the train through burned fields and towns that had been put to the sword by one army or another. The train and its passengers overtook people on foot, or fleeing in wagons piled high with goods: mattresses, wardrobes, a pianoforte once, stoves and skillets and butter churns and pigs and angry-looking geese. Sometimes the train stopped while men got out and examined the tracks and made repairs. They did not stop at any stations, although there were people waiting, sometimes, who yelled and ran after the train. No one got off. There were fewer people up in the mountains, when they got there. Instead there was snow. Once Onion saw a wolf.

"When we get to Qual," one of the rich women, the older one, said to Onion's aunt, "my sister and I will set up our establishment. We'll need someone to keep house for us. Are you thrifty?" She had Bonti on her lap. He was half-asleep.

"Yes, ma'am," Onion's aunt said.

"Well, we'll see," said the woman. She was half in love with Bonti. Onion had never had much opportunity to see what the rich thought about. He was a little disappointed to find out that it was much the same as other people. The only difference seemed to be that the rich woman, like the wizard's secretary, seemed to think that all of this would end up all right. Money, it seemed, was like luck, or magic. All manner of things would be well, except they wouldn't. If it weren't for the thing that was going to happen to the train, perhaps Onion's aunt could have sold more of her children.

Why won't you tell them? Halsa said. *Soon it will be too late.*

You tell them, Onion thought back at her. Having an invisible Halsa around, always telling him things that he already knew, was far worse than the real Halsa had been. The real Halsa was safe, asleep, on the pallet under the wizard's stairs. Onion should have been there instead. Onion bet the wizards of Perfil were sorry that Tolcet had ever bought a girl like Halsa.

Halsa shoved past Onion. She put her invisible hands on her mother's shoulders and looked into her face. Her mother didn't look up. *You have to get off the train,* Halsa said. She yelled. GET OFF THE TRAIN!

But it was like talking to the door at the top of the wizard's tower. There was something in Halsa's pocket, pressing into her stomach so hard it almost felt like a bruise. Halsa wasn't on the train, she was sleeping on something with a sharp little face.

"Oh, stop yelling. Go away. How am I supposed to stop a train?" Onion said.

"Onion?" his aunt said. Onion realized he'd said it aloud. Halsa looked smug.

"Something bad is going to happen," Onion said, capitulating. "We have to stop the train and get off." The two rich women stared at him as if he were a lunatic. Onion's aunt patted his shoulder. "Onion," she said. "You were asleep. You were having a bad dream."

"But—" Onion protested.

"Here," his aunt said, glancing at the two women. "Take Mik for a walk. Shake off your dream."

Onion gave up. The rich women were thinking that perhaps they would be better off looking for a housekeeper in Qual. Halsa was tapping her foot, standing in the aisle with her arms folded.

Come on, she said. *No point talking to* them. *They just think you're crazy. Come talk to the conductor instead.*

"Sorry," Onion said to his aunt. "I had a bad dream. I'll go for a walk." He took Mik's hand.

They went up the aisle, stepping over sleeping people and people stupid or quarrelsome with drink, people slapping down playing cards. Halsa always in front of them: *Hurry up, hurry, hurry. We're almost there. You've left it too late. That useless wizard, I should have known not to bother asking for help. I should have known not to expect you to take care of things. You're as useless as* they *are. Stupid good-for-nothing wizards of Perfil.*

Up ahead of the train, Onion could feel the gunpowder charges, little bundles wedged between the ties of the track. It was like there was a stone in his shoe. He wasn't afraid, he was merely irritated: at Halsa, at the people on the train who didn't even know enough to be afraid, at the wizards and the rich women who thought that they could just buy children, just like that. He was angry, too. He was angry at his parents, for dying, for leaving him stuck here. He was angry at the King, who had gone mad; at the soldiers, who wouldn't stay home with their own families, who went around stabbing and shooting and blowing up other people's families.

They were at the front of the train. Halsa led Onion right into the cab, where two men were throwing enormous scoops of coal into a red-black, boiling furnace. They were filthy as devils. Their arms bulged with muscles and their eyes were red. One turned and saw Onion. "Oi!" he said. "What's he doing here? You, kid, what are you doing?"

"You have to stop the train," Onion said. "Something is going to happen. I saw soldiers. They're going to make the train blow up."

"Soldiers? Back there? How long ago?"

"They're up ahead of us," Onion said. "We have to stop now."

Mik was looking up at him.

"He saw soldiers?" the other man said.

"Naw," said the first man. Onion could see he didn't know whether to be angry or whether to laugh. "The fucking kid's making things up. Pretending he sees things. Hey, maybe he's a wizard of Perfil! Lucky us, we got a wizard on the train!"

"I'm not a wizard," Onion said. Halsa snorted in agreement. "But I know things. If you don't stop the train, everyone will die."

Both men stared at him. Then the first said angrily, "Get out of here, you. And don't go talking to people like that or we'll throw you in the boiler."

"Okay," Onion said "Come on, Mik."

Wait, Halsa said. *What are you doing? You have to make them understand. Do you want to be dead? Do you think you can prove something to me by being dead?*

Onion put Mik on his shoulders. *I'm sorry,* he said to Halsa. *But it's no good. Maybe you should just go away. Wake up. Catch fish. Fetch water for the wizards of Perfil.*

The pain in Halsa's stomach was sharper, as if someone were stabbing her. When she put her hand down, she had hold of the wooden doll.

What's that? Onion said.

Nothing, Halsa said. *Something I found in the swamp. I said I would give it to the wizard, but I won't! Here, you take it!*

She thrust it at Onion. It went all the way through him. It was an uncomfortable feeling, even though it wasn't really there. *Halsa,* he said. He put Mik down.

Take it! she said. *Here! Take it now!*

The train was roaring. Onion knew where they were; he recognized the way the light looked. Someone was telling a joke in the front of the train, and in a minute a woman would laugh. It would be a lot brighter in a minute. He put his hand up to stop the thing that Halsa was stabbing him with and something smacked against his palm. His fingers brushed Halsa's fingers.

It was a wooden doll with a sharp little nose. There was a nose on the back of its head, too. *Oh, take it!* Halsa said. Something was pouring out of her, through the doll, into Onion. Onion fell back against a woman holding a birdcage on her lap. "Get off!" the woman said. It *hurt*. The stuff pouring out of Halsa felt like *life,* as if the doll was pulling out her life like a skcin of heavy, sodden, black wool. It hurt Onion, too. Black stuff poured and poured through the doll, into him, until there was no space for Onion, no space to breathe or think or see. The black stuff welled up in his throat, pressed behind his eyes. "Halsa," he said, "let go!"

The woman with the birdcage said, "What's wrong with him?"

Mik said, "What's wrong? What's wrong?"

The light changed. *Onion,* Halsa said, and let go of the doll. He staggered backward. The tracks beneath the train were singing *tara-ta tara-ta ta-rata-ta.* Onion's nose was full of swamp water and coal and metal and magic. "No," Onion said. He threw the doll at the woman holding the birdcage and pushed Mik down on the floor. "No," Onion said again, louder. People were staring at him. The woman who'd been laughing at the joke had stopped laughing. Onion covered Mik with his body. The light grew brighter and blacker, all at once.

"Onion!" Halsa said. But she couldn't see him anymore. She was awake in the cubby beneath the stair. The doll was gone.

Halsa had seen men coming home from the war. Some of them had been blinded. Some had lost a hand or an arm. She'd seen one man wrapped in lengths of cloth and propped up in a dogcart that his young daughter pulled on a rope. He'd had no legs, no arms. When people looked at him, he cursed them. There was another man who ran a cockpit in Larch. He came back from the war and paid a man to carve him a leg out of knotty pine. At first he was unsteady on the pine leg, trying to find his balance again. It had been funny to watch him chase after his cocks, like watching a windup toy. By the time the army came through Larch again, though, he could run as fast as anyone.

It felt as if half of her had died on the train in the mountains. Her ears rang. She couldn't find her balance. It was as if a part of her had been cut away, as if she were blind. The part of her that *knew* things, *saw* things, wasn't there anymore. She went about all day in a miserable deafening fog.

She brought water up the stairs and she put mud on her arms and legs. She caught fish, because Onion had said that she ought to catch fish. Late in the afternoon, she looked and saw Tolcet sitting beside her on the pier.

"You shouldn't have bought me," she said. "You should have bought Onion. He wanted to come with you. I'm bad-tempered and unkind and I have no good opinion of the wizards of Perfil."

"Of whom do you have a low opinion? Yourself or the wizards of Perfil?" Tolcet asked.

"How can you serve them?" Halsa said. "How can you serve men and women who hide in towers and do nothing to help people who need help? What good is magic if it doesn't serve anyone?"

"These are dangerous times," Tolcet said. "For wizards as well as for children."

"Dangerous times! Hard times! Bad times," Halsa said. "Things have been bad since the day I was born. Why do I see things and know things, when there's nothing I can do to stop them? When will there be better times?"

"What do you see?" Tolcet said. He took Halsa's chin in his hand and tilted her head this way and that, as if her head were a glass ball that he could see inside. He put his hand on her head and smoothed her hair as if she were his own child. Halsa closed her eyes. Misery welled up inside her.

"I don't see anything," she said. "It feels like someone wrapped me in a wool blanket and beat me and left me in the dark. Is this what it feels like not to see anything? Did the wizards of Perfil do this to me?"

"Is it better or worse?" Tolcet said.

"Worse," Halsa said. "No. Better. I don't know. What am I to do? What am I to be?"

"You are a servant of the wizards of Perfil," Tolcet said. "Be patient. All things may yet be well."

Halsa said nothing. What was there to say?

She climbed up and down the stairs of the wizard's tower, carrying water, toasted bread and cheese, little things that she found in the swamp. The door at the top of the stairs was never open. She couldn't see through it. No one spoke to her, although she sat there sometimes, holding her breath so that the wizard would think she had gone away again. But the wizard wouldn't be fooled so easily. Tolcet went up the stairs, too, and perhaps the wizard admitted him. Halsa didn't know.

Essa and Burd and the other children were kind to her, as if they knew that she had been broken. She knew that she wouldn't have been kind to them if their situations had been reversed. But perhaps they knew that, too. The two women and the skinny man kept their distance. She didn't even know their names. They disappeared on errands and came back again and disappeared into the towers.

Once, when she was coming back from the pier with a bucket of fish, there was a dragon on the path. It wasn't very big, only the size of a mastiff. But it gazed at her with wicked, jeweled eyes. She couldn't get past it. It would eat her, and that would be that. It was almost a relief. She put the bucket down and stood waiting to be eaten. But then Essa was there, holding a stick. She hit the dragon on its head, once, twice, and then gave it a kick for good measure. "Go on, you!" Essa said. The dragon went, giving Halsa one last reproachful look. Essa picked up the bucket of fish. "You have to be firm with them," she said. "Otherwise they get inside your head and make you feel as if you deserve to be eaten. They're too lazy to eat anything that puts up a fight."

Halsa shook off a last, wistful regret, almost sorry not to have been eaten. It was like waking up from a dream, something beautiful and noble and sad and utterly untrue. "Thank you," she said to Essa. Her knees were trembling.

"The bigger ones stay away from the meadow," Essa said. "It's the smaller ones who get curious about the wizards of Perfil. And by 'curious,' what I really mean is hungry. Dragons eat the things that they're curious about. Come on, let's go for a swim."

Sometimes Essa or one of the others would tell Halsa stories about the wizards of Perfil. Most of the stories were silly, or plainly untrue. The children sounded almost indulgent, as if they found their masters more amusing than frightful. There were other stories, sad stories about long-ago wizards who had fought great battles or gone on long journeys. Wizards who had perished by treachery or been imprisoned by ones they'd thought friends.

Tolcet carved her a comb. She found frogs whose backs were marked with strange mathematical formulas, and put them in a bucket and took them to the top of the tower. She caught a mole with eyes like pinpricks and a nose like a fleshy pink hand. She found the hilt of a sword, a coin with a hole in it, the outgrown carapace of a dragon, small as a badger and almost weightless, but hard, too. When she cleaned off the mud that covered it, it shone dully, like a candlestick. She took all of these up the stairs. She couldn't tell whether the things she found had any meaning. But she took a small, private pleasure in finding them nevertheless.

The mole had come back down the stairs again, fast, wriggly, and furtive. The frogs were still in the bucket, making their gloomy pronouncements, when she had returned with the wizard's dinner. But other things disappeared behind the wizard of Perfil's door.

The thing that Tolcet had called Halsa's gift came back, a little at a time. Once again, she became aware of the wizards in their towers, and of how they watched her. There was something else, too. It sat beside her, sometimes, while she was fishing, or when she rowed out in the abandoned coracle Tolcet helped her to repair. She thought she knew who, or what, it was. It was the part of Onion that he'd learned to send out. It was what was left of him: shadowy, thin, and silent. It wouldn't talk to her. It only watched. At night, it stood beside her pallet and watched her sleep. She was glad it was there. To be haunted was a kind of comfort.

She helped Tolcet repair a part of the wizard's tower where the stones were loose in their mortar. She learned how to make paper out of rushes and bark. Apparently wizards needed a great deal of paper. Tolcet began to teach her how to read.

One afternoon when she came back from fishing, all of the wizard's servants were standing in a circle. There was a leveret motionless as a stone in the middle of the circle. Onion's ghost crouched down with the other children. So Halsa stood and watched, too. Something was pouring back and forth between the leveret and the servants of the wizards of Perfil. It was the same as it had been for Halsa and Onion, when she'd given him the two-faced doll. The leveret's sides rose and fell. Its eyes were glassy and dark and knowing. Its fur bristled with magic.

"Who is it?" Halsa said to Burd. "Is it a wizard of Perfil?"

"Who?" Burd said. He didn't take his eyes off the leveret. "No, not a wizard. It's a hare. Just a hare. It came out of the marsh."

"But," Halsa said. "But I can feel it. I can almost hear what it's saying."

Burd looked at her. Essa looked, too. "Everything speaks," he said, speaking slowly, as if to a child. "Listen, Halsa."

There was something about the way Burd and Essa were looking at her, as if it were an invitation, as if they were asking her to look inside their heads, to see what they were thinking. The others were watching, too, watching Halsa now, instead of the leveret. Halsa took a step back. "I can't," she said. "I can't hear anything."

She went to fetch water. When she came out of the tower, Burd and Essa and the other children weren't there. Leverets dashed between towers, leaping over one another, tussling in midair. Onion sat on Tolcet's throne, watching and laughing silently. She didn't think she'd seen Onion laugh since the death of his mother. It made her feel strange to know that a dead boy could be so joyful.

The next day Halsa found an injured fox kit in the briar. It snapped at her when she tried to free it and the briars tore her hand. There was a tear in its belly and she could see a shiny gray loop of intestine. She tore off a piece of her shirt and wrapped it around the fox kit. She put the kit in her pocket. She ran all the way back to the wizard's tower, all the way up the steps. She didn't count them. She didn't stop to rest. Onion followed her, quick as a shadow.

When she reached the door at the top of the stairs, she knocked hard. No one answered.

"Wizard!" she said.

No one answered.

"Please help me," she said. She lifted the fox kit out of her pocket and sat down on the steps with it swaddled in her lap. It didn't try to bite her. It needed all its energy for dying. Onion sat next to her. He stroked the kit's throat.

"Please," Halsa said again. "Please don't let it die. Please do something."

She could feel the wizard of Perfil, standing next to the door. The wizard put a hand out, as if—at last—the door might open. She saw that the wizard loved foxes and all the wild marsh things. But the wizard said nothing. The wizard didn't love Halsa. The door didn't open.

"Help me," Halsa said one more time. She felt that dreadful black pull again, just as it had been on the train with Onion. It was as if the wizard were yanking at her shoulder, shaking her in a stony, black rage. How dare someone like Halsa ask a wizard for help. Onion was shaking her, too. Where Onion's hand gripped her, Halsa could feel stuff pouring through her and out of her. She could feel the kit, feel the place where its stomach had torn open. She could feel its heart pumping blood, its panic and fear and the life that was spilling out of it. Magic flowed up and down the stairs of the tower. The wizard of Perfil was winding it up like a skein of black, tarry wool, and then letting it go again. It poured through Halsa and Onion and the fox kit until Halsa thought she would die.

"Please," she said, and what she meant this time was *stop*. It would kill her. And then she was empty again. The magic had gone through her and there was nothing left of it or her. Her bones had been turned into jelly. The fox kit began to struggle, clawing at her. When she unwrapped it, it sank its teeth into her wrist and then ran down the stairs as if it had never been dying at all.

Halsa stood up. Onion was gone, but she could still feel the wizard standing there on the other side of the door. "Thank you," she said. She followed the fox kit down the stairs.

The next morning she woke and found Onion lying on the pallet beside her. He seemed nearer, somehow, this time. As if he weren't entirely dead. Halsa felt that if she tried to speak to him, he would answer. But she was afraid of what he would say.

Essa saw Onion, too. "You have a shadow," she said.

"His name is Onion," Halsa said.

"Help me with this," Essa said. Someone had cut lengths of bamboo. Essa was fixing them in the ground, using a mixture of rocks and mud to keep them upright. Burd and some of the other children wove rushes through the bamboo, making walls, Halsa saw.

"What are we doing?" Halsa asked.

"There is an army coming." Burd said. "To burn down the town of Perfil. Tolcet went to warn them."

"What will happen?" Halsa said. "Will the wizards protect the town?"

Essa laid another bamboo pole across the tops of the two upright poles. She said, "They can come to the marshes, if they want to, and take refuge. The army won't come here. They're afraid of the wizards."

"Afraid of the wizards!" Halsa said. "Why? The wizards are cowards and fools. Why won't they save Perfil?"

"Go ask them yourself," Essa said. "If you're brave enough."

"Halsa?" Onion said. Halsa looked away from Essa's steady gaze. For a moment there were two Onions. One was the shadowy ghost from the train, close enough to touch. The second Onion stood beside the cooking fire. He was filthy, skinny, and real. Shadow-Onion guttered and then was gone.

"Onion?" Halsa said.

"I came out of the mountains," Onion said. "Five days ago, I think. I didn't know where I was going, except that I could see you. Here. I walked and walked and you were with me and I was with you."

"Where are Mik and Bonti?" Halsa said. "Where's Mother?"

"There were two women on the train with us. They were rich. They've promised to take care of Mik and Bonti. They will. I know they will. They were going to Qual. When you gave me the doll, Halsa, you saved the train. We could see the explosion, but we passed through it. The tracks were destroyed and there were clouds and clouds of black smoke and fire, but nothing touched the train. We saved everyone."

"Where's Mother?" Halsa said again. But she already knew. Onion was silent. The train stopped beside a narrow stream to take on water. There was an ambush. Soldiers. There was a bottle with water leaking out of it. Halsa's mother had dropped it. There was an arrow sticking out of her back.

Onion said, "I'm sorry, Halsa. Everyone was afraid of me, because of how the train had been saved. Because I knew that there was going to be an explosion. Because I didn't know about the ambush and people died. So I got off the train."

"Here," Burd said to Onion. He gave him a bowl of porridge. "No, eat it slowly. There's plenty more."

Onion said with his mouth full, "Where are the wizards of Perfil?"

Halsa began to laugh. She laughed until her sides ached and until Onion stared at her and until Essa came over and shook her. "We don't have time for this," Essa said. "Take that boy and find him somewhere to lie down. He's exhausted."

"Come on," Halsa said to Onion. "You can sleep in my bed. Or if you'd rather, you can go knock on the door at the top of the tower and ask the wizard of Perfil if you can have his bed."

She showed Onion the cubby under the stairs and he lay down on it. "You're dirty," she said. "You'll get the sheets dirty."

"I'm sorry," Onion said.

"It's fine," Halsa said. "We can wash them later. There's plenty of water here. Are you still hungry? Do you need anything?"

"I brought something for you," Onion said. He held out his hand and there were the earrings that had belonged to his mother.

"No," Halsa said.

Halsa hated herself. She was scratching at her own arm, ferociously, not as if she had an insect bite, but as if she wanted to dig beneath the skin. Onion saw something that he hadn't known before, something astonishing and terrible, that Halsa was no kinder to herself than to anyone else. No wonder Halsa had wanted the earrings—just like the snakes, Halsa would gnaw on herself if there was nothing else to gnaw on. How Halsa wished that she'd been kind to her mother.

Onion said, "Take them. Your mother was kind to me, Halsa. So I want to give them to you. My mother would have wanted you to have them, too."

"All right," Halsa said. She wanted to weep, but she scratched and scratched instead. Her arm was white and red from scratching. She took the earrings and put them in her pocket. "Go to sleep now."

"I came here because you were here," Onion said. "I wanted to tell you what had happened. What should I do now?"

"Sleep," Halsa said.

"Will you tell the wizards that I'm here? How we saved the train?" Onion said. He yawned so wide that Halsa thought his head would split in two. "Can I be a servant of the wizards of Perfil?"

"We'll see," Halsa said. "You go to sleep. I'll go climb the stairs and tell them that you've come."

"It's funny," Onion said. "I can feel them all around us. I'm glad you're here. I feel safe."

Halsa sat on the bed. She didn't know what to do. Onion was quiet for a while and then he said, "Halsa?"

"What?" Halsa said.

"I can't sleep," he said apologetically.

"Shhh," Halsa said. She stroked his filthy hair. She sang a song her father had liked to sing. She held Onion's hand until his breathing became slower and she was sure that he was sleeping. Then she went up the stairs to tell the wizard about Onion. "I don't understand you," she said to the door. "Why do you hide away from the world? Don't you get tired of hiding?"

The wizard didn't say anything.

"Onion is braver than you are," Halsa told the door. "Essa is braver. My mother was—"

She swallowed and said, "She was braver than you. Stop ignoring me. What good are you, up here? You won't talk to me, and you won't help the town of Perfil, and Onion's going to be very disappointed when he realizes that all you do is skulk around in your room, waiting for someone to bring you breakfast. If you like waiting so much, then you can wait as long as you like. I'm not going to bring you any food or any water or anything that I find in the swamp. If you want anything, you can magic it. Or you can come get it yourself. Or you can turn me into a toad."

She waited to see if the wizard would turn her into a toad.

"All right," she said at last. "Well, good-bye then." She went back down the stairs.

The wizards of Perfil are lazy and useless. They hate to climb stairs and they never listen when you talk. They don't answer questions because their ears are full of beetles and wax and their faces are wrinkled and hideous. Marsh fairies live deep in the wrinkles of the faces of the wizards of Perfil and the marsh fairies ride around in the bottomless canyons of the wrinkles on saddle-broken fleas who grow fat grazing on magical, wizardly blood. The wizards of Perfil spend all night scratching their fleabites and sleep all day. I'd rather be a scullery maid than a servant of the invisible, doddering, nearly-blind, flea-bitten, mildewy, clammy-fingered, conceited marsh-wizards of Perfil.

Halsa checked Onion, to make sure that he was still asleep. Then she went and found Essa. "Will you pierce my ears for me?" she said.

Essa shrugged. "It will hurt," she said.

"Good," said Halsa. So Essa boiled water and put her needle in it. Then she pierced Halsa's ears. It did hurt, and Halsa was glad. She put on Onion's mother's earrings, and then she helped Essa and the others dig latrines for the townspeople of Perfil.

Tolcet came back before sunset. There were half a dozen women and their children with him.

"Where are the others?" Essa said.

Tolcet said, "Some don't believe me. They don't trust

wizardly folk. There are some that want to stay and defend the town. Others are striking out on foot for Qual, along the tracks."

"Where is the army now?" Burd said.

"Close," Halsa said. Tolcet nodded.

The women from the town had brought food and bedding. They seemed subdued and anxious and it was hard to tell whether it was the approaching army or the wizards of Perfil that scared them most. The women stared at the ground. They didn't look up at the towers. If they caught their children looking up, they scolded them in low voices.

"Don't be silly," Halsa said crossly to a woman whose child had been digging a hole near a tumbled tower. The woman shook him until he cried and cried and wouldn't stop. What was she thinking? That wizards liked to eat mucky children who dug holes? "The wizards are lazy and unsociable and harmless. They keep to themselves and don't bother anyone."

The woman only stared at Halsa, and Halsa realized that she was as afraid of Halsa as she was of the wizards of Perfil. Halsa was amazed. Was she that terrible? Mik and Bonti and Onion had always been afraid of her, but they'd had good reason to be. And she'd changed. She was as mild and meek as butter now.

Tolcet, who was helping with dinner, snorted as if he'd caught her thought. The woman grabbed up her child and rushed away, as if Halsa might open her mouth again and eat them both.

"Halsa, look." It was Onion, awake and so filthy that you could smell him from two yards away. They would need to burn his clothes. Joy poured through Halsa, because Onion had come to find her and because he was here and because he was alive. He'd come out of Halsa's tower, where he'd gotten her cubby bed grimy and smelly, how wonderful to think of it, and he was pointing east, toward the town of Perfil. There was a red glow hanging over the marsh, as if the sun were rising instead of setting. Everyone was silent, looking east as if they might be able to see what was happening in Perfil. Presently the wind carried an ashy, desolate smoke over the marsh. "The war has come to Perfil," a woman said.

"Which army is it?" another woman said, as if the first woman might know.

"Does it matter?" said the first woman. "They're all the same. My eldest went off to join the King's army and my youngest joined General Balder's men. They've set fire to plenty of towns, and killed other mothers' sons and maybe one day they'll kill each other, and never think of me. What difference does it make to the town that's being attacked, to know what army is attacking them? Does it matter to a cow who kills her?"

"They'll follow us," someone else said in a resigned voice. "They'll find us here and they'll kill us all!"

"They won't," Tolcet said. He spoke loudly. His voice was calm and reassuring. "They won't follow you and they won't find you here. Be brave for your children. All will be well."

"Oh, please," Halsa said, under her breath. She stood and glared up at the towers of the wizards of Perfil, her hands on her hips. But as usual, the wizards of Perfil were up to nothing. They didn't strike her dead for glaring. They didn't stand at their windows to look out over the marshes to see the town of Perfil and how it was burning while they only stood and watched. Perhaps they were already asleep in their beds, dreaming about breakfast, lunch, and dinner. She went and helped Burd and Essa and the others make up beds for the refugees from Perfil. Onion cut up wild onions for the stew pot. He was going to have to have a bath soon, Halsa thought. Clearly he needed someone like Halsa to tell him what to do.

None of the servants of the wizards of Perfil slept. There was too much work to do. The latrines weren't finished. A child wandered off into the marshes and had to be found before it drowned or met a dragon. A little girl fell into the well and had to be hauled up.

Before the sun came up again, more refugees from the town of Perfil arrived. They came into the camp in groups of twos or threes, until there were almost a hundred towns-people in the wizards' meadow. Some of the newcomers were wounded or badly burned or deep in shock. Essa and Tolcet took charge. There were compresses to apply, clothes that had already been cut up for bandages, hot drinks that smelled bitter and medicinal and not particularly magical. People went rushing around, trying to discover news of family members or friends who had stayed behind. Young children who had been asleep woke up and began to cry.

"They put the mayor and his wife to the sword," a man was saying.

"They'll march on the King's city next," an old woman said. "But our army will stop them."

"It *was* our army—I saw the butcher's boy and Philpot's middle son. They said that we'd been trading with the enemies of our country. The King sent them. It was to teach us a lesson. They burned down the market church and they hung the pastor from the bell tower."

There was a girl lying on the ground who looked Mik and Bonti's age. Her face was gray. Tolcet touched her stomach lightly and she emitted a thin, high scream, not a human noise at all, Onion thought. The marshes were so noisy with magic that he couldn't hear what she was thinking, and he was glad.

"What happened?" Tolcet said to the man who'd carried her into the camp.

"She fell," the man said. "She was trampled underfoot."

Onion watched the girl, breathing slowly and steadily, as if he could somehow breathe for her. Halsa watched Onion. Then: "That's enough," she said. "Come on, Onion."

She marched away from Tolcet and the girl, shoving through the refugees.

"Where are we going?" Onion said.

"To make the wizards come down," Halsa said. "I'm sick and tired of doing all their work for them. Their cooking and fetching. I'm going to knock down that stupid door. I'm going to drag them down their stupid stairs. I'm going to make them help that girl."

There were a lot of stairs this time. Of course the accursed wizards of Perfil would know what she was up to. This was their favorite kind of wizardly joke, making her climb and climb and climb. They'd wait until she and Onion got to the top and then they'd turn them into lizards. Well, maybe it wouldn't be so bad, being a small poisonous lizard. She could slip under the door and bite one of the damned wizards of Perfil. She went up and up and up, half running and half stumbling, until it seemed she and Onion must have climbed right up into the sky. When the stairs abruptly ended, she was still running. She crashed into the door so hard that she saw stars.

"Halsa?" Onion said. He bent over her. He looked so worried that she almost laughed.

"I'm fine," she said. "Just wizards playing tricks." She hammered on the door, then kicked it for good measure. "Open up!"

"What are you doing?" Onion said.

"It never does any good," Halsa said. "I should have brought an ax."

"Let me try," Onion said.

Halsa shrugged. Stupid boy, she thought, and Onion could hear her perfectly. "Go ahead," she said.

Onion put his hand on the door and pushed. It swung open. He looked up at Halsa and flinched. "Sorry," he said.

Halsa went in.

There was a desk in the room, and a single candle, which was burning. There was a bed, neatly made, and a mirror on the wall over the desk. There was no wizard of Perfil, not even hiding under the bed. Halsa checked, just in case.

She went to the empty window and looked out. There was the meadow and the makeshift camp, below them, and the marsh. The canals, shining like silver. There was the sun, coming up, the way it always did. It was strange to see all the windows of the other towers from up here, so far above, all empty. White birds were floating over the marsh. She wondered if they were wizards; she wished she had a bow and arrows.

"Where is the wizard?" Onion said. He poked the bed. Maybe the wizard had turned himself into a bed. Or the desk. Maybe the wizard was a desk.

"There are no wizards," Halsa said.

"But I can feel them!" Onion sniffed, then sniffed harder. He could practically smell the wizard, as if the wizard of Perfil had turned himself into a mist or a vapor that Onion was inhaling. He sneezed violently.

Someone was coming up the stairs. He and Halsa waited to see if it was a wizard of Perfil. But it was only Tolcet. He looked tired and cross, as if he'd had to climb many, many stairs.

"Where are the wizards of Perfil?" Halsa said.

Tolcet held up a finger. "A minute to catch my breath," he said.

Halsa stamped her foot. Onion sat down on the bed. He apologized to it silently, just in case it was the wizard. Or maybe the candle was the wizard. He wondered what happened if you tried to blow a wizard out. Halsa was so angry he thought she might explode.

Tolcet sat down on the bed beside Onion. "A long time ago," he said, "the father of the present King visited the wizards of Perfil. He'd had certain dreams about his son, who was only a baby. He was afraid of these dreams. The wizards told him that he was right to be afraid. His son would go mad. There would be war and famine and more war and his son would be to blame. The old King went into a rage. He sent his men to throw the wizards of Perfil down from their towers. They did."

"Wait," Onion said. "Wait. What happened to the wizards? Did they turn into white birds and fly away?"

"No," Tolcet said. "The King's men slit their throats and threw them out of the towers. I was away. When I came back, the towers had been ransacked. The wizards were dead."

"No!" Halsa said. "Why are you lying? I know the wizards are here. They're hiding somehow. They're cowards."

"I can feel them, too," Onion said.

"Come and see," Tolcet said. He went to the window. When they looked down, they saw Essa and the other servants of the wizards of Perfil moving among the refugees. The two old women who never spoke were sorting through bundles of clothes and blankets. The thin man was staking down someone's cow. Children were chasing chickens as Burd held open the gate of a makeshift pen. One of the younger girls, Perla, was singing a lullaby to some mother's baby. Her voice, rough and sweet at the same time, rose straight up to the window of the tower, where Halsa and Onion and Tolcet stood looking down. It was a song they all knew. It was a song that said all would be well.

"Don't you understand?" Tolcet, the wizard of Perfil, said to Halsa and Onion. "There are the wizards of Perfil. They are young, most of them. They haven't come into their full powers yet. But all may yet be well."

"Essa is a wizard of Perfil?" Halsa said. Essa, a shovel in her hand, looked up at the tower, as if she'd heard Halsa. She smiled and shrugged, as if to say, *Perhaps I am, perhaps not, but isn't it a good joke? Didn't you ever wonder?*

Tolcet turned Halsa and Onion around so that they faced the mirror that hung on the wall. He rested his strong, speckled hands on their shoulders for a minute, as if to give them courage. Then he pointed to the mirror, to the reflected Halsa and Onion, who stood there staring back at themselves, astonished. Tolcet began to laugh. Despite everything, he laughed so hard that tears came from his eyes. He snorted. The wizard's room was full of magic, and so were the marshes and Tolcet and the mirror where the children and Tolcet stood reflected, and the children were full of magic, too.

Tolcet pointed again at the mirror, and his reflection pointed its finger straight back at Halsa and Onion. Tolcet said, "Here they are in front of you! Ha! Do you know them? Here are the wizards of Perfil!"

KELLY LINK is the author of two story collections, *Stranger Things Happen and Magic for Beginners*. She and her partner, Gavin J. Grant, live in Northampton, Massachusetts, where they publish books as Small Beer Press, produce the zine *Lady Churchill's Rosebud Wristlet* (www.lcrw.net), and coedit (the fantasy half of) *The Year's Best Fantasy and Horror* with Ellen Datlow. In late 2008, Viking will publish her first YA story collection, tentatively titled *The Wrong Grave and Other Stories*.

Kelly once won a free trip around the world by answering the question "Why do you want to go around the world?" with "Because you can't go through it."

Her Web site is **www.kellylink.net**.

AUTHOR'S NOTE

For about five or six years, I've had this picture in my head of a city of wizards. They live at the very top of impossibly tall towers and employ children to run up and down the stairs, fetching water and food and books and letters. But it wasn't really a story. It was just a very strange picture.

The first time I wrote "The Wizards of Perfil," it was Onion's story. He went off with Tolcet, and then the story just sat there. This wasn't Onion's fault: he was so happy to be working for wizards that the story got kind of boring. And I was sorry that Halsa and her brothers and mother went off on the train to be killed. So I put "The Wizards of Perfil" aside and went and wrote another story, "The Constable of

Abal," which takes place in the same world, I think, although it's either somewhat earlier or later. It's a story about gods, ghosts, and a murder, and I was still so preoccupied with the problem of Onion that it was a breeze to write. And by the time I'd finished the new story, I'd figured out some things about "The Wizards of Perfil." ["The Constable of Abal" appears in Ellen Datlow and Terri Windling's anthology *The Coyote Road: Trickster Tales* (Viking).]

So I came back, looked at the beginning again, and realized that I liked Halsa as much as I liked Onion, partly because she wasn't a likable character at all. So I sent her off with Tolcet instead, put Onion on the train, and then I could write the story.

I should also say that I wrote this story while sitting in the Haymarket (a coffeehouse in Northampton) and drinking smoothies with the writer Holly Black. I don't think I could have finished it without her or the smoothies.

Patricia A. McKillip

Jack O'Lantern

Jenny Newland sat patiently under the tree in her costume, waiting for the painter to summon her. Not far from her, in the sunlight, one of the village girls sneezed lavishly and drew the back of her wrist under her nose. A boy poked her; she demanded aggrievedly, "Well, what do you want me to do? Wipe me nose on me costume?" Jenny shifted her eyes; her clasped fingers tightened; her spine straightened. They were all dressed alike, the half-dozen young people around the tree, in what looked like tablecloths the innocuous pastels of tea cakes.

"Togas?" her father had suggested dubiously at the sight. "And Grecian robes for the young ladies? Pink, though? And pistachio . . .?" His voice had trailed away; at home, he would have gone off to consult his library. Here, amid the pretty thickets and pastures outside the village of Farnham, he could only watch and wonder.

He had commissioned the renowned painter Joshua Ryme to do a commemorative painting for Sarah's wedding.

Naturally, she couldn't wear her bridal gown before the wedding; it was with the seamstress, having five hundred seed pearls attached to it by the frail, undernourished fingers of a dozen orphans who never saw the light of day. Such was the opinion of Sylvester Newland, who claimed the sibling territory midway between Sarah, seventeen, and Jenny, thirteen. It was a lot of leeway, those four years between child and adult, and he roamed obnoxiously in it, scattering his thoughts at will for no other reason than that he was allowed to have them.

"Men must make their way in the world," her mother had said gently when Jenny first complained about Sylvester's rackety ways. "Women must help and encourage them, and provide them with a peaceful haven from their daily struggle to make the world a better place."

Jenny, who had been struggling with a darning needle and wool and one of Sylvester's socks, stabbed herself and breathed incredulously, "For this I have left school?"

"Your governess will see that you receive the proper education to provide you with understanding and sympathy for your husband's work and conversation." Her mother's voice was still mild, but she spoke in that firm, sweet manner that would remain unshaken by all argument, like a great stone rising implacably out of buffeting waves, sea life clinging safely to every corner of it. "Besides, women are not strong, as you will find out soon enough. Their bodies are subject to the powerful forces of their natures." She hesitated; Jenny was silent, having heard rumors of the secret lives of women, and wondering if her mother would go into detail. She did, finally,

but in such a delicate fashion that Jenny was left totally bewildered. Women were oysters carrying the pearls of life; their husbands opened them and poured into them the water of life, after which the pearls . . . turned into babies?

Later, after one of the pearls of life had finally irritated her inner oyster enough to draw blood, and she found herself on a daybed hugging a hot water bag, she began to realize what her mother had meant about powerful forces of nature. Sarah, tactfully quiet and kind, put a cup of tea on the table beside her.

"Thank you," Jenny said mournfully. "I think the oysters are clamping themselves shut inside me."

Sarah's solemn expression quivered away; she sat on the daybed beside Jenny. "Oh, did you get the oyster speech, too?"

She had grown amazingly stately overnight, it seemed to Jenny, with her lovely gowns and her fair hair coiled and scalloped like cream on an éclair. Sarah's skin was perfect ivory; her own was blotched and dotted with strange eruptions. Her hair, straight as a horse's tail and so heavy it flopped out of all but the toothiest pins, was neither ruddy chestnut nor true black, but some unromantic shade in between.

Reading Jenny's mind, which she did often, Sarah patted her hands. "Don't fret. You'll grow into yourself. And you have a fine start: your pale gray eyes with that dark hair will become stunning soon enough."

"For what?" Jenny asked intensely, searching her sister's face. The sudden luminousness of her beauty must partially be explained by Mr. Everett Woolidge, who had already spoken to Sarah's father, and was impatiently awaiting Sarah's eighteenth birthday. "Is love only about oysters and the water of life? What exactly was Mama trying to say?"

Sarah's smile had gone; she answered slowly, "I'm not sure yet, myself, though I'm very sure it has nothing to do with oysters."

"When you find out, will you tell me?"

"I promise. I'll take notes as it happens." Still a line tugged at her tranquil brows; she was not seeing Jenny, but the shadow of Mr. Woolidge, doing who knew what to her on her wedding bed. Then she added, reading Jenny's mind again, "There's nothing to fear, Mama says. You just lie still and think of the garden."

"The garden?"

"Something pleasant."

"That's all it took to make Sylvester? She must have been thinking about the plumbing, or boiled cabbage."

Sarah's smile flashed again; she ducked her head, looking guilty for a moment, as though she'd been caught giggling in the schoolroom. "Very likely." She pushed a strand of hair out of Jenny's face. "You should drink your tea; it'll soothe the pain."

Jenny stared up at her, fingers clenched, her whole body clenched, something tight and hot behind her eyes. "I'll miss you," she whispered. "Oh, I will miss you so. Sylvester just talks at me, and Mama—Mama cares only about him and Papa. You are the only one I can laugh with."

"I know." Sarah's voice, too, sounded husky, ragged. "Everett—he is kind and good, and of course ardent. But I've

known you all your life. I can say things to you that I could never say to Mama—or even to Everett—" She paused, that faraway look again in her eyes, as though she were trying to see her own future. "I hope he and I will learn to talk to one another . . . Mama would say it's childish of me to want what I think to be in any way important to him; that's something I must grow out of, when I'm married."

"Talk to me," Jenny begged her. "Anytime. About anything."

Sarah nodded, caressing Jenny's hair again. "I'll send for you."

"Why must he take you so far away? Why?"

"It's only a half day on the train. And very pretty, Farnham is. We'll have long rides together, you and I, and walks, and country fairs. You'll see."

And Jenny did: the village where Mr. Woolidge had inherited his country home was charming, full of centuries-old cottages with thick stone walls, and hairy thatched roofs, and tiny windows set, with no order whatsoever, all anyhow in the walls. The artist, Mr. Ryme, had a summer house there as well. Jenny could see it on a distant knoll from where she sat under the chestnut tree. It was of butter-yellow stone with white trim, and the windows were where you expected them to be. But still it looked old, with its dark, crumbling garden wall, and the ancient twisted apple trees inside, and the wooden gate, open for so long it had grown into the earth. The artist's daughter Alexa was under the tree as well, along with four comely village children and Jenny. The village children with their rough voices and unkempt hair would have horrified Mama. Fortunately she had not come, due to undisclosed circumstances that Jenny suspected had to do with oysters and pearls. Sylvester was away at school; Mr. Ryme would add their faces to the painting later. The governess, Miss Lake, had accompanied Jenny, with some staunch idea of keeping up with her lessons. But in the mellow country air, she had relaxed and grown vague. She sat knitting under a willow, light and shadow dappling her thin, freckled face and angular body as the willow leaves swayed around her in the breeze.

The artist had positioned Jenny's father on one side of the little rocky brook winding through the grass. The wedding guests, mostly portrayed by villagers and friends of the painter, were arranged behind him. The wedding party itself would be painted advancing toward him on the other side of the water. A tiny bridge arching above some picturesque stones and green moss would signify the place where the lovers Cupid and Psyche would become man and wife. Papa wore a long tunic that covered all but one arm, over which a swag of purple was discreetly draped. He looked, with his long gold mustaches and full beard, more like a druid, Jenny thought, than a Grecian nobleman. He was smiling, enjoying himself, his eyes on Sarah as the artist fussed with the lilies in her hands. She wore an ivory robe; Mr. Woolidge, a very hairy Cupid, wore gold with a purple veil over his head. At the foot of the bridge, the artist's younger daughter, golden-haired and plump, just old enough to know how to stand still, carried a basket of violets, from which she would fling a handful of posies onto the bridge to ornament the couple's path.

Finally, the older children were summoned into position

behind the pair. Mr. Ryme, having placed them, stood gazing narrowly at them, one finger rasping over his whiskers. He moved his hand finally and spoke.

"A lantern. We must have a lantern."

"Exactly!" Papa exclaimed, enlightened.

"Why, Father?" the artist's daughter Alexa asked, daring to voice the question in Jenny's head. She thought Mr. Ryme would ignore his daughter, or rebuke her for breaking her pose. But he took the question seriously, gazing at all of the children behind the bridal pair.

"Because Cupid made Psyche promise not to look upon him, even after they married. He came to her only at night. Psyche's sisters told her that she must have married some dreadful monster instead of a man. Such things happened routinely, it seems, in antiquity."

"He's visible enough now," one of the village boys commented diffidently, but inarguably, of Mr. Woolidge.

"Yes, he is," Mr. Ryme answered briskly. "We can't very well leave the groom out of his own wedding portrait, can we? That's why he is wearing that veil. He'll hold it out between himself and his bride, and turn his head so that only those viewing the painting will see his face."

"Oh, brilliant," Papa was heard to murmur across the bridge.

"Thank you. But let me continue with the lantern. One night, Psyche lit a lantern to see exactly what she had taken into her marriage bed. She was overjoyed to find the beautiful face of the son of Venus. But—profoundly moved by his godhood, perhaps—she trembled and spilled a drop of hot oil on him, waking him. In sorrow and anger with her for breaking her promise, he vanished out of her life. The lantern among the wedding party will remind the viewer of the rest of Psyche's story."

"What was the rest, Mr. Ryme?" a village girl demanded.

"She was forced to face her mother-in-law," Alexa answered instead, "who made Psyche complete various impossible tasks, including a trip to the Underworld, before the couple were united again. Isn't that right, Father?"

"Very good, Alexa," Mr. Ryme said, smiling at her. Jenny's eyes widened. She knew the tale as well as anyone, but if she had spoken, Papa would have scolded her for showing off her knowledge. And here was Alexa, with her curly red-gold hair and green eyes, not only lovely, but encouraged to reveal her education. Mr. Ryme held up his hand before anyone else could speak, his eyes, leaf green as his daughter's beneath his dark, shaggy brows, moving over them again.

"Who . . ." he murmured. "Ah. Of course, Jenny must hold it. Why you, Jenny?"

Behind him, Papa, prepared to answer, closed his mouth, composed his expression. Jenny gazed at Mr. Ryme, gathering courage, and answered finally, shyly, "Because I am the bride's sister. And I'm part of Psyche's story, as well, like the lantern."

"Good!" Mr. Ryme exclaimed. His daughter caught Jenny's eyes, smiled, and Jenny felt herself flush richly. The artist shifted her to the forefront of the scene and crooked her arm at her waist. "Pretend this is your lantern," he said, handing her a tin cup that smelled strongly of linseed oil from his paint box. "I'm sure there's something more appropriate in

my studio. For now, I just need to sketch you all in position."
He gestured to the dozen or so villagers and friends behind
Mr. Newland. "Poses, please, everyone. Try to keep still. This
won't take as long as you might think. When I've gotten you
all down where I want you, we'll have a rest and explore the
contents of the picnic baskets Mr. Woolidge and Mr. Newland
so thoughtfully provided. I'll work with small groups after we
eat; the rest of you can relax unless I need you, but don't vanish. Remember that you are all invited to supper at my cottage
at the end of the day."

Jenny spent her breaks under the willow tree, practicing
historical dates and French irregular verbs with Miss Lake,
who seemed to have been recalled to her duties by the references to the classics. At the end of the day, Jenny was more
than ready for the slow walk through the meadows in the long,
tranquil dusk to the artist's cottage. There, everyone changed
into their proper clothes, and partook of the hot meat pas-
tries, bread and cheese and cold beef, fresh milk, ale, and
great fruit-and-cream tarts arrayed on the long tables set up
in the artist's garden.

Jenny took a place at the table with Sarah and Mr.
Woolidge. Across from them sat Papa and Mr. Ryme, working
through laden plates and frothy cups of ale.

"An energetic business, painting," Papa commented approvingly. "I hadn't realized how much wildlife is involved."

"It's always more challenging, working out of doors, and
with large groups. It went very well today, I thought."

Jenny looked at the artist, a question hovering inside her.
At home, she was expected to eat her meals silently and grace-

fully, speaking only when asked, and then as simply as possible. But her question wasn't simple; she barely knew how to phrase it. And this was more like a picnic, informal and friendly, everyone talking at once, and half the gathering sitting on the grass.

"Mr. Ryme," she said impulsively, "I have a question."

Her father stared at her with surprise. "Jenny," he chided, "you interrupted Mr. Ryme."

She blushed, mortified. "I'm so sorry—"

"It must be important, then," Mr. Ryme said gently. "What is it?"

"Psyche's sisters—when they told her she must have wedded a monster . . ." Her voice trailed. Papa was blinking at her. Mr. Ryme only nodded encouragingly. "Wouldn't she have known if that were so? Even in the dark, if something less than human were in bed with her—couldn't she tell? Without a lantern?"

She heard Mr. Woolidge cough on his beer, felt Sarah's quick tremor of emotion.

"Jenny," Papa said decisively, "that is a subject more fit for the schoolroom than the dinner table, and hardly suitable even there. I'm surprised you should have such thoughts, let alone express them."

"It is an interesting question, though," Mr. Ryme said quite seriously. "Don't you think? It goes to the heart of the story, which is not about whether Psyche married a monster—and, I think, Jenny is correct in assuming that she would have soon realized it—but about a broken promise. A betrayal of love. Don't you think so, Mr. Newland?"

But his eyes remained on Jenny as he diverted the conversation away from her; they smiled faintly, kindly. Papa began a lengthy answer, citing sources. Jenny felt Sarah's fingers close on her hand.

"I was wondering that, myself," she breathed.

Mr. Woolidge overheard.

"What?" he queried softly. "If you will find a monster in your wedding bed?"

"No, of course not," Sarah said with another tremor—of laughter, or surprise, or fear, Jenny couldn't tell. "What Jenny asked. Why Psyche could not tell, even in the dark, if her husband was not human."

"I assure you, you will find me entirely human," Mr. Woolidge promised. "You will not have to guess."

"I'm sure I won't," Sarah answered faintly.

Mr. Woolidge took a great bite out of his meat pie, his eyes on Sarah as he chewed. Jenny, disregarded, rose and slipped away from her father's critical eyes. She glimpsed Miss Lake watching her from the next table, beginning to gesture, but Jenny pretended not to see. Wandering through the apple trees with a meat pie in her hand, free to explore her own thoughts, she came across the artist's daughter under a tree with one of the village boys.

Jenny stopped uncertainly. Mama would have considered the boy unsuitable company, even for an artist's daughter, and would have instructed Jenny to greet them kindly and politely as she moved away. But she didn't move, and Alexa waved to her.

"Come and sit with us. Will's been telling me country stories."

Jenny glanced around; Miss Lake was safely hidden behind the apple leaves. She edged under the tree and sat, looking curiously at Will. Something about him reminded her of a bird. He was very thin, with flighty golden hair and long, fine bones too near the surface of his skin. His eyes looked golden, like his hair. They seemed secretive, looking back at her, but not showing what they thought. He was perhaps her age, she guessed, though something subtle in his expression made him seem older.

He was chewing an apple from the tree; a napkin with crumbs of bread and cheese on it lay near him on the grass. Politely, he swallowed his bite and waited for Jenny to speak to him first. Jenny glanced questioningly at Alexa, whose own mouth was full.

She said finally, tentatively, "Country tales?"

"It was the lantern, miss." His voice was deep yet soft, with a faint country burr in it, like a bee buzzing in his throat, that was not unpleasant. "It reminded me of Jack."

"Jack?"

"O'Lantern. He carries a light across the marshes at night and teases you into following it, thinking it will lead you to fairyland, or treasure, or just safely across the ground. Then he puts the light out, and there you are, stranded in the dark in the middle of a marsh. Some call it elf fire, or fox fire."

"Or—?" Alexa prompted, with a sudden, teasing smile. The golden eyes slid to her, answering the smile.

"Will," he said. "Will o' the Wisp."

He bit into the apple again; Jenny sat motionless, listening to the crisp, solid crunch, almost tasting the sweet, cool juices.

But these apples were half-wild, her eye told her, misshapen and probably wormy; you shouldn't just pick them out of the long grass or off the branch and eat them . . .

"My father painted a picture of us following the marsh fire," Alexa said. "Will held a lantern in the dark; I was with him as his sister. My father called the painting *Jack O'Lantern*."

"What were you doing in the dark?" Jenny asked fuzzily, trying to untangle the real from the story.

"My father told us we were poor children, sent out to cut peat for a fire on a cruel winter's dusk. Dark came too fast; we got lost, and followed the Jack O'Lantern sprite, thinking it was someone who knew the path back."

"And what happened?"

Alexa shrugged slightly. "That's the thing about paintings. They only show you one moment of the tale; you have to guess at the rest of it. Do you want to see it? My father asked me to find a lantern for you in his studio; he won't mind if you come with me."

Jenny saw Miss Lake drifting about with a plate at the far end of the garden, glancing here and there, most likely for her charge. She stopped to speak to Sarah. Jenny swallowed the last of her meat pie.

"Yes," she said quickly. "I'd like that." It sounded wild and romantic, visiting an artist's studio, a place where paint turned into flame, and flame into the magic of fairyland. It was, her mother would have said, no place for a well-brought-up young girl, who might chance upon the disreputable, unsavory things that went on between artists and their models. Jenny couldn't imagine the distinguished Mr. Ryme doing unsavory things in his studio. But perhaps she could catch a glimpse there of what nebulous goings-on her mother was talking about when she said the word.

"You come, too, Will," Alexa added to him. "You don't often get a chance to see it."

"Is there a back door?" Jenny asked, her eye on Miss Lake, and Alexa flung her a mischievous glance.

"There is, indeed. Come this way."

They went around the apple trees, away from the noisy tables, where lanterns and torches, lit against insects and the dark, illumined faces against the shadowy nightfall, making even the villagers look mysterious, unpredictable. Alexa, carrying a candle, led them up a back staircase in the house. Jenny kept slowing to examine paintings hung along the stairs. In the flickering light, they were too vague to be seen: faces that looked not quite human, risings of stone that might have been high craggy peaks, or the ruined towers of an ancient castle.

Will stopped beside one of the small, ambiguous landscapes. "That's Perdu Castle," he said. He sounded surprised. "On the other side of the marshes. There's stories about it, too: that it shifts around and you never find it if you're looking for it, only if you're not."

"Is that true?" Jenny demanded.

"True as elf fire," he answered gravely, looking at her out of his still eyes in a way that was neither familiar nor rude. As though, Jenny thought, he were simply interested in what she might be thinking. He was nicer than Sylvester, she realized suddenly, for all his dirty fingernails and patched trousers.

"When you saw it, were you looking for it?"

"Bit of both," he admitted. "I was pretending not to while I searched for it. But I was surprised when I found it. I wonder if Mr. Ryme knew it was there before he painted it."

"Of course he did," Alexa said with a laugh. "Great heaps of stone don't shift themselves around; it's people who get lost. My father paints romantic visions, but there's nothing romantic about carrying a paint box for miles, or having to swat flies all afternoon while you search. He'd want to know exactly where he was going."

She opened a door at the top of the stairs, lighting more candles and a couple of lamps as Jenny and Will entered. Paintings leaped into light everywhere in the room, sitting on easels, hanging in frames, leaning in unframed stacks against the walls. The studio took up the entire top floor of the house; windows overlooked meadow, marsh, the smudges of distant trees, the village disappearing into night. Richly colored carpets lay underfoot; odd costumes and wraps hung on hooks and coatracks. A peculiar collection of things littered shelves along the walls: seashells, hats, boxes, a scepter, crowns of tinsel and gold leaf, chunks of crystals, shoe buckles, necklaces, swords, pieces of armor, ribbons, a gilded bit and bridle. From among this jumble, Alexa produced a lamp and studied it doubtfully. One end was pointed, the other scrolled into a handle. Gleaming brass with colorful lozenges of enamel decorated the sides. It looked, Jenny thought, like the lamp Aladdin might have rubbed to summon the genie within. Alexa put it back, rummaged farther along the shelves.

Will caught Jenny's eye then, gazing silently at a painting propped against the wall. She joined him, and saw his face in the painting, peering anxiously into a wild darkness dimly lit by the lantern in his hand. Alexa, a lock of red hair blowing out of the threadbare shawl over her head, stood very close to him, pointing toward the faint light across murky ground and windblown grasses. Her face, pinched and worried, seemed to belong more to a ghostly twin of the lovely, confident, easily smiling girl searching for a lamp behind them.

Something flashed above the painting. Jenny raised her eyes to the open window, saw the pale light in the dense twilight beyond the house and gardens. Someone out there, she thought curiously. The light went out, and her breath caught. She stepped around the painting, stuck her head out the window.

"Did you see that?"

"What?" Alexa asked absently.

"That light. Just like the one in the painting . . ."

She felt Will close beside her, staring out, heard his breath slowly loosed. Behind them, Alexa murmured, "Oh, here it is . . . A plain clay lantern Psyche might have used; no magic in this one. What are you looking at?"

"Jenny!"

She started, bumped her head on the window frame. Miss Lake stood below, staring up at them. Will drew back quickly; Jenny sighed.

"Yes, Miss Lake?"

"What are you doing up there?"

"I'm—"

"Come down, please; don't make me shout."

"Yes, Miss Lake. I'm helping Alexa. I'll come down in a moment."

JACK O'LANTERN

"Surely you're not in Mr. Ryme's studio! And was that one of the village boys up there with you?"

Mr. Ryme appeared then, glanced up at Jenny, and said something apparently soothing to Miss Lake, who put a hand to her cheek and gave a faint laugh. Jenny wondered if he'd offered to paint her. They strolled away together. Jenny pushed back out the window, and there it was again, stronger this time in the swiftly gathering dark: a pulse of greeny-pale light that shimmered, wavered, almost went out, pulsed strong again.

"Oh . . ."

"What is it?" Alexa demanded beside her, then went silent; she didn't even breathe.

Behind them, Will said softly, briefly, "Jack O'Lantern."

"Oh," Jenny said again, sucking air into her lungs, along with twilight, and the scents of marsh and grass. She spun abruptly. "Let's follow it! I want to see it!"

"But, Jenny," Alexa protested, "it's not real. I mean it's real, but it's only—oh, how did my father put it? The spontaneous combustion of decayed vegetation."

"What?"

"Exploding grass."

Jenny stared at her. "That's the most ridiculous thing I've ever heard."

"It is, a bit, when you think about it," Alexa admitted.

"He obviously told you a tale to make you stay out of the marshes." Her eyes went to the window, where the frail elfin light danced in the night. "I have to go," she whispered. "This may be my only chance in life to see real magic before I must become what Mama and Miss Lake and Papa think I should be . . ."

She started for the door, heard Will say quickly, "She can't go alone."

"Oh, all right," Alexa said. Her cool voice sounded tense, as though even she, her father's bright and rational daughter who could see beneath the paint, had gotten swept up in Jenny's excitement. "Will, take that lantern—"

Will put a candle in an old iron lantern; Jenny was out the door before he finished lighting it. "Hurry!" she pleaded, taking the stairs in an unladylike clatter.

"Wait for us!" Alexa cried. "Jenny! They'll see you!"

That stopped her at the bottom of the stairs. Alexa moved past her toward the apple trees; Will followed, trying to hide the light with his vest. As they snuck through the trees, away from the tables, Jenny heard somebody play a pipe, someone else begin a song. Then Alexa led them through a gap in the wall, over a crumbled litter of stones, and they were out in the warm, restless, redolent dark.

The light still beckoned across the night, now vague, hardly visible, now glowing steadily, marking one certain point in the shifting world. They ran, the lantern Will carried showing them tangled tussocks of grass on a flat ground that swept changelessly around them, except for a silvery murk now and then where water pooled. Jenny, her eyes on the pale fire, felt wind at her back, pushing, tumbling over her, racing ahead. Above them, cloud kept chasing the sliver of moon, could never quite catch it.

"Hurry—" Jenny panted. The light seemed closer now, brilliant, constantly reshaped by the wind. "I think we're almost there—"

"Oh, what is it?" Alexa cried. "What can it be? It can't be—Can it? Be real?"

"Real exploding grass, you mean?" Will wondered. The lantern handle creaked as it bounced in his hold. "Or real magic?"

"Real magic," Alexa gasped, and came down hard with one foot into a pool. Water exploded into a rain of light, streaking the air; she laughed. Jenny, turning, felt warm drops fall, bright as moon tears on her face.

She laughed, too, at the ephemeral magic that wasn't, or was it? Then something happened to the lantern; its light came from a crazy angle on a tussock. She felt her shoulders seized. Something warm came down over her mouth. Lips, she realized dimly, pulling at her mouth, drinking out of her. A taste like grass and apple. She pushed back at it, recognizing the apple, wanting a bigger bite. And in that moment, it was gone, leaving her wanting.

She heard a splash, a thump, a cry from Alexa. Then she saw the light burning in Will's hand, not the lantern, but a strange, silvery glow that his eyes mirrored just before he laughed and vanished.

Jenny stood blinking at Alexa, who was sitting open-mouthed in a pool of water. Her eyes sought Jenny's. Beyond that, neither moved; they could only stare at each other, stunned.

Alexa said finally, a trifle sourly, "Will."

Jenny moved to help her up. Alexa's face changed, then;

she laughed suddenly, breathlessly, and so did Jenny, feeling the silvery glow of magic in her heart, well worth the kiss snatched by the passing Will o' the Wisp.

They returned to find the villagers making their farewells to Mr. Ryme. Mr. Woolidge's carriage had drawn up to the gate, come to take Sarah and Jenny, Papa and Miss Lake to his house.

"There you are!" Sarah exclaimed when she saw Jenny. Alexa, staying in the shadows, edged around them quickly toward the house. "Where have you been?"

"Nowhere. Trying to catch a Will o' the Wisp."

Her father chuckled at her foolishness, said pedantically, "Nothing more, my dear, than the spontaneous combustion—"

"Of decayed grass. I know." She added to Mr. Ryme, "You'll have one less face to paint in the wedding party. Will won't be coming back."

"Why not?" he asked, surprised. His painter's eyes took in her expression, maybe the lantern glow in her eyes. He started to speak, stopped, said, "Will—" stopped again. He turned abruptly, calling, "Alexa?"

"She's in the house," Jenny told him. "She slipped in a pool."

"Oh, heavens, child," Miss Lake grumbled. "It's a wonder you didn't lose yourselves out there in the marsh."

"It is, indeed, a wonder," Jenny agreed.

She stepped into the carriage, sat close to Sarah, whose chilly fingers sought her hand and held it tightly, even as she turned toward the sound of Mr. Woolidge's voice raised in some solicitous question.

PATRICIA A. MCKILLIP was born in Salem, Oregon, received an M.A. in English literature from San Jose State University in California, and has been a writer since then. She is primarily known for her fantasy, and has published novels both for adults and young adults. She is a two-time winner of the World Fantasy Award: for *The Forgotten Beasts of Eld* and *Ombria in Shadow* (which also won the Mythopoeic Award). Her many other novels include the *Riddle-Master* trilogy, *The Changeling Sea*, and the science fiction duo *Moon-Flash* and *The Moon and the Face* (reissued by Firebird as *Moon-Flash*). Her recent novels include *Winter Rose*, *Od Magic*, and *Solstice Wood*. Her short fiction is collected in *Harrowing the Dragon*. She and her husband, the poet David Lunde, live on the Oregon coast.

AUTHOR'S NOTE

I've been doing research lately into the Pre-Raphaelite painters, who worked in mid-1800s England, and who dedicated themselves to reviving fantasy and wonder with their art. One of the paintings I learned about, by Arthur Hughes, is called *Jack O'Lantern*. This surprised me because I thought that was a particularly American term signifying fiery, grinning pumpkins on Halloween. So I did more research, and incorporated that painting into my version of the Pre-Raphaelite world, with its mystical, romantic, and otherwise unconventional views occasionally hampered by the stricter and stodgier beliefs of the Victorians.

Carol Emshwiller

Quill

Mother says, "Don't sing. Don't dance. Don't wear red." She says, "Simplify!" She says, "We don't eat bugs. We don't eat crawdads." Aren't they simple enough? She says, "We . . . our kind . . . doesn't do *that,* doesn't do *this.*" We heard it in the egg—so to speak. So to speak, that is.

We do eat eggs.

Sometimes when we're playing too vigorously, Mother says, "No high notes."

Mother says we're unique. We don't know whether to feel left out or included in with special people. We keep wondering, if we climbed high enough up or far enough down, we'd find another group like us just as special and if they'd be all right to make friends with. We plan to go find out but right now the littlest one of us would need help.

A stranger came out of the woods and stared at us. We were dressed right, yet he watched as if we were strange. We acted normal. We played human-being games just to prove we were completely proper. I'm too old for this kind of play but the little ones like me to do it. I was the man this time, though I'm female. I stamped around and took big steps. But how many times have we seen a man?

But this stranger isn't the first, though he's come the closest to our houses. Not long ago we saw three men, climbing up along the stream. At first we didn't know what they were. We thought some sort of humped-back creatures. But then they took their packs off and we saw they were men. They didn't see us, though we followed them all the way up.

They had beards. We laughed but only afterwards so they wouldn't hear. Mother wondered what was so funny. We made up something else even sillier than beards.

Tom, though. He's getting hair on his upper lip. I saw him cutting it off with little scissors he stole from Mother's sewing kit. They don't work very well for that, so there's some of it still there. That's called a mustache.

This other man that stared . . . We saw him first from across the lake, the one we call Golden because of the golden eyes of the frogs. Mother doesn't like us to call it that. The idea of gold makes her gloomy. The river we call Silver, though that's where gold is. We found some but we knew better than to tell Mother. We hardly tell her anything in case what we do "just isn't done." Or maybe "just isn't talked about."

We have to be out here by ourselves so as not to be tempted by the way other people live. We might do what they do and "they're not our kind." But we couldn't be a different kind if we wanted to. We don't know how.

Mother says, "Every day is a lesson." We knew that a long time ago. Jumping rock to rock is a lesson, especially when we fall. Not testing stepping-stones before you step on them—that's a lesson. Watching lightning strike the tallest trees, though not always. Building a little hut of reeds. Making fires in the rain. You have to know how.

Mother doesn't know any of those lessons. I'll bet she couldn't even make a fire when it *wasn't* raining. I wonder if she even knows how to swim. I've never seen her near the lake except to gather rushes for mats or cattails for supper—those, our kind is allowed to eat. She hates to get her feet muddy.

We have secret places for dancing and singing. We stole a pan for a drum. We have scraping sticks. We clack stones. We only make our music beside the stream so as to hide the sound in case Mother should come out that far, though that's unlikely.

Morning is lessons. Numbers mostly. You can't fault numbers. Some of us are not good at them. If we complain, Mother says, "That's the way it is." Spelling . . . I'm not good at that. Geology I'm good at. It's all around us. I like to know how things got this way.

Mother wants us to know things such as honesty and generosity, but we had that all figured out on our own a long time ago. We know what's fair and what's not. We know you have to give to get. Sometimes we argue all afternoon about the rules of whatever we're playing and never get to play it, so we know we have to give up and give in.

Afternoons, when Mother takes a nap, we rush out before she can think of something else for us to do. We don't come back till dusk and sometimes later. Now and then some of us spend all night in the woods. We've built ourselves little houses of reeds or twigs and branches. We know all the caves and cozy piles of rocks. She doesn't worry if a few of us are missing. We wonder, though, if she knows how many we are.

Every day, first thing, we're supposed to give thanks for what we have, but also that we have but little. Thanks for beans and corn and apples, and especially for living right here in a safe place. And thanks to Mother for the simple life. And thanks to Mother for Mother.

That stranger walked into our part of the forest, sat down, and stared. He has paper and pencil. He might be writing or drawing. We can't tell from here.

But we quacked when we should have cawed.

He knows there are no ducks around. We came out in plain view then. Across the lake from him. That's when we did what people do. Except instead of talking, we quacked.

It's not far across the lake at that point. He got a good view. He watched the whole time. He must like our looks. We liked his looks, too. We liked his big hat. His shirt is red. Except for our collections of feathers and flowers, we don't have any red.

Tom is the best at everything. Of course, since he's the oldest. He dances now. Just look at Tom's fast footwork and how he can leap. The man stares. He even looks at us through things Tom says are binoculars. And he has another thing. Tom says that's a camera and he's taking our picture. We've seen pictures in our books. He'll have us on paper to take home to his house.

Where the river comes down to the lake, you have to cross on the stepping-stones to get to our side. It looks as if that man is coming over. There's a couple of wobbly stones we set up on purpose. We didn't want Mother crossing without us knowing it.

Those flat stones look as if they're there to be stepped on, but they're really there to trip you up. So down he goes right in the middle of the stream, backpack and all. I'm not happy about him getting his paper wet. How much paper is there in the world? I'll ask Tom. Or maybe I'll ask this man.

We save our laughing for later. We only caw a little bit.

He sloshes out.

He knows that was on purpose—that those two middle rocks were set there so as to teeter.

He takes off his big black hat and empties out the water, puts it back on. Then he sits on the bank and examines his ankle.

We crowd around and look, too. His ankle is already starting to swell and turn black. Others of us skip back and forth across the stream. We don't avoid the center stones, we just go really fast over them.

He has tape just for this. He wraps up his ankle, twisting the tape here and there. He's better at it than Tom ever was with our sprained ankles. Here's another lesson for all of us.

What if we bring this man to our little homemade huts or our cave? We could hide him from Mother and have him to ourselves. Or what if we bring him home to Mother?

When he gets up, we get up, too. He limps. He follows our path from the stepping stones. If we don't watch out he'll be right at Mother's in ten minutes. Well, at this rate, twenty.

Tom says, "Lean on me," but he won't. Tom says he's angry. Tom says, "If we had fathers, that's who he'd be limping off to see. He wants us punished."

We do wonder about fathers. Why don't we have them? Even Tom doesn't know, and Mother won't talk about it.

We can let him limp along the path to home, or sidetrack him to our cave. Tom says, "Let him go on home. We'll get to see what Mother does."

Pretty soon our regular houses come into view. They're good houses, not only thatched roofs, but thatched sides, too. Maybe we shouldn't call it thatch. It's made of tule rushes. Mother's house is made of stone and is much bigger. Tom says she made it by herself. He remembers thinking he was helping, though now he doesn't think he could have helped much. He was only three or four.

At our clearing, the man stops and looks.

Chickens in the yard have already cackled a warning that a stranger is coming—or a fox. We know Mother's hiding behind the door of her house looking out the little peephole. I'll bet she has the bar down.

The man keeps standing at the edge of our clearing, just looking.

Usually we hear the clanking of her loom, but lately she's been making moccasins. The simple life seems awfully complicated to Tom. The rest of us don't know any other way, though we try to guess. Tom says you don't even have to build a fire or light the lamps. He says clothes and shoes are just there, and he's told us all about electricity.

"Mother!" That's Tom. He goes to the door. "Don't worry. He's hurt."

"Tell him to go away."

"We want him."

"He's not the right sort."

"Come and see for yourself."

"I can tell from here."

"Please come. He can hardly walk. He has paper and pencil."

"We don't need it."

How can she say that? It's what I want the most.

"And he has a camera."

We hear the bar fall away and the door opens. Out she comes.

She's pretty much covered up, big baggy shirt. She's the only one we know with breasts, though I seem to be getting something like that now. I hide it from the others. I wish she'd give me a shirt like the one she's wearing. If I get any lumpier, I'll need that. It's a wonder I even know about them, but we do have books with pictures. Mother gave me a talk. It sounded silly. I don't know whether to believe her or not.

Usually Mother dresses so you can tell more about her body. Now she's different. And her hair is pulled back tight like it never is. She looks angry and worried. We just can't keep track of all the things we're not supposed to do. As we think up new things, new ones keep turning out to be bad. It even surprises us older ones. But now we do know. We never should have let the man come this far. Mother knows to blame Tom and me.

Tom and I are getting sick of not knowing more things about more places. It's a good thing Tom once was someplace else or we wouldn't even know there was another place. He came up here with Mother before any of us were born. He says Mother was looking for the simple life. He says that's what we're doing now.

He remembers lots of things from before. He had a father who left and Mother went around punching things when she wasn't lying on the couch. Finally she came up here with Tom. She said she didn't like the world the way it is and she was going to live a different way. But Tom doesn't know where the rest of us come from. He doesn't remember me coming. Suddenly I was here.

The man must like Mother. He looks relieved. As if everything is all right now.

When Mother steps out, Wren, right away, grabs Mother's skirt and Loon hides behind her. Mother couldn't save us from anything. Only Tom could do that. You'd think they'd know by now.

Mother looks horrified. "You can't stay here. Tom, take the camera."

"I've sprained my ankle—maybe broken it," says the man. "I need to impose on you. I don't think I'll be able to climb down for a while."

"You can't stay!"

Tom says, "We'll keep him with us. You'll hardly know he's here."

"He can't stay. You know that as well as I do. Think, for heaven's sake!"

The rest of us say, "Why?" but Tom says, "All right, all right. We'll send him on his way."

We didn't know Tom would be so cruel, nor Mother either.

The man looks upset. He hands Tom the camera. He says, "It got wet."

Tom gives it to Mother. Mother opens it and pulls out the insides.

The man says, "I can't climb down now."

Mother says, "You have to."

"Can I at least stay the night?"

"That's impossible."

We all say (except Tom), "Why not?"

But right away the man turns and starts hobbling down the trail.

Tom goes to help him and this time the man lets him. Tom is exactly as tall as the man.

A little ways down we turn off the path. Tom tells the man, "Only a little farther now." Then, to the younger ones, "If anybody says anything to Mother, I'll take your gold."

I know what's happening. It's off to our cave, sitting around the campfire, and crawdads for supper. Maybe even frog's legs. Nothing better. Nothing more fun.

Our cave has thick beds of ferns. Much better than our beds at home. And we have really soft rabbitskin blankets we made ourselves. Tom and I sewed them up. We chipped out little pockets in the walls so we could have feathers and flowers all over. But it's shallow. When it rains the rain blows all the way in, but when it's clear, if you lie with your head toward the entrance, you can see the stars as you go to sleep. Sometimes the moon's so bright it wakes you up when it pops up over the mountain. There's a sort of porch in front where we made a fireplace and put logs around it to sit on. That porch has a good view over the whole valley.

I say, "Isn't this nice?" The man is impressed.

We build a little fire and send everybody out to catch things or dig things up. They're so excited to be doing it for the man. On the way back they pick big stalks—taller than they are—of fireweed in bloom just for looks.

He can't stop saying, Thank you, and keeps asking what can he do for us. We say, Don't worry, we'll think of things. He asks our names. His is Hazlet, but people call him Haze. He asks our ages but we're not sure. Asks where our fathers are. We say we don't have any.

"One mother for all these little ones?"

We don't know. Sometimes little ones just appear—in the chicken coop. Mother takes them in.

We talk about paper. He'll set his out to dry tomorrow. We'll help. He's going to draw us all as presents to each of us. And he'll give us all the leftover paper when he leaves.

Tom and I stay out all night with the man but we make the little ones go home.

Haze asks a lot of questions. Some are the same ones we ask ourselves, like, "Where's our father? How long have we lived up here? Why are we here in the middle of nowhere?"

(We think it's as much a place as anyplace else.)

We tell him Mother doesn't want us to get to be like other people.

He thinks that can't be the only reason, though he sees her point. He says we're turning out a lot better than some.

We like him. We say, "Stay. We need another grown-up. The only one we know is Mother."

He says both I and Tom are not far off from being grown.

Of course he has to stay until his ankle gets better, but we want him after.

Next day first thing he spreads the paper out to dry with a rock on each one. We help. It hurts him to walk, so he mostly crawls. Then he picks good pieces of charcoal out of the fireplace. He'll show us how to use them for drawing.

The little ones come rushing down. Some wanted to come so badly they didn't even have their breakfast.

As soon as the paper dries, Haze draws. He draws me and Tom first, and then Henny and Drake. Then the little ones sitting in a row on the logs on the stone porch. Sometimes he draws with the charcoal he picked out of the fireplace. "They'll smear," he says. "Be careful."

We hang the drawings at the back of the cave, high so the little ones won't mess them up. Me he draws again in pencil and rolls it up and puts it in his pack.

We want to show them to Mother, we wonder if she's seen anything like it, but we don't dare. It might be one of those things we're not supposed to do. Besides, the man is supposed to be gone by now.

Haze shows us how to use the binoculars. We look around at everything. To the side we see those three men . . . or, rather, their little tents—up along the silver river. We're good at taking turns. When we're not looking, we draw. He gives us lessons. I'm good at it already. I thought I would be.

We have lots of days of drawing and looking while Haze gets better. He even shows us how to make paper out of weeds. Lumpy, but better than nothing.

Tom makes a good strong staff for Haze. Haze says that'll be good even when his ankle is better. The rest of the time we gather cattail roots and lily roots and Solomon's seal along with the frog's legs and crawdads.

Then one time when Haze is much better he says, "I always wanted to go up to your glacier. Have you ever gone that high?"

We haven't, but we've thought about it. "We see lights up there sometimes."

"Good, we'll go. You and Tom. The little ones can spend the day with your mother."

"They won't unless we threaten to take away their gold."

"Gold?"

But we're not thinking gold, we're thinking how we'll be getting out of here, farther than we ever have. We're so happy we put out our traps and catch rabbits. Mother doesn't need to know about it. We stretch the skin for ourselves and dry the meat for our trip.

Tom and I skip morning lessons all the time now and stay down with Haze. We're learning more from him in just a few weeks than we ever did from Mother. He shows us all about maps on his maps. We pick out what looks like the best route up to the glacier. He shows us all about his compass. He thinks it odd that we never saw a flashlight till now. He's got two, one you fit on your head and another you hold.

We start out while it's still dark. Haze wears the flashlight on his head and goes first. He gives the other to me and I go last. Tom and I each carry a little rabbitskin blanket. Haze has a bag for sleeping. He has the cane Tom made him and his maps. His backpack is full. He even brought paper in case he wants to draw. He has this waterproof stuff that he wrapped his food in before. Now he wraps the paper in it. He feels about paper as we do. We'd rather have paper than gold. He says he would, too.

We top our pass and dip into the next valley at sunrise, or what would have been sunrise if it hadn't been for the mountain in the way. This mountain is much higher than the ones near us. That's why you can see the glacier from our house.

Tom and I had hoped to find people in this valley, but there's nobody. Still the path goes on. From here you get a really good view of the glacier. It's been melting away. Haze gives us a lesson on glaciers. There's a lot of debris at the sides. That's called lateral moraine, at the end it's called terminal. I already knew that, though I never saw it until now.

The glacier's a lot bigger than we thought. Back home we can only see the top. We had no idea it had all this junk around it and came down so far into this other valley.

We spend the night right where we are, partway down the

second pass, and by afternoon next day, we're at the glacier and its river trickling out.

This valley has a lot fewer trees in it and those are all stunted. Haze points out odd stuff. To us everything is odd. He says, "Look at the peculiar shapes of those rocks. They look like a whole row of skyscrapers."

They sure seem like they're scraping the sky, but we know the sky is way, way, way up, all the way to the stars.

We climb the sideways debris to get a good look around. Then Haze sees what he thinks might be the mouth of a cave.

He tells us to stay back, but we don't want to. "Why come all this way and not see everything?"

"All right, but stay behind me."

It's not a cave but a doorway of some sort into a big, long, long bluish white house, hugging up close to the glacier. Until you get close, it just looks like more glacier.

At the door, Haze doesn't even knock. He just opens it in a careful sneaky way.

Mother never likes that. She wants us to know how to be courteous. Tom and I look at each other. Haze doesn't know how to be polite.

Haze opens the door all the way and we go in. Tom and I don't want to be sneaky, but we don't know what else to do except go with him.

It's warm in there. We were getting cold. We had wrapped our rabbitskin blankets around us. Haze is wearing his jacket filled with little feathers. He showed us. "Down is the warmest there is," he said, "but you know that already." Only we didn't. He wanted me to trade my rabbit skins with his jacket so I'd be warm as we crossed the high places but I said maybe later, and we should all have a turn with it.

Through that door, we aren't anywhere at all, but there's another door. We open that one and it's even warmer. It's large and dim. At first we don't know what the room is all about, then we see it's a whole room full of eggs. Really big ones. There must be ten or fifteen. They're nested in white stuff. Warm air blows over us and them. Tiny feathers are flying around. Not a lot, just here and there.

Haze keeps saying, "My God. My God."

We're not as surprised as he is—after all, we gather chicken's eggs every day, just not such big ones. And there's feathers in our henhouse, too, but these are all the ones Haze calls "down." They're like what's on my head, but mine are black. Tom told me that when I first came, mine started out yellow.

Then we're even more surprised. Haze takes off his jacket, grabs the closest egg, wraps it in the jacket, and we hurry out. It's so big it'll be a meal for more than just us three. But we have plenty of food with us. Besides, no pan to cook it in.

It's not like our usual eggs. It has a leathery shell.

Haze holds the egg close to his chest to keep it warm. We go back to the edge of the valley.

Tom says, "Are you going to hatch it?"

"Well, I'm not going to eat it. Did you think I would?"

We like Haze. We didn't think he would but we weren't sure.

It's getting dark. It's too late to start home now. We build a little fire and eat our dried rabbit. Haze keeps the egg in his lap and takes out paper and sketches the big room full of eggs from memory. He also marks on the map where the cave is. Tom and I curl up by the fire. I fall asleep right away but then I hear Haze ask, "Does your mother know about all this?"

That's what I was wondering. I think she does. But I won't say. Tom says, "Maybe."

And I know . . . I *think* I know what's in this egg. My little brother or little sister, I suppose.

Haze says, "It's a smart way to get a lot of them . . . of you . . . in a hurry." Then: "Maybe only takes one mother for the lot."

Just when I'm falling back to sleep he says, "Not clones either. Easy to see that."

The egg hatches next day when we're on the way home. The cutest little thing I ever saw. All golden. It's cute even before it dries off. It's one of the scaly ones with a feathered cap like I have, though I don't have many scales. Just in a few spots. It's a little on the duck-like side. Much more than me. We don't know yet if it's a boy or girl. Mother can tell right away.

Since I'm a girl I think I ought to get to carry it, but Haze thinks it's safer if he does.

"What do they eat?" he asks.

"Just regular food. Like everybody else. We can give it some of our rabbit. Look, it has all its baby teeth."

Now Haze is saying, "My God, my God, my God," again, then, "I suppose they crashed."

He says Mother is right to keep us away from the rest of

the world. He says, again, he has to admit we're, all of us, very nice children.

He jumps from one idea to another. He says, except for Tom we're all half-breeds. He says, "It's a good way to endure here. He says, "Maybe they think we won't kill any creatures that are half our own." Then he says, "When has that ever stopped us? Killing our own is what we do best."

Haze says I was hatched up there. He says he can't imagine what kind of creature my father is.

I get to feed the baby. (Those sharp little teeth are better at chewing rabbit than mine.) I get to have his first smile. And I get to sleep with him. Haze wraps us both in his down jacket. He keeps the fire going all night. I don't think he sleeps much. I don't sleep well either, but that's because the baby is wiggly. It doesn't seem to know it's night. Or maybe it's been sleeping so much in the egg so that now it wants to do things.

One of those funny things Mother told me turns out to be true. There's blood. So not only do I have to figure out how to keep the messes of the baby from getting all over, but I have to figure out what to do about my mess. I take pieces from our rabbit skins. I pretend it's all for the baby, but some is for me. I wonder if those breast things are any bigger than they were. I hope not. But I guess Mother is right about that, too. They will get bigger. This baby, though, is one of the ones that doesn't need them.

I lag behind though Haze carries the baby and we've already eaten most of our food so nobody has much to carry.

I'm cold even in Haze's jacket. My stomach feels funny. I sit down on a rock to rest and think.

But somebody is coming from behind. A tall creature with long thin legs that bend the way fox legs do. At first I think it's wearing a beautiful feathered hat, red and gold, but as it gets closer I see it's a topknot and that what I think is a black and red suit is feathers all over. When it sees me, the topknot lifts higher, widens. It's iridescent. There's blue and green in it, too. The creature spreads its arms. There's a row of red along its sides. I never saw anything so beautiful.

Someone has been in the nest. Our soft warmth has been intruded upon. Entered by they of those that can't smell. They think we won't know. As if we don't smell everything that happens.

Worst of all, my own little loved one, on the edge of hatching, stolen. A precious being in the making.

Strange and stranger land of much pain and so little softness in it. So few spots in which to hesitate and love.

I go to speak of my love for my own kind and even for their kind if need be speaking of it. Say it with nodding of head sky to ground, sky to ground, as if their yes and not sideways, east and west.

I lean forward so as to speed. Also lean so as to catch the scent. I smell not only my little one but also my biggest one, and she's ready to lay. Our first layer among the half-ones. A precious dear. I can't wait to speak of the future of us all. So much depends on her willingness, though why not? Offspring this way is so much easier than the way of mammals.

My tender feelings come with the good smell of myself on her. I breathe of myself all along the trail. Strange and dangerous as this place is, I'm happy. Strange as even my own is, I'm happy.

But what of these harsh creatures? Even without moving from our wreckage, we've seen what they do—seen from their own technology. We know who they are. We've heard both war and music. Dance. At least they dance.

Now a whole new way to egg which only our knowledge makes possible. Not as pleasurable but necessary. But here's my daughter, though she, my dear one, is more of them than of me.

Our kind is not unknown here, though they never had a chance to develop. Had they come to full flower, we'd have landed among friends instead of among these odd intelligent mammals. It's too bad we didn't come earlier to help those like us achieve their full potential. We could have egged with them and raised them to our level.

Strange that this world took such a different turn. Hardly logical that eggless ratlike things would grow so large. Though even our own mammals get into everything, and some are smart enough to have made themselves into the little companions of our kitchens and the darlings of the nurseries.

I have wished my first daughter could be beautiful—more like me. Still I love her. I can be in love by smell alone. So much love I found it hard to bring her down to her mother. And when she smiled, like ours always do—the first conciliation, the first appeasement—I found myself in every way, her doting father.

It was Quat called us. The intruding mammals didn't see him in the dim nesting light. One of them was half us—Quat could smell that—and two were of their kind. One a full grown male not known to us. Quat said that male knows too much. Everything is vulnerable.

I've watched the offspring dance. Life will be hard for them, but at least they have the joy of dance. Now, to my own young one, I'll display. I'll strut. Though with these creatures it seems it's more the female's role to lure with colors and tall shoes. Still, I will display.

It calls, "Quill, Quill." It sounds like quacks but I'm used to that from some of the little ones—I can tell it's my name. It has a loud echoing voice. I don't know how far Tom and Haze have gotten, but for sure they'll hear. For sure they'll come, though I wonder if I want them to.

At first it doesn't come close. It stands, silent, below me on the trail so as to let me get used to it. I look. That's what it wants me to do. Its scales only show at its neck and clawed hands and feet. It turns sideways and shows off its topknot, up and out and then down, then up and out again. None of the little ones have anything at all like that topknot, though I realize now that some have the beginnings of one.

It comes closer. It makes more quacking sounds. Again, not too different from the way lots of the little ones talk. It says, "I'm your father."

I shout, *"Yes!"* He's so beautiful I can't help it. I've been wondering and wondering all this time. I can't conceive of a better father than this one.

"May I sit beside you for talking?"

I move to make room. He sits on my rock and we both look back toward the glacier.

He touches my hand with his and it feels terrible. His claws prick and his skin is scaly. That's all right, except when he turns it the wrong way it scratches. Some of the little ones are like this, too. I hide that I don't like it like I do with them.

He says he loves me. I can see that in the way he looks at me. He calls me consort, but I don't know what that means. He says I'm old enough now. I don't know what that means either. But maybe I do. It's about the crazy things Mother told me. Which are coming true.

Then he asks about the baby. "He hatched. Did he? I saw where it happened. Or was that a . . . killing?"

"No, we wouldn't. I wouldn't let them. He hatched. He's fine."

I hope so. I think Haze will keep him safe. But Haze seemed pretty worried. He never stopped saying *My God,* and he couldn't sleep. Maybe I should have made him let me carry the baby.

"Did the baby smile at you first?"

"I guess so."

"Are you caught in his smile?"

"Yes, but I liked him even before he smiled."

"Excellent!"

Then he grabs my wrist, hard. It hurts.

"Come. You'll like it. Keep warm in the nursery. My friends will make you happy."

I try to twist away, but he's too strong, and twisting makes his hand scratch all the more. I think how glad I am that I hardly have any scales at all except a little on my back and the backs of my hands.

"I saw how you were. You like little ones. Come and make more."

"No!"

"We're from a far place. We crashed. We thought the glacier, so white and blue, was a dump of discarded nursery feathers. We slammed and slid and died. We can't go home. We made our conveyance into a nest. Had we even one female of our own kind, it would have changed everything. But here was your mother. Willing. Like you are."

But I'm yelling, "No. No!" and I'm yelling for Haze.

"You've no place on this world but with us. They'll never accept you. They hate the different. They never heard of one like you."

"Is that true?"

"The whole world is them."

"It's not. It can't be. How can that be?"

"My dear, dear one, it *is*! You're the first of your kind. Your mother has kept you hidden from the world so as to save you for us and save you for yourself."

He's loosened his grip and I manage to twist away and start running—up the trail toward Tom and Haze, but he catches me with no trouble. His legs are so long.

But Tom and Haze have turned back. They see me struggling. I yell for them to help.

Haze has something he never showed us. I've heard of that, it's like Mother's rifle but smaller. *Pop, pop,* and my father falls. Just like that. Into a fancy bundle of shiny black and red and iridescent. His hand still grips me. Haze has to pry open his fingers.

Tom sits me down and gives me a drink from the canteen. Haze is looking over my father's body. Examining everything, the clawed hands and feet, the topknot. I see him looking at the sex, which is mostly covered with down. Then Haze actually sits down and starts to draw him. I'm not sure how I feel about this. It's true, he's beautiful, but Haze isn't drawing a portrait like he did of us. It's more diagrams, my father's different parts all laid out, a hand, then a foot, the topknot, the beak.

But I want to get away from here. I want to get home tonight. I need to talk to Mother—mostly about myself. I didn't listen when she talked about blood. It sounded too ridiculous. And how come my father knew that right away? Or maybe it was these lumps on my chest that made him say I'm ready for egging.

But I'm shaky and I do need to rest. I don't say, "Let's go." Not even to Tom.

We're so late we have to camp again. And practically right away, as soon as we leave my father's body. Haze says we should camp off the trail and hide. We find a place in among rocks.

I'm still all trembly. I just found a father and lost him right away. Some of the little ones squeak when they're sad and don't have tears, ever, but I'm one of the ones that cries. I cry, but I don't think the others know. I sleep with the baby. I need to. I need something warm and cuddly to hug.

The baby isn't as wiggly as he was when he was so happy to be out of the egg. I guess he stayed awake all day, looking around at everything, and now he's tired. Haze props himself against a rock and puts the gun in his belt, ready to shoot somebody. He looks as if he's going to stay awake to guard us, but he starts to snore right away.

I cry for a while. The baby clings to me as though he wants to comfort me. After I stop I look up at the starry sky. It's so beautiful it makes me cry all over again. No matter what it looks like from down here, it's full of faraway suns, some even bigger than our own. We know all that because Mother taught us. "Who knows," Mother said, "what other kinds of life swirl around those suns?" She said, "Who knows, there might be a world where the dinosaurs didn't die out." I think now she was preparing us for strangers like my father. I wish I'd listened instead of looking out the window and wanting to be off in the woods.

Just when I finally start to fall asleep, Tom wakes me. He says Haze will tell about what we found. That's why he made the drawings. Tom says at first nobody will believe him . . . that there could exist creatures like us, so Haze will take us down to the real people. We'll get examined by policemen. Tom doesn't want that to happen. He likes us and he's always taken care of us—more than Mother has. He says he's not sure if Mother isn't crazy. Now that *we're* here, he knows why she has to live out here, but in the beginning she was angry at everybody and everything.

He talks as if my father was right. We won't be let anywhere near our nice home. There'll be nothing but buildings, and we'll never be able to come back. We might even be put in a zoo. The best thing to do is to get rid of Haze and then our life will stay the same.

"But how?"

"Easy. We'll just use that gun he has."

"I don't want to. I like him."

"Liking has nothing to do with it. It's your whole future. Mother's future, too."

"Let's wait and see what happens when we get back. We can always do it later if we have to."

"It might be too late then."

"I don't see why. Mother doesn't want him around either. She'll be on your side. She'll get out her hunting rifle and kill him herself."

So Tom says, "All right. We won't do it yet."

Next morning we come down, all of us together, straight to Mother's. Even Haze walks right in with us.

Mother comes out from her stone house looking shocked. I start crying right away. I never used to cry much, but now I seem to cry at everything. I don't even know why. I wonder if that's because I'm a grown-up now. I hope that's not the reason.

I run to Mother and hug her tight. We're breast against breast. I say, "I have to talk," and she says, "I should think so! What are you thinking? Can't you see? Couldn't you tell?"

She pulls away and slaps me. So hard she almost knocks me over. She's never done that before. I've never seen her so angry. I'm afraid to ask her anything, but there's nobody else to ask the kind of things I need to know. I don't think she'll ever want to talk to me—especially not about what I want to talk about. I wonder if it's in our anatomy book and I didn't notice it before because I didn't want to.

She snatches the baby from Haze—so hard the baby starts to squeak and won't stop. Talk about high notes! That's the first he's squeaked in all the time he's been with us. I snatch him right back and he stops squeaking right away, which is a relief to all of us. I stop crying, too. That's the end of me crying. I won't do it anymore, especially not in front of Mother.

Mother tries to snatch him back but I won't let her. She says, "You have no idea. None of you do. Look what you've done! All our lives I've worried this would happen—someone like this man would come. It's over and done for. Do you think we can live the way we do after this? It's *over!*"

I don't know who we ought to get rid of, Mother or Haze or maybe both.

Haze says, "It doesn't have to be over. It can be just begun. I can take Quill and the baby down and bring them right back."

Mother says she doesn't want us made into a sideshow. She says they'll wipe out the whole enterprise. She says what she's always said before, that she knows how the world is, which is why she's living up here. "My innocent Quill," she says. (She never has called me hers before. I don't know what to think, and just after she slapped me.) "My little Quill, corrupted."

Little! Can't she see anything? Not even my breasts?

Tom says, "It doesn't have to be over. It can be like it always is. Wait! Mother! Everything will be like you want it to be. I can fix it." He gives Mother a look. Says, *"Wait!"* again.

I go stand in front of Haze just in case it happens right now. But I don't want Haze to get suspicious. I don't *think* I want Haze suspicious. I'm not sure of anything anymore.

I'm not even sure if I might not want to go down and see the zoo.

Haze says, "You'll be found out sometime no matter what I do. Strange that you've lasted all this time as it is."

I don't see why Tom gets to be the only one who knows about down there. I might go with Haze, like he said, just me and the baby. Down to Haze's home forest. Who would have to know about us? Maybe it would be like our cave. Nobody but us would ever go there.

I should tell Haze to go home to his home right away, and he should keep watch over his little gun.

But I don't have a chance to tell him anything. He knows. We . . . Tom and I and Haze and the baby . . . We say we're going down to spend the night in the cave and that we'll eat supper there, but Haze goes right on past, without a word, not even to me. We're all worn out, but he just goes, even without supper, and he's going fast. Tom follows without a single word to me, and I follow Tom. I keep well back because of the baby, though the baby doesn't sound any different from the birds. The birds are settling down for the night so there's lots of chirping. The baby's settling down, too, with little night songs.

Haze has his lights, both of them, and Tom and I don't have anything, so we're a lot slower.

Pretty soon I decide I just have to rest. I think Haze will have to rest, too. I hope he finds a place where Tom can't get at him.

The baby and I move off the trail and cuddle up.

When I wake and look out, I'm way up on the side of a mountain and I can look down on a whole other valley with a big
town there. I'm so happy. I start chirping to myself along with
the baby. I'm getting somewhere really interesting. I'm going
to know things Tom knows.

The baby and I pick elderberries and mountain currants for
breakfast. I'm not in a hurry anymore. There's the town and
I have plenty of time to get there. I don't care if I ever catch
up to Haze or Tom.

But Tom waits beside the trail and jumps out at me. And
right away tells me I have to go home. "You mustn't let people
see you and especially not let anybody see the baby. He'll
scare them to death."

"How can a baby scare anybody?"

"He, and even you, but he especially . . . you don't belong
on this world."

How can he say such a thing? "Of course I do."

"You don't understand anything."

"I wasn't going to show myself right away. I thought to take
a look around and maybe go to the zoo and see the animals.
And then come home."

"People will see you for sure."

"What's so bad if they do see us?"

"Quill!"

"We're just other human beings."

"Well, that's the problem."

"Aren't we?"

"You've been protected from the real people."

"I'm real."

"Look at yourself. You're them. You may be a *being* but you're not a *human* being."

"I am so."

"You belong in the zoo."

"I wouldn't mind."

"There's no zoo in that little town anyway. They're only in big towns."

"That doesn't look little to me."

"Believe me, it is."

I suppose he's right. He usually is.

"Well, I won't go home. Not when I'm so close to seeing new things."

"You won't get far with that baby on your back."

"Lots of people must have babies down there."

"Not one like that."

"I'm not going to argue, I'm just not going to go home until I see this town."

"Go ahead, then, but it's the end of all of us. Though . . . I'm tired of it, too. Let's end it. Or I'll tell you what, go on down. Wear my hat pulled low and see if you can get away with it. And they might have a little zoo with maybe four or five animals in some park or other, but don't go into town till it's dark. I'll keep the baby. You'll never get away with it with him."

"All right, if the baby doesn't mind."

I do want to see that town. I start right away. It'll be getting dark by the time I get there.

Pretty soon the trees get fewer and there's fields of stuff growing. I begin to see cows and horses. I've only seen those in books. I stop at the edge of one of the fields and two horses come over to me as if to say hello. At first I think they might bite, but there's the fence between us and you can tell they're friendly right away. They lean to be touched and I touch them.

Right after, there begins to be houses. All nicer even than Mother's. Some with one floor on top of another. I know all about that. I've seen pictures. There's some with different colors and bobbles hanging all over them. I never knew a house could be so pretty. I'm already glad I came.

When I get to the edge of town it's pretty dark. I pull my hat down even lower and walk on. The people are all Tom's kind of people just like he said. Nobody is as beautiful as my father. There aren't any feathers at all.

I come to a little park with swings and slides. I've seen pictures of those. There's nobody there. I guess it's too late for young ones to be out. I try all the things. I can't believe I'm learning so much in such a hurry. These last few days it's been one new thing after another.

There's streetlights. You don't need those lights Haze has. I come to a big street with stores all along it. Most of them closed. Some have prices in the windows. Money! I hadn't thought of that.

I walk all the way down the main street. It must be a mile long. Shops all along the way. I don't care what Tom says, it's a big town to me. I look in the store windows. The clothes look different from the ones Mother makes. And shoes . . . so fancy and slick, some with funny little heels. There's a store full of beautiful shiny pots and pans never used, cups and plates neither tin nor wood nor clay.

There's a bigger park at the other end of town. It even has a swimming pool. All blue and smells funny. I'm thirsty but I don't drink there. There's a river running through the park and that's where I drink. There's no zoo that I can find. I was so hoping there'd be one. I want to see monkeys and tigers and elephants. I wonder how far a bigger town is. If I knew which direction to go in, I might head for that town.

I see people on the porch of an eating place eating with forks. I see two women clacking along in high-heeled sandals. I see cars and trucks. All this even though you'd think people would be in bed. I get honked at. I jump away and quack back.

Then Haze is here. He must have been following me all this time. Even though my hat is pulled down low, he knows it's me.

I say, "Don't tell," and he says he won't. I don't know if I should believe him or not, but it looks as if he won't tell *right now,* anyway.

"You look exhausted. Are you hungry? Come home with me."

Haze's house is like I've never seen before. There's rugs and a couch. There's even a little room that's just for me, but I don't want it. I've never slept by myself before and I'm scared to. Haze makes me up a mattress on the floor next to him. The food is odd, too. I don't know what it is but I eat it anyway. Except for bugs, Haze ate what we ate. That was like Mother, too. She hated for us to eat bugs. There's also a little room for an outhouse that's not even *out.* I learn to flush. I learn to turn on the water, cold *and* hot.

But next morning breakfast is just like at home, oatmeal. I ask Haze, "What are you going to do about us? You killed my father. You might do anything."

"You were yelling, Help. Your father was trying to take you back. I thought I was helping. I didn't know it was your father. But I don't know. What *should* I do?"

"I don't know either."

"You're going to be discovered no matter what I do. Might as well be now as later. Might as well be me as somebody out to make a buck."

"How come we've not been discovered all this time?"

"Your mother picked a good hiding place."

"Tom said it was the end of all of us. Tom said our lives depend on you."

"I won't let anybody hurt you."

"You have drawings of everything."

"You're scientifically important. You're *all* important. They'll need to study you."

You wouldn't think so many things could happen so fast. It all comes about in a couple of days. Even the destruction of the fathers, which they did to themselves. I'm glad the regular human beings didn't do it. I don't know what I would have thought if they had.

The fathers knew what would happen. They know about human beings. When Haze and the others . . . the scientists and the army and police get out to the ship, it's destroyed. The nest and eggs and all the creatures with it. There's nothing left of them but us.

Mother must have known. Even if we didn't hear the blast

down in town, she's so much closer she must have heard and known. They found her body washed down our Silver river. She had made us all moccasins and lined them up along the table, all exactly the right size. She loved us but she needed for things to stay the same.

Now she'll never find out how we got taken into this school. A farm kind of school off in the middle of nowhere, with all kinds of animals. But also a scientific school with lots of geology and biology, so someday I can be a scientist in a zoo. I'll probably have to be *in* the zoo myself. I know that. Even now people keep coming to take blood and study us. I don't mind. I'm studying myself myself and them, too.

Haze took all our gold, but he's using it for us. He's paying for the school.

He says, "The fathers were scared of us." When he says "us," he means the human beings. He says, "And rightly so. They thought we wouldn't accept them and we wouldn't. They knew their nests and eggs were easy to destroy. But having living dinosaurs . . . Feathered . . . Think of the experiments . . . And studying . . . them and their ship . . ."

And he keeps saying, "Just think . . . think, there's been contact with aliens all these years and nobody knew it."

I don't feel like an alien. I think I belong here just as much as anybody.

CAROL EMSHWILLER is the author of many acclaimed novels and story collections, including *Carmen Dog*, *The Start of the End of It All* (winner of the World Fantasy Award), *I Live with You*, *The Mount* (winner of the Philip K. Dick Award and a Nebula Award Finalist), *The Secret City*, and *Mister Boots*. She divides her time between homes in New York City and California.

Her Web site is **www.sfwa.org/members/emshwiller**.

AUTHOR'S NOTE

Quill's strong voice made the tone—the *surface* of the story—interesting to me, so it was fun writing it. It was because of her voice that I went on with the story.

I usually don't write such a science fiction-y story, but the idea of beautiful, feathered dinosaurs pleased me. That is, after I got to them. I didn't know there were going to be dinosaurs in the story until I got to their cache of eggs. Then I had to go back and make the earlier parts match.

I always write that way: give myself hints of a mystery and then have to solve it after I've set it up. That means there's almost always an OH MY GOD NOW WHAT'LL I DO place in every story. I find my plots come out better when I don't know where I'm going.

Francesca Lia Block

BLOOD ROSES

Every day, Lucy and Rosie searched for the blood roses in their canyon. They found eucalyptus and poison oak, evening primrose and oleander, but never the glow-in-the-dark red, smoke-scented flowers with sharp thorns that traced poetry onto your flesh.

"You only see them if you die," Lucy said, but Rosie just smiled so that the small row of pearls in her mouth showed.

Still, the hairs stood up on both their arms that evening as they sat watching the sunset from their secret grotto in the heart of the canyon. The air smelled of exhaust fumes and decaying leaves. The sky was streaked with smog and you could hear the sound of cars and one siren, but that world felt very far away.

Here, the girls turned dollsize, wove nests out of twigs to sleep in the eucalyptus branches, collected morning dew in leaves and dined on dark purple berries that stained their mouths and hands.

"We'd better get home," Lucy said, brushing the dirt off her jeans.

They would have stayed here all night in spite of the dangers—snakes, coyote, rapists, goblins. It was better than the apartment made of tears where their mother had taken them when she left their father.

Their mother said their father was an alcoholic and a sex addict, but all Lucy remembered was the sandpaper roughness of his chin, like the father in her baby book *Pat the Bunny*, when he hugged her and Rosie in his arms at the same time. He had hair of black feathers and his eyes were green semiprecious stones.

Lucy and Rosie loved Emerson Solo because like their father he was beautiful, dangerous and unattainable. Especially now. Emerson Solo, twenty-seven, had stabbed himself to death in the heart last month.

You really have to want to die to be successful at that, their mother said before she confiscated all their Solo albums and posters. Lucy understood why she'd done it. But still she wanted to look at his face and hear his voice again. For some reason he comforted her, even now. Was it because he had escaped?

Lucy and Rosie were in the record store looking through the Emerson Solo discs. There was the one with the black bird on the cover called *For Sorrow* and the one called *The White Room*. There was a rumor that the white room was supposed to be death. The store was all out of *Collected* with the photo of Emerson Solo holding a bouquet of wildflowers with their dirty roots dragging down out of his hands.

A man was standing across the aisle from them, and when Lucy looked up he smiled. He was young and handsome with fair hair, a strong chin.

"You like him?" he asked.

Rosie said, "Oh, yes! Our mom threw out all his CDs. We just come and look at him."

The man smiled. The light was hitting his thick glasses in such a way that Lucy couldn't see his eyes. Dust motes sizzled in a beam of sunlight from the window. Some music was playing, loud and anxious-sounding. Lucy didn't recognize it.

"My uncle's a photographer. He has some photos he took of him a week before he killed himself."

Lucy felt her sinuses prickling with tears the way they did when she told Rosie scary stories. Her mouth felt dry.

"You can come see if you want," he said. He handed Lucy a card.

She put it in her pocket and crumpled it up there, so he couldn't see.

One of Emerson Solo's CDs was called *Imago*. The title song was about a phantom limb.

She wondered if when you died it was like that. If you still believed your body was there and you couldn't quite accept that it was gone. Or if someone you loved died, someone who you were really close to, would they be like a phantom limb, still attached to you? Sometimes Rosie was like another of Lucy's limbs.

◻ ◻ ◻

Rosie was the one who went—not Lucy. Lucy was aware
enough of her own desire to escape, to let herself succumb
to it. But Rosie still believed she was just looking for ways to
be happier.

When Lucy got home from school and saw her sister's
note, she started to run. She ran out the door of thick, gray
glass, down the cul-de-sac, across the big, busy street, against
the light, dodging cars. She ran into the canyon. There was
the place where she and Rosie had seen a rattlesnake block-
ing their path, the turn in the road where they had seen the
baby coyote, the grotto by the creek where the old tire swing
used to be, where the high-school kids went to smoke pot and
drink beer. There was the rock garden that had been made
by aliens from outer space and the big tree where Lucy had
seen two of them entwined in the branches early one Sunday
morning. Lucy skidded down a slope causing an avalanche of
pebbles. She took the fire road back down to the steep, quiet
street. She got to the house just as Rosie knocked on the tall,
narrow door.

Rosie was wearing a pink knit cap, a white frilly party dress
that was too small, too-short jeans, ruby slippers, mismatched
ankle socks—one purple, one green, and a blue rhinestone pin
in the shape of a large butterfly. No wonder people teased her
at school, Lucy thought. She wanted to put her arms around
Rosie, grab her hand, and run, but it was too late to leave
because the man opened the door right away as if he had been
waiting for them all that time.

He didn't ask them in but stood staring at them and twisting his mouth like he wanted to say something. But then another man was standing at the top of the steep staircase. The girls couldn't see his face. He was whited out with light.

Lucy knew two things. She knew that she and Rosie were going to go inside the house. She knew, too (when she saw it in a small alcove as she walked up the stairs) that she would take the screwdriver and put it in the pocket of her gray sweatshirt.

The walls were covered with plastic. So was all the furniture. Plastic was stretched taut across the floor. The walls were high, blond wood. There were skylights between the ceiling beams. Fuzzy afternoon sun shone down onto the plastic skins.

There was a long table. The older man stood at one end, watching. It was still hard to see what he looked like. The young man offered the girls pomegranate juice in small opalescent glasses. Lucy put her hand on Rosie's arm, but her sister drank hers anyway. Then Rosie walked out of the room.

"Rosie," Lucy whispered.

The young man said, "Do you know there's this dream that Jeffrey Dahmer had? He dreamed he was in this big, fancy hotel lobby with all these beautiful people wearing evening dresses and tuxedos. They were all pounding on the marble floor and screaming. But he was just standing there, not moving, not saying anything. He had on a leather jacket. It was like his skin."

Lucy felt for the screwdriver in her pocket. "I'm going to get my sister," she said.

But Rosie was back now. Her eyes looked brighter. She sat on a stool next to Lucy. She kept wetting her lip with her tongue.

The older man left the room.

"He's going to check on his photos," the younger man said. "You didn't take anything, did you?"

Rosie shook her head no.

"I have another story. It's about Richard Ramirez. When he went to this one lady's house, she kept him there like half an hour talking. Then he left. He didn't touch her. Do you know what she said to him? She said, 'My God, what happened to you?' And she listened. That was the main thing, she listened."

"What happened to you?" Lucy whispered.

The light in the room changed. It turned harsh. Emerson Solo was reclining on a chair. His skin was broken out, his hair was greasy, hanging in his eyes, and he had a bottle in one hand. His long legs were stretched out in front of him. A blue butterfly was inside the bottle.

"Get the fuck out of here," the younger man said, very softly. He was not looking at Lucy. The light was in his glasses. He was being swallowed up by the strange light.

Lucy felt the spell crack apart like an eggshell. She grabbed Rosie's hand. She pulled Rosie up from the stool. Rosie felt heavier, slower. Lucy dragged her sister out of the room. There was another staircase leading down to a back door.

Lucy flung herself down the staircase, pulling Rosie behind her.

"Lucy!" Rosie said.

A photograph had fallen out of Rosie's pocket. It was of Emerson Solo sitting on a chair with his legs stretched out in front of him.

Rosie tried to grab the photo but Lucy kept dragging her down the stairs. Their footsteps pounded, echoing through the house. Lucy fell against the door with her shoulder and jiggled the lock. The door opened.

They were in a strange, overgrown garden. They tore through brambles. Lucy saw a crumbling stone staircase. She pulled Rosie down it, deeper into the bottom of the garden. A palm tree was wearing a dress of ivy. There was a broken swing moving back and forth. A white wrought-iron bench looked as if it had been thrown against a barbed wire fence. The bougainvillea had grown over it, holding it suspended.

The barbed wire was very intricate, silvery. It was like metal thorns or jewelry. There was one small opening in the bottom. Lucy crawled through. Rosie followed her. But then she stopped: her ankle was wreathed in a circlet of spikes. Lucy dropped to the ground and carefully slipped the anklet off her sister, not cutting her, not even catching her mismatched socks.

She pulled Rosie to her feet. They were standing on the road, across from the wilds of the canyon. There were no cars. Not even the sound of cars. The sky was blue and cloudless. Lucy felt a buzzing sensation in her head like bees or neon.

She dragged Rosie across the road into the trees. The light kept buzzing around them.

Lucy reached into the pocket of her gray sweatshirt. It was empty. She reached into the other pocket and felt around. Nothing. The screwdriver was gone.

Gone, Lucy thought.

Rosie dropped to her knees on the soil.

"Lucy, look."

"What?" Lucy said. Her mouth felt numb, it was hard to talk.

"Blood roses."

"They don't grow here."

"I know that. "

The two sisters looked at each other, waiting for the shivers to graze their arms, making the hairs stand up, but instead they felt only a strange, unnatural warmth as if spring had seeped into them and would stay there forever.

FRANCESCA LIA BLOCK is the acclaimed, best-selling author of over fifteen works of fiction and nonfiction, including the beloved Weetzie Bat books, and has received the Margaret A. Edwards Award for the body of her work. Her latest novel is *Pyche in a Dress*. She lives in Los Angeles.

Visit her Web site at **www.francescaliablock.com**.

AUTHOR'S NOTE

"Blood Roses" came to me in a dream, even down to the details, like the screwdriver and the chain link fence. I rarely dream so vividly, and certainly never with this much plot. I had been experiencing a lot of conflicts in my life. I am sure this stress added to the dark tone of "Blood Roses." My response to Elliott Smith's death was another factor in the dream and the story. By writing this piece I believe my brain was trying to create some grace, order, and beauty out of sorrow. That is the power of art, and of dreaming.

I am grateful to Sharyn November for asking me to write something; the dream came right after this request. I believe that a wonderful editor is a huge part of the alchemy of creativity. Sometimes just a word can spark something that might never have come into existence.

Kara Dalkey

HIVES

The girl curled up on the battered couch wanted to die. I understood. I'd been there myself.

"Get me her rig, doc," I said.

The thirtysomething juvie psychologist standing beside me turned and scowled. "That'd be giving a junkie a fix, wouldn't it, Mitch?"

I couldn't blame her 'tude. Dr. Sophie McGlynn had seen bad stuff in her work. Me, I was Michelle Rodriguez, a seventeen-year-old smart-ass who just happened to be the niece of the head detective in the Chelliwah Police Department. Uncle Ted had asked me to come down to the station, thinking I could help the girl on the couch. He liked Dr. Sophie, though, so I'd promised him I wouldn't act up . . . much.

"Works if you want the junkie's attention," I said. "Look, I can reach her, doc. But I need her rig."

Doc Sophie sighed and rubbed her face. "Can't you just talk like a normal person?"

My turn to sigh. "Once you've been a hive-girl, Doc, outside talk doesn't seem as real. She could tune me out like I was no more than a fly buzzing. An ESP call, though, she can't ignore."

Something I said must have connected. Doc Sophie drew her lips tight with a quick nod. "Guess we have to try." She walked out, shoulders slumped. Couch girl must have been a hard case.

I walked across a floor of peeling paint, a floor that had felt the feet of too many sad people on their last legs. The girl on the couch didn't deserve to be here. Her only crime had been wanting to belong.

I crouched down beside her. Her name was Angela and she was fourteen. She had honey-brown hair and a face that was an ordinary sort of pretty. Probably she only saw the ordinary part when she looked in the mirror. Angela had tried to make herself into an all-meat patty by jumping off the 605 overpass. But a cop watching for speeders had seen her straddle the railing and got to her in time. She was lucky, though I bet she didn't think so.

I gently stroked her hair and said, "Hi, Angela." She curled up tighter, pretending she didn't hear me.

Doc Sophie walked back through the door and handed me Angela's headset, still looking dubious. "This better be legit or your uncle Ted will hear about it. Don't think I don't know *your* history, girl."

"Thanks for the vote of confidence," I said, reaching up to take the coppery pink headset. I was proud that my hand only shook a little and that I stared for only a few moments, caught up in the junkie's fascination with her drug.

A wonder of technology is the ESP, the Ebisu SonoPhone. It looks like an old-style set of music headphones, but instead of earpieces, it has a pair of pads that press against the skull behind the ears. The ESP conducts sound waves through the bone, so that the voice or voices calling you sound like they're in your head. Clear and close as your own thoughts. The added features include the throat pad that allows you to subvocalize. With practice, you can talk with no one "outside" hearing you. To dial, you can use a wafer-thin tongue pad that sits on the inside of your lower jaw or up on your palate. My generation is as quick with our tongues as our parents were with their thumbs. And, yeah, I've heard the nasty jokes so stuff 'em.

Girls love phones. Girls love friends. Girls love being tight with the coolest clique. Put it all together with an ESP private network and you've got yourself a hive. All friends, all the time, right there with you, no matter where you are. Some hive-girls even sleep with their rigs on. I had, for a while. The ESP has really caught on—everyone from gangbangers to cops to biz-geeks to chatline callers love the ESP. Its popularity is even moving down the age ladder. There's a company that sells a clip-on accessory that looks like a princess's tiara. Oh yeah, they know their market. Bastards.

Being in a hive is the sweetest thing in the world to a lonely girl. If you don't like yourself or your life, you don't have to think about it. Your friends are always there to fill your thoughts, to make you feel like you belong. Until something happens. Maybe you say the wrong thing, or your Queen Bee suddenly decides you're not cool enough. You get Cut. Your conference code no longer works. And then you go crazy. Because the voices in your head *stop*. You're left with that horrible silence, those lame, desperate thoughts. Nothing but you, despicable you. And you just want to die.

I put the speakers on Angela's scalp, behind her ears. She stirred a little. Using my thumbs (okay, so sometimes I'm old-fashioned), I called up a readout on her mouth pad and got her rig's number. I slung my backpack off my back, unzipped it, and pulled out my old silver-and-powder-blue rig. It looked clunky compared to Angela's newer model.

My heart began to pound. I'd begged Uncle Ted to let me keep the ESP rig, even after my own crash and burn. "For emergencies," I'd said. I swore I'd never do a hive again, and I meant it. And I'd been good, really good—hadn't used it since. I'd kept it mostly as a reminder . . . of just how horrible some people can be. And Uncle Ted had trusted me. But he probably had checked the rig now and then to keep me honest.

I slipped the rig on quick, turning to face the wall so that Doc Sophie wouldn't see how hard I was controlling my breathing. *I can do this,* I thought. *It's just one girl. Not a hive thing. I'm maybe saving her life. It'll be okay.*

I popped in the tongue pad (I wear mine left-lower). I tasted the sharp tang of the embedded disinfectant—the most delicious taste in the world to a hive-girl. I dialed Angela's number and heard a riff from Frivolous Genocide's latest track. *The tone quality has gotten better,* I thought, though that one was probably an illegal download. A click of connection. "Angela," I said.

Her whole body jerked. She blinked and sat up, eyes wide,

suddenly very alive. Now somebody was home. "Who are you?" she asked. It was strange hearing her voice in front of me and inside my skull at the same time. Like her voice totally surrounded and soaked through me. Sweet/scary memories of hive life flooded back. I didn't know whether to scream or cry.

I closed my eyes, clenched my palms, and tried to ignore the rush of adrenaline. "My name's Michelle Rodriguez," I said. "Most people call me Mitch. I wanted to talk to you."

"Me? Why?" She didn't say it, but I could hear the "I'm nobody" loud and clear.

"Because you're going through something awful. And I've been through the same thing."

"What, being rescued when you didn't wanna be?"

I shook my head and grasped Angela's shoulder gently. "You got cut out of a hive, didn't you?"

She stared at me as though I'd accused her of eating baby seals for lunch. Then she looked down and gave a slight nod.

"It's okay, Angela. That happened to me, too, about three years ago. I know how it feels. It was the worst thing that ever happened to me, worse even than losing my parents. I know what it's like, Angela—that awful silence in your head."

Angela looked away, her face screwed up like she was going to cry. What she finally blurted out, though, surprised me. "It's all my own fault!" The wail echoed through my head, bringing back even more memories. Helplessness. Rejection.

"It is *not* your fault, Angela!"

"Yes, it is! There was this boy I liked, and this girl that Sarah liked was all flirty with him. So I . . . I called her a slut!"

KARA DALKEY

"Well, calling other girls sluts isn't a good thing, but it doesn't get you the death penalty, last I heard. So. You think you made your queen bee mad, huh?"

Angela shrugged. "I guess. I guess I wasn't good enough for them. I should have known."

"Bullshit."

"No, really, I should have *known!*" She pounded her fist against the old couch, and I had to turn down the volume on my headset.

"Stop blaming yourself."

"That's not it." She looked down again. "I should have known because . . . I wasn't the first."

"The first what?"

Her fingers tore at the already shredded upholstery. "Wasn't the first girl Sarah cut from the hive."

"You mean, just suddenly, no warning, like you were?"

Angela nodded. "Two other girls, one of them about three months ago, the other just last month. But I thought I'd be different."

Yeah, don't we all? I thought in sympathy. "Sounds like your queen bee is a flaky bitch. Well, you can find new friends. Join a school club or something."

"Hah. Not at Condoleezza Rice."

"Oh. Shit." A public school. A holding pen for kids not rich enough to go to a Corp or Church school. Poor Angela. Maybe her folks weren't rich enough for Microsoft Academy, but they could have at least tried for Wal-Mart High. Hell, even some Jimmy Bob Jones Praise Jesus school would've been better.

In public school, you were lucky if there were only fifty students per class. Lucky if you could hear the teacher talking through the bulletproof glass. Lucky if the teacher got to teach at all and not just be floor warden until the bell rang and the doors unlocked. No arts, no sports, no frills. No wonder she'd been desperate to join a hive.

"Mom doesn't have much money," Angela said, shrugging. "Dad left when I was ten. It was so cool when Sarah and the others . . . they seemed to really like me. And they watched my back. Made sure I didn't get beat up." Tears started to roll down her cheeks.

I put my arms around Angela and let her head fall onto my shoulder. "It wasn't your fault and you're not alone, Angela. Getting cut from a hive is like heartbreak. Lots of girls go through it. Just like I did." Not all people get addicted to ESP networks, just like not every beer drinker becomes an alkie. And not every heartbroken lover becomes a police statistic. Just the lonely ones, the shy ones, the geeky ones, the ones who think they deserved the rejection. The ones who had never felt such intense closeness—and figure they never will again.

My memory tossed up a vision of my former queen bee, Patty Nguyen's cute, freckled sneer as she told me I wasn't getting the new conf code. Her laughter had been like knives in my chest. All I did was cry as she and Cynthia and DaShauna and the others walked away, tossing their heads and laughing.

"Ow?"

I pulled back, realizing that I'd been gripping Angela's shoulders way too hard. "Sorry."

"Yeah. Must have been easy for you. You didn't kill yourself."

"I tried. I woke up that night in a hospital with my stomach being pumped."

Angela raised her head from my shoulder and looked me in the eye. I didn't really like the props I saw her giving me. "No shit?"

"No shit. No fun either. I learned my lesson."

Angela sat back, disappointed. "So you didn't try again."

"Still here, aren't I? No, I got too pissed off at what my hive did to me. What they nearly made me do. Anger kept me alive, Angela. Get mad at this Sarah person, that's what you have to do. What your hive did wasn't right. They promised to look after you and they didn't."

Angela sighed and rested her head back on my shoulder. "No. It's someone else's turn now."

"Hey, survival is the best revenge. Get a zPod, fill your head with your favorite music—"

"It's not the same."

"Well, then, find those other girls that your queen bee cut, be friends with them. Make a new hive."

"I can't. They're dead."

A prickle danced down my spine and my stomach went cold. "Whoa, whoa, whoa, *what*?"

"They succeeded," Angela went on with a grim smile of respect. "One hung herself. The other slit her wrists in a bathtub. They weren't stupid like me."

"Stop this!" My grasp on her wrist grew tighter and I shook her a little. "My God, didn't anyone at your school notice this was happening?"

"'Leezza Rice, remember?"

I sighed. "Shit. They probably get three dead kids a week from one thing and another. And kids run away all the time. Nobody'd fuss about two or three more, would they?"

Angela shrugged. "They'd be happy for the space."

My thoughts started clicking together like a Tau-Ka-Chi puzzle. After moving in with Uncle Ted the Detective, I read a lot of his books that weren't exactly kid-appropriate. Psychological profiles, rambling prison confessions, tabloid tales of murder. "Angela, before you joined this hive, when the other girls who were cut . . . died, how did this Sarah and the other girls react when they found out? Were they sad at all?"

"Ha. Sad?" Angela snorted. "No. Maybe the others, but not Sarah. She was kinda . . . smug. Like she knew a cool secret. I think she liked it."

"Uh-huh." This queen bee was a killer bee. Angela was right. If this Sarah had gotten a taste for taking lives, it was going to be some other poor girl's turn soon.

Doc Sophie walked in once more and her face brightened with surprise. She gave me a nod of respect before saying, "Hello, Angela. I'm Dr. McGlynn. Your mom is here. She'll be taking you over to Seacrest Hospital in just a little bit. Mitch, let me talk to Angela privately for a few minutes?"

"Sure. You stay strong, Angela, okay?" I gave her arm one last squeeze and stood up to walk out.

"Oh, and Mitch," Doc Sophie added, "take off the rig."

"But I . . ."

"Detective Rodriguez will have my hide, and yours, if he sees you wearing it."

I sighed loudly, wanting to say something really nasty back.

She was sweet on Uncle Ted, I knew it, and I could—but then realized it was my phone jones reacting. "Yeah. Sure. Okay." I reached up for my headset.

"Don't leave me!" Angela cried out, her voice so full of pain, it was like a physical punch to my chest. I felt hot tears start to well up in my own eyes.

"It'll be okay, Angela," I said softly. "Hold on. Just hold on. Remember, get angry. Survive. It'll be worth it." It was hard, but I did it. I took off the rig.

Doc Sophie reached for Angela's headset. "No!" Angela wailed. She fell over sideways on the couch and curled up again. I stuffed my rig in my backpack and left to the sound of Doc Sophie's gently cajoling voice, which now seemed weirdly flat and phony after the resonance of Angela in my head.

I almost slammed the holding room door behind me as I walked out into the busier station area. I leaned back against the cold painted-plaster wall beside the door and closed my eyes a moment. I breathed deeply, trying to ignore the echoing silence in my skull. It was all I could do not to jam the rig back on and call somebody, anybody—a phone psychic, a porn line, some stupid corporate voice-mail system. Anything.

I opened my eyes and saw a sad-faced woman wearing a faded coat sitting in one of the station's cheap plastic chairs. She was staring, absorbed, into her Styrofoam coffee cup, completely ignoring the raving Oxy-head going by on the arm of a cop. I went and sat in the chair next to her. "You must be Angela's mom, right?"

She looked up with the same "lights on" expression Angela had when I called her rig. "Oh! Yes . . . how is she?"

"She'll be okay," I said, totally lying. "She just needs, you know, some time."

"Of course, of course," murmured the woman.

What were you thinking? I wanted to scream at her, *Sending your precious girl to 'Leezza Rice?* But, as Detective Uncle Ted always says, "Don't get mad, get information." So instead, I asked her, "Was Angela happy at school?"

She did the one-shoulder shrug thing. Like daughter, like mom. "No more than other kids. Until recently, like a month ago? She'd found some new friends. Suddenly she was happier than I'd seen her, well, since she was just a little girl. She got that new phone in a school raffle drawing—"

Probably stolen by her hive sisters, I thought sourly.

"—and her grades went up and she couldn't wait to get to school. I always knew she was a real smart kid and I was so pleased to see her finally applying herself. That's what I don't understand about all this. She was so happy."

"Uh-huh." It was odd that Angela's grades had gotten better; usually hive-girls become total slackers. They're having too much fun in their heads. Unless Angela wasn't just studying for one. "Do you happen to remember a name or have a phone number of her new friends because, you know, I'd like to contact them. Maybe they could cheer her up or at least explain why she suddenly changed. It could really help."

"No . . . she hadn't brought her new friends home yet. I remember one of them was named Sarah. Angela seemed in awe of her. What we used to call a girl-crush, I guess. Do you go to Condoleezza Rice, too?"

"Uh, no. Homeschooled. Passed my GED last year." There

had been just enough money left from my parents' life insurance that Uncle Ted could hire tutors after my one-night stand with Mr. Death. I was hoping to get into Skagawit Community College next year. They have a great preforensics program.

"Well, good for you, I guess," Angela's mom rambled on. "I think it's such a shame that so much of the country has given up on public education."

Reality check, lady. It's your daughter's life you're playing politics with here. But I didn't say that aloud. My folks taught me some manners.

The holding room door opened again and Doc Sophie peered out. "Mrs. Smith? Would you like to speak to Angela now?"

"Oh! Oh yes! Thank you!" She stood suddenly, and the Styro cup fell to the floor, spilling the few remaining drops of her coffee. She remembered her own manners at the last minute, turning to say, "Nice to meet you, um . . ." and then hurrying off for some long overdue bonding with her daughter. Doc Sophie gave me a tired smile before going in after the mom.

I looked down and saw a colorful backpack leaning against the wall. It had a 3-D photo of the latest pop-hottie, Aramus James, printed on it. Hmmmmm. I doubted it was the mom's. As my uncle Ted once told me, I'm a good girl with bad girl instincts. I wondered how long the mom would be in the holding room. Well, couldn't let some Oxy-head walk off with Angela's backpack, could we?

I picked it up, set it on my lap, unzipped it, looked around. Nobody was watching me. I hang out in the station all the time, I'm like furniture there. I pulled a battered old e-pad out of the backpack. Mrs. Smith must have bought it used—stores don't even sell 'em anymore.

I pressed the "on" button and selected _Search: Sarah_. The screen shimmered and scrawled writing flowed to the surface. Right there I found what I wanted. Girls get name fetishes. Angela had written over and over, "Sarah Potosi is cool!" and "Sarah Potosi Rules!" and "Callie Harris + Angela Smith = friends forever!"

I checked the memory use. Sheesh, hardly forty gig. I don't have the freshest wrist pad, myself, but it's got fifty times the space of an old e-pad. Fortunately Angela's was just new enough to have wireless tech. I was able to beam the entire contents into my wrist pad in less than five minutes. Then, being the good girl, I slipped the e-pad back into the backpack and walked up to the front desk.

Betsy Huang was just coming on duty. She's no nonsense. I like her. I handed her the backpack, saying, "The lady visiting her daughter in the holding room left this out here. Could you keep it up here for her?"

Betsy nodded once and that was that.

I went across the street and waited in Harriet Mizuki's diner for Uncle Ted to get off work, as I often did when I came down to the station. I sipped at a lemon mushroom tea and did a few searches on my download of Angela's e-pad. I checked her calendar. Pretty blank, except for a few notes here and there, like "4:30 see Mr. Wasserman about test. 8:00 ask Mrs. Cambert about homework. Zeek—4:00 Comp Lab 201!" whatever that meant.

Angela had a "Poetry" file full of haikus of confusion and self-hate. I felt a pang at the all-too-familiar words that mostly added up to a big *why me?* Why were you born with a "kick me" sign on your back, kid? Don't know, but it happens to more of us than you'd think.

The poems turned suddenly hopeful, warm odes to togetherness and friendship and I looked at their entry date. Jeez, she'd only been in her hive six weeks.

There was a photo file, though it was awkward to look through it on my wrist pad's tiny pop-up screen. Pre-hive, Angela's pictures were of houses, parks, cats, anything but people, except for a few of her mom. Then there were several pics of a group of girls in a tight hug grinning at the camera. A couple of them had fashionable gold tooth rings and circular cheek scars. Yeah, this was the hive. I was betting the tall girl with long black hair in the middle was Sarah. Maybe it was just what Angela had said, or my imagination, but their smiles reminded me of a pack of wolves staring at a trapped rabbit.

"Hey, Mitch!" Uncle Ted slapped his hand down on my shoulder and I jumped.

"Hey, hi! God, you startled me!" I switched off my wrist pad and let the screen sink back into the unit.

"Ready to go home?" He must have had a court day because he was wearing a suit. Uncle Ted's fortyish face was more rumpled than his jacket and that's saying a lot. But it's the handsomest face I know, anyway.

"Longtime ready." I followed him out to his battered old Toyota Prius. I made myself comfortable in the passenger seat as he worked on coaxing the car to life.

"Sophie says you got somewhere with the girl from the freeway," Uncle Ted said as he pulled into traffic.

"Yeah, some." I still felt a strange lump of guilt in my stomach at having disconnected from Angela. From being disconnected at all. I sensed Uncle Ted's X-ray gaze on me. "What?"

"You don't look too happy. Was it a mistake, honey? Hit too close to home?"

I shrugged, "Nah, it was all right. Just . . . really sad, you know? I felt sorry for her."

"Uh-huh. Sophie said you didn't want to take your rig off."

Anger flashed through me. "Hey, I just forgot it was on, okay? I'm cool. No problem."

After a pause, Uncle Ted said, "You're a tough girl, Mitch, and I trust you. And you know you can trust me. You can tell me anything, whatever. You know I'll listen."

"'Course, Uncle Ted." I get a lump in my throat when he talks like that. Best uncle a girl could ever have. I cleared my throat and changed the subject. "So, you ask Sophie out yet? She's dying to date you, you know that."

He gave me a mind-your-own-business glare that could make a perp cry. Then he just growled "Awww," and flapped his long-fingered hand as he looked away. He still wasn't over Aunt Dolores. Cousin Rosa says he still calls Dolores once in a while, hoping she'll come back.

"So what's for dinner?" I asked.

"Macaroni and cheese," he announced, as if it were a special on the board at Delamino's.

"Cool." It's always either mac and cheese, tuna casserole, or chicken fingers. Uncle Ted squeezed every dime he could to send Cousin Rosa to St. Margarite's boarding school, even though it was way down in Tacoma, so we didn't get to see her much. God bless Uncle Ted.

"Sure there isn't something on your mind?" he said.

God damn Uncle Ted—it's like he's psychic sometimes. So I opened up. "Okay, so it's like . . . this queen bee of Angela's—that's her name, the girl who tried to jump off the overpass—anyway she, that is Sarah, the queen bee, like, cut two girls before Angela, just weeks before, and the girls *killed* themselves just like Angela was going to, and she's going to do it again, and—"

"Whoa, whoa, slow down, kid! That sentence is like a Christmas tree, you got so many clauses hanging on it. Start over. What's this about Angela?"

"The girl off the overpass."

"Right, the one you were talking to."

"Told me about Sarah, the queen bee of her hive."

"That's the girl who's kinda leader of the pack, right?"

"Right. Her name's Sarah Potosi. Anyway, Angela thinks Sarah deliberately cut two other girls out of the hive just because Sarah liked the power of making them go nuts."

"Well, that sounds pretty rude."

"*Rude?* Uncle Ted, those other girls killed themselves just like Angela tried to. This Sarah is a killer queen, Uncle Ted!"

"Whoa, don't be throwing words like *killer* around me."

"But it's true! Angela says Sarah's gonna do it again. We've got to stop her!"

At a red light, Uncle Ted turned and squinted at me. "Let me get this straight. Two other girls from the same hive have committed suicide?"

"Yeah."

"And Angela was going to be the third."

"Yeah. And there's probably gonna be more."

He sighed and stared out the windshield. "Shit."

"Isn't there some way you can charge this Sarah with murder? Or manslaughter at least?"

Uncle Ted sighed and shook his head. "No way you could prove it."

"Aw, come on! You mean she can get away with it? Think about it, Uncle Ted!"

"You think I didn't think about it after I picked you up from the hospital three years ago?"

I paused. "You did?"

"'Course I did. Nobody treats my favorite niece like that." He made a disgusted face and looked away from me as he drove. "But incitement to suicide as murder? Impossible to prove. Especially when the victim's a teen. Too many other factors the defense can bring up. You'd need a confession from the perp to even get it before a judge."

"Well, how about possession of stolen ESPs at least, or illegally setting up a cell network?"

He sighed heavily again. "Yeah, well. Let me talk to the guys. They'll work it, honey, but it'll take some time. Just don't expect much, okay?"

"Yeah. I understand." Like our cops don't have enough to do, what with mall bombings and ricin in the mail. Lonely girls offing themselves weren't going to get much priority. I sighed, and stared out my window, watching the decaying suburb roll by. "What's it take to get people to pay attention? Does another girl have to die?"

"You don't know that's gonna happen."

"My gut tells me it's true, and you always said I should trust my gut."

"Yeah, well, guts aren't always right. And as *Papá* used to say, they often lead to something messy."

"I'm right, Uncle Ted. I know it."

He stopped the car in the middle of the street and turned to me, angry. "Look, what are you saying we should do? I asked you to be a friend to that girl, not be her avenging angel. You didn't promise anything to that Angela, did you?"

"I didn't promise nothing!"

"All right, then. Forget about it. Sometimes you gotta let other people take care of their own problems, okay?"

I let a long, silent moment pass before saying, "So there's no justice, huh?"

"Leave perfect justice to the next world, *chica*. We just do what little we can in this one."

"After all you've been through, you still believe?"

"If I didn't, I'd go crazy."

"Lotta that going around," I said softly. I remembered the sight of Angela falling back on the couch. I felt awful. "Every school has suicide awareness alerts. You can at least do that, can't you?"

"Yeah." He sighed heavily again. "Yeah, I guess I can put one of the boys on that. What school does she go to again?"

"Condoleezza Rice."

"Shit. It'll have to go through the mayor's office. But, yeah, I can do that. First thing tomorrow, okay?"

"Okay. You're the best, Uncle Ted."

"Yeah, right."

That night, we were pretty quiet over our mac and cheese. Uncle Ted left shortly after because he was meeting his cousin, former colonel "Skip" Alvarez, for a beer. Cousin Skippy was one of those guys every cop knows—someone who says he's former Special Forces, SEAL, CIA spook, what-have-you. Half the stories they tell you're sure aren't true, and the other half you're scared sick just might be. Cousin Skippy was the Black Ops sheep of the family, and I wished I could go along, but Uncle Ted said, "You don't have the clearance rating for his secrets, and you aren't old enough to drink. Don't wait up for me."

We live in a highly secure condo, so I feel safe when he has to leave me alone. I'd told Uncle Ted I was going to spend the evening studying the want ads online. See, I have a hard time keeping summer jobs. The last one Uncle Ted got me, data entry at the district attorney's office, well, I lost that one when I got caught paying too much attention to the data. Turns out the attorneys don't like their admins playing girl detective. Who knew?

But instead of the want ads, I spent the evening studying my download of Angela's e-pad. I was hoping she'd entered the name of the spyder that had set up the network for Sarah's hive. Techie kids made a lot of side money and loads of new friends by becoming spyders—setting up the illegal webs, the free hive conference connections. The really clever ones pirated satellite relays, sometimes hosting it all themselves over their family TV dish and computer, some piggybacking on their neighborhood cell tower. I'd heard rumors of one girl at 'Soft Academy who'd been caught with a transmitter in her backpack. The network provider corporations are rabid over this, but even their hired PIs learn that spyders are tough to find.

I Googled under *spider, spyder, spidey,* anything, but all I found were gushing love notes about the hottie new actor in *Spider-Man X.* I flung myself down on my bed in frustration.

What I hadn't told Angela was that, though I'd gotten over getting cut, I hadn't let the anger go. Last I'd heard about Patty Nguyen, she'd moved down to L.A. and was dating movie stars.

I threw a pillow against the wall, but it didn't help. Another girl was going to die. Like I almost did. Like Angela almost did. Like two girls already had. And what was I going to do about it?

I went to my desktop. Yeah, still got one of those. I'm so prehistoric. It's got a nice old plasma monitor that still works well, though. I went online and looked at the Ebisu Web site. Not sure why. Maybe hoping to see a confession of guilt, some hint that they knew what their little toy was doing. A pretty Asian anime lady popped up wearing a rig, purring, "With an Ebisu headset and wireless network, now you can get closer than ever before!" Yeah, helping to crush the egos of girls worldwide.

The home page had a cute little story about Ebisu's latest

promotional contest, for the farthest separated conf group. The runner-up team had a person on each continent. But the winners were a group of Chinese scientists with a man at each pole and one taikonaut on the moon. Kinda seemed like cheating, to me.

There was much burbling about how Ebisu's stock was taking off and would be "a wise choice for savvy investors." Farther down the page was a nice picture of the Ebisu North American CEO shaking hands with the director of Homeland Security. "Ebisu is helping to make the world safer!" the caption said. Right. How effective would it be for an interrogator or torturer to be speaking in your head? Bet Cousin Skippy would have some ideas about that. But I didn't want to save the world, just the life of one girl.

I Googled the blogosphere for a spyder at 'Leezza Rice. No self-respecting net-weaver would out himself in public, but geek boys feud like pit bulls. From the slime they sling at one another you can sometimes tell who's up to what if you read between the lines. Sure enough, there was some jerk handled Snotwire ragging on a guy named Zeek who'd been getting all high and mighty. Zeek . . . where had I seen that before?

I went back to Angela's data on my wrist pad. It was that entry in her calendar . . . it was right about the date she would have gotten in the hive. "Zeek—4:00. Comp Lab 201." With a bright red exclamation point beside it. Well, well. Wonder if Zeek made a habit of hanging at the computer lab at Angela's school?

I made my decision. I was going in.

The next morning Uncle Ted woke me just before he left for work. He still smelled of cigarette smoke and beer. I got up and dressed for invisibility in gray sweats, black T-shirt, and a gray hoodie. I threw random books in my old backpack, wolfed down a couple of toaster tarts, and hopped the city bus to 'Leezza Rice.

The old brick school was surrounded by a high chain-link fence topped by razor wire. There were only two gates that I could see; each had a grimy white electronic sensor arch. Half the time, the sensors in the arches didn't work and the schools were too underfunded to fix them, so their deterrent factor was kinda lost. Besides, they mostly scanned for guns and sniffed for drugs or bombs and I was carrying none of that.

Supposedly students had to wave their IDs as they went in, but I arrived at crunch time just before the first period, when everybody crammed through the gates to get in before lockdown. I let myself be caught up in the crushing flow of bodies, getting the breath squeezed almost out of me as we stampeded through the gate. I waved my learner's permit card as if it was an ID, but nobody cared. I was in.

And I was reminded why I was so glad I left school. The halls were narrow, crammed with lockers and kids and reeking of wet clothing and sweaty bodies and girls overdoused with pheromone perfume. The girls shrieked their greetings and threats, the guys glowered and shoved one another—you almost couldn't tell a friendly hit from an angry one. Lots of them wore hive rigs, some with eye-screen attachments for TV or vid. One hulking gangbanger glared at me through a GPS display over his right eye. I felt my stomach tighten, even though this was not my crowd, no longer my world. I hunched my shoulders and pulled the hood down on my head, slogging along like a slacker too lowered with seds or too short on sleep to be worth the bother.

I'd sussed out Angela's class schedule from the info I'd downloaded, so I followed that. First hour was Spanish. I'd have aced this if I cared. The class was huge . . . a hundred kids at least in a big stadium seating room. The party-hearties sat way up in the back, the kids who wanted to learn anything sat way down front. I sat upper middle with the sleepers and stoners who gave me a companionable nod as I joined them. "You a narc?" one of them slurred at me.

"No. New transfer."

"Oh. S'cool."

There was a ruckus down front and I saw a posse of girls swagger in, just as the hour chimed. Well, well. I recognized the tall girl with long black hair and circular cheek scars. Angela's notes hadn't mentioned she shared classes with Sarah. The killer queen bee was holding hands with a small Asian girl who was staring up at Sarah with near adoration. The rest of the hive—a redhead, a blonde, and two black girls standing behind the Asian girl—could barely hide their cruel amusement. *So she's the next one*, I thought, my skin going cold.

The teacher, a haggard, thin woman with short gray hair, stepped into the safety booth at the front of the room and called for order. Hardly anyone listened. Somebody dropped a book, and the woman flinched. "Ha!" cackled the boy beside me. "Gun-shy."

The teacher called out *"Buenos días,"* in a shrill voice. Only half the class responded. She asked everyone to put their thumb on the chair pad for roll call. I noticed the glowing blue circle on the chair arm. I noticed a lot of other chairs had blue circles that weren't glowing. I noticed a lot of students weren't bothering to log in, so I didn't feel so bad about not doing it either.

Sarah and her posse sat down front with their new pet, brazenly ignoring the teacher. I wondered what the hell I was going to do, how was I going to warn the new girl? If I could just get her name, I might be able to get her e-mail address. I could write: "Hi, you don't know me but you are in grave danger." Yeah, like she'd believe that. These were the happiest moments of her short, miserable life. But she wasn't wearing a rig yet, so there still might be time.

I nudged the slumped-over guy next to me. "Who's that girl down there with Sarah Potosi?"

"I dunno," the guy slurred at me with a rude glare.

'Course not. Who knew anybody in this hell pit?

I suffered through the Spanish class as the poor teacher tried to get some *palabras* through to a class that didn't care. I hunched down in the too-small seat and watched Sarah and her hive fuss and coo over the new girl like she was the latest Supersinger. Oh yeah, Sarah had It, the coolness that attracts no matter what they're like on the inside. I stuffed my fists in my pockets and ground my teeth. Jealous, me? Nah, just a little pissed off. Sarah turned her heavily made-up face my way, her eyes squinting. Uncle Ted had told me that people have this animal sense—they know when they're being stared at. One predator knows another. I looked away, hoping she hadn't seen me.

When the chime ended the class, I was suddenly sorry I'd chosen to sit in the back. The aisles were jammed with kids fleeing for the door and a few moments of freedom. I'd hoped to follow the hive, maybe pull the Asian girl into a doorway when no one was watching and give her the whole story. She could believe me or not, but at least I'd have tried. I squeezed through the crowd, getting called bitch and worse, but by the time I got to the front of the classroom, Sarah, the hive, and their new prey were gone.

I followed the rest of Angela's schedule for the day, but didn't see any of the hive again. Not even in the lunch room or lavatories. I didn't feel like asking around after Sarah. Word might get back to her, along with a description of me. As Uncle Ted says, sometimes it pays to be paranoid.

Besides, I had a date with a datageek. Around 2:00, as most of the school was emptying out, I went down to the computer lab and hung out near Room 201. One of the scrawny guys passing by said, "Can I help you with something?" in that combination of arrogance and abject terror that geeks display around girls.

"Lookin' for Zeek," I mumbled.

His expression lost every shred of hope. "Yeah. 'Course you are. They're always looking for Zeek. Down there." He made a weird, exaggerated nod down the hall. "In the radio lab."

"This school has a radio station?"

"Not so's you'd notice." The kid wandered off and I walked down the hall. There was an open door to a ratty-looking studio with an old-style soundboard and chewed-up foam padding on the walls. No one in it. The next door down was slightly open and I peered in.

It was no bigger than a closet, maybe five by five, walls floor to ceiling lined with electronic sound and computing equipment from I'd swear the last hundred years. Wouldn't have been surprised to see an old CD player or even an eight-track. The rest of the space inside the room was filled by a tall, skinny kid with brown skin and shoulder-length brown hair that couldn't decide whether to dread or 'fro, sitting on a rickety wheeled office chair. His big brown eyes gazed at me with wary intelligence and his smile wasn't exactly welcoming.

"'S up?" he asked.

"Zeek?"

"Maybe."

"Hear you know something about hive-nets."

"Maybe."

"Well, do you or don't you?"

"Who says I do?"

I paused. What the hell. "A friend of Sarah's."

"Sarah P.?"

"Yep."

"Well, this friend of Sarah P. better watch her mouth. Come in and close the door."

I squeezed in, feeling pretty uncomfortable in the tight space. "You like it in here?"

"More cozy than home. Now what you want?"

"I wanna start my own hive."

"Heh." He chuckled. "Hope you got the leafy, girl. You don't exactly look dressed for success."

"My 'rents are Frugies." They hadn't been Frugalists, actually, one of the most hated movements in America, but I figured it might get me some sympathy.

"Dude, that's ugly."

"Tell me."

"How many?"

"In my family?"

"In your *hive*, emptywig."

"Oh. Maybe four."

"Probably cost you four Ronnies, then. Not including the rigs."

"Four hundred dollars! I could get a legit net for that!"

"On setup, maybe, but then you'd keep paying every month. Not to mention DHS, NSA, PTA, and God knows who all able to listen in and track. Spyder nets you pay only once and there's no Big Brother hanging on. Got it?"

"Yeah. But I don't got that kind of leafy right now."

"Then why are we still talking?"

I was staring at all the equipment. What a perfect place to hide a phone net transmitter. Who would know, or even care? "Did Sarah pay that much?" I asked, stalling.

Zeek chuckled again and his eyes became sly and knowing. "Sarah takes some of it out in trade, know what I'm sayin'?"

I didn't want to know what Sarah traded. "Yeah, right. Probably all HUAC anyway."

"Hey, you doubt me, ask around at the Crazy C. See what it gets you."

Probably beaten the crap out of, was my guess. The Crazy C was a downtown hangout not known for checking ID too closely, or noticing what the patrons might be doing. It seemed to be protected by all sorts of strange zoning codes. Lots of towns have such a place, Uncle Ted says, and how long they last depends on how long they keep the money flowing to local politicos. Anyone asking too much about spyders or Sarah at the Crazy C was not going to be mistaken for a friendly. "Never mind. I gotta think about this."

"Get out, then, bitch, and don't come back until you're richer. Better yet, don't come back." This was said without anger, by a king secure in his kingdom, even if it's a five-by-five closet paneled with silicon and steel and smelling of ozone and sweaty socks.

I slipped out the door and slung the backpack over my shoulder. Leaving the school was easy, so long as it was after class hours. They only try to keep you in while they're being paid to. I trudged across the asphalt yard, feeling only semi-successful. I'd found the spyder, but so what? I'd seen the new victim-to-be, but so what? I hadn't solved anything yet.

Out of the corner of my eye, I saw a familiar car rolling up to the curb as I went out the security archway. A *real* familiar car. My stomach sank and I sighed as I got into the Prius. "Hey, nice of you to come pick me up, Uncle Ted."

As he glared at me, I could almost see the anger radiating off him like the squiggly heat lines in cartoons. He jerked the wheel hard and the car lurched back into the street. "What. The hell. Do you think. You are doing?"

"Well, I told you I was job-hunting. I thought maybe they might need a new lunch lady or something . . . "

"*Michelle!*" he roared. Uncle Ted never calls me Michelle. And he never roars. His fingers were white on the steering wheel.

I slumped down in the seat. "I was investigating Angela's hive."

"God damn it!" He struck the steering wheel so hard I could swear I heard it crack. A horn blared behind us. Uncle Ted leaned out his window and yelled stuff in Spanish and English that could cause a plaster Maria to burst into flame. The car behind sped around us with a squealing of tires. And then he turned back to me. "People. Get hurt. Doing this sort of thing. People. Get killed. Doing this sort of thing. I should know. I got scars. Most of my friends got scars. Some of them got headstones. You hearing me?"

"I hear you."

"So what the friggin' hell were you doing?"

I took a few deep breaths and said, "I know who Sarah's next victim is."

"No, you don't know!"

"Yes, I do! I saw her. I saw Sarah the killer queen fuss over her. I've been there. I know what's going on, Uncle Ted!"

"Did this Sarah see you?"

"I don't think so."

"Damn it, Mitch. Is that all?"

I paused a little longer. "I know who the spyder is."

"Did you talk to him?"

"Yeah."

"Shit."

"It's cool. He just thought I was an unhappy potential customer."

Uncle Ted shook his head. "You have no idea what you're doing. I should never have let you talk to that Angela."

"Uncle—"

"You are so grounded. Two weeks!"

"What? Uncle Ted, I'm not a child!"

"Then stop acting like one!"

"I am not! That's unfair!"

"I am one seriously pissed off grown-up! That entitles me to be unfair!"

I crossed my arms on my chest and let my jacket hood slip down over my eyes. "How did you know I was at the school?"

"I got a buddy who's a narc there."

"You're shittin' me."

"Watch your mouth. You would not make your mother proud saying such words."

Yeah, like he should talk. The powers that be could spare money to track down every ounce of weed but couldn't spare the time to save the life of one girl. I stared out the window, feeling a good sulk coming on. Then I noticed something. "Hey, this isn't the way home."

"I gotta stop by the office. Doc Sophie wanted to tell me something."

"She couldn't use the phone?"

"She wanted to talk in person."

On a better day, I would have teased him about Sophie wanting face time, but this was not that day.

We pulled up into the parking lot of the station. Doc Sophie was standing on the sidewalk and came over to the car, her arms wrapped tightly around her chest. When she saw me her eyes widened. Uncle Ted got out even before the engine shuddered to a halt, asking, "Sophie, what's wrong?"

Still staring at me, Doc Sophie said, "You're even more psychic than usual, Theodore. Still, I guess it's just as well you brought her."

That extra sense must run in the family. I jumped out of the car, asking, "It's about Angela, isn't it?"

Sophie nodded and looked down at the ground. "She got up to the top floor of the hospital. No one knows how. She—"

"Is she okay?"

Sophie shook her head. "She's dead."

"No!"

Uncle Ted grabbed me and held me while I pounded his chest with my fists. "No, damn it, no!" I yelled, still hearing Angela in my head, saying, "Don't leave me!"

"I'm sorry," Sophie whispered. "You tried, Mitch. I know you did. Sometimes, when a person is just determined—"

"There was nothin' you could do, honey," Uncle Ted said.

"There was plenty I could have done! I should have stayed connected to her longer, I should have—"

"Could you have replaced her hive?" asked Sophie.

I stopped, remembering the emptiness. No one voice from the outside could have filled it. "No," I admitted. Then I turned to Uncle Ted. "So. Looks like Sarah bagged herself another victim, doesn't it?" I snarled at him.

"What?" asked Sophie.

"Mitch is just upset. Never mind. Thanks, Sophie. We'll talk later, okay?"

Sophie nodded and Uncle Ted practically forced me back into the car. I felt my old buddy Anger come roaring back, filling every bone and muscle.

"God, I'm sorry, Mitch. God, I'm sorry," Uncle Ted said as we drove on to the apartment. I wiped a few tears, but I didn't say anything. I was scared of what might jump out of my mouth.

Uncle Ted took a call on his cell—a job had come up. When he dropped me off at home, he turned and looked at me, worry all over his face. "I gotta go to work. You gonna be okay, honey?"

"Sure, fine," I growled. "Am I still grounded?"

"'Fraid so, honey, more than ever. You've got every right to be upset, but I don't want you doing anything stupid."

"I won't." I got out and slammed the car door.

He got out partway and shouted, "Mitch, I love you. I just . . . don't want you getting hurt."

That made me pause. Uncle Ted never says "I love you." I turned and looked back at his sad, weathered face. "Too late for that," I said. Then I added, softer, "Thanks," feeling the tears flow again. "Love you, too."

"I'll see you later, honey."

"Yeah."

He slipped back into the Prius and roared off. I dragged myself up into the apartment, wishing I had a boatload of tissues to wipe my face. Uncle Ted sure knew how to take the air out of a case of righteous rage. But it was still there, simmering below the surface. One way or another I was going to get Sarah and her hive. Just a matter of when and how.

I sat on my bed and tried to calm my thinking, trying to channel the anger into something useful, like a plan. The phone rang, jangling me out of my fine meditation of hate. I could have just let the machine get it, but I was hoping it was one of those phone evangelists now oh-so-protected by free speech amendments, 'cause I was spoiling for a fight.

"Hey," I snapped at the receiver as I picked it up.

"Sugar pie, is that you?" It was Skippy Alvarez. He'd spent too much time in a platoon of Southerners, and therefore called women by the most syrupy crap. "Is Teo there?"

"Naw, Unk is at work, you might try his cell."

"Don't wanna bother him. Just thought we might get together one more time before I left town. Tell him I called, will ya?"

"Wait! Cousin Skip, can I ask you something?"

"Sure, sweetie, ask anything."

"Skip . . . what do you know about cell phones?"

An hour later, Skippy was sitting in front of me in the living room. He was short and broad and looked like he could pick up a tank if he had to. His salt-and-pepper hair was cropped in a short flattop, and his eyes were flinty black, but held a glint of worldly amusement. He pushed a white cardboard box, about the size of a small brick, across the coffee table at me. "Just so you know, it's a felony to have one of these."

I didn't pick the box up right away. "A felony to carry a jammer?"

Skip nodded. "FCC takes its rights seriously. Doesn't keep them from coming in, though. This one's Italian make.

They use them in churches over there and in Mexico."

I gently opened the box, like it was a bomb or something.

"Mind you, that one's been a little . . . modified."

I jerked my hands away. "Modified how?"

Skip shrugged. "It's also a booster. Helps when the signal is weak in some areas."

"Spook modified?"

He winked at me. "It's got its tweaks. Mind you, I don't know all the mechanics of the ESP, so I can't guarantee how it will interact. This stuff you've been telling me about the girls dying . . ."

"Killing themselves, Skip. It's ugly."

He bit his lower lip and shook his head. "I always wondered when something like this would happen."

"What do you mean?"

He folded his thick fingers in his lap and leaned toward me. "Back in the 1960s, there was this guy, Dr. Allen Frey, who was involved in some studies called Project Pandora for the Department of Defense. He discovered a thing they called 'microwave hearing.' Seems you can beam radio frequencies at a person, do it just right it sounds like words inside their head. Artificial telepathy."

I sat back. "You don't even need a phone?"

"Not for limited purposes, no. They found there were all kinds of . . . effects you could get by using the right frequencies. It was a real active area of study for a while among the non-lethal weapons people. Almost mind control, you could say."

I sucked my breath in. "Holy shit."

"Pretty unholy, if you ask me. Anyway, Project Pandora is long gone and many of the scientists moved on to the corporate world. I guess it was only a matter of time until some of their findings found . . . commercial applications."

My thoughts spun like tires on ice. "The addictiveness of the ESP . . . do they know . . . did they plan . . . ?"

He shrugged again. "Who can say?"

"Do they *want* to kill girls?"

Cousin Skip shook his head. "It's not profitable to kill off your customers, sugar pie. No, I figure that's a side effect the developers hadn't counted on. There's a saying from back in your grandfather's time: 'The street finds its own uses for technology.' This hive queen of yours is just taking advantage of a hidden . . . feature."

"Shit," was all I could say.

He pushed the box closer to me. "Use it, but use it wisely and in good health. Maybe you can bring a little more attention to this whole mess." He took out the slim, black bar about the size of my grandfather's cell phone, and showed me the controls. "This switch is the jammer. The range is set at about a twenty-foot radius. You don't want larger than that, or you might call attention to yourself. That's the booster dial. Keep it low, if you need it . . . set too high, something might break. Got it?"

"Yeah."

He paused and looked at me. I had the feeling he was sizing up my courage. "Take care of yourself, Mitch. It's a more dangerous world than you know."

"So I'm learning."

"Good. I gotta scoot." He stood and swiftly but quietly headed toward the door. "Oh, and remember . . ."

"You never gave me this and you were never here."

"That's my girl." He kissed my forehead and slipped out the door. I watched from the living room window as he walked down the sidewalk, casually looking around, checking to see if he was observed. He'd probably parked a block or two away. Once a spook, always a spook.

I hid the jammer in a sock in my dresser drawer for the night. I had a weapon. I figured, if nothing else, maybe I could give Angela's old hive-girls a taste of their own medicine. Maybe, if I timed it right, I could ruin their plans to cut the next girl. Now I just had to wait for those two things Uncle Ted relies on—luck and inspiration.

When Uncle Ted came home, late, I told him that Skip had called, but just left a message.

Uncle Ted nodded, distracted. "You okay?"

I shrugged. "As okay as anyone who couldn't stop a murder."

Uncle Ted sighed and rubbed his stubbly chin. "I had some boys check out that computer lab at 'Leezza Rice."

My heart rose. "Yeah?"

He sighed more heavily. "They found nothing. No transmitter. Guess your guts aren't always right, honey. Well, I gotta sleep. You too. Get to bed."

"Oh. Yeah. Sure, Uncle Ted." I went to bed but didn't sleep for a long time. I was too busy hitting my pillow with my fist.

I slept in and vegged the next day, Saturday. Late afternoon, Uncle Ted called—he still had to work, said they'd found a big meth lab, dealers shot, and he had to tie it all to terrorism to get enough funding from Homeland Security to tide the department over for the year. I commiserated, told him politics sucked while inwardly I crowed for joy. Grounding or no, I was going out tonight.

I dressed for blending in—jeans, camo T-shirt, and a scarred-up leather jacket. At about nine, I slipped out the back door of the apartment complex. Yeah, there were cameras and Uncle Ted could've requested the tape, but if things got that far he'd already know. I caught a bus two blocks away and took it downtown.

The Crazy C was in a low brick building, wedged between a shabby used bookstore and an even shabbier teriyaki place. I was early, for the crowd, so I had no problem slipping up to the bar and ordering a beer. Hey, I was already violating curfew, what was another broken rule? Besides, the bartender didn't even ask for my fake ID. I felt slightly insulted. I settled onto a stool in the corner and pretended I was a chameleon.

There was a small stage against the back wall and a group of gangly, scruffy guys were setting up band equipment. When they set up the stands with the funny-shaped knobs on top, I muttered, "Who uses mikes on stands anymore?"

"Didja bring your rig?" asked the barrie.

I jumped, spilling some beer. His question was a little too pertinent. "Uh, yeah. Matter of fact I did. Why?"

"Well, put it on, *chica*. Those are BrainBombs they're setting up. Make the music sound inside your head. Really cool. Band starts in about forty-five. Stick around."

"Yeah, think I will, thanks." I took another swig of beer to hide my surprise. *The street finds uses for technology.* No wonder Zeek and the hive-girls liked this place.

A few minutes later, one of those same hive-girls strode in, but it wasn't Sarah. It was one of her underlings, whom I'd only seen in a couple of Angela's photos—a blonde with shoulder-length, curled hair, wearing a bangly crop top and jeans. Not the brightest of the bunch, according to Angela's notes. The blonde was also wearing her rig, and I could see her throat bobbing a bit. She was sub-voking, probably to the rest of the hive. I tried to practice some of Uncle Ted's technique of watching without seeming to. I fetched my old rig out of my backpack, now feeling self-conscious about how out-of-date the phone was. I slipped the headset on and flipped my hair over the pads.

The place was starting to fill up, but I still didn't see Sarah. Hive-girl was starting to look a little anxious, too. I wondered what was up. I saw her head to the bathroom, and on a whim, I followed her.

She stood by the sink, fussing with a make-up bag while I went into a stall. I heard her whisper audibly, "Are you there? Sarah? Renee?" Hmmm . . . reception problems. That gave me an idea. I took the jammer out of my backpack and clipped it on to my belt at the small of my back, beneath my leather jacket. Then I turned the jammer switch on.

"Hello? Hello, Sarah?" Hive-girl's voice became panicked and louder. "Sarah, don't *do* this! Shitshitshitshitshit!"

I gotta admit, for several seconds I drank in the delightful draft of vengeance. Poor miss co-conspirator now thinks she might be victim number four. Awwwww. I let her panic rise a few seconds more, then my delicious joy made me bolder. Why stop at that?

I flushed and stepped out of the stall. Hive-girl was stabbing at her rig with the business end of a pair of tweezers. "Having problems?"

"Shut up."

I ignored her rudeness. "Oh, hey, you got one of those Cayce 1500s."

"I said shut *up*! Go away."

"I know how to fix those. These new rigs are touchy, they need a lot of tweaking. But I know a few tricks."

She finally looked up and noticed me, blue eyes slightly red around the rims. She looked so young—what, fourteen, maybe fifteen, tops? "You can fix it?"

"Maybe." I almost felt sorry for her...and then imagined Angela taking a nosedive off the hospital roof.

"But you're wearing an old rig."

"Yeah, well, I find the old ones are more stable. These new ones are hot, but they need a little extra loving care. Want me to have a look at it?"

She stared at me with fear, distrust, hope, and desperation warring in her eyes. "Yeah, okay, but do it fast." She yanked the rig off her head, pulling out a few golden hairs with it, and handed the rig to me.

"Sure. And ice out. It should just take a sec." I took her silvery-opalescent rig in one hand and slipped my other hand behind my back, to pull a toothpick out of my back jeans pocket. I slid open the panel where the headset widens to get at the command pad. Just like cell phones have always had, there's a place you can look up the last number dialed. And thanks to hive-girl's desperation, I was pretty sure the six-digit number repeating over and over on the screen was the conf code. I quickly memorized it and the phone number, pretended to tweak some more, then slid the toothpick back in my back pocket, turning off the jammer as I did so. "There ya go. Should be workin' now."

Hive-girl swiftly slipped the rig back on, redialed with her tongue. "Hey? Hey?" I swear tears slid down her cheeks and a smile ten miles wide crossed her face. She jumped up and down and flashed me a high sign before dashing out the bathroom door giddy with joy.

I wasn't sure whether to laugh or puke. Sad thing was, I was jealous.

The room was packed when I came out, and a too-angular-to-be-cute young man was standing at the BrainBomb. "Are you ready to get Beamed?" he teased the crowd.

"Yeah!" they all cheered back as one.

"Headsets on, space cadets. Here comes the noise." He jammed his fist down across his guitar strings. The jangling chord resounded in my brain, filling every neuron. He played a long, trilling riff and I felt his fingers playing the nerves up my spinal column. I blinked in astonishment. The drummer began a rhythm on his bass drum pad that replaced my heartbeat in the center of my chest.

I didn't want to be distracted like this, not when there was information to get and deeds to be done. But the music might make good cover. Before my personality was completely wiped by waves of sound, I tongued in the phone number of the hive, then, at the prompt, the conf code.

Just in time as another power chord washed through me.

"We're here," I heard Sarah's husky voice rasp amid the music. In my head, as if she spoke from the center of my cerebellum.

—"by the door," said another hive-girl.

—"was waiting so long. What *took* you?"

—"we had take care of—oh!"

Another chord crashed like an ocean wave in a storm. Thoughts flew from my brain and all that was left was the sound. The drums started their pulsing beat again and my body moved, no longer entirely under my control. I swayed and shook, my hair standing on end, my skin tingling. The hive-girls began chanting in my brain, "Yeah . . . yeah . . . yeah," over and over, an affirmation of the high of sound, the high of togetherness, "yeah . . . yeah . . . yeah," they sighed in ecstasy, and it was so good, this oneness filling the void in me, that I began to whisper with them, "yeah . . . yeah . . . yeah," my breath their breath, my words their words.

"Who's there?" Sarah snapped sharply, cutting across the music.

—"Who?"

—"What?"

—"Someone's cutting in . . . I don't know that voice."

—"That girl from the bathroom—"

Oh my God. It took all my will to force my waving arms up to my head to yank off my headset. I began to shake uncontrollably in panic. *How could I be so stupid? How could I?*

The music still reverberated inside me but no longer controlled my limbs. I was able to slip, hunched over, through the writhing, oblivious bodies to the bar. I didn't see any of the hive-girls, so I hoped they couldn't see me. I drank down the last gulps of my beer, trying to calm my nerves. I must have looked like a spastic wreck, but the bartender was so caught up in the music, he didn't care. Desperate to get my brain cells back, after a couple of minutes, as the song the band played was ending, I put my rig in my backpack and slipped out the back door.

A chill northwestern drizzle was falling. I leaned back against the brick wall and let the drops flow down on my face and neck. It felt good, and I could finally think again. Okay, I'd been stupid, but they didn't know who I was. I hadn't learned anything useful about soon-to-be-victim girl. And Sarah was probably going to change the conf code right away. Oh, well, live to fight another day and think of something else. I sighed and stepped away, turned right into the small passageway beside the building.

They were waiting for me. By the few beams of light that escaped the painted windows of the Crazy C, I counted five of them, Blondie on my far right, Sarah in the middle. The others, two black girls and a redhead I recognized from Angela's Spanish class.

"That's her," said Blondie. "The one who fixed my phone."

"Stole our number, you mean," growled the redhead.

"Well, aren't you the clever bitch," said Sarah, striding languidly toward me.

"Let's rip her!" said one of the black girls.

Sarah stopped and held up her right hand.

"She don't do that to you," the black girl protested. "Nobody does that to you. Not and live to tell about it."

I thought hard about running, but I could hear the other black girl circling quietly behind me. I wouldn't get far.

There was a silent pause, which I figured was filled with them sub-voking at one another. Then Sarah tilted her head at me. "Before you receive your just punishment, bitch, I just want to know why. Are you such a loser that you have to hijack other people's hives?"

"I'm here for Angela," I snarled back.

"Angela?" Sarah acted as though she didn't recognize the name.

"You know who she is. You cut her, didn't you? Angela threw herself off a building and now she's *dead,* thanks to you."

"Oh. Angela. She's dead? Oh, I'm *so* sorry." Sarah didn't even try to hide her laughter. She was really enjoying the news.

Blondie chimed in, "Well, Angela was such a waste of skin."

"Pathetic. Better off dead, really," said the redhead.

"Shut up!" I yelled.

"Oh, was Angela a . . . *friend* of yours?" cooed Sarah, as if Angela couldn't possibly have had worthwhile friends.

That's when I reached back behind my jacket with my right hand. Time to give them a taste of their own medicine. And maybe distract them just long enough to have a chance to run away.

"Watch it, she's packing!" said the black girl now in front of me.

"It's not a gun." I sneered at her. My fingers touched the jammer switch.

"Better show us what it is, then, bitch." She grabbed my arm and yanked on it. My fingers scraped across the box, dragging against the booster switch and the volume wheel. I heard the band strike another chord inside the bar. A loud hum erupted in my head that I'm sure didn't come from the band's equipment.

For a moment, Sarah and the hive-girls stood absolutely still. Then their hands flew to their heads, but they didn't take off their rigs. Their knees buckled, and one by one, each girl sank to the ground. Blondie began to twitch as if in the throes of an epileptic fit. Sarah began mewling like a lost, confused kitten, her eyes wide. The other girls were shaking and flailing, too.

I fumbled for precious seconds with the jammer, my hands shaking horribly. Finally I toggled the booster switch and the volume wheel. The hum in my head went away. It was off.

But the girls on the ground didn't get up. Two of them stopped moving altogether. Sarah continued her strange, sick cries. I swallowed hard, and like a gutless coward, I ran. At a gas station I called 911, then I grabbed a bus for home.

Thank God Uncle Ted wasn't in when I got there. I dashed for the bathroom and puked my guts out. I threw the jammer back in the dresser, as if it were hot to the touch. Then I paced and paced the apartment, hugging myself to control my shaking. Then I crawled into bed. When the adrenaline was finally spent, I fell into sleep as fast as falling off a building.

When I woke up, it was already bright morning. I heard a

rustling sound and glanced up. Uncle Ted was standing in the bedroom doorway, staring down at me. I wondered how long he had been there. "Morning," I mumbled.

"I got news," he said, walking farther into my room. He turned his back to me and ran his gaze lightly over the poster-covered walls, the bookshelves. His fingers idly played with a few papers on my desk. As if he were seeing the place for the first time. As if examining a perp's lair.

"What . . ." My voice rasped and I had to clear my throat. "What sort of news?" I sat up, drawing my knees up to my chin beneath the covers.

"You know that Sarah Potosi, the one you thought was a killer hive queen?"

"Yeah?"

"Seems she and four of her hive mates were found in the alley beside the Crazy C last night."

"Is she . . . are they okay?" I really did want to know. And much to my own disgust, I also wanted to know . . . *did they talk?*

"No," Uncle Ted said, leaning heavily on my desk with both hands. He still didn't look at me. "They're not okay. Best as anyone can figure, something went wack with their ESPs. Girls got a huge jolt of RFs right to the brain." He waggled his hands over his ears. "Fried the synapses in their amygda-lawhatsis. They got serious memory loss. Some loss of limb control. Worst of all, they got hit in the parts of the brain that deal with sound. They'll be totally deaf the rest of their lives. Not even able to hear their own thoughts, the docs say. Already the parents are screaming lawsuit and lawyers are circling the hospital like buzzards. It's a crappy thing, but thanks to this there's a chance this whole hive addiction business will be blown into the open."

"Wow." I didn't know what else to say.

His gaze fell on my rig headset hanging out of my backpack on the floor. He snatched up the rig and began to methodically snap the plastic headgear in many places. "You. Will. Not. Ever. Wear. One of these. Again. Understood?"

"Y-yeah, Uncle Ted. Sure. I understand."

Uncle Ted flung the rig in the wastebasket, turned, and walked back to the door, still not meeting my eyes. Pausing in the doorway, he said softly, "You wanted justice, sweetheart. You got it." Then he left, closing the door behind him.

I should have felt righteous joy. I should have pumped my fist in the air, saying "Yes!" Instead, I felt sick to my stomach again, and I curled back up under the covers, hiding my face from the light of day.

A week and a half later, on a miserable May afternoon, I took the ferry from Seattle to Bainbridge. Halfway across, I dropped the jammer into Puget Sound. It didn't make a noise over the hiss of the wake and the rumble of the ferry's engine. I watched the churning water behind the boat as the ferry plowed into the fog ahead. Maybe I wasn't cut out for this girl-detective stuff. Maybe it was time to get some new goals.

I'd tried to tell Uncle Ted what happened, but he made it clear he did not want to hear it. Did he know? Did he not know and not want to know? It made my brain hurt. I wondered if I'd been set up by Cousin Skip. Had he used me to expose Ebisu? Seemed like a long shot to just give me the jammer and hope for the best. Unless there was something to all this mind control shit . . .

I shook my head as if I could get the memories out of my mind. But they wouldn't leave, playing on endless loop. I could hear Angela saying "Don't leave me!", hear the power chords from the BrainBombs, replay the hive-girls chanting their glorious "yeah . . . ," replay Sarah's mewling as her brain melted down. Replay the stricken tone of Uncle Ted's voice as he told me the news about the hive, and the fact they couldn't hear their own thoughts anymore.

And I've decided that, those girls now living in utter silence? I envy them.

KARA DALKEY is the author of fifteen novels and a dozen short stories, all fantasy, historical fantasy, or science fiction. Her most recent publications have been *Water,* a trilogy of young adult novels she describes as "the Atlantis and Arthurian myths in a blender." Her short story "The Lady of the Ice Garden," which appeared in *Firebirds,* was selected for the James Tiptree, Jr., Award shortlist. Kara lives in the Pacific Northwest, land of overly caffeinated creative people. On the side, she plays electric bass in an oldies rock band and spends too much time playing computer games.

AUTHOR'S NOTE

"Hives" came about as the result of several ideas colliding. The little SF I write tends to be stories about ordinary folk, and how technology may enhance or, more likely, complicate everyday life. "The street finds uses for technology," as the saying goes, but those uses are not always benign.

There's been a lot of attention in the media in recent years on young girls in groups, and how the competition for status in the schoolyard pecking order can damage a girl's psyche. This theme is addressed in such books as *Odd Girl Out* by Rachel Simmons and *Fast Girls* by Emily White, as well as the movie *Mean Girls.*

Cell phones are a technological marvel whose unexpected consequences are showing up all over, from buses becoming rolling phone booths for commuters to the "flash crowds" that a certain candidate made use of in the last presidential primaries. And, of course, cell phone use is growing fast among teenagers, whose need to connect to friends was already well established with old-style landline phones.

Curiously, one study I read about noted that most cell phone calls are not for emergencies, but instead for the most ordinary of communications—just keeping in touch. Like the *baaa*s within a herd of sheep, indicating "I'm here. We're all here. It's okay. All's well." Constant reassurance for social creatures is key.

And young girls are intensely social. So for teen girls, especially the shy and awkward, wouldn't it be wonderful, even addictive, to be in constant, voice-in-head-close contact with their friends, their clique, their in-group? It would be like heaven . . . until it stops. And then it's hell.

The additional note of "telepathic sound" was something I came across on the Internet. Given the wide-open range of stuff you find on the Web, all must be taken with a grain of salt until corroborated, but there were enough other references that it carried the whiff of truth, and added a healthy dose of paranoia to the plot.

So all these factors came together in the writing of "Hives." Curiously, not long after I'd finished the first draft of the story, I saw a commercial on TV for A Major Phone Carrier. This ad described a woman setting up a prototype cell network on her home computer. Her teenage daughter notices and asks how it works. Then promptly borrows it to get her friends together for an afternoon outing. Gave me chills. Looks like phone "hives" could be just a few years away. I just hope the dark side of the story doesn't happen, too.

Alan Dean Foster

Perception

Stefan didn't want the assignment to Irelis. He didn't
want to work at the Outpost. He'd seen pictures of
Irelis, and the Outpost, and the Allawout natives, and
found all of them unpleasant in equal measure. But advancing up the company ladder meant climbing the rungs in
order. Skipping one now and then, if you were fortunate. For
a young apprentice such as himself, Irelis was a rung that
couldn't be skipped.

So it was that he found himself installed for a year at
the Outpost, a self-contained subdivision of the larger Irelis
station set in the middle of a swamp. It could as easily have
been anywhere on Irelis except at the poles. Swamp or
savanna, take your choice: they were what covered nearly all
of Irelis except for the murky, algae-coated oceans. Of the
two, the savannas offered the more pleasant prospect, with
drier, cooler weather. Unfortunately, humans weren't the
only ones who preferred the plains to the swamps. So did
the several dozen species of ferocious biting arthropods that

drained body fluids without discriminating between planets of origin.

The Allawout got around the swamps on primitive flat rafts fashioned from fiberthrush and covango saplings fastened together with strong, red looporio vine. Ages ago, some Allawout Einstein had figured out that if you built the rafts with points at both ends, not only would they go faster through the tepid, turgid water, but you wouldn't have to turn them around to reverse direction. That discovery represented the height of Allawout nautical technology. The idea of a sail was beyond them. Ignoring directives that forbade supplying indigenous aliens with advanced knowledge, visiting humans who observed the locals struggling with poles and paddles had taken pity on them and introduced the concept of the rudder, an innovation that the natives readily adopted and for which they were inordinately grateful.

To the Outpost the Allawout brought the pleasures and treasures of the Irelis hinterlands: unique organic gem material; seeds from which exotic spices were extracted; sustainable animal products; barks and resins and flowers from which were derived uniquely unsynthesizable pharmaceuticals; and their own fashionable primitive handicrafts. Widely scattered and hard to find, located in disagreeable, dangerous country, these diverse products of Irelis found their way into the insatiable current of interstellar trade through the good offices of the dirt (literally) poor natives. Everyone benefited, and the Commonwealth government was happy.

Stefan was not happy. He did not quite hate Irelis, but he disliked the place intensely. The swamp, for one. There was nothing in the way of entertainment. Worst of all was having to work with the locals. None of the Allawout stood taller than a meter in height—if you could call it standing. In the absence of anything resembling legs or feet, it was hard to tell. They slimed their way along, their listless pace in perfect harmony with their sluggish metabolisms. A quartet of narrow but strong tentacles protruded from their cephalopodian upper bodies. These were covered in a fine, hairless, slick skin not unlike that of a frog or salamander. From the center of the upper bulge that was not quite a proper head, two large round eyes marked by crescent-shaped pupils took in the swamp that was their world. They had no external ears, no fur or horns, and wore no clothing. Not that there was much to cover.

When they burbled at one another in their rudimentary, vowel-rich language, bubbles frothed at the corners of their lipless mouths. They had no proper teeth and subsisted on a wide variety of soft plant life, supplementing this with the occasional freshwater mollusk that did not require overmuch chewing. Soon after arriving, Stefan had had the opportunity to see them eat. It was not a pretty sight.

It did not take him long to learn from his three coworkers that the Allawout were as oblivious to human sarcasm as they were to much of the world around them. Making fun of the slow-moving, slow-thinking natives was one of the few spontaneous entertainments available to the Outpost's inhabitants. Except when a supervisor came visiting, it was a sport they indulged in shamelessly, taking care to do so only out of range of the station's largely humorless scientific complement. By the time Stefan's tour of duty was half over, his own personal file of Allawout jokes had grown as fat as one of the natives.

Not that they were inherently unlikable, he mused as he lazed his way through his daily turn at the trading counter. On his right was a projector that could—magically as far as the Allawout were concerned—generate a three-dimensional, rotatable image of anything in the Outpost's warehouse. Visiting natives who made endless demands of the device simply for its entertainment value soon found themselves cut out of the trade loop. Once word spread among the local clans, this abuse stopped. The Outpost, they learned, was a place in which to conduct serious trade.

The tripartite clan that was now leaving carried between them several parcels sealed in the ubiquitous, biodegradable plastic wrap that was used to package all trade goods. As he watched them depart, Stefan directed the room's air purifier to grade up a notch. Allawout body odor was no more pleasing than their appearance. In a few minutes the atmospheric scrubber would have removed the last lingering traces of the clan's visit.

Pervasatha waited for the cheerful, noisily bubbling family to exit before coming in. Despite his special cooling gear, he was sweating profusely. A number of visiting supervisors and scientists felt that would have been a better name for the planet: Sweating Profusely. It was certainly more descriptive than Irelis IV.

"Got something for you, Stef." Perv, as his friends and coworkers called him, leaned on the counter. The corners of his mouth twitched. He seemed to be striving hard to repress a grin.

"Not another carved Ohrus tooth." Stefan eyed the other young man warily. "They're pretty, but we've already got a boxful."

"Nope. Better than that." The grin escaped its bounds. Perv gestured toward the door. "Enter! Come inside."

A native slid slowly inward on the familiar, disgusting trail of lubricating gunk. Behind it, the floor did its best to clean up after the visitor. Unfeeling mechanical though it was, Stefan still felt sorry for the autocleaner. Unlike the rest of them, it could never look forward to a day off. Not on Irelis.

Perv's grin was wider than ever. "You remember that directive? Not last week's—the one before. Page twelve. 'All company Outposts must strive where possible to encourage local life-forms to participate in the ongoing activities of a given station, with regard to maintaining and enhancing benign relations between the human and native populations.'"

"Yeah," Stefan replied guardedly. "I remember it. So what?" He slapped at his forehead, smashing something small, irritating, and resistant to the cocktail of insecticides that he had liberally applied earlier.

Perv gestured grandly at the newcomer, who was gazing around at the interior of the station with eyes that were even wider than normal. "Meet your new native assistant!"

Stefan blanched, recovered when he thought it was a joke, eyed his friend in disbelief when it began to sink it that it was not. "Don't try to be funny, Perv. It's too hot today."

"And it'll be too hot tomorrow, and the day after that, and the one after that also. But this is still your new assistant. Morey says so."

"Screw Morey!" As if the native were not present, Stefan gestured in its direction. "We don't have indigenous assistants. No local works inside the Outpost."

"We do now," Perv shot back. "They do now."

The other man's eyes narrowed. "Then where's *your* assistant?"

"Regulations say that, at this point in the Outpost's development, we only need one. She's it. She's yours." His smile flattened. "Lack of seniority says so."

"'She'?" A dubious Stefan studied the lumpish native, who continued to ignore the two young humans as she gawked at the interior of the trading room. "I thought the biologists hadn't figured out how to sex them yet."

Perv stood away from the counter. "Far as I know, they haven't. But that's the classification I've been given." He winked and turned to go. "I'll leave you two alone now."

The other man gestured wildly. "Hey, wait a minute! What am I supposed to do with this—with 'her'?"

Perv kept walking. "Not my concern. Morey says she's your new assistant. Get her to assist. Me, I've got work to do on the bromide concentrator or the delay'll go down on my record." He exited at a brisk clip, not looking back.

Stefan was once again alone in the room. Well, not quite.

Maybe if he ignored the native, it would go away. Sitting back down, he muttered the "unpause" command and resumed watching the game he had been engrossed in prior to the trading clan's arrival. Images danced in the air half a meter in front of his eyes. After a while, he became aware that he was not alone. As was often the case, it was the smell that tipped him off.

Advancing silently on its sheet of motive slime, the Allawout had sidled up as close behind him as it dared, and was dutifully gazing up at images whose origin, meaning, and purpose must be as alien to it as tooth gel.

Nostrils flaring in revulsion, he looked over his shoulder and down at the creature. Morey had declared it was his new assistant. Until he could make the notoriously gruff Outpost administrator see reason, Stefan realized with a sinking feeling that he was probably stuck with the creature. (But fortunately, he told himself, not *to* it.) If he abused it physically, there could be trouble. Members of the station's scientific contingent, who infrequently mixed with the much-younger and less experienced team of trader apprentices, would report him. His advancement up the company ladder would be questioned, and he might even be dropped down a rating or two. That could not be allowed to happen. Not after the horrid half year he had already been forced to put in on Irelis.

Swallowing his distaste, he asked in Terranglo, "Do you have a name?"

The dumpy alien quivered as if trying to slough off its skin. Flesh-protecting mucus oozed from pores and slid down its sides. "I am chosen Uluk."

At least it could talk a little, Stefan thought. Come to think of it, the staff would not have selected one to work inside the station, with humans, unless it had acquired at least some facility with the visitors' language. Then something happened that completely broke his train of thought.

Raising a tentacle, the Allawout pointed at the hovering wordplay image and said, "Pretty—what means it?"

It was the first time in nearly six months that Stefan had heard a local ask a question not directly related to trading. Minimal fluency he had expected; intellectual curiosity, if such it could be called, was something new. Without pausing to wonder why he was bothering to reply, he struggled to explain something of the subtle nature of a wordplay.

She did not understand. That was not surprising. Had she comprehended even his childishly simple explanation, he would immediately have passed her along to the scientific staff as an exemplar of Allawout acumen. On the indigenous scale of intelligence, she doubtless qualified as quite bright. About at the level of a human eight-year-old, only without any book learning to draw upon. It was unlikely she would grow any smarter.

But as the months progressed, she did. Or at least, her vocabulary increased. Struggling with the most fundamental concepts, she did everything he asked of her, from laboriously dragging trade goods into the back chamber to be sorted, cataloged, prepriced, and packaged for shipment off-world to making suggestions to visiting locals about what goods the strange dry-skin folk preferred and would pay well for.

It was funny to see how the other natives deferred to her. Even mature males, thick of tentacle and sharp of eye, seemed to shrink slightly in her presence. For a wild moment he thought she might be some kind of local equivalent of royalty, much as the notion of an Allawout princess seemed a contradiction in terms. Belleau Lormantz, one of the xenologists, assured him that could not be the case.

"In the nearly twenty years there has been a human

presence on Irelis, no evidence has surfaced of any level of government above that of the extended family or clan. They haven't even achieved the tribal level yet. They're just starting to emerge from the hunter-gatherer stage." Belleau had a nice voice, Stefan mused. About the nicest voice on Irelis. And unlike most of the scientists, she was nearly the same age as he was.

They were sitting together on one of the elevated walkways built atop balumina pilings that had been driven down through water and muck into the reluctant bedrock far below. Irelis's sun, redder than that of his homeworld, was setting behind red and yellow fiberthrush, the light peeking through the fronds to illuminate the station's sealed-together, prefabricated modules. Belleau was almost as reflective as the metal walls, he decided.

A voice sounded behind them, plaintive yet insistent. "Stef-han, what should I do with kaja bowls just buying today?"

He looked around irritably. "They go in the back, on the bottom shelves on the right-hand side. You know that, Uluk!"

Her tone did not change, and she had no expression to alter. "Yes, Stef-han. I will make it so." It took her several minutes to slip-slide back inside.

He returned to contemplating the sunset, the violet underside of the evening cumulus filling his head with thoughts that did not belong in as unpleasant a place as the Outpost.

"I hear that you're leaving the station."

She nodded. "Sabbatical. On Rhenoull V. To consolidate my reports, put some into book form, give lectures—that sort of thing. I think I'll be back, to start in on my advanced work.

There's a lot about these creatures we still don't know."

"Is there that much more to learn?" When she did not comment, he added, "How do I know you're coming back, Belle?"

"Because I say so. Because my work is here."

He peered deep into her eyes. Perspiration glistened on her forehead and cheeks. She was wet, tired, unkempt, and beautiful. "Is that the only reason?"

She turned away from him, to the sunset. "I'm not sure—yet," she replied candidly. "I like you, Stefan. I like you a lot. But I'm so deep into my work that much of the time I feel like I'm drowning."

"Drown in me," he told her with more intensity than he intended.

Her hand slipped sideways to cover his. "Maybe when I come back," she told him frankly. "When I have more confidence in my own future. Then, maybe—we'll see. You're a little young for me, Stefan."

"I'm not that young." When he reached for her, she leaned away, laughing affectionately.

"No, not now. As sweaty as we are, if we hold each other too tightly, we're liable to slip right past each other and into the water."

He laughed, too, and settled for squeezing her hand, and waiting for the alien sun to finish its day's work.

He sweated out another six months, her absence made all the more frustrating by his having to deal with Uluk. Just when it seemed she was acquiring some real skill, she would do something supremely stupid. He was forced to reprimand her, sigh in exasperation, and explain the procedure all over again. She would listen patiently, indicate understanding, go along fine for a while, and eventually repeat the same mistake. Something about the Allawout seemed to render them incapable of retaining any pattern of information for more than a few weeks at a time. It was as if the entire species was afflicted with Attention Span Deficit Disorder.

To make matters worse, he had to endure the endless jokes and gags the rest of the staff enjoyed at his expense. His only compensation was the occasional reluctant, approving grunt from Administrator Morey, who recognized the strain his most junior employee was operating under, plus praise from the scientific staff. The behaviorists in particular would seek him out to query him endlessly about his conversations with the Allawout.

"Look," he would object in exasperation, "we don't have 'conversations.' I give the thing orders, and she carries them out. Except when she forgets what to do, which is all the time, and I have to explain them all over again. Slowly and repeatedly, in the simplest terms possible."

"But within those constraints," a much older xenologist had pressed him, "the native in question *is* capable of performing the complex tasks she is assigned by you."

"Sure," he said, "if you can call stacking carvings and sorting voull horns 'complex.' Anything that involves actually thinking I have to guide and help her with. Initiative doesn't exist among the Allawout. Except when it involves food and shelter, I personally don't think they have any understanding of the concept."

"Yet the other locals obviously respect her deeply," the persistent scientist had insisted.

"Sure!" Stefan agreed. "She's big stuff because she has a job in the House-of-Wonders-That-Stands-in-Water, and speaks freely to the visitors from the cloud rafts. I suppose," he conceded, "that gives her some kind of rank, or status, that raises her up a notch or two above her fellow weed munchers." A few such carefully chosen comments were usually sufficient to send the behaviorists on their contemplative way, muttering to themselves.

One nice thing about Stefan's assistant, as far as Morey was concerned, was that the native never questioned her status. She accepted payment in trade goods, never asked for a change in the amount or kind of remuneration, worked silently and steadily, and was a real help in communicating the wants of the human traders to the natives. She slept in an old concentrate barrel Perv had welded to one of the balumina stilts, just above the waterline. Each morning she would ooze out of the plastic cylinder, drop into the water to clean herself, and then squirm up the ramp that had been erected to provide her kind with easy access to the station. With their strong tentacles the Allawout could easily climb a ladder, but that would not allow them to bring goods into or take them out of the Outpost.

Stefan had despaired of ever seeing Belleau again. Then one day, slightly less than a month before his tour was up and he was due to be promoted off-world, suddenly she was there, having arrived without notice on the monthly shuttle. They did not exactly fall into each other's arms—not with Customs officials and everyone else watching. But their eyes met, spoke, and smiled. Certain decisions were reached without the use of words.

"I told you I'd come back," she whispered to him later that morning.

"To resume your work?" He left the question hanging, too fearful to add the other question he was burning to ask.

"To do that, yes—and perhaps," she added mischievously, "to attend to other matters."

"I'm finished here in a few weeks." They were standing in the Outpost, its familiar hothouse surroundings for once the equal and not the excess of what he was feeling inside. "The Company has offered me promotion from apprentice and my choice of positions. On civilized worlds, at a proper salary. I have a lot of flexibility."

"Hmm. That does open certain possibilities, doesn't it? For example, I've taken a lectureship on Mathewson III."

His expression did not change. "There are two Company operations on Mathewson. Big ones."

She nodded thoughtfully. Then she leaned forward, kissed him once, adequately, and almost ran from the room. He remained behind, dazed and relieved and overflowing with satisfaction.

Behind him, a familiar odor preceded a question. "Stef-han is happy?"

His expression fell. The wondrous contentment rushed away like water out of the bottom of a broken jar.

"Yes, Uluk. Stefan happy. Stefan go away soon."

"Go away?" Crescent pupils swam within disk-like eyes. "Why Stef-han go away?"

"It's time to go," he muttered irritably. "All sky folk eventually go from Irelis. Go back to home." At her uncomprehending silence he added, "Back to own home-raft."

She considered this. "Outpost not Stef-han's raft?"

"No, dammit. Don't you have something to do?"

"Yes. I forget."

Lifting his eyes heavenward, he moved to check the duty scan for the day. But nothing, not even Allawout dullness, could entirely diminish the joy of Belle's return.

The next several weeks passed in a haze that was more a consequence of his reestablishing his relationship with Belleau than of the heavy atmosphere. They spoke of her science and his business, and how the two might complement each other on a world like Mathewson III. When it was clear that the positives outweighed the negatives, their delight was mutual. Though young, they were both very practical people.

When it was time to go, to finally leave behind Irelis and its miasmatic swamps, bug-ridden savannas, melancholy atmosphere, and multifarious stinks and smells, it was almost an anticlimax. Complaining a little less than usual, Administrator Morey was there to see them both off and to wish them well. The grumpy old Company man was unable to look his former apprentice in the face for fear of giving way to an actual smile. Pervasatha was long gone, having been promoted ahead of Stefan, but several others among the scientific and commercial community who had established friendships with the personable young trader on his way up turned out to see the two of them off.

They were waiting for the skimmer that would ferry them

out to the distant shuttle site, an artificial island built out in the middle of a spacious lake, when it occurred to Stefan that something was missing. A certain—stench.

"Funny," he mused aloud, "I thought she'd come to say good-bye."

"'She?'" Belleau's tentative tone mimicked one he himself had used some time ago.

"My native assistant. An Allawout named Uluk. You met her. Or at least, you encountered her."

"Oh yes, of course. I only saw her a couple of times. She was usually working in the rear storeroom whenever I came into the Outpost."

He found himself searching the station's walkways, then the grubby muck below. "I thought she'd be here." He shrugged. "Oh well. No matter. She probably forgot." Turning back to Belleau, he smiled affectionately. "After a year here I don't know how I'll cope with a normal, Earth-type climate."

"I give you about two days to become fully acclimated," she replied softly.

Henderson came huffing and puffing down the walkway. Reaching out, the panting behaviorist caught his breath as he shook first the apprentice's hand, then Belleau's. "Wanted to wish luck to you both. I'm sure you won't need it."

Stefan nodded his thanks, looked past the scientist. "Say, you haven't by any chance seen Uluk around today?" He hesitated slightly. "I sort of . . . wanted to say good-bye."

"Your native assistant?" Henderson's expression fell. "Oh. I thought you knew. They found her yesterday, about half a kilometer from the station. On Islet Twelve. Dead. Self-inflicted killing wound, the biologists tell me. Sorry."

A very strange feeling tightened in the younger man's gut. The longer he thought about it, the worse it got. "That's—too bad. I wonder what happened."

Henderson cast a quick glance in Belleau's direction before replying. Though much younger, she was a fellow scientist, after all, and the incident was an interesting comment on indigenous behavioral patterns.

"You really didn't know, did you? No, you wouldn't, always paying attention to commerce, and trade balances, and the like. An Allawout's individual focus is on its extended clan. Alpha males and females, Beta juniors, and so on. Didn't you ever notice that Uluk was never seen interacting with a family grouping?"

Stefan looked blank. "You're right, I didn't. But I never thought about it. She lived at the station. That was her choice. Mr. Morey, myself, everyone else—we all thought that was her choice."

"Oh, it was, it was," Henderson hastened to assure him. "I spoke to her several times, you know. As part of my work," he added almost apologetically. "You didn't realize that instead of one of her own kind, she had chosen to focus on *you*?"

The apprentice eyed the behaviorist uncertainly. "On me? Why would I notice something like that?"

Belleau's response was more understanding. "Are you saying that this Uluk individual chose to imprint herself on Stefan in lieu of a normal Allawout extended family grouping?"

"They worked together. Almost every day." Henderson looked apologetic as he regarded the younger man. "I thought surely you would have perceived something, or I would have mentioned it to you. It makes for a very interesting case history."

Stefan swallowed hard. "You're not saying that in some crazy kind of way she got, uh, attached to me, or anything weird like that?" In his mind he conjured up an image of the misshapen, slimy alien. But for some reason, it did not repulse him quite as much as it once had.

He found himself scanning the vegetation of the distant, fetid swampland. He remembered how Uluk had hovered about him, lingering in his vicinity even when her work was done; watching him operate the projector and the viewers; asking questions to which he was sure she already knew the answers. How she was always there waiting for him in the mornings, and leaving reluctantly when it was time for her to retire to her barrel under the Outpost.

He thought about how he had treated it—her—with casual indifference, even contempt. Memories of the time he had spent in her company came flooding back to him. They did not make him feel better. Surely he wasn't—responsible. He forced himself to ask as much.

Henderson considered. "Your announcement that you were leaving, permanently, no doubt came as a shock. In the absence of any other extended family connection, it's not uncommon for an Allawout to opt for self-termination instead of attempting to impose himself on another family or clan."

"You're saying," Belleau ventured, "that what happened was something like a dog pining away for its master?"

"Well, hardly." Henderson drew himself up slightly. "The Allawout may be a little slow on the uptake, but they're far from unaware." He turned back to the suddenly silent, staring apprentice. "It's not your fault, you know. Happens all the time with these clans. Self-termination is a well-documented means of controlling the population and maintaining the available food supply."

"Oh, I know." Stefan pushed away the sad thoughts. "It's too bad. She was nice enough—except for the smell. I can't help it if she was somehow attracted to one of the 'sky people.' To me." The oddest sensation was spreading through him. It made him angry, but try as he might, he found he could not suppress it.

"'Attracted'?" Henderson stared at him. "You really *didn't* perceive much, did you? Uluk wasn't 'attracted' to you. We spoke about many such things, and I remember quite clearly that she told me once she thought you were the ugliest living thing she had ever set eyes upon. Even uglier than any of the other humans she had met. *That's* why she stayed at the Outpost so long, and close to you. She felt it was something she needed to do. And then when you ignored her, and what she was doing for you, I guess she felt that all her efforts on your behalf were being rejected."

"Rejected?" Stefan frowned. "'Doing for *me*'? I was tolerating *her*. What did she think she was 'doing' for me?"

Wiping his eyes, the behaviorist blinked back the unforgiving rays of the setting violet sun. "She didn't stay close to you because she was attached to you, Stefan. She stayed because she felt sorry for you."

ALAN DEAN FOSTER's first stories appeared in *The Arkham Collector* and *Analog* in the late 1960s. His first novel, *The Tar-Aiym Krang*, was bought by Betty Ballantine and published by Ballantine in 1972. It is still in print. His short fiction has appeared in all the major magazines and numerous anthologies. Six collections of his short-form work have been published.

Foster has written more than one hundred books (science fiction, fantasy, mystery, western, historical, and contemporary fiction, as well as nonfiction) and his work has been translated into more than fifty languages. He is the author of screenplays, radio plays, talking records, and the story for the first *Star Trek* movie. His work has won awards in Spain and Russia in addition to the Southwest Book Award for Fiction (*Cyber Way*, the first work of science fiction ever to do so). A world traveler, explorer, and scuba diver, he has spent time in more than eighty countries.

Alan Dean Foster and his wife live in Prescott, Arizona. Visit his Web site at **www.alandeanfoster.com**.

AUTHOR'S NOTE

It's bad enough growing up without being one of the "in" kids. Not popular, not with it, not invited to parties, etc. What's even worse is being treated as though you don't exist. Having the boy or girl you worship from afar totally ignore you in the halls, in class, or out on the street. Sometimes all you want from someone is an acknowledgment that you're alive. A polite word or two would be fine . . . just a smile and a "hello" or "how you doin' today?"

But what happens when that special someone does acknowledge you . . . only not with a smile or a greeting, but with contempt. As if the world would be a better place if you didn't exist, because that person thinks you're too dumb, too ugly, or simply too not in the know to be worthy of anything less than a casual insult.

Life can be heartless.

Something to keep in mind when we start exploring the universe, lest we find another species out there that looks at us the way the captain of the football team or the head cheerleader looks at you.

Tanith Lee

tHe House on tHe Planet

PLANET DATE: YEAR 3
Part One—Pioneers: Zelda

The journey, even with FLJ,* took over three months. But the ship was okay. Lots of places to roam around, a huge game room with everything from flyball to Computace, a movie theater, and a solar garden that, if you didn't think too much about it, did just about resemble someone's really wonderful backyard.

Then they landed.

Zelda looked at the spaceport—bleak and windswept, with cold-eyed buildings.

The sky was green.

Oh, God.

"Tell me again why you wanted to come?"

"Oh, Zelda." Moth and Dad, exasperated.

The transport raced over rolling hills too fast to see a thing.

"When'll we *get* there?" sang Joe.

* Fast Light Jump

"Soon, honey."

"No, but *when*?"

Joe grinned secretly at Zelda. He was eight now. He only acted up to be annoying.

"One hour exactly. In fact"—Dad checked the speed monitor—"fifty-seven minutes."

Joe went back to his laptop game.

Zelda, who was fourteen, repeated her own unanswered question: "Why are we here?"

"It's an opportunity, the chance of a lifetime, Zel," said Dad. "We explained, didn't we? A whole new world to open up. Aren't you the least bit excited?"

"*I'm* excited!" sang Joe noisily.

Zelda thought of home, the whitewashed house on Anchor Street, of the sunny town, of saying good-bye to her friends at school, who had looked at her with a mixture of awe, jealousy, and sorrow. Zelda—off to another planet. Amazing Zelda, lucky Zelda, Zelda-who-was-doomed. Zelda thought of a *blue* sky.

"It'll be great," said Moth.

"Try to enjoy yourself," said Dad.

"Are we there yet?" added Joe.

They lived, ate and slept in the transport while the machines built the house. (The transport, unlike the ship, was cramped.)

Their robot, Plod, oversaw the building, now and then coming to Dad with a query—where the yard trees should go, how many windows in the kitchen, and so on.

Joe *liked* Plod. He tagged along with the seven-foot, gray, two-headed, four-handed metal man, asking endless questions. Plod never grew tired of Joe. Well. Plod was a robot.

Zelda, when not engaged in chores, sat on the stoop of the transport, looking narrowly at the view.

"Isn't it *beautiful,* Zelda?"

"Yes, Moth. I suppose." Was it? Or ugly?

"Oh, *Zelda.*"

The hills were behind the house. Machines were already out front, marking out the plan of fields and orchards, fencing in the herd animals that had arrived one day by helejet. The animals were *planet* animals. Dad thought they were terrific, Moth thought they were very big, Joe thought they were fascinating. Zelda stood at the neat white fence and stared.

"What *are* they? Are they supposed to be *cows*?"

"Tappuls. A type of bovine animal, yes."

The tappuls, one hundred in number, were each about the size of a small adult Earth elephant. They were brown, with large brown eyes, and long yellow horns. They could be machine-milked, and the milk was both calcium-rich and thick with benign amino acids. The tappuls had a heavy smell, not nasty but—weird.

"They're very docile, Zelda."

I'm docile, Zelda thought morosely. *I'm spineless. I let you bring me here against my will.*

There were other planet animals. The newly planted fields were soon full of plays, which looked like rabbits with one single upright ear. Unlike rabbits, they did little damage to the crops. In fact, their droppings gave useful natural fertilizer. Joe liked the plays. He kept trying to catch one as a pet.

"Suppose it bites you?" Zelda snapped at him.

"Wouldn't matter. They're not poisonous."

"How do you know? Everything here could be. Even the air could be full of some poison the machines just don't recognize. We may all get sick, or evaporate, or turn into mush."

Having said that, watching his bright face crunch up, she felt sorry in case she'd really scared him.

But then he poked out his tongue at her. "Balls," said Joe, as he was *never* allowed to.

Day followed day, and night followed night. Same old thing.

They moved into the new house with its wide, airy rooms and brilliant self-cleaning, shockproof glass windows. Moth and Dad hung up the new white drapes.

"Doesn't it look fine?"

Chilly evenings, they lit the self-renewing pine logs on the big stone hearth.

"It's really getting to be homey now."

Outside in the darkness, strange things whiffled and chattered, just as they did by day. But here, the birds sang all night.

There were no dangerous animals in the region. Even if there had been, the fences and the house area walls had infallible devices for keeping any bad problems out.

In every window, the rolling blue hills, the rolling blue plain dotted with fields of white or red alien grain, with trees that would make pink and orange fruits and were already covered with pink and staring purple blossom. Machines roved, walking the land. Above, the green sky, lit by a sun that was not the sun of Earth. And at night, a green-black sky, lit by two tiny moons. Even the stars were wrong.

One night, Zelda dreamed she flew out over the hills. In the dream she didn't mind them so much. When she woke, the dream disgusted her.

"You'll be at school soon," said Dad, riding in on the cultivator machine, so cheerful Zelda wanted to hit him.

"That'll be *so* nice."

"Now, why be sarcastic? Lots of new friends to make."

"I liked my old friends."

Dad frowned and swung off the machine. He came over and stroked her hair. "It takes a while for the Ipsi-mail* to come through. You'll have some letters soon."

"It's been over a month, Dad."

"Well . . . I guess maybe . . . "

"They don't know what to say to me. I don't either, Dad."

He sat beside her on the porch. She could smell the three Earth trees that had been planted in the yard, especially the pine—if she shut her eyes she could pretend. But what was the use? If she opened them, the truly blue hills reached to the truly green sky. The sun was sinking in the front, over the fields, turning the hills to a mauve as raucous as a loud noise.

"Honey, look. You know how tight money was. We tried to tell you. We couldn't have kept going—we'd have had to move—take some tiny apartment in the city—my firm folded, I'd lost my job, Zelda, remember? And then this opportunity—government sponsored—perfect . . ."

"Yeah, Dad. It's okay."

"I know it isn't, honey. Not for you. Not yet."

* Interplanetary Satellite Intercommunication

"I'll get used to it," said Zelda grimly.

Dad sighed, and went into the house, and again, seeing his bowed head, she was sorry. Till she heard him laughing with Moth at the stove.

In two years I'll be sixteen. I'll take some kind of job—who needs college? I'll save. I'll catch the first ship out I can. I'll go home.

If only the night birds would shut up. They sat on the trees along the wall, even came in and sat on the Earth trees in the yard below Zelda's window. *Twindle-twindle tweety trrr,* they went. "Our own nightingales," Moth had said, pleased. But their song was thin, like wires in Zelda's ears.

She put in her music plugs not to hear the birds.

Tomorrow the house transport would run her to the school in the nearby town. It was, by Earth measurement, miles and miles away, but the transport would get her there in twenty minutes. She dreaded it

The planet had no human life other than the human life that, for the past three years, had come here from Earth. Moth and Dad were two of the last batch of "settlers" who had taken up the government's offer to help develop the land. Everyone else at school would have been here a *long* time.

Aliens. Like everything else.

I'd run away, but where'd I go? There's only here now.

In sleep, one of the music plugs was dislodged. In sleep, she began to hear the *twindle-twindle* birds. In sleep, she threw stones at them, which, awake, she never would have done. In sleep, anyhow, she missed.

Joe dissolved in tears when Zelda started to leave for school. Astonished, they all stood gawping at him.

"What's wrong, baby?" cried Moth, trying to resist gathering him into her arms.

"Zelda!" wailed Joe. "Don't wan' Zelda go!"

"But, honey—she has to—"

"She don' wanna!" yodeled Joe, absurd, funny, heartbreaking. "Don' make 'er—"

Zelda stepped forward. She just knew how ashamed he would be of this in ten minutes' time. She grabbed him by the shoulders.

"I *do* want to, you pest. Do you think I want to hang around here all day with *you*? And where's that stupid play rabbit thing you promised to catch for us? When I get back tonight you'd better have caught one—or two, that'd be better. Get two, Joey. If you think you *can*."

Joe stared at her. The tears dried on his face in the heat of his fury. "What ya bet, huh?"

"Ten Earth bucks."

"Zelda!" shrieked Moth. Dad restrained her, grinning.

"You are *on*," snarled Joe.

Zelda swept into the house transport and was whisked away.

She thought of Dad, his face so pale when he'd first told them he'd lost his job. She thought of Moth, being so determined to make the best of it. And Joey, always ready for something new. And herself, Zelda, sticking tight, refusing to move an inch.

She had never felt so alone. She couldn't even talk about her feelings now, in case she upset Joe. She just hated it when he cried. She would have to pretend from now on everything was fine, just fine.

Zelda pretended.

She pretended she hadn't dreaded the school, had been looking forward to it. She marched in, looking coolly pleased. When spoken to, she was friendly. She absorbed all the new instructions, the new schedule, gazed at the subjects of the classes, pinned on her grade badge, did what everyone else did. At lunchtime she went into the school yard, which was absolutely an alien garden. On the soft blue grass court, she played flyball with a girl called Patty. They were both pretty good.

"What color would you say this grass is?" Patty asked as they ate their food under a tree like a giant zucchini.

"Blue?"

"What shade of blue?"

"Well—kind of dark blue—"

"*I'd* say," said Patty, "it's the shade of Todd Ariano's eyes."

"Who?"

"Look. Over there."

Zelda looked. Just then Todd Ariano looked back at them and smiled.

Patty was totally right.

The planet grass was Todd-Ariano's-eyes blue.

Zelda kept on pretending. She pretended very hard. She pretended to Dad and Moth and Joe. At school and at home. Indoors and out. Even to Plod, she pretended. "Listen, Plod! Those birds are really singing today!"

It grew easier. Like something she'd wear on her wrist, at first too tight, loosening up over time.

She joined the chess club and the drama club at school and the flyball team. Patty did, too. So, for that matter, did Todd Ariano. Why not? It was okay.

She thought about home—that was, the house on Anchor Street, which they would have had to leave anyhow. And about the town and the big city they'd have to have moved to, crowded, often dangerous, alarms going off and sirens every place, and police cordons. She thought of the blue sky of Earth that could also turn gray or yellow with heat and pollution. She thought of Dad, tired and sullen, Moth looking angry or sad. Joey had always been the happiest there, maybe—but Joey hadn't made any fuss at all. He'd just said, "When are we going?" and gone to pack his games and toys.

Zelda had started to notice some things, almost as if she hadn't seen them before.

How not only was the grass the color of Todd Ariano's eyes but the purple blossom was like raspberry Jell-O, or sometimes violets.

The new town was clean and painted in different colors, too, hot colors and refrigerated colors.

Here and there Earth plants, which had been put in a year or so ago, were beginning to grow to great height, glossy-leaved, liking the soil, and the sun that was always warm, never too hot.

"This place is like heaven, my mother says," admitted Todd as a group of them walked to the transport bay.

"*Heaven?*"

"Yeah, I know. Mom uses words like that. But I like it here."

"Me, too," said Zelda, pretending, since now she must never say, except to her own heart, that she *didn't* like the planet.

"Wait till you see the wild roses in the spring," said Todd, truly surprising her. "But, you know, there's something even better."

"What?"

"The new ice-cream place on the corner of Foundation."

Zelda sat and thought in the window of her room, too.

She wondered why there was no humanlike life, no so-called Higher Intelligent life here.

This, so far, had been common to all the planets discovered, which was why, apparently, it was all right to colonize them. Earth had gotten so small, so crammed with people. There had to be somewhere else to go.

Earth.

The sunset touched the hills. Mauve.

Zelda glared at the color. Outside, the *twindle-twindle* birds twittered and trilled.

A couple of plays were actually *playing* in the backyard, closely watched by Joe. He crept toward them. Zelda could see from the angle of the two single upright ears that they knew exactly what he was doing, but they let him get way close before they darted off under the gap in the fence Joe had made to lure them in. There they went, along the outer wall and through the gate—Zelda laughed. She guessed her ten bucks were still safe.

A few months more, she'd be fifteen.

I can wait. Fifteen, sixteen—then she could start to get ready to go—home.

The rains came, and high winds, and Zelda stayed at the house, doing schoolwork through the compulink.

In the evenings she saw how the twindle birds sat out, soaking and beak-dripping, in the cover of the stout planet trees by the wall. They still bravely sang, through wind and rain, *twindle-twindle tweety trrr.*

"Moth—do you think we should put out some food for them? They look so—*wet.*"

They put out food for the twindle birds. (Their real name was auxicaps—"twindle" was much better.) The birds fed, and fluttered around the yard. They never left droppings. Apparently they only ever had to—er—*drop* stuff about once every five or six days, so you were unlucky if it fell on you or the lawn.

It was that day when Zelda stopped hearing them. Worried, she glanced out the window. Then she could see—and hear— they still sang. She had simply stopped hearing it, unless she listened.

An Ipsi-mail torrent of letters to Zelda fell into the home computer as the torrents of rain drummed down. She answered them slowly, carefully. Everyone wanted to know everything— the way the planet was, the animals, the people. Zelda sat for hours, telling them, telling them all about it. Describing the colors, the moons, the sky.

Outside in the sheets of rain, the huge forms of the tappuls grazed and slowly moved, unconcerned, calm. Several had new calves.

Joe, unable to hunt plays in the weather, sat drawing up battle plans of capture. He and Plod—or, rather, Plod with Joe jumping around him—had already constructed a large, luxurious enclosure for the one-eared rabbits.

Seeing Joe hunched over his plans, just after she and Todd had read through their parts for the drama club on the voice-view link, Zelda said, "Joey—thanks."

"What? Thanks 'cause I didn't catch a play yet and cost ya ten bucks? Just wait."

"No. Thanks for caring about me."

"You?" he asked with utter scorn.

The wind and rain faded back up into the sky. The world was glassy and clear, smelling of salad and flowers.

Zelda walked between the fields, the wet, Todd's-eyes-blue grass tinkling with a few last cascades, the grain heavy in the head, tall now as any corn in the fields of Earth.

That night, her ears unstoppered by the music plugs, sleeping, Zelda heard the twindle birds singing again. She was glad they sang. Why shouldn't they?

She thought, in her sleep, *See, there* is *a poison in the air. It makes you* like *this place even when you hate it.*

In the dream, she flew up above the plain once more, gazing at the house below, lit not by moonlight but by the sunset. How—*beautiful* it was after all, the light of the sun on the faces of the house and the hills, not lurid, but a color like lavender.

Zelda flew over the dream hills. She watched the dream moons rise, one, two. She looked at the clever pattern of the stars.

Next week I'll be fifteen.

Only one more year then before she could begin to think about leaving the planet. She could get through it. Just a year.

Down in the dream she swooped, to peer into the house. She saw Moth and Dad and Joe sitting watching an old classic movie, *Pirates of the Caribbean.* Joe nearly *had* caught a play today. Better save her money.

She thought, *I'm dreaming this. It's so real. It's like—home.*

Something in the air, she thought.

In her sleep, she smiled, and turned over.

Outside the twindle birds sang solemnly on through the night.

PLANET DATE: YEAR 31
Part Two—Present Tense: Harrington

In the end the farmers on the plains made their money and moved away. Some went back to Earth, but most went to the great cities that now stood proudly up on the planet. Meanwhile, the little towns swelled. New streets bloomed and ran like vines. Stretching out over the plains and hills, they closed around the solitary houses of the first pioneers, turned their farmlands to parks and neat backyards, enclosed everything in neighborhoods.

The house stood on Pine Street now. On either side were other houses, and across the street Pioneer Park, with a fine view of the overhead train.

A nice area. Good to bring up kids.

Their mother had thought that, Harrington guessed, when she and Pop bought the house eight years ago. Mom usually went by "Annie," now that Harrington had turned fifteen. Pop, though, had ceased to have a name or to be Pop. He'd left them one month after they'd moved in.

Then eventually there had been Annie's other guy.

Harrington—thirteen back then—hadn't liked the Guy much. But he was soon gone, though he'd left behind a souvenir.

Harrington looked at it now, this keepsake of Annie's sudden short love affair.

It was crawling along the rug, looking adorable. Harrington wanted to throw up.

Its real name was Jasselly. It couldn't speak even, not

properly, not yet. A girl who was almost two, Annie's second daughter, Harrington's sister.

"Oh, Harry—couldn't you have kept an eye on her?"

"I have to practice piano, don't I?"

"Yes—but—oh—come here, baby baa-baa," cooed Annie, scooping the crawling atrocity off the floor.

Annie didn't—*couldn't*—see, apparently, that Harrington did not care about It, that frankly, if It had crawled right out the front door and away down the block, Harrington would not have been exactly *upset*. She knew she *should* be. But why tell yourself lies?

It was a pain.

"When I think," said Annie, rocking the object, "buying this house—do you remember?"

"Not much. I was seven."

"And their daughter was married—I remember the live-view showing it—what was her name? She's a writer—Zelda, that's it. Zelda Ariano—she married the male flyball champion . . . And the son, what was he doing? A naturalist with Government Survey. No wonder they all moved away to someplace more fancy. But it was so lucky for us. The house going so cheap and all—"

"Yeah, we were really lucky. We moved in, Pop moved out, you got together with that Guy and we ended up with It—" All this was under Harrington's breath as she began to let loose rills of Chopin from the piano.

Annie put It back in the enclosure.

Really, the enclosure was like the ones the plays had, Harrington thought.

They had two plays, mostly to amuse It, though Harrington

was quite fond of them, too. They were very affectionate and intelligent for one-eared rabbits, and you could let them roam free outside when they wanted, like cats. Unlike cats, they did no damage, though the people next door always seemed to think they would.

Not *It*, though. *It* must not roam free. *It* had to be protected.

Which was why the Hedge was coming today.

"It's so clever," said Annie. She didn't mean the baby, but the Hedge, or what the Hedge could do.

"Sure, Annie."

"What are you playing so loud?" cried Annie as Jasselly started to wail.

"Chopin, Mom. 'The Funeral March.'"

"You'd never know it wasn't real, would you, Mrs. Riveras?"

Mrs. Riveras stared through the eyehole in the Hedge.

"No, Annie. It sure blocks out the sun like it's real. I'd a thought you had enough big things growing in there already with that pine tree."

"Well, the Hedge is only for one hour in the morning and one in the late afternoon."

"I guess that'll have to be okay, then."

"What we agreed, Mrs. Riveras."

Mrs. Riveras frowned. She was a thin old woman with a bitter face. She didn't think much of Annie, and she lived right next door. On the other side were Mr. and Mrs. Oplough. When Annie had explained to them about getting the Hedge, they had both peered at her as if she were crazy.

"It ain't allowed," said Mr. Oplough. "No way on Earth."

He had cackled at his joke. He had been an engineer ten years back; now he was retired and he knew his rights.

"Twelve meters high, you say?" quavered Mrs. Oplough. "Virgil, that's thirty-nine feet, isn't it?"

"Yes," said Virgil Oplough, scowling.

"Just from nine till ten in the morning," pleaded Annie. "Then just four till five. It's to keep the baby safe."

"Babies!" snorted Virgil. "Some folks don't know when to call it a day with babies."

But it was nearly impossible to insult Annie when she was trying to be sweet.

Harrington had watched from the back door. She'd wanted to shout at Mr. Oplough. Yes, even though all this fuss was for *It*.

Now the Hedge had been put in. That had taken all morning, with the soft but intrusive buzz of subsaws and whine of electrasonics. The neighbors hadn't liked that, and the Oploughs had come out to squawk *How long would this racket go on?*

When the Hedge was installed, Annie hit the button to bring it alive.

The Hedge stayed invisible, and in fact actually not *there*, when it was switched off. Switched *on*, it leaped instantly into being. Thirty-nine feet of darkest green-blue foliage, so dense there were the preordered peepholes to see through. Among the mat wove the *appearance* of wild planet roses the color of strawberries, and Earth-type ivy. Then Mrs. Riveras's face had appeared, unroselike, in the little hole nearest the house. (At the same moment Harrington heard, on the Oplough side, a door open, a gasp gasped, and a door slammed.)

"Only two hours a day," sweet-talked Annie. "Mrs. Riveras—there'll even be days it won't be on at all."

"I'm timing you, Annie," said Mrs. Riveras, worryingly. "I'll keep track of your hours. If you go over time—"

"I won't. I promise."

Harrington wanted to throw something at Mrs. Riveras, too. Yes, even though, again, it was all for *It*.

The Hedge was a molecule construct, one of the latest things, and had cost two thousand IPU dollars,* which they couldn't afford. But what the heck.

Harrington had to admit she was quite impressed.

There was *really* nothing there but airwaves, and the original low fence, just reinforced slightly to stop the plays straying into the neighbors' yards, and the plays preferred to go to the park anyhow. Yet when that button was pressed, the Hedge towered, casting a rich green shadow, cool and safe, for the baby to crawl out of the direct sunlight, and with no apparent way for her to get out. Or anything else to get in. The Hedge *felt* of hedge, too. If you touched it, it felt real—leaves, roses. They even had a scent. The Hedge felt as if you couldn't push through it—it resisted, held you back. It seemed to do that with the sun, too—though in fact there was only a shadow because of something to do with the activated molecules "bending light."

Annie was as strict as Mrs. Riveras. On a corner of the home computer she faithfully marked off the two hours, nine till ten, sixteen (four) till seventeen (five) in the afternoon—

* Interplanetary Union

except every tenth day when she left the Hedge completely switched off, and Jasselly had to stay inside.

The plays didn't bother with the Hedge at all. Ignored it.

But Harrington noticed that birds had started to fly over.

A lot of the birds and animals had been driven out of the area as the town grew. There wasn't enough space for them and human disturbance wasn't what they liked. People didn't seem to care. They had their pets. Sometimes in the parks you spotted wild plays or foxiles, a lizard or two.

Birds, though . . . there weren't many birds at all.

Harrington, gazing up at the birds dark on the pale green young summer sky, realized abruptly that she had only ever really seen birds in books or on a screen.

"Mom?"

Annie looked around. Being called "Mom" by Harrington usually meant something was going on—good or bad.

"What, Harry?"

"Come see."

Annie, despite her major faults of (1) losing Pop, (2) liking the Guy, and (3) producing It, still had some plus points. If you said something like "Come see" in the right kind of "come see" voice, she went with you to look.

They stood in the yard.

The Hedge was on, and Jasselly was lying asleep on a big cushion. Harrington, sitting outside to draw, had been "keeping an eye" on her. Sort of. *Touching, really, how Annie trusts me . . .*

"Up there."

They both gazed upward.

On top of the Hedge a large bird had perched, balancing on the joined-up molecules that felt like solid twigs and leaves, fanning its feathers in blissful ignorance.

"Wow," said Annie.

"It's been there fifteen minutes. Why 'wow'?"

"Well, when did we last see a bird that close?"

"It's forty feet up!"

"Yes."

"You're not scared it'll pounce and peck Jass's eyes out?"

"Oh no, honey," said Annie. "I recall these birds from years back when your pop—when I lived more outside the town. They're called—what are they called?"

The bird pecked at the Hedge, and though nothing came off it into the bird's beak, it seemed convinced and pecked a bit more. Another bird just like it flew down and settled by the first bird. They began to make a noise. *What* a noise.

"Like rusty nails on a glass," exclaimed Harrington.

"No, it's more like—like tuning a guitar—"

Twindle-twindle, went the birds, *tweety trrr.*

"Auxicaps!" cried Annie.

"Gesundheit!" Harrington laughed.

Annie laughed, too. They stood laughing, looking up at the birds singing their twindle song on the Hedge above the sleeping baby.

Mr. Oplough stood the other side of the right-hand boundary, looming over the low fence. Demonstrating without meaning to how excellent it was when the Hedge was there and they didn't have to see him.

"I'd like a word with you, Annie."

"Yes, Mr. Oplough."

"I have a vegetable patch just along here."

"Yes, Mr. Oplough? That's great."

"No, it ain't. Your damned Hedge is cutting off my sun."

"Only for two hours a—"

"And my planet tomatoes are going blue."

"But—they *do*, don't they, Mr. Oplough?"

"Nah. I bred it outta the darn things, till you started with that Hedge." Mr. Oplough glowered. "And besides, it ain't hardly two hours now, is it?"

Annie all innocence, Harrington all astonished.

"No, I been countin' them hours, Annie. *Three* hours yesterday. And *two* this morning."

"It's because of the birds, Mr. Oplough," said Annie, beaming at him.

"What birds? What're you talking about? And who wants birds anyhow, dropping their dirt all over my yard—"

"Oh, they hardly ever do, Mr. Oplough—only every six days. No need for you to get all tense."

Annie pointed.

Twelve meters up, two birds flew over and over where the Hedge had been, circling like moving paintings of birds on a green plate of sky.

"You're nuts!" declared Mr. Oplough. "You're a darn nuisance. Why don't you get back to Earth where you belong, causin' all this trouble for proper folks, litterin' this clean new world with fatherless kids—"

Speechless, they watched him tramp away, and the door slammed loud as thunder.

"I guess the gloves are off," said Annie thoughtfully. "Mrs. Riveras told me yesterday—after we had the Hedge on too long—she's going to L-mail* the Town Authority. She says she plans for us to be thrown out of the house. It seems we've ruined the neighborhood."

"She can't!"

"Maybe she can."

They too went back—into what was still their house.

Annie set the stove to fix tea and the Ice-it to ice it.

They sat on the living room floor while Jasselly played quietly with her fur bear. Annie and Harrington drank their tea and watched the birds circle over the lawn, through the wide window.

Annie put down her glass.

"Yes?"

"*Yes,*" said Harrington.

Jasselly looked up at the excited voices of these people she had come to live among. She smiled. "Yeff," agreed Jasselly, nodding both her head and the toy bear's.

Annie rose in her graceful way. She had been a dancer in live theater before Pop and Harrington. She strode to the button panel on the wall and pressed the brand-new button.

Outside, the two walls of Hedge sprang gloriously sunward, and after about five minutes more, the auxicaps floated down.

"I've always liked my tomatoes blue," said Harrington.

* Local Mail

"Boo," said Jass with approval. "Thom-*aif*-oos."

Three persons united against the world.

They were building a nest. They thought the Hedge was completely there, but maybe not quite, because they brought in the nesting material from elsewhere—twigs and leaves from the park, hair from Mr. Brand's dog four doors down. The nest was a huge unwieldy thing, big enough for a legendary roc's egg, Annie remarked. The birds sat on the nest in turns by day. In the evening they groomed each other with their beaks and snuggled up. They sang all night—if singing was what you could call it.

"It says in this book that they nest for ten to fourteen days, and then the eggs will be laid."

"Is that quick?"

"I don't really know, Harry. I don't know anything about birds, just that I like them."

"How many eggs?"

"Between two and six."

"Hey!"

By night, as the birds sang, the stars and moons shone down, and the Hedge gleamed as if moon-polished and star-gemmed, unseen (they had closed the eyeholes), they heard Mrs. Riveras's silent purse-mouthed rage and Mr. Oplough's trumpetings of fury. The birds sang louder and louder.

"You know, it's not so bad, the way they sing."

"Like badly tuned nightingales."

"What's a nightingale, Mom?"

"A bird that sings."

"Come on!"

"I said. I don't know a thing about birds."

"Look," said Harrington, "she's asleep with the rabbits."

"Yes. Real rabbits—I don't know that I'd risk a baby around them. But plays are fine. Gentle. *Careful.*"

"Was I *ever* that small?" asked Harrington, staring at Jasselly in her molecule-guarded sleep.

"Was *I*?" said Annie. Harrington stared at her mother. Once Annie had been a kid, too. As if she read thoughts, Annie added, "Hated my younger sister and all. I used to plan to kill her. Never did. Decided she was okay in the end. She's on Earth—I'd love to see her again . . . Maybe one day."

The tall man walked into the house and looked about him. His name was Dennis Rooney. He was very good-looking, but he came from Town Authority. Mrs. Riveras and Mr. Oplough had summoned him.

"Is that the Hedge? Yes, it's high. You can get slightly shorter models, though not by much. The shortest is, I understand, eight meters. And the cost's the same. It would cause the same problem, too. Block out neighbors' view and sunlight. Not everyone wants to know everybody else's business, of course, or get fried."

"I didn't mean to upset them," Annie said. "But those are living things up there. They've produced *seven* eggs—that's unusual."

"How'd you know there are seven?" He smiled at Annie.

"I hired a tiny elevcam and sent it up. They didn't notice—I mean the birds."

"Seven," Dennis repeated. "That *is* impressive."

Harrington broke in. "You sound like you don't think we did anything wrong."

"Harry, sshh. Wait."

"No, it's okay, Annie—may I call you Annie?"

"Yes, Dennis," said Annie, and blushed.

"You see, I'm less interested in the neighbors' gripes than in someone who's gotten these birds to breed again. They seemed to be dying out. As for Oplough and Riveras, they've already told me they want to move. They don't like children or animals so close. We can always pay them compensation and buy them out—then we can locate people who'll be happy to live in the two houses with a big Hedge on one side and some rare birds."

"What about," said Annie, "the other neighbors—Mr. Brand and the rest of them?"

"Oh, they're fine. Mr. Brand actually asked me to ask you if he could drop by sometime, take a closer look at the auxies. Won't bring the dog, he swore to me. *Or* his robot."

"The dog is welcome," said Annie. "And Mr. Brand, too."

"So there's just this form on the carry-com to sign, if that's okay? Read it all first."

Annie began to read. She looked up, very pale where she had been pink. "You're *paying* us to look after the birds?"

"Sure thing. Government grant concession Number X112, Rare and Endangered Indigenes, subclause 6."

Harrington saw her mother was gazing at Dennis from Town Authority spouting jargon and numbers as if he were reading her an ancient love lyric from Lord Byron. Ever the soul of tact she knew herself to be, Harrington led Jasselly into the Hedge-safe yard, where they sat in the cool and watched the birds nesting and twindling high above.

"How many do you think will hatch, Jass?"

"Eighfs," announced Jass.

"Don't be crazy—eight? There are only seven eggs."

"Eighfs," insisted Jass, who, having found speech, wasn't going to have it challenged.

In any case, she was right. When the eggs did hatch, out tottered eight balls of fluff with beaks, who solidified enough inside a few hours to fly down with their parents to the lawn, for the bird food TA had supplied. One egg had been a double. It made the planetwide NewsNet.

PLANET DATE: YEAR 103
Part Three—Thinking Future: Lute

Riding there in her single-person hoverjet, Lute heard the melody and words of old songs running through her brain.

The jet didn't go so fast she couldn't take in the rolling prairie, dotted with ripening fruit trees and untended stands of grain, the wild herds of tappuls grazing, and whitehawks idling over the sky.

It had been government policy since the fiftieth year on-planet to let certain areas go back to the wild, let the land renew itself and give the local animal life a chance to regain habitat.

The town of Pioneer Pines was the first of these projects. And by now, according to the information site, most of the town was gone, smothered in mutating trees and rioting vines, with creatures lairing in the remains of the houses. There were even some dangerous critters now, the site overview had told her—felinxes, for example, the nearest thing to bobcats the planet had. Lute had brought a Planet League Approved stunner along with her bag, her rob, and her guitar.

"Why in hell do you want to go there?"

That had been the question one or two had asked her, in the city.

Because, she thought, *it's about as far away as I can get from here.*

She was seventeen, adult status. Nobody could stop her.

To be polite, she said some of the truth: "It's where Harrington Rooney lived, before she moved south."

Harrington Rooney was the movie actress who had been the star of so many of the early planet-made movies. Lute had always admired her.

"Wasn't her sister a mathematician, Lute?" inquired one of the "bright" girls.

Lute didn't answer, but someone else did. "Jasselly? She still is."

"She must be old . . . They both must be—"

"Kicking eighty or ninety, I guess," said the someone else. "But Zelda Ariano lived in that house, too, didn't she—different time, same place, right, Lute?"

Once more Lute said nothing.

Inside she said this: *I just want to get away so bad.*

To get away—

But you couldn't. Not really. For wherever Lute went, the memory went with her. The memory of Cholan.

The rob was the first out of the jet. It trundled lightly down Main Street, navigating between arching tree roots, clumps of huge flowers, and heaps of metallic rubble. The houses and stores had been designed to break down over a period of years if unmaintained. But enough of them were still standing to get in the rob's way.

The town looked weird. Hollow, yet choked with growing stuff.

Having parked the jet, Lute toted her bag and the guitar, the stunner slung over her other shoulder.

The morning was peaceful. Nothing moved.

Then—

Out of the tunnel of trees shot the rob, its metal box shape whirring with dials and lights. It raced toward her in robotic panic. Lute dropped her bag and pulled the stunner around.

"What is it?"

A scarlet light lit: *unfriendly life form*—that's what the light meant.

The rob was flinging itself for shelter against her ankles.

Lute braced herself for the biggest felinx on-world to burst from the trees.

Next moment the unfriendly life did erupt out of there.

"Oh, rob. That's only—it's only *plays*, that's all."

The three one-eared rabbits dashed up, turned a couple of somersaults over one another, and darted away again into the undergrowth.

The rob made ticking complaining noises. Embarrassed?

Lute raised her eyebrow. "It looked like they were teasing you, pal!"

Guided by the old street plan, Lute found the Ariano-Rooney house just after noon. Like everything else, it was tented in by vines. One wall had crumbled down, and most of the strong, unbreakable window glass had given way, as it always did without mechanical care.

In what had once been a pretty backyard, now part of the neighborhood jungle, a single tall Earth pine, slightly tinged with blue, lifted its dark pagoda to the sun.

Lute made her camp in the house. She was not without company. Pale-furred rodents lived in various holes, and a foxile kept a single-fox apartment on the top floor—she soon grew used to its slim orange shape padding to and fro. She would try not to disturb them all, but they might not mind her too much. It had been noted that the planetary animals had a great tolerance for small groups of people, only shying away from the vast sprawls of populated towns and cities. Even there, though, you sometimes found them, and they seemed prepared to adopt Earth humans. So many of them had become companionable pets, rivaling the cats, monkeys, mice, and dogs the settlers had first introduced.

This house had even been the site of a breeding pair of auxicaps, who had built their nest in a molecular Hedge for six years running, producing a whole flock of new birds that bred in turn.

The auxicaps had been thought to be an endangered species. They were the most selective, and would never go just anyplace. They avoided most fully built-up areas. But they had always seemed to like Pioneer Pines. It was now quite a center for them—another reason why people had been encouraged to move away. So far Lute, always a city girl, had never seen an auxicap, except in a book or on a screen.

In the fading light, Lute sat by her little portofire, cooking her hamburger in a responsible way, the prewashed salad in its bowl, the glass of sparkling Plancola to hand.

Now and then she touched the guitar. She didn't play it. *Not yet. One day. When I can.*

She had been promising that for months.

The rob scuttled around. It had taken a dislike to the harmless white rats now. Whenever one appeared, the rob would launch itself off its resting pad and trundle toward the rat over the roots and broken floor. She would have to reprogram it in the morning. A city machine. It had clearly gotten hysterical out here.

Machines did have personalities, robs definitely, especially if they were with you a long time. She had argued about that such a lot with—

Such a lot with—

With Cholan.

Lute thought about Cholan. Let herself do it. The memories poured in like a sea gushing from a giant faucet, drowning her. Before Cholan, despite her many friends—none of whom had been close—she had been alone. Her parents had left her college *in loco parentis* and had "gone home" to Earth.

Then, a year ago . . .

He'd come to see her at the stadium, one more fan of double-line soccer, with a program for her to sign. She was the Green Tigers' main striker, and she'd spun three balls in the net. She always tried to be decent to any fan. Happy with her score, she was laughing and joking with all of them. Then Cholan was in front of her. Lute had fallen silent.

He held out the program in his long, dark-fingered hand. She signed, and glanced up into his face, and he smiled. Lute smiled back. At first she wasn't sure she'd be able to. It was as if she recognized him—*knew* him. But they'd never met before. Their fingers brushed as he took the program back from her, and they both started. "Electric," he said. Lute nodded. That was it.

Few things had been so simple. So good.

That year. That perfect almost-year. With Cholan.

She saw him nearly every day, and in the evenings they went dancing at the rinks, or drank sodas, or sat listening to music in the clubs. Cholan taught her how to really play a guitar. He would move her hands, and where he placed them on the instrument, she could suddenly make music—music that *shone*. He, too, could play guitar, and asera, drums, sax, and seventeenth-century mandolin. They sang together. His voice—velvet, dark as coffee.

The ones who knew about them figured that, once Cholan and she were seventeen—their birthdays were only five days apart, hers first—they'd marry.

Simple.

They even talked about it sometimes, but it didn't seem to matter. Being *together* mattered. But the strange thing was, Lute felt she was with him even when they were apart. Somehow.

They seldom argued, except about things like robots, or soccer tactics.

Once he said to her, standing in daylight under the city clock, "You're like a part of me, Lute." And she replied, "Me, too."

She'd left him only two hours before. She was sitting up in her bed, reading a novel that never after would she remember, when something happened inside her head.

It scared her stupid. It was like a light going out. A kind of blindness.

She jumped out of bed, ran halfway across the floor, wishing that her parents had not left her on-planet without them, wishing that someone in the sorority house was someone she could really confide in. She thought of her friends. They all seemed like cardboard cutouts. All but Cholan. But where she looked for *him* in her mind, she couldn't see him anymore. He had vanished.

That was when she knew he was dead.

An automated door on the city's overhead train had given way. Such an accident had never happened before, was thought impossible. Two or three people had been slightly hurt. Cholan was killed.

It was that *simple*.

Lute wrapped herself in steel. She was cool and hard and distant. No one could get in. She didn't *want* them in.

She wanted Cholan, and he was gone. Forever.

Her friends, teachers, teammates, all the people she knew, they were concerned about her, tried to help, grew tired with trying and with her new steel surface. They gave up.

On her own, Lute seldom cried, and then only quietly, not wanting to be heard.

She began to hate the city. The city had killed him. She would leave, go somewhere she could cry really loud if she wanted, somewhere she could scream, and no one would hear.

Odd, though, now she was here in Pioneer Pines, she couldn't cry at all. She had held it back so long, the pain, too, had changed to steel.

For several days Lute camped in the house on Pine Street that had had such famous people grow up in it.

She explored the town, striding up into the hills, which were going back to grass now, blue as Todd Ariano's famous eyes.

She was okay if she kept busy.

At night, worn out from her long treks, she let the rob run her a bath in the portable unfolding tub, cooked supper, ate it. Reprogrammed, the rob was now sulky. It knew it had been stopped from doing what it wanted, which was to have hysterics every time a rat walked past or the foxile trotted up the stairs.

Once Lute saw two felinxes down among the crumbled stores on Main Street. They paid her no attention.

It wasn't till twelve days had gone by that Lute saw her first auxi.

The bird flew in out of the green sky and landed in the pine tree. But the needles weren't to its liking, obviously. After a moment it sailed down to the back porch.

Strange birds, the auxies. Weird.

And then the song began.

Twindle-twindle tweety trrr.

Lute stared at the auxi. Her eyes bulged. She stood up, her mug falling to the floor, spilling the hot tea.

Twindle-twindle—

"No," said Lute. "I'm not going out of my mind. No. I'm just—imagining—"

"You're not," said the auxicap, poised in the open doorway. "You can hear me perfectly plainly. I said, 'Hi, there.'"

Lute shook her head. She turned in horror to stumble away.

That was when she felt the edge of the auxicap's wing brush, gentle and smooth, over the surface of her brain. Immediately Lute grew calm. Her eyes cleared.

She gazed back at the bird.

Twindle, it said.

No. It said, "That's more comfortable, I hope."

"I don't—"

"Most humans we talk to don't hear the words. They just pick up the ideas. But we can help them to feel a little better, if they're receptive. You, though, Lute, are *very* receptive. You have the musician's ear. Maybe that's why."

Lute sat down.

The bird hopped slowly through the room. Meeting the rob—which had frozen to the spot just as Lute had—the auxi tapped it with its beak. The rob let out a little twitter, went to its resting pad, and sat still.

"Machines sometimes respond, too," said the auxi.

"Uh—good . . ."

The auxi perched beside her. It began to tell her of many things about the past of the planet. And of its own kind. Higher Intelligent life existed here. It was the animals who were intelligent, all of them to varying degrees. But the strongest minds existed among the auxicaps. "That isn't our name, of course. Would you care to know the real name of my kind?"

"Y-es—"

"Naturally it's in a different language from those of your own planet, but I think you *do* hear me in your own language? Good, then. The real name for the auxicaps, what we call ourselves, is the Human Race. Shall I tell you," it added, gentle and somehow smiling there in her ears and her mind, "what we call this planet?"

"What?" whispered Lute.

"Earth," said the human auxicap. "It's what most species call their own home place, you know."

When the bird went away, flying off into the sky, Lute still felt calm. But she told herself she'd been dreaming.

That night she did dream. She dreamed she and Cholan were flying together on broad wings over the sky. When she woke, she cried for hours. It was like rain after a dry season.

She saw the auxi—the *human*—only once more. It perched neatly on the top of the unprotesting rob, and told her that, along with the ability to help, its kind—the *human* kind of *this* planet—could often bring out the talents of the other humans, the colonists who had settled here. It told Lute she already had a major talent for music.

"I can't play anymore," said Lute.

She thought, *Here I sit, confiding in a bird.*

It's all right.

The human auxi said, "Is that since Cholan died?"

"Yes. I should forget—I should get over it—but I can't— how can I?"

"You will never forget Cholan, or loving him," said the auxi softly. "So your job now is to make all the world know and love and remember him, with you. Even all those he never met."

"How?" she asked.

"Through your talent. How else? Through songs you'll write and sing. Through the music of your guitar. Your love can't die, even though Cholan died. Let it live, then. Tell it to the world. That's your future—think! Even your name is a musical instrument of your Earth—isn't it? A lute. Play it, then. Play all your music for *him*."

As she rode back toward the city, new shiny songs ran through Lute's mind.

She saw the rolling hills and plains, the prairies starred with fire-colored flowers under the wide green sky.

Pioneer Pines was full of humans again—*auxi* humans.

Who would ever believe it? No one. Don't try to tell.

The rob stirred in the back of the hoverjet.

Twindle, said the rob. *Twindle tweety trrr.*

Are we there yet? the rob had asked her, like a child. And she had understood.

"Soon, rob. Only a few hours. Go to sleep now."

See, Cholan, see, they're kind of alive, too. And maybe you're alive? Someplace else?

He was with her again. She could feel he was, there in her brain that the auxicap had brushed with its wing and opened up like a planet to new songs and new dreams. Cholan was with her. She wasn't alone.

TANITH LEE was born in 1947 in London, England. She was unable to read until almost the age of eight and began writing at the age of nine. After she left school, she worked as a library assistant, shop assistant, a filing clerk, and a waitress. She spent one year at art college.

To date she has published almost eighty novels, thirteen short-story collections, and well over 250 short stories. Four of her radio plays were broadcast by the BBC and she wrote two episodes of the BBC TV cult SF series *Blake's Seven*. She has twice won the World Fantasy Award for short fiction, and was awarded the August Derleth Award in 1980 for her novel *Death's Master*.

Tanith Lee lives with her husband, the writer and artist John Kaiine, on the southeast coast of England.

Her Web site is **www.tanithlee.com**.

AUTHOR'S NOTE

The idea for this story came, like about half of what I write, out of "nowhere." First I got the image of the place—green sky, small township growing and then going back to the wild. *Then* the three heroines arrived, complete with their names and characters. Zelda is named for the wife of F. Scott Fitzgerald, Lute for her music . . . Harrington, I'm not sure. I think I just liked the sound of a girl with a guy's name! I wrote the story in a few days. But I really want to go back to that planet. So sometime it will feature in a longer work.

Pamela Dean

COUSINS

Kisandrion's mother was fond of saying that water always rolled downhill. When Dri was smaller, this fondness had led to a number of juvenile attempts to cause water to do something else. Only twice had the water done anything else.

On the first of these occasions, Dri's older brother chose a sandy hill, and the water at once sank into the sand without a trace. After the argument about whether sinking down into the sand was the same thing as rolling downhill, and the conclusion that sinking was not rolling and that straight down for—here came a subsidiary argument about how far water would sink into sand—that straight down was not the same as downhill, the four of them, Dri and her older brother and younger brother and sister all took the broiling paved road to the top of Mystery Hill. There they conducted an argument about whether it might not be better just to drink the water, which was sensibly resolved by drinking most of it but leaving a spoonful for the experiment.

Dri was nine years old at the time, and believed firmly that any place called Mystery Hill must surely cause everything to behave differently from usual. The water, however, ran down into a crack in the pavement, and its faint trail had dried entirely by the time the other three were done rehashing the argument about how much more water they should have saved.

Later that day, while their mother was putting smeary stuff on their sunburns, she remarked, "You do know that's a metaphor, don't you?"

"It's an analogy, surely?" said their father.

Then it was necessary to go get out their books to find out what an analogy was; and the next day to go call upon a friend who worked in the Levar's Library. When they finally had the matter sorted out to their own satisfaction, Dri's mother attempted to explain over their usual Sunday dinner of fish and sea grass that when she said "water rolls downhill," she meant, roughly, that many small things could invisibly join together to suddenly fall on one's head in a surprising fashion, and that one might be less surprised if one bore this in mind.

The eldest child, Kiffen, and the youngest child, Sinja, had agreed, but Dri and Melandin, the middle children, as well as their father, argued that while resentment or a failure to react promptly might well be mitigated by bearing such things in mind, the initial moment of sheer surprise could not be so easily affected. The experience of Kiffen, who was a newly trained member of the Scarlet Guard, was sifted in the course of this discussion, as well as that of a neighbor who was a retired City Guard. The discussion alone proving unsatisfactory, Dri and Melandin spent a week leaping out at the other members of their family from dark corners and from under the stairs and, once or twice, from behind trees or walls far from home, and then pointing out triumphantly that their beleagured family members ought to have expected them to do so by now and yet were still surprised. No conclusions were reached, but a house rule had to be made about leaping out at people while they were carrying fragile or liquid loads, and another about following family members about the city to surprise them while defaulting on one's own academic or professional duties.

Nobody else's family argued so much as the Dorlianishes did. The upstairs neighbors, who took a dim view of all the discussion even though very little of it involved shouting, felt that the Hrothvekan origins of Dri's mother must explain the Dorlianish family's strange tendency to talk so much and so directedly. Dri had once tried to tell them that her aunts hardly talked at all, let alone directedly, but the upstairs neighbors were too pleased with their own reasoning to notice that they were being argued with.

It was her experience with arguments that got Dri a position in the Red Temple. After a year or so in the Scarlet Guard, Kiffen became an enthusiastic convert to the Faith of the Twin Forces. There was not much religion in Dri's family. A visiting nonarguing aunt had once opined that argument was their religion. As a small child, Dri had found priests of any temple rather unnerving. They all dressed alike and looked so full of concentration. Seeing them made her feel as if a collection of painted soldiers had grown to life size and was looking for her.

Kiffen, however, came home from his training overflowing with enthusiasm. "They give you your very own spiritual adviser!" he informed his intrigued family over their usual Rainday meal of potboil. "And she has to listen to whatever you say about yourself! And she has to figure you out! And if you don't argue she tells you to do it!"

"How would you know what she does if you don't argue?" said Melandin.

"Jairy told me. Jairy makes a mussel look wide open."

"Why does Jairy talk to you, then?" inquired Sinja.

"Because I just keep saying things until he can't keep still anymore."

"Goodness, child, what do you say?" asked his mother.

"I say nice things about people he hates," said Kiffen, with a limpid look.

"How do you know he hates them, if the only way you can get him to talk is to—"

"I observe his expressions."

"When I hate people," remarked Dri, "I don't let them have any expressions of mine."

"Why, Dri," said her mother, "whom do you hate, and why?"

Dri was thinking of a certain fruit merchant who did not fall in with the usual City custom of letting children take the bruised fruit without paying. But Kiffen said, "She hates our aunt Mininu."

"I certainly do not!"

"You certainly do," said Kiffen. "Whenever she comes to visit, your face looks just like a statue."

"Kisandrion Dorlianish! You must not hate your aunt!" said her mother.

"Why not?" said Kisandrion, who did not actually hate her aunt but was deeply in awe of her, which was a very uncomfortable feeling; hatred would have felt cozier. "I don't have to live with her."

"You may one day."

"Why?"

"Should the pot of Liavekan politics ever boil over," said her mother, "I'll send you all to her by the fastest way."

"If the pot boils over," said Kiffen, while Dri stared horrified, "will the water run downhill?"

"Indeed it will," said their mother.

"What if potboil runs downhill?" cried Sinja.

"What if Dri came to work with me after school?" said Kiffen.

"I don't want to be a guard," said Dri.

"They want another clerk in the library. You could do that."

"Would I get to read the books?"

"They haven't books, really, they have archives."

"But would I get to read them?"

"I don't know, Dri. Come to work with me and find out."

So Dri, whose childhood ambition had been to own and pull a footcab, catching nefarious villains in the process, came to work for the Red Temple. She did not ask about reading the archives. Mundri, the chief librarian of this branch of the

Red Temple's documents, was almost as forbidding as Dri's not-hated, nonarguing aunt. Mundri did not brook much argument either. When Dri pointed out that one's spiritual advisers told one to argue, Mundri said dryly that Dri could argue with the priests all she liked, but she was not to argue in the library.

Dri liked her priest, a young placid woman called Atliae. Atliae argued with her, but Atliae also let her talk. At home, unless one happened to be bleeding heavily or running a fever, it was more or less impossible to speak more than a sentence without having it discussed in detail. Their mother had had to be very firm repeatedly before the bleeding and the fevers were let off the general requirement of discussion. Dri enjoyed home quite a lot, but talking about herself in paragraphs was enchanting, like eating as many cinnamon cakes as you wanted and neither being scolded nor ending up with a stomachache.

This happy state of affairs lasted for a month or two, and then the stomachache showed up. Atliae greeted Dri one Luckday morning by saying, "You have got on so well that we can go on to the second chapter of your training sooner than usual."

In the second chapter, Dri did not get to talk about herself in paragraphs; instead, she got to tell Atliac about five choices she had made in the preceding week, and Atliae would then tell her why the choices were not good ones. For every choice she had made, whether it was to lie to her mother about whom she fancied at work or school, to tell her sister the truth about who ate the last cinnamon cake, to buy her mother a bottle of lavender water or to adopt a litter of kittens that were living under the house, to read a poem or write one, to write a letter to her country cousins or to throw a tantrum about the necessity of doing so, she had to contrive a deed that was that choice's opposite in magnitude and nature, and then do that.

They had a terrific shouting match about the kittens. Dri's first suggestion was that she put them and their mother back under the house, and she had to suffer a long and, for Atliae, impassioned lecture about how impossible it was to undo anything, ever, under any circumstances. Dri did not much heed this at the time because she wondered whether Atliae had somehow divined her intention of continuing to feed and brush the kittens even when they were back under the house.

Her second suggestion, that she give away the cat puppets that had taken a lot of her time and thought before she found the kittens, evoked a much calmer but equally long lecture about the inefficacy of symbolism and substitution in such a situation. Dri finally suggested that she give Sinja away instead. Atliae said briefly, "Sinja is not yours to give." Dri had no way of telling whether Atliae knew the suggestion was not serious or whether, much more intriguing, she would have entertained it if Sinja had been Dri's child instead of her sister.

"What do you suggest, then?" demanded Dri.

"You could find another litter of kittens and drown it," said Atliae.

Dri got up. "No," she said.

"Sit down, Dri; we haven't finished."

"I am not sitting down with a drowner of kittens."

"No, indeed now you are not, though certainly you have done so many times unknowing."

"Good people don't let their cats have dozens of kittens!"

Atliae looked dubious. Dri, her belief in Atliae's wisdom eroding rapidly, said in exasperation, "All you have to do is give them Worrynot."

"Some people's cats don't like the taste," said Atliae. Dri opened her mouth to provide a list of methods of giving medicine to cats whether the cats liked the taste or not, but Atliae went on, "In any case, a person can be too good."

"Well, I know that," said Dri, thinking of her eldest cousin on her father's side, who was a model of deportment, according to himself and also to Dri's parents. Then she thought through this initial thought, as Atliae had taught her to do. What was good about deportment, after all? You could bet that it didn't feed anybody—in fact, it slowed down how well you could feed yourself at the table—and it didn't save any kittens either. "Good at what?" she said cautiously.

Atliae grinned at her. She did not look like a person who would drown kittens. "That is a useful distinction," she said—this being perhaps the highest praise Atliae could bestow on a remark as opposed to a deed, "but it is sideways to our purposes. Hark now."

At this signal of a long speech, Dri sat down with her feet on the floor and put a cushion firmly behind her back. Atliae did not like it if you let your feet go to sleep and then tried to wake them up again while she was talking.

"Here is the fashion of the world," said Atliae. She was not a very dramatic speaker, but her voice took on a faint tinge of the storyteller's rhythm. "Two great forces there are, continually at war. We call the one Good, and the other Evil; and yet they remain upright only by virtue of the pressure that they exert, the one upon the other. Should either of them vanish or be vanquished, the other would collapse. Whether the other force would vanish also or merely assume a form so alien that the world would fail, we do not know, though many rolls of paper and gallons of ink have been expended in essays to prove the inevitability of one or the other event."

Dri was thrilled. She thought of the two forces as astrological drawings, their forms imposed on the wandering patterns of the stars, one gold and one red, arms upraised, eyes shut in concentration, each forcing the other upright so that the world of kittens and sand and spicy lentils and family and rain and railroads might continue.

"We are all part of this struggle," said Atliae. "In each of us it goes on in miniature."

Dri thought of herself as a dollhouse with the sky painted on the wall. She was somewhat less thrilled.

"And though few of us could bring down the world entire, we can all bring down the world that is our particular self."

I'd rather bring down the world entire, thought Dri. Atliae probably knew this, but Dri preferred not to say it just the same.

"The Twin Forces of good and evil must be balanced," said Atliae. "They must be truly twins. You must strive to keep them equal in yourself."

That said, Dri was still deeply preoccupied with the kittens. She knew without having to consider the matter that she was going to keep them and was not going to harm them. If behaving so brought down the equally braced forces of her particular self, perhaps it would be interesting to see what that was like. But her decision did not matter to whether the argument must go on. "If I found a sick cat," she said, "and took it to a healer and it had to be put down . . ."

"I'm afraid you are very literal," said Atliae, shaking her head.

Dri had heard this before from her parents and was not much impressed. In fact, as usual, a comment upon her literalness made her take it further. "Well, if you won't let me do anything opposite," she said, "what if I rather sneaked up on the middle again in little steps by doing smaller and smaller good things until I did a not-good, not-bad thing?"

Atliae actually clapped her hands and exclaimed, "Well done, well done!" This was when Dri realized that the Faith of the Twin Forces was made for her.

Matters proceeded in this pleasing fashion for most of a year. The kittens grew long-legged and were given to the baker on Dri's street, whose cat was getting too old to be interested in mousing; to the healer two streets over, who looked lonely to Dri; and, astonishingly, to Mundri, who, it developed, liked cats much better than she liked people. Dri was left with the ugliest kitten, not having troubled to mention his patient disposition. He even let them see whether water would roll downhill on his fluffy unevenly striped tail. It was lucky that nobody thought of seeing if potboil would boil downhill on his tail, because he would probably have let them try that, too. He was much interested in all family activities, and was so often tripped over that they named him after Ghologhosh, the god of small curses.

Not long after the making of this momentous decision, suddenly it was the twelfth day of the month of Flowers, and Dri turned fourteen years old. She was not interested in her inborn luck; the danger and trouble of investing it into a usable object so that she could perform magic did not seem to her worth the rewards. She thought that she would prefer to rely on her wits. There had been, naturally, a great deal of argument about this decision all through her childhood, but after this birthday, nobody brought up the subject again.

She did not talk about it with Atliae, and perhaps oddly, Atliae did not ask her about it either. Dri puzzled herself over the matter for some little time. Surely it was a momentous decision, to abandon one's birthright and decline the acquisition of power. But like the decision to take care of the kittens, it seemed to be beyond argument, a thing she would simply do, like breathing. She did, once her birthday was a week or so past, ask Atliae whether a thing that seemed as natural as breathing might be viewed as a choice by the Twin Forces.

Atliae, after a much longer pause than usual, said that one should strive to make as few of one's actions in life like breathing, and as many like taking a life or having a child, as possible. Dri remarked that many people did both those things pretty much as if they were the same as breathing, and Atliae was rather short with her instead of arguing. Dri put this down to the late Spring heat, which Atliae didn't like, and thought that she would wait to bring the matter up again until Fog or even Frost.

Once her birthday was weeks and weeks past, her family became so embroiled in enthralling discussions of what should happen at her coming-of-age party that neither water's running nor potboil's boiling was mentioned at all except in purely practical terms.

When the pot did boil over, it was not the entire pot of Liavekan politics, but a different pot. It was the Red Temple.

Dri's experience of the Red Temple was limited to her brother, Atliae, Mundri, and her fellow clerks, who acquired their positions and left them with irregular frequency, usually after either repeatedly professing boredom or having a huge battle with Mundri over some minor detail. People did come to use the library, but it was always Mundri who talked to them. Kiffen, however, saw and spoke to ten times as many inhabitants of their faith as Dri did, and he always kept her well informed of all the gossip. So she knew quite well that the head of the whole affair, His Scarlet Eminence, Regent of all Liavek until the Levar came of age, was named Resh, and was both soft-spoken and much feared. She did not specifically fear him herself, since he did not seem to be interested in her library, and since Mundri's behavior and remarks implied strongly that among Mundri's high and sacred duties was the doling out of a proper amount of fear in His Scarlet Eminence's direction. He seemed more an eccentricity of Mundri's than an active force.

On a dazzlingly hot day in the month of Fruit, Kiffen came breathlessly into the library. Even in the midst of crisis, he upheld Mundri's rules. He came in at the beginning of the recess allowed Dri for her luncheon, and he said nothing to her until they were outside the library proper. Then he took her elbow and hustled her out into Gold Street. "We're going home," he said.

"I haven't time to—"

"We must go home."

Dri contemplated him. He looked as if his cat had died. She hoped hers was all right. If not, though, surely he would just say so. She fell into step with him. She did not stop arguing, but she did not stop walking either. They went home through the empty noontime streets, squinting at the dancing of dust motes in the dry bright air.

Their mother was preserving garlic, but did not scold them for interrupting. She put down her knife.

"Resh is dead," said Kiffen.

Their mother slid off her high wooden stool, picked up the jug of vinegar, put it down again. "Quick, Dri, bring me my pen and ink," she said.

Dri, going, heard Kiffen say in a voice that began low and firm and squeaked halfway through, "I can't leave the City."

Sinja had borrowed the ink again, and had also sequestered the paper under her bed. While discovering these facts, Dri thought that she could not leave the City either. Her work, her cat, her coming-of-age party; the necessity of preventing Melandin from disgracing them all or killing himself accidentally; the necessity of educating Sinja not to be like Melandin; fireworks in the Levar's Park and the long-legged white cadies wading in the Salt Marsh; the escaped white geese and the wild white ducks on the Cat River; her friends in the next street, all condemned to years more of school to become apothecaries, who listened so breathlessly to her tales of the real outside world. No, she could not leave the City.

When she returned to the kitchen with the objects she had been sent to fetch, Kiffen was sitting at the table with a lowering expression and her mother had filled up two more jars of garlic. "I am writing to your aunts," said her mother. "Go and fill one pack for each of you. Dri, I will be good to your cat."

"Why can't I take Golly with me?" demanded Dri, and was immediately aware of having made a mistake.

"Don't fret, Dri, I'll look after him," said Kiffen.

Dri opened her mouth and then shut it again. She had always felt, even before first Kiffen and then she came of age, that their arguments had force, that they were attended to, if sometimes laughed at, that they helped to keep the house standing and people in a right relation to one another. But the way her mother was writing and not attending, as if she had suddenly gone deaf, made speaking seem useless. Kiffen's blithe tactic, of speaking as if what he wanted had already been accomplished, usually got him just what he wanted, to Dri's intense annoyance; but it was not working now. She thought there must be a thing to say that would restore rightness, but she did not know what it was.

Sinja arrived at that moment with a tremendous noise of slapping sandals, ready for her lunch. She looked around and did not ask why it was not ready. She edged up under her mother's unoccupied elbow and announced, "I didn't do anything wrong."

"Sinja can help me look after your cat," said their mother, still writing.

"Why can't Dri—"

"Because she is going to the great plains on a visit."

"Why?"

"Because His Scarlet Eminence is dead."

"Dri! Did you kill him?"

Dri sat down and laughed. There was nothing else to do except pack. After half a moment's serious consideration, she packed her cat. If she carried the bag in her arms instead of pulling the drawstring tight and putting it over her shoulder, he would be able to breathe. She put only a shirt or two of her own in the bottom of the bag. She had the vague impression that farmers were very poor—a great many stories told in the marketplace began, *Once, my excellencies, there was a poor farmer who*—But if she must go about wearing a flour sack, it was all the same to her. Who would see her in the country, after all?

She got Sinja's attention while their mother was talking Kiffen out of taking his entire wardrobe, and showed her Golly curled in the pack, and told her to wait until after dinner and then tell her mother where the cat was. Sinja's ordinary response to being told anything at all was to balk, but she nodded solemnly, rubbed Golly's nose, and said, "After dinner and before sweets, or after sweets, too?"

"After sweets, too, unless she asks you," said Dri.

In other circumstances, the journey might have been exciting and full of interest. Dri did her best to be excited and interested. Riding out of Liavek in a cart full of cloth and earthenware was nothing new. She had done it many times on her own, staying at the shore or in the marsh for the day and making her return trip in a cart full of cabbages or mint or fish. Kiffen had shown her how it was all done. He had shown her hawks, dragonflies, river rats, sea otters, blackbirds, bluebirds, redbirds, and mockingbirds. He had discoursed on the military difficulties of the desert and the tides in the Saltmarsh and the building of the railroad.

Now, however, as they rode in a small cart and then a large cart and then a very small cart, farther and farther into a huger and huger blue sky, while the accustomed shapes of the earth dwindled and flattened and the road narrowed to a point like an impossibly long waxed-paper cone of soup bought in some giants' version of the Levar's Park, Kiffen did not discourse. He sulked. Dri showed him a red hawk and a blue dragonfly and a running camel, possibly the one carrying a mailbag that included her mother's letter to the aunts, warning of her and Kiffen's coming. But he did not even look at her.

Her cat was not troubled by the first cart, from whose driver one could purchase tidbits of fried fish; nor by the larger cart, which was full of dried seaweed; but even though the smallest cart held jars of cream, oddly being driven away from the City rather than toward it, he protested about every bump and jostle, and did not purr at anything. By the time the driver put them down on a crossroads distinguished from all the others by a clump of three gnarled trees and a parcel of goats, they were a disheveled and grumpy bunch. Before they could also become lost, Mininu stood up from where she had been talking to the goats and walked to meet them. In the City she had always looked to Dri like the goddess of night, so tall and so dark with flecks of white like stars in her crown of black hair. Under the empty sky of the country, in her brown tunic and leggings with a cap on her hair, she seemed smaller and more like a person.

They must both have looked quite fretful, because her first words were, "Never worry, I have your mother's letter." She added as she touched her forehead in greeting and then patted their shoulders, "She didn't say that you were bringing any more livestock."

"He's very clever," said Dri, "and I'll keep him out of trouble. He's very meek with other cats, they don't mind him."

"Oh, we have no cats. Your cousins will be happy to see him. I suppose he sleeps on your bed. You will want to talk to Numa about that." She relieved Kiffen of his huge pack, removed Dri's smaller one from her shoulder with her other hand, and walked off down the northern road, leaving them to follow. Golly bumped his head under Dri's chin, which was an improvement on his behavior of the previous day and night.

The walk took perhaps as long as it would to go from Dri's house to the far end of the Levar's Park, but it was otherwise unlike any walk she had ever taken. The road was made of gravel, like the gardens at the Tichenese Embassy, except that their gravel was black and red and green and pure white, and this was a dusty gray. The land looked as flat as a griddle, but from time to time one's legs would give notice that in fact the road was going up and then down and then up again, in a stealthy fashion.

Dri did not realize that they were near the house until they were almost upon it. It was screened from the north and east by a triple row of mixed cedar trees, which Dri recognized, and leafy ones shaped like an elongated drop of water, which she did not. The house was made of cedarwood and gray and white stone, with a roof of cedar. It had no upstairs, and was very well supplied with windows. When Kiffen remarked on this, Mininu said, "Yes, this country has never been fortified. We have been the cause of many wars, but they all took place on the seas."

Mininu, who came from Ombaya, was their thin aunt. Their other aunt, their round aunt, their mother's sister, was called Sinja, and Dri's sister had of course been named after her.

The elder Sinja came running out of the house, trailed by two people taller than she was and one much shorter. Mininu and Sinja were raising three children, two from Ombaya—the tall ones, a boy and a girl called Wari and Welo, respectively—and one from Liavek—the short one, a much younger girl who was called Numa.

Dri had expected a great many farmhands, and not only cats but dogs. There were none of these, and this seemed a small family to do the work of a farm. They were all usually busy doing something or the other, and whenever Kiffen and Dri, who stayed together like each other's shadow for the first few days, came across them, work was offered, but smilingly and offhandedly. Apples appeared in bins and goat's milk in churns, and sometimes even cheese upon the table, without Dri's being able to see that anybody had picked any apples or milked any goats.

Fields of tall grass were mown and the grass gathered in cunning hillocks that, Wari explained proudly, would shed even the heaviest rain. But Dri had seen none of the family in the hayfield. The goats moved here and there, but nobody seemed to be telling them what to do. Then again, they were goats. The chickens were another matter, though. She had been shown how to feed the chickens that first night, but two mornings later she forgot and rushed out in a panic, followed by a mewing cat also with a point to make about his own late breakfast, and the chickens were pecking at corn that she had not scattered. She knew where her cousins and aunts had been all morning. Perhaps they worked all night, sneaking out of the children's common sleeping room after their soft city cousins were asleep. Dri stayed awake as long as she could on the fourth night, but nobody left the room.

Dri settled down insofar as she knew how to pump water for a bath and where the woodpile was, but she felt, on the whole, unsettled. There seemed to be nothing in the house to read but schoolbooks. She missed the library and the orderly progression of her work there. She even missed Mundri. When she sat or worked with her thin cousins, she felt like one of many nails made without much thought by a skilled smith, or a paper lantern of the cheaper sort that nobody had bothered to paint a special flower or character on. It was Kiffen with his round face and heavy shoulders who looked special. She wondered if she should be eating twice as much as usual, but that had never made any difference before.

Besides, she hated the food. It was all animal stuff: chicken, eggs, chicken fat, egg fat for all she knew; milk and cheese and milk fat; sometimes goat, and of course goat fat. And it had no flavor to speak of other than its own fat animal flavor. Once they had a dish of lentils and she pounced on it with glee, only to find it coated with chicken fat and bits of meat, and quite inedible.

Golly loved the food, and began to look rather round himself.

In addition to being thin while eating fat, her cousins did not talk. This was the way Dri put it to herself. They did talk, really. That first evening at dinner, they exclaimed over Golly and asked his history and his habits; they asked after young Sinja and Melandin and their parents; they asked about Kiffen's work and Dri's work and what the railroad was like. They seemed to want only description, though. Dri and Kiffen's energetic disagreement about the amount of money the Red Temple possesed elicited only a polite silence.

Ending this silence none too soon for Dri, Mininu said, "Your mother's letter was rather hurried. I see that the Red Temple is now without a leader."

"Well, of course Resh's deputy Pitullio would—" began Kiffen.

"I think it would be just as well," said Mininu, "if this news were kept within the family for the time being. It will arrive from the City by a myriad of means soon enough, but I would prefer that nobody speak of it to anyone until one of us has heard it as gossip first."

"But we may whisper it at bedtime," said Wari.

"I think not for the present," said Mininu.

"May I ask one thing?" said Numa, the youngest cousin.

Dri's only memory of her was of a two-year-old screeching because she was afraid of the black dragonflies in the Saltmarsh, but she seemed steadier now.

"If your question is kept nameless," said Sinja the aunt.

"Why did our cousins' parents send them out of the City?"

Dri was much interested, since she was the one whose life had been upended. She watched Sinja and Mininu exchange glances and then nods. How could they talk without talking?

"A great leader, good or ill," said Mininu after this silent communication was concluded, "is like the keystone of an arch. Remove her and stones will fall."

"Water always rolls downhill," said Numa.

"Very sensible, Numa," said Sinja.

"But how can you be prepared for that kind of surprise?" demanded Dri.

Her aunts and cousins looked at her as if she had spoken in Ombayan—except that they knew Ombayan. Tichenese, perhaps. Kiffen said thoughtfully, "Really, you know, how can it be a surprise if it always happens?"

"Well, silly," said Dri, exasperated, "if it happens whenever there is an occasion for it to happen but there is not often an occasion."

"It's better not to call names," said Sinja, very kindly.

Dri looked at Kiffen, who gave her a very slight shrug. Neither of them said anything else. There seemed a kind of resistance against speech in the room itself, so that to consider speaking was like pushing against a stuck door.

They had arrived on a Luckday, and after almost a week

of the relentless sameness of meals, Dri had begun to think
that she would starve or survive on windfall apples and the
occasional potato rescued from being boiled, mashed, and
smothered in sour cream. Then Rainday came around. For
breakfast, there was congee. Dri approached it warily, expecting a huge blob of butter or sour cream or chicken fat, but
it was quite innocent of these embellishments. It was full of
parsley, chives, and spinach rather than ginger, green onion,
and seaweed, but she didn't care. She devoured three bowl-
fuls, and Mininu looked at her thoughtfully.

At lunch they had a stew of potatoes, green beans, carrots,
and mushrooms, with garlic and brown sauce. Dri wondered
if she could save the leftovers under her bed and eat them
all week. Brown sauce was very preserving, her mother said.
Unfortunately, Golly liked it. At dinner they had sour cabbage
soup with wheat dumplings. Sour cream was offered, but it
was not assumed to be everybody's favorite.

She was trying to concoct a way to ask about the abrupt
change of menu, and whether it might last a long, long time,
without sounding snooty, judgmental, whiny, or spoiled, when
Wari, the eldest, heaved a gigantic sigh and proclaimed, "How
I hate Raindays!"

Both aunts looked at him warningly; he pushed out his
lower lip and, ostentatiously reaching for the bowl of sour
cream, covered the surface of his soup with it. Welo rolled her
eyes in a sisterly fashion.

That seemed to settle that. In a normal family, Dri would
have asked what was so special about Rainday, but here that
would probably be done in sign language of some sort. She

might raise her eyebrows, and perhaps one aunt or another would give her a little book for farm children, and the answer would be in the last chapter. This thought amused her so much that she laughed, and got two warning looks of her own.

"I love Rainday," she said calmly.

"There, Wari, you see," said Sinja.

Wari rolled his eyes again. Dri bit her tongue on the remark that he wouldn't see much for long if he kept doing that.

She tried to repeat this witticism to Kiffen later, but Kiffen was proving a frail reed. Not only did he love the fat animal food, he very shortly vanished into this new family culture as if he had been born to it. Dri wondered if he would even want to come home with her. She caught him in the apple orchard that Rainday evening and asked him outright.

"Do try not to be insane," he said, an old family remark that cheered Dri quite a lot. "Of course I wouldn't want to stay here always. It would be like one endless Festival Week—no proper work and rich food, day after day."

"And no proper talk," said Dri wistfully.

"Yes, truly, a fine meditative silence."

"There is nothing fine about it."

"Not being challenged to a duel every five seconds is fine."

"Do try not to be insane," said Dri, but her heart was not in it.

Kiffen said comfortingly, "I would like to be at my work this moment."

"Kiffen," said Dri, and had to pause and breathe as if she had been running. She wanted to ask a question, but it was very hard. Finally she said, "I think that you know what happened to Resh, and I want you to tell me."

"I don't precisely know," said Kiffen. "I have an idea. One hears stories, you know, and perhaps I put them together in the wrong order. But Resh wanted the Red Temple to be first in Liavek. He wanted to drive the other temples out. When he was a little drunk, my captain said that Resh had given the orders that destroyed the Gold Temple. I think that perhaps he tried to drive out some faith or god that was stronger than he was."

"But, Kiffen! There is nothing one could do that would balance an act like that." Dri looked up at the sky; she felt that it ought to be falling.

"I don't believe that we really understand others' acts," said Kiffen. "We only understand how those acts would be if we had done them ourselves. So you or I, we couldn't balance a huge act like that. But we are not Resh."

"And Resh is dead," said Dri. She thought of a dollhouse, a tall and imposing and richly furnished dollhouse, its rooftree upheld by the striving figures. Resh had ordered the destruction of the Gold Temple; the red figure, then, might hook its heel behind the ankle of the gold one, and then the house would fall on them both. What need of a stronger god to seek revenge when one could bring down all by oneself? She shivered.

They were looking at each other, feeling at a loss, when they heard their names being called. Welo, who tended toward dreaminess, was trudging through the orchard, calling without bothering to look. Kiffen hailed her, and she looked startled. "It's Rainday," she said. "Come back to the house for the Affirmation."

She walked off again, and they followed after a moment. Dri said to her brother, "I wonder if the Twin Forces are here, too."

"The Twin Forces are everywhere. They hold up the world. They are in all of us."

"I wonder if they are in the Way of Herself."

"Of course."

"I think the Ombayans would say the Way of Herself was in the Twin Forces."

"They can say what they like," said Kiffen.

Dri glared at him. That was not a cooperative remark. It discouraged argument. He was ingesting more than the wrong food. The effort was great, but she said, as she would have said without a second thought at home, "I thought there were different gods in different places."

"There are," said Kiffen briefly, "but the Twin Forces are above gods."

"There is no way to know that," said Dri, who was not actually possessed of such firm opinions but could think of no better way to phrase her real question.

"It's obvious," said her brother loftily.

They had almost reached the house, and Wari was already holding the door open for them. This gesture looked polite but actually, Dri and Kiffen had privately agreed, indicated impatience. Dri said hurriedly, "We don't know what they do on Rainday."

"If they don't tell us, it's their fault," muttered Kiffen.

This was not comforting. However, the Affirmation was

brief and wordless. Dri and Kiffen went to stand with the cousins in the big room with windows on three sides where the weaving and reading were done. Mininu and Sinja had taken a red cloth from a wooden chest and opened the lid to reveal a collection of candles and cups stored in a carved tray made of dozens of small sections. They bowed to the children and to one another, lit candles, poured water into various vessels and finally onto the floor, and then lifted a large wooden cup between them and drank from it one after the other. Sinja brought the goblet to Wari; he drank and passed it to Welo, who drank and passed it to Numa; and so it came finally to Kiffen, who sipped cautiously and gave Dri a reassuring wink along with the goblet.

Dri took a cautious sip of her own and almost gasped. The water was cold and had a complicated flowery flavor. The room was stuffy and warm, and she would have liked to gulp from the goblet, but nobody else had. So she refrained.

People separated to their various occupations without speaking, but Dri lingered in the big room while Sinja briskly packed everything into the trunk again. She had never participated in a religious ritual before and wanted to think about it. The Red Temple did have rituals involving the Twin Forces, but Atliae had told her that she was not ready for the large public ones, let alone anything smaller and more secret. This first experience had been so everyday and matter-of-fact, except for the shock of the water.

"I hope that you have something to do, Dri," said Sinja.

This meant, "Try not to be idle," but it was also an inquiry into her well-being.

"I was going to read some history while the light lasts," said Dri. Her cousins had settled on the idea that the library she worked in was for historians, and they seemed concerned that she would forget her knowledge if not gently nagged.

"Good, good. There are plenty of candles," said Sinja, and went out. She had not wiped up the spilled water.

Dri walked over to the place where Mininu and Sinja had been standing. The water had reached out a long finger toward the south, and another to the east. Dri was surprised. She took from her pocket a marble that she kept in case Golly should want more amusement than he could provide for himself. She bent and put the marble on the polished wide board next to the pool of water. It rolled north and fetched up under Sinja's loom. Having done this, Dri was not sure what she had discovered. After a moment she got the largest of the history books and studied the map in the middle of it. Ombaya was south of the plains the farm stood on, and Liavek was to the east. Dri retrieved Golly's marble and went to get herself a drink of ordinary water from the pump in the kitchen.

Then she went about the house, with the pewter cup of ordinary water in her hand. In all the rooms that she entered, the water from the pump that she poured out of the pewter cup spread slowly or ran eagerly in the same direction as the marble rolled. The floors of the house were like the land about it; they seemed flat but were really made of a great many small ups and downs. Golly appeared, stretching, about halfway through her activities, and aside from one moment when he rolled in the water and was affronted, he was useful in that he could always find the marble and bat it back to the center of the room. His mishap also made her think of what would happen if anybody slipped on the water she had left, so she went about wiping up all the pools she had left behind. The pool of water from the Affirmation had somehow disappeared on its own.

She was obliged to omit the kitchen and the room where all the children slept from her roster, since that was where people were in the evenings. She dealt with the sleeping room the next morning by being late to breakfast, but she despaired of the kitchen's ever being empty. Someone was almost always cooking something or making bread or preserving fruit or using the large table for carving or writing.

Her natural impulse in such a puzzlement would have been to consult Kiffen, but she felt somewhat hurt over their conversation in the orchard. A little pondering, however, provided her with a very likely idea of what he would have suggested.

So that night she kept herself awake by reciting songs and poems to herself, and when her supply of these ran dry, by naming all the rivers and mountains in and around Liavek. Then she tried to list all the Levars of Liavek, and their Regents, where those had been necessary. Her knowledge was still too imperfect to let her make much of a list, so she considered instead her scheme to find out which way water ran in all the rooms of the house. She thought that perhaps she had been driven to action because it was so hard to simply ask questions in this house. But there was something homelike, too, in seeing what water would do, even if she had no family members to help her.

Her brother and cousins were asleep very soon, but she could hear Sinja and Mininu moving about the rest of the house, and then the murmur of their voices, and then silence. Some time passed. The air sliding through the open windows became cool, the leaves of the oak trees rustled, and finally, caught in their branches, she saw the bright fat crescent that was the waning moon. She got up carefully. Golly stood up from his position at her feet and settled onto her pillow while she was still looking for her slippers.

Even after such long staring into the dark, she could not see very much. It was fortunate that on account of the food's disagreeing with her in the first days of her visit, she had been told to change beds with Numa so that she might sleep nearer the door. She made her way very slowly, if not patiently, to the kitchen, mostly holding her breath. She had pumped a cup of water after dinner and left it behind a stack of bowls in a lower cupboard. She got it out with only a single ring of pewter against earthenware. It sounded like the largest gong owned by the Red Temple to her, but nobody seemed to stir after.

Dri tilted the cup, and stopped, wanting very much to laugh. She had forgotten that she would need light. What a pity I never invested my luck, she thought. Almost any street magician can make a little light. She put the cup down on the table and groped in the table's drawer for a candle. The fire in the stove never went out; Mininu had told her so, during that first day when it had been permitted for the cousins to ask about Liavek and for Dri and Kiffen to ask about the house. She opened the oven door. A red glow came out, but no heat. She hoped it would light her candle. It did, with a whoosh that made her jump back, feeling glad that she had laid hold of a long, new candle rather than a stub.

Finally, finally, she was able to sit firmly on the worn stone floor with cup, candle, and marble, and make her investigation. The flickering thread of water moved, unsurprisingly, toward the hollow worn in front of the stove by several generations of cooks. The marble followed. Something white streaked through the candlelight, pounced on the marble, and knocked it with an enormous clang into the iron base of the oven. Dri muffled her squeak of surprise. I thought cats were stealthy, she thought at Golly. He was waiting for her to pick up the marble, and she did so, and put it in her pocket. Luckily for her, he was not a talkative cat and merely stared and followed her when she went to sit down at the table and get her breath back.

The big squares of the windows were pale. Dri looked up and out and saw, over the flat land with no intervening towers or hills, the fat crescent moon lighting up the whole eastern sky. It would be dawn soon. Her startlement had thoroughly woken her up. She would go out with her cat and watch the sun rise.

There was a welcome chill in the air. All the grasses and little trees were drenched in dew. Golly came out of the grass after a single exploration, shaking his paws and ears, and thereafter stayed on the path with Dri.

In Liavek, if you wanted to watch the sun or moon rise or set, you went up a hill, or if you did not want to walk so far, you went up on the roof of any building you could get to, preferably one with a garden and seats. She was not sure what to do here. The sky was so much larger that perhaps it hardly mattered. The apple orchard was on a south-facing slope of what passed for a hill. The eastern slope of that hill was a garden of onions, in raised beds. She could sit on the stone edge of a bed and have a good view.

When she had settled there, in the strange half-light, Dri felt exposed. It was as bad as the sea and somewhat worse than the desert. It was so very flat. Parts of Liavek were flat, but there were buildings and trees breaking up the sky, providing shade and concealment. She didn't know what she thought was going to catch her, but here, whatever it was, if it wanted to come out of the sky and pluck her up as a hawk does a mouse, where could she hide?

At least, she thought, sitting straight on the cold stone of the garden edge and glaring at the huge colorless bowl above her, she would hear the hawk coming. The silence was as enormous as the flatness. And yet her ears were so unattuned to it, perhaps she would not after all hear the hawk. Because she had always lived in the City, she knew how to listen for voices, footsteps, drunken brawls and drunken revelry; wheels, hooves, paws; windows opening, nails going into wood, water sloshing in buckets, students of music practicing the flute and professionals playing the drum; the clatter of dishes and tiles, the shriek of the train whistle and the singing rumble of the train. Here in the country, she knew that the wind was making a sound in the grass, but her ears dismissed it as a barrier to hearing the sounds that she wanted, which were not there.

But we are there, she did not hear but heard somehow, and then, not believably, *If we were there, she would hear us, so where are we? Or where is she?* It was the kind of thing she thought all day long, taken out of her head and put into the rustle of the dry grasses in the ceaseless breeze. Was this how it was to be insane?

This thought upset her so much that she took a great breath and spoke to the grass and the apple trees and the empty air. If one were going to be mad, one might as well do the thing thoroughly. Mundri was always intent on doing anything thoroughly. "I want to know who you are," she said.

The wind stopped making the grasses hiss. Now it was truly silent, a silence that made Dri feel even more as if she might fall off the unsafe flat surface of the earth and into the great beckoning sky. Her cat had disappeared. She wanted to clear her throat, to shout, to scuff her boots in the dry grass. But something was waiting to speak; she felt it.

When it spoke it was much more like a voice, alive in the chilly moving air. "The stranger should rather say than ask."

Oh, thought Dri, is that why it is so hard to ask anything? They might have said something before. She said, "I am Kisandrion Dorlianish, and I come from the City of Luck."

"Ahhhhh," said the voice, said several voices, unless it was only the wind.

"You sound as if you know my city," she said.

"We are exiles therefrom."

"So am I," said Dri, and sighed.

"Why so?"

"My mother thought it wasn't safe for my brother and me to stay."

The wind began again, hiss, rustle, whisper, scratch. It

sounded like a gigantic grassy conference. Maybe it was. Dri did not know what lived out here that was not people or domestic animals and birds. In the mountains were the shy gray mountain folk; in the sea were Kil; in the desert were trolls. But here among the farms, all the stories were simple and prosaic. Magical beans, golden duck eggs, cows that gave an endless amount of cream, talking goats, silver apples, geese that riddled and pigs that sang. But wait, the wind voice was not a thing native here; it had said that it was an exile from the City. She frowned, thinking. The City was full of everything, of course, from far and near, and an exile might not mean a native creature, just an accustomed one. Still, what had the City itself that might speak with the voice of the grass, unseen? Chipmunks, she thought, and giggled.

The wind stopped at once; the grass was silent. The sun had come up; she had not noticed. Dri's impulse was to speak, to repeat her question, to explain why she was laughing. But people hereabouts did not seem to use speech as she and her family used it. She hugged herself in the chill and tried not to think of chipmunks. The oldest, most luck-soaked things in Liavek were all remnants of the older city on whose site Liavek was built; but older than that were the chipmunks. They had their own god, Rikiki, who was blue, and irresistibly funny as long as you stayed out of his way. Her imagination peopled the brown and green and golden landscape around her with blue chipmunks, and she giggled again.

"Is exile a matter for laughter?" said the voice.

"No," said Dri hastily.

"What is, then?"

"I was thinking of chipmunks," said Dri, feeling somewhat helpless. She was so tired of not being able to ask questions that it was a relief to answer anybody who did.

"Do you follow Rikiki?"

"No," said Dri. "But I like the chipmunks in the Levar's Park. Once one of them ran up my leg and stole a roasted potato from my hand."

She felt entirely foolish as soon as she had made this childish remark, but the voice said, "A wise denizen, indeed," and did not seem sarcastic.

Dri put her hand to her forehead in formal acknowledgment, and said, "I thank you."

There was a brief pause in which the sky seemed less full of threats.

"We had hoped for better news," said the dry voice suddenly; Dri jumped. "We had hoped to hear that the City was safer."

"Well, mothers have particular ideas, you know," said Dri. "The City seemed just the same to me. And if Resh was so dangerous, I would think the City was safer without him."

The drooping grasses around her stood up straight, like the hair on a cat's back when the cat is angry. "Do you tell us that Resh has left the City?"

"He's dead," said Dri.

The grass crackled. Dri was tolerably sure that it was not supposed to do that. She stood up.

"Rumor hath many tongues," said the voice.

"I know, but I work for the Red Temple and I was told this by my brother, who was in His Eminence's special guard."

The grass around her still crackled. She took a few steps, looking around her. She saw the small trees on the little hill shake, and then all the grass flatten as if a huge invisible beast were striding across the fields from west to east. All the grass within her view lay down. Dri sat down on the path herself, feeling it prudent, and just as she did so, a wall of air pushed her backward. She lay there for some time after it had passed, because it smelled of home. Not the dry grass, warm earth, leaf-mold smell of the plains, but wet stone, cold metal, hot oil and spices, roasted potatoes and roasted nuts, flowers grown out of season and put out in their pots on warm days, even a faint whiff of sewage unmodified by the application of luck—all flowed over her and lingered in the air when it was still again.

In time, the smell of home wore thin and vanished. Dri sat up, and stood up, and stood still. Everything was the same, and not the same. She turned slowly in a circle. The orchard, the onion garden, the small hill with oak trees and the mass of trees that marked the strange low farmhouse were all there. They looked the wrong color. She took a step or two, and a mouse ran across the packed dirt in front of her. Two more followed it, and another. Dri went on cautiously, wishing for her cat. She called him, but he did not appear.

Before she reached the house, she had seen several more dark-colored mouselike animals with short tails, several rabbits in several sizes, something that might have been a rat, and a smooth brown blunt-headed animal larger than a cat.

The house, like the landscape, looked as if some sparkle had gone from it, although it was basking in early sunshine.

Inside, it felt stuffy. Dri went into the kitchen. Everyone was there, sitting around the big table peeling apples. They looked as they often had before, and yet they did not. Dri slid into her assigned seat. Wari passed her a knife and bowl. They knew that she did not have the knack of peeling apples, but some feeling of invisible pressure in the air made her forbear to speak. This sensation of having inquiry stifled was much harder to bear after the free speaking in the orchard.

She made a slow careful start on the nearest apple, but had to stop. The atmosphere was so strong that she felt she must keep a close eye on everyone. Kiffen looked as she felt, alert and wary. Mininu and Sinja had serene faces, but they kept exchanging glances. Dri felt that in a more outward family, they would be talking at the tops of their voices and gesturing. All three of their children were watching them, and had a general air of injured virtue.

"Dri," said Sinja, in her usual gentle tones, "I have not seen Golly these two hours."

"He was in the onion beds just now."

Sinja smiled at her, and finished removing the peel from an apple in one long curling piece.

"I hope he hasn't done anything bad," said Dri.

"Not that I know of."

"I could go and fetch him."

"No, I think he will manage on his own."

"There was a very large wind just now," said Dri. When nobody made any reply, she pulled in the air for the enormous effort necessary and asked, "Did you feel it?"

"This is a very windy place," said Mininu.

If Sinja had said that, Dri might, she thought, have had the courage to describe the wind and how it was different from the ordinary wind of the plains; but Mininu was truly formidable, all without even raising her voice.

That was the most conversation they had all day. Dri had thought it a house devoid of conversation already, but that day even the nods and raised eyebrows and smiles and half sentences were absent. The faint pressure she had always felt, oppressing her desire to ask a thousand questions, to question every statement, and to dissect every definition, had grown heavier and firmer, and sat on her chest like an older brother in an evil mood.

When Dri went to take her bath, the tub was full of spiders and there was a mouse on the windowsill. She backed out slowly. Not much later she heard Numa cry from the big room, "Min, Min, there is a snake in my chair!" Mininu came striding past Dri and toward the big room, but no other words passed.

Dri sank down on her bed, checking it for previous occupants first, and marveled at a family that could be silent in the face of this invasion. After she had marveled, she felt grateful. Her conscience was not easy. Mininu had asked her not to tell anyone about Resh's death, and she had blurted it out the first chance she got. Whether a disembodied voice could be defined as "anyone" might be open to debate, if anybody ever would debate in this house, but she still was not easy. If the exiled Liavekan spirits had kept the spiders and other creatures away, and if they had gone back to the City on hearing that Resh was dead, the invasion of all the vermin was Dri's doing.

COUSINS

She wanted to lie down and take a nap, but somebody might think to ask her some pointed questions at any moment. Without thinking much about it, she climbed out of the window and went away toward the hill with the small oak trees atop it. There were piles of last year's leaves there, nicely dry by now. She could sleep and return to the house with more of her wits in working order.

It was a still day with no wind, but Dri kept hearing sounds anyway, rustlings and scrapings and slidings. She supposed the grass was full of spiders and mice and snakes now, just like the house. This made her think twice about curling up in a pile of leaves. When she got to the top of the hill she perched herself on a protruding boulder and tried to examine her intended bed from a safe distance. She was distracted from this pursuit by the sight of Sinja, Mininu, Kiffen, all the cousins, a flock of chickens, and some five or six goats, who were all gathered at the back of the house. Mininu was talking vigorously. Everyone looked very solemn, even the chickens. After Mininu had spoken, Sinja sang a song that sounded Ombayan, and then Mininu sang a song that Dri recognized. She could not make out the words, but the tune was that of "Potboil Blues," which Mininu had once irritably referred to as "that all-too-typically-Liavekan catch." Dri was afflicted with a desire to giggle.

A striped snake slid across the rock at her feet, which was not so funny. She watched the group near the house narrowly. If they went far enough off, perhaps she could sneak back in and sleep in her bed. A bed seemed unlikely to hold as many snakes as a pile of leaves, so she had better settle for that.

With luck, whatever they were doing would send the snakes and other creatures back to where they had been before, before, before Dri had told the exiled Liavekan voices the secret that Resh was dead. If others undid the results of one's choice, how did that affect the figures striving to keep one's self upright?

The party below was marching around the house rightward, scattering clouds of yellowish matter, except for the chickens and goats, who were eating it. Therefore, it must be grain. Numa had a shining object in her hand and might have been pouring water from it.

"Oh no," said Dri. Perhaps it was not her speaking to spirits, but her going about the house pouring water, that had let all the creatures arrive. Even ordinary Plains water. Perhaps it was both. She could not unpour water, she could not unspeak secrets. As Atliae had taught her, the only way was forward.

"I hope you are here," she said firmly. "Spirits of my city, I hope that you are." She was being as foolish as the people below, but at least nobody could see her.

"They are all gone into the world of stone," said a furrier, cracklier voice. Dri's breath unlocked. She could speak in her native language. I must be careful, she thought. She said, "Do you mean the City?"

"Verily."

"Oh, but the City isn't only stone. It's wood and tile and water and grass and trees and what it really is, is people."

"Do you taste and smell stone when it is by, does it dazzle your eyes and befuddle your mind?"

Dri, sorting swiftly through a number of remarks about jewels and avarice, finally answered, "Not entirely."

"To us, the City is the world of stone."

"I'm sitting on a stone."

"You appear as a voice from a burning light."

Dri got up and moved carefully to her left, since she thought that the voice might be more leftward than not.

"What am I now?" she asked.

"A voice in the quiet air."

"Who are you? Can I see you?"

"We are before you in the air."

"I guess I can't," said Dri, staring before her. She saw only the air, just as they did when they looked at her. She spared a glance for the group down at the house. They were now hidden by the windbreak, but she could hear them singing something.

"But who are you?" she repeated firmly.

"If you cannot see us, you will not hear our names."

"What do you do?"

"What we are bid."

"Really!" said Dri, entertained. "I know a great many parents who would trade their children for you."

Several laughs overlapped in the empty air. The same voice said, "That is not bidding as we mean it."

"Do you mean luck, magical bidding?"

"No, luck has no power over us."

"Really!" said Dri. She felt warmed, released, returned to herself. All the questions she had suppressed since she arrived, in the shut-door pressure of that house below, seemed to make a pressure of their own in her heart, pushing these new questions before them. "What about the Twin Forces?" she said. "Do they have power over you?"

"Power over us is held by water, word, and will."

Dri looked again at the house. The group of people and animals had come around to where they started, and Mininu was speaking again.

"Is that what they are doing down there? Getting power over you?"

The several laughs came again. Dri wondered how she knew it was laughter. It was more like, like, she was not sure what. But she felt laughter. The voice said, "They do not know us. They seek those who have fled."

"The city spirits?"

"Our cousins of the stone, indeed."

Dri swallowed hard. "Why did your cousins leave?"

"That which drove them out has in its turn been driven."

"Oh," said Dri.

To speak to the voices of the air had been an action like breathing, an unconsidered choice. But Atliae might say that it should have been considered more than it was. She was glad that Atliae was far away. She wished that she knew of a way to tell whether one of the striving figures in herself was about to hook the feet from under the other. What would it feel like? She felt more herself than she had since they left Liavek. Perhaps some previous choice had made her totter and now she had restored herself. Would Atliae know? Dri did not know what she thought.

"What did they do, your cousins," she asked, "when they were here?"

"All tasks of ours; to guide the grain, to guard the house from moth and mold and the garden from mouse and mold and moth, to guard all things and yet harm none."

"Is that really possible?"

"If we are well bid."

"But they didn't bid you, they bid your cousins from the City?"

"Their bidding is too—sly."

"Oh!" cried Dri, and clapped her hands. "It is, it is, it truly is! They say that they hope you have an occupation when they want you not to be lazy, they, they, oh, yes, *sly* is a grand word!"

"They have need of us now," said the voice, "but they know not how to make us love them."

Dri sobered at once. "Why don't they, do you suppose?"

"They do not know that they have the need; even knowing, their way is not our way."

"Is that the Ombayan way?"

"We have toiled and created for Ombayans who were not sly, but there are many Ombayan ways. What would you call a Liavekan way? Our cousins of the City were as sly as yours of the plains."

"Things are always more complicated than you believe they are," agreed Dri.

"Unless they are simpler."

"Do you think we never see things truly, then?"

"We do not know. When we say 'we,' we have not been accustomed to think of the creatures of the earth in that wind. And yet you speak as properly as could be wished."

"Not if you ask Mininu," said Dri.

"It is she who must ask us."

Dri sat down on a fallen branch, staring down at the antics of her family and the animals. She no longer wanted to laugh. Their way was not her way, but she could tell well enough from her week's stay that they were happy in it. It had fed and clothed them, and had put horrid goat cheese and disgusting chicken eggs in the market for people who liked them; it had tended apple trees and barley fields; it had put that now missing sparkle in the landscape. She had wrecked it. However her interior structure might feel, it was necessary to restore the wreckage. She wondered what Atliae would say, but, as with tending to the kittens, what Atliae would say did not matter. Dri rubbed her tired eyes and firmly addressed the air.

"Do you live here, on their—on this land that they live on?"

"We do, and have always."

"Do you like your tasks, when you are well bidden; do they please you and feed you, and make things beautiful?"

"They do, and have always."

"You can't have had a very happy time of it, can you, while your cousins were here," said Dri.

"We cannot."

"Tell me, then," said Dri, "who is it that may bid you well?"

Before she went down the hill and back to the house, she scuffed thoroughly through the brown tea-smelling oak leaves that she had thought to take a nap in. On the bare earth thus revealed she saw a few affronted worms and some hastily retreating roundbugs, just as she might find in her father's garden at home. Those would be good for growing things, she supposed. There were no snakes or mice.

"Thank you," she said to the air, not for the first time, but she had no reply. Her companions were busy.

Dri started down the path with a sigh. If she were behaving in Mininu's way, she would need to say nothing of what had passed. But since she must behave in her own way to restore what she had damaged, she must tell Mininu everything. Now that order was restored, she could only feel chastened for a few moments before she wanted, once again, to laugh. Mininu would be able to do as she liked, as she always did, in her household, but to conciliate the resident spirits of the air, she would have to ask questions and make statements and even, from time to time, to argue. "I am in such a great leafpile of trouble," she said, having gotten used to talking to the air in the past few hours. "I wonder what they will do to me."

Perhaps they would send her home.

She smiled at the thought, and then stopped smiling. Perhaps they would call her back once every year, to speak as Mininu would not, and eat fat cheese except on Raindays.

Golly came trotting out of the tall grass with a mouse in his mouth.

"That will be the last of those you see hereabouts," Dri told him.

But perhaps they would send her home first.

PAMELA DEAN is the author of six fantasy novels and a handful of short stories; five of the stories are set in the same world as "Cousins."

Firebird has reissued her Secret Country Trilogy (*The Secret Country*, *The Hidden Land*, and *The Whim of the Dragon*) and *Tam Lin*; a reissue of *The Dubious Hills* is forthcoming. She is currently working on *Going North*, a sequel to both the Secret Country books and *The Dubious Hills*.

She lives in Minneapolis with some congenial people, a lot of cats, and an overgrown garden. You can find a few photographs, links to interviews with her, a bibliography, and the occasional announcement at **www.dd-b.net/pddb**.

AUTHOR'S NOTE

Sharyn says I should tell you why I wrote this story. There isn't one reason, of course. I wrote it because she asked me to; and because I loved the first *Firebirds* anthology and wanted to be in such good company. But the reason that those other reasons could be gratified is that Kisandrion, my protagonist, had a story in her. She and her family come from a novel I'm writing. It's set in a shared world called Liavek, about which five volumes of stories were published in the 1980s. The other characters in that novel are people I've written about before, but she was new, and she had a lot of opinions. The novel is mostly about other people, so that her opinions about family and food and how to conduct a conversation, about religion and how one chooses right actions, did not have very much room to grow. I wanted to give her a landscape to try her thoughts out on. I also wanted to write a story that did not have certain usual complications, so that other complications caused by Kisandrion's opinions could also have room. I wanted the story to have no romantic element and not much darkness in it. When I began to write, I thought that when Kisandrion got to the country she would learn to garden. I had no notion at all that she would talk to the air, or what would happen when she did.

Emma Bull

What Used to Be Good Still Is

Porphyry is a volcanic rock. Maybe that's why it happened. Maybe it was because the hill that became a pit was named Guadalupe, for the Virgin of Guadalupe, who appeared in a vision to a Mexican peasant a long time ago. Maybe it's because walls change whatever they enclose, and whatever they leave out.

And maybe it could have happened anywhere, anytime. But I don't believe that for a second.

I expect I wouldn't have taken too much notice of Sara Gutierrez if my pop hadn't. I was a senior at Hollier High School, varsity football first string, debating team, science club. Sara was the eighth-grade sister of Alfred Gutierrez, who I knew from football. But the Gutierrezes lived in South Hollier, down the slope from the Dimas shaft, on the other side of Guadalupe Hill, and we lived on Collar Hill above downtown with the lawyers and store owners and bankers. Alfred and I didn't see much of each other outside of football practice. The only time my father saw Alfred's father was when Enrique Gutierrez had his annual physical at the company hospital, or if he got hurt on the job and Pop had to stitch him up.

But one night I was up studying and heard Pop in the kitchen say, "I don't know if that youngest Gutierrez girl is simple or plain brilliant."

Pop didn't talk about patients at home as a rule, so that was interesting enough to make me prick up my ears.

"Probably somewhere in between, like most," Mom said. Mom didn't impress easily.

"She came into the infirmary today with her chest sounding like a teakettle on the boil. If I can keep that child from dying of pneumonia or TB, I'll change my name to Albert Schweitzer." He paused, and I knew Mom was waiting for him to come back from wherever that thought had led him. She and I were used to Pop's parentheses. "Anyway, while I'm writing up her prescription, she says, 'Dr. Ryan, what makes a finch?'"

"I don't suppose you told her, 'God,'" Mom said with a sigh.

"I didn't know what to say. But when she saw I didn't get her drift, she asked why are house finches and those little African finches that Binnie Schwartz keeps in her parlor both finches? So I started to tell her about zoological taxonomy—"

"I just bet you did," Mom said. I could hear her smiling.

"Now, Jule—"

"Go on, go on. I won't get any peace till you do."

"Well, then she said, 'But the finches don't think so. We're human beings because we say we are. But the finches don't think they're all finches. Shouldn't that make a difference?'"

A pause, and the sound of dishes clattering in the wash water. "Sara Gutierrez spends too much time on her own," Mom said. "Invalids always think too much."

I don't remember what Pop replied to that. Probably he argued; Pop argued with any sentence that contained the word *always*.

By the time I came home for the summer after my first year of college, the matter was settled: Sara Gutierrez was bright. She'd missed nearly half her freshman year in high school what with being out sick, but was still top of her class. Pop bragged about her as if he'd made her himself.

She was thin and small and kind of yellowish, and you'd hardly notice if she was in the same room with you. The other girls in town got permanent waves to look like Bette Davis. Sara still looked like Louise Brooks, her hair short, no curl at all. But that summer I saw her at the ballpark during one of the baseball games. She looked straight at me in the stands. There was something in her eyes so big, so heavy, so hard to hang on to that it seemed like her body would break from trying to carry it.

Nobody ever suggested that Sara was bright at anything likely to be of use to her. A long while later I looked her up in the *Hollier Hoist*, the high school yearbook, to see what her classmates must have made of her. She'd been a library monitor. That was all. No drama society, no debating team, no booster club, no decorating committee for the homecoming dance.

I guess she saved her debating for me. And she danced, all right, but you won't find that in the yearbooks.

WHAT USED TO BE GOOD STILL IS

Hollier was a mining town—founded in the 1880s by miners and speculators. The whole point of life here was to dig copper out of the ground as cheap as possible, and hope that when you got it to the surface you could sell it for a price that made the work worthwhile. The town balanced on a knife edge, with the price of copper on one side, and the cost of mining it on the other.

And that didn't apply only to the miners and foremen and company management. If copper did poorly, so did the grocers, mechanics, lawyers, and schoolteachers. What came up out of those shafts fed and clothed us all. Pop was a company doctor. Without copper, there was no company, no one to doctor, no dinner on the table, no money for movies on Saturday, no college tuition. He used to say that Hollier was a lifeboat, with all of us rowing for a shore we couldn't see. The company was the captain, and we trusted that the captain had a working compass and knew how to read it.

Underground mining's expensive. The shafts went deeper and deeper under the mountains following the veins of high-grade ore, the pumps ran night and day to pump out the water that tried to fill those shafts, and the men who dug and drilled and blasted had to be paid. But near the surface, under what farmers call dirt and miners call "overburden," around where the rich veins used to run, there was plenty of low-grade ore. Though it didn't have as much copper in it, it could be scraped right off the surface. No tunnels, no pumps, and a hell of a lot fewer men to pay.

Guadalupe Hill was a fine cone-shaped repository of low-grade ore.

The summer after my sophomore year at college, I came home to find the steam shovels scooping the top off Guadalupe Hill. You could see the work from the parlor windows on Collar Hill, hear the roar and crash of it funneled up the canyon from the other side of downtown. Almost the first thing I heard when I got off the train at the depot was the warning siren for a blast, and the dynamite going off like a giant bass drum. From the platform I could see the dust go up in a thundercloud; then the machinery moved in like retrievers after a shot bird.

As Pop helped me stow my suitcase in the trunk of the Hudson, I said, "I'd sure like to watch that," and jerked my head at Guadalupe Hill.

"I'd take you over now, but your mother would fry me for supper."

"Oh, I didn't mean before I went home." I would have meant it, but I knew he'd be disappointed in me if I couldn't put Mom before mining.

Once I'd dropped my suitcase in my room and given Mom a kiss and let her say I looked too thin and didn't they feed me in that frat house dining room, Pop took me down to watch the dig.

It was the biggest work I'd ever seen human beings do. Oh, there'd been millions of dollars of copper ore taken out of the shafts in Hollier. Everyone in town knew there were a thousand miles of shafts, and could recite how many men the company employed; but you couldn't *see* it. Now here was Guadalupe Hill crawling with steam shovels and dump trucks, men shouting, steam screeching, whistles, bells. It went as smooth and precise as a ballet troupe, even when it looked and sounded like the mouth of hell.

And the crazy ambition of the thing! Some set of madmen had wanted to turn what most folks would have called a mountain inside out, turn it into a hole as deep and as wide as the mountain was tall. And another set of madmen had said, "Sure, we can do that."

Later I wasn't surprised when people said, "Let's go to the moon," because I'd seen the digging of Guadalupe Pit. It was like watching the building of the Pyramids.

Pop stopped to talk to the shift boss. Next to that big man, brown with sun and streaked with dust, confident and booming and pointing with his square, hard hands, Pop looked small and white and helpless. He was a good doctor, maybe even a great one. His example had me pointed toward pre-med, and medical school at Harvard or Stanford if I could get in. But looking from him to the shift boss to the roaring steam shovels, I felt something in me slip. I wanted to do something big, something that people would see and marvel at. I wanted people to look on my work and see progress and prosperity and stand in awe of the power of Man.

Over dinner, I said, "It makes you feel as if you can do anything, watching that."

"You can, if you have enough dynamite and a steam shovel," Pop agreed as he reached for a pork chop.

"No, really! We're not just living on the planet like fleas on a dog anymore. We're changing it to suit us. Like sculptors. Like—"

"God?" Mom said, even though I'd stopped myself.

"Of course not, Mom." But I'd thought it, and she knew it. She also knew I was a college boy and consequently thought I was wiser than Solomon.

Conversation touched on the basketball team and the repainting of the Women's Club before I said carefully, "I've been wondering if I'm cut out for med school."

Guess I wasn't careful enough; Pop gave me a look over his plate that suggested he was onto me. "Not everyone is."

"I don't want to let you down."

"You know we'll be proud of you no matter what," Mom replied, sounding offended that she had to tell me such a thing.

"I'm thinking of transferring to the Colorado School of Mines."

"Might need some scholarship money—being out of state," said Pop. "But your grades are good. The company might help out, too." He passed me the mashed potatoes. "You don't have to be a doctor just because I am."

"Of course not." I needed to hear him say so, though.

We sat in the parlor after dinner. Pop got his pipe going before he said, "The Gutierrez family isn't doing so well. Tool nippers got laid off at the Dimas shaft, and Enrique with 'em. I think it hit Sara hard."

At first I thought he was talking about Mrs. Gutierrez; I don't know that I'd ever heard her first name. Then I remembered Sara.

"You might take the time for a chat if you see her." He took his pipe out of his mouth and peered at it as if it were a mystery. "She asks about you."

If there's a young fellow who can remain unmoved by the knowledge that a girl asks about him, I haven't met him.

Sara was working in the Hollier Library for the summer. I found an excuse to drop in first thing next day. I came up to the desk and called to the girl on the other side who was shelving reserved books, "Is Sara Gutierrez working today?"

Of course it was her. When I look back on it, it seems like the most natural thing in the world that the girl would straighten up and turn round, and there she'd be. Her hair still wasn't waved, and she wasn't pink and white like a girl in a soap ad. But she wasn't thin anymore, either. Her eyes were big and dark under straight black brows, and she looked at me as if she were taking me apart to see what I was made of. Then she said, without a hint of a smile, "She'd better be, or this whole place'll go to the dickens."

I'd planned to say hello, pass the time of day for a few minutes. But a little fizz went up my backbone, and I heard myself say, "Must be awful hard for her to get time off for lunch."

"She'd probably sneak out if someone made her a decent offer."

"Will the lunch counter at the drugstore do?"

Sara looked at me through her eyelashes. "Golly, Mr. Ryan, you sweet-talked me into it."

"I'll come by for you at the noon whistle."

She had grilled cheese and a chocolate phosphate. Funny the things you remember. And she said the damnedest things without once cracking a smile, until I told her about my fraternity initiation and made her laugh so hard she skidded off her stool. By the time I asked for the check, I'd gotten a good notion of how to tell when she was joking. And I'd asked her to go to the movies the next night, and she'd said yes.

I picked her up for the movie outside the library, and when it was over, I proceeded to drive her home. But at the turn-off for the road to South Hollier, she said, "I can walk from here."

I turned onto the road. "Not in the dark. What if you tripped in a hole, or met up with a javelina—"

"I'd rather walk," she said, her voice tight and small.

I didn't think I'd said or done anything to make her mad. "Now, don't be silly." I remembered Pop saying that Sara seemed to take her father's layoff hard. Was that what this was about?

"Really—" she began.

In the headlights and the moonlight I could see two tall ridges of dirt and rock crossways to the road on either side, as if threatening to pinch it between them. Two corrugated iron culvert pipes, each as big around as a truck, loomed in the scrub at the roadside.

"Where'd that come from?"

She didn't answer. The Hudson passed between the ridges of dirt, and I could see the lights of the houses of South Hollier in front of me. I pulled over.

"Are they building something here?" I asked.

Sara sat in the passenger seat with her hands clenched in her lap and her face set, looking out the windshield. "It's Guadalupe Hill," she said at last.

"What?"

"They have to put it someplace. The tailings will make a

new line of hills around South Hollier on the east and south."

I tried to imagine it. North and west, the neighborhood ran right up to the mountain slopes. This would turn South Hollier into the bottom of a bowl with an old mountain range on two sides and a new one on the others.

"What about the road?"

"That's what the pipes are for."

"You mean you'll drive through the pipe, like a tunnel?"

"One for each direction," she answered.

"Well, I'll be darned." The more I thought about it, the cleverer it was. Wasn't it just like mining engineers to figure out a way to put a tailings dump where it had to go without interfering with the neighborhood traffic?

Sara shook her head and pleated her skirt between her fingers. I put the Hudson into gear and drove down the road into South Hollier.

At her door, I asked, "Can I see you again?"

She looked up into my face, with that taking-me-apart expression. At last she said, "'May I.' College man."

"May I?"

"Oh, all right." Her eyes narrowed when she was teasing. Before I knew what had happened, she was on the other side of her screen door. Based on her technique, I was not the first young man to bring her home. "Good night, Jimmy."

I drove back to Collar Hill with vague but pleasant plans for the summer.

She met me for lunch a couple times a week, and sometimes she'd let me go with her and carry her packages when she had errands to the Mercantile or the Fair Store. Once she wanted sheet music from the Music Box, and she let me talk her into a piano arrangement of a boogie-woogie song I'd heard at a college party.

"Should I hide it from my mama?" she asked, with her eyes narrowed.

"I'll bet she snuck out to the ragtime dances."

"Oh, not a good Catholic girl like my mama."

"Mine's a good Catholic girl, too, and she did it."

Sara smiled, just the tiniest little smile, looking down at the music. For some reason, that smile made my face hot as a griddle.

Sara wouldn't go to a movie again, though, or the town chorus concert or the Knights of Columbus dance. I asked her to the Fourth of July fireworks, but she said she was going with her family.

"I'll look for you," I said, and she shrugged and hurried away.

The fireworks were set off at the far end of Panorama Park, down in the newer neighborhood of Wilson, where the company managers lived. Folks tended to spread their picnic blankets in the same spot every year. The park divided into nations, too, like much of Hollier. A lot of the Czech and Serbian families picnicked together, and the Italians, and the Cornishmen; the Mexicans set up down by the rose garden, at the edge of the sycamores. The Gutierrez family would be there.

I got to the park at twilight, and after saying hello to a few old friends from high school, and friends of Mom and Pop's, I pressed through the crowd and the smells from all those picnic dinners. When I got to the rose garden it was almost dark, but I found Alfred Gutierrez without too much trouble.

"You looking for Sara?" he said, with a little grin.

"I told her I'd come round and say hi." I was above responding to that grin.

"She's around here someplace. *Hola, Mamá,*" he called over his shoulder, "where'd Sara go?"

Mrs. Gutierrez was putting the remains of their picnic away. She looked up and smiled when she saw me. "Hello, Jimmy. How's your mama and papa?"

"They're fine. I just wanted to say hello . . . "

Mrs. Gutierrez nodded over her picnic basket. "Sara said she had to talk to someone."

Was it me? Was she looking for me, out there in the night, while I looked for her? There was a bang—the first of the fireworks. "Will you tell her I was here?"

Alfred grinned again, and Mrs. Gutierrez looked patient in the blue light of the starburst.

I watched the fireworks, but I didn't get much out of them. Was Sara avoiding me? Why wouldn't she see me except when she was downtown, in the daytime, but never the evenings? Could it be she was ashamed of her family, so she wouldn't let me pick her up at home? The Gutierrez family wasn't rich, but neither were we. No, it had to be something about me.

It wasn't as if we were sweethearts; we were just friends. I'd go back to college in September, she'd stay here, and we'd probably forget all about each other. We were just having fun, passing the time. She was too young for me to be serious about, anyway. So why was she giving me the runaround?

By the time the finale erupted in fountains and pinwheels, I'd decided two could play that game. I'd find myself some other way to pass the time for the next couple months, and it wouldn't be hard to do either.

That was when I saw her, carried along with the slow movement of people out of the park, her white summer dress reflecting the moon and the streetlights. She was holding someone's little girl by the hand and trying to get her to walk, but the kid had reached that stage of tired in which nothing sounded good to her.

"Hi, Sara."

"Jimmy! I didn't see you there."

I wanted to say something sophisticated and bitter like, "I'm sure you didn't," but I remembered that I'd resolved to be cool and distant. That's when the little girl burst into noisy, angry tears.

"Margie, *Margarita,* I *can't* carry you. You're a big girl. Won't you please—"

I scooped the kid up so quickly that it shocked the tears out of her. "A big girl needs a bigger horse than Sara," I told her, and settled her on my shoulders, piggyback fashion.

We squeezed through the crowd without speaking until we got to Margie's family's pickup truck. The Gutierrez family was riding with them, and I had to see Alfred smirk at me again. Folks started to settle into the back of the truck on their picnic blankets. Something about Sara's straight back and closed-up face, and the fact that she was still not talking, made me say, "Looks kind of crowded. I've got my pop's car here . . . "

Mrs. Gutierrez looked distracted and waved her hands over picnic basket, blankets, sleeping kids, and folded-up adults. "Would you—? Sara, you go with Jimmy. I don't know how . . . " With that, she went back to, I think, trying to figure out how they'd all come in the truck in the first place.

Sara turned to me, her eyes big and sort of wounded. "If you don't mind," she mumbled.

We were in the front seat of the Hudson before I remembered my grievance. "Now look, Sara, you've been dodging me—"

She was startled. "Oh, no—"

"I just want to say you don't have to. We've had some fun, but if you think I'm going to go too far or make a pest of myself or hang on you like a stray dog—"

The force of her head shaking stopped me. "No, really, I don't."

"What's up with you, then? We're just friends, aren't we?"

Sara looked at her knees for a long time, and I wondered if I'd said something wrong. "That's so," she said finally. "We are."

She sounded as if she were deciding on something, planting her feet and refusing to be swayed. I'd only started on my list of grievances, but her tone made me lose my place in the list. "I guess I'll take you home, then."

We talked about fireworks as I drove: which we liked best, how we'd loved the lights and colors but hated the bang when we were kids, things we remembered from past July Fourths in the park. But as I turned down her road and headed toward South Hollier, Sara's voice trailed off. At the tailings ridge, I stopped the car.

"Darn it, Sara, why should I care where you live? Is that what this is about, why you go all stiff and funny?"

She stared at me, baffled-looking. "No. No, it's that . . . " She reached for the door handle. "Come with me, will you, Jimmy?"

In the glare of the headlights, she picked her way up to the foot of the tailings. I was ready to grab her elbow if she stepped wrong; the ground was covered with debris rolled down from the ridge top, rocks of all sizes that seemed to want to shift away under my feet or turn just enough to twist my ankle. But she went slow but steady over the mess as if she'd found a path to follow.

She stopped and tipped her head back. The stars showed over the black edge of the tailings, and I thought that was what she was looking at. "Can you tell?" she asked.

"Tell what?"

Sara looked down at her feet for the first time since she got out of the car, then at the ridge, and finally at me. "It doesn't want to be here."

"What doesn't?"

"The mountain. Look, it's lying all broken and upside down—overburden on the bottom instead of the top, then the stone that's never been in sunlight before. It's unhappy, and now it'll be a whole unhappy ring around South Hollier." She turned, and I saw two tears spill out of her eyes. "We've always been happy here before."

For an instant I thought she was crazy; I was a little afraid of her. Then I realized she was being poetic. Pop had said her dad's layoff had hit her hard. She was just using the tailings as a symbol for what had changed.

"You'll be happy again," I told her. "This won't last, you'll see."

She looked blank. Then she reached out toward the slope as if she wanted to pat it. "This will last. I want to fix it, and there's nothing . . ." She swallowed loudly and turned her face away.

I couldn't think of a way to fix things for her, and I didn't want to say anything about her crying. So I turned back to the tailings ridge, textured like some wild fabric in the headlights. "That gray rock is porphyry, did you know?"

"Of course I do." The ghost of her old pepper was in that. I suppose it was a silly question to ask a miner's daughter.

"Well, do you know it's the insides of a volcano?"

She looked over her shoulder and frowned.

"The insides of a want-to-be volcano, anyway," I went on. "The granite liquefies in the heat and pushes up, but it never makes it out the top. So nobody knows it's a volcano, because it never erupted."

Sara had stopped frowning as I spoke. Now she turned back to the tailings with an expression I couldn't figure out. "It wanted to be a volcano," she murmured.

I didn't know what else to say, and she didn't seem to need to say anything more. "I ought to get you home," I said finally. "Your mom will be wondering."

When we stopped in front of her house, Sara turned to me. "I only told you that, about the . . . about the mountain, because we're friends. You said so yourself. I wouldn't talk about it to just anybody."

"Guess I won't talk about it at all."

She smiled. "Thank you, Jimmy. For the ride, and everything." She slid out of the passenger side door and ran up to her porch. She ran like a little kid, as if she ran because she could and not because she had to. When she got to the porch she waved.

I waved back even though I knew she couldn't see me.

Mom asked me the next day if I'd drive her up to see her aunt in Tucson. We were halfway there before she said, "Are you still seeing Sara Gutierrez?"

I was about to tell her that I'd seen her the night before, when I realized that wasn't how she meant "seeing." "We're just friends, Mom. She's too young for me to think of that way."

"Does she think so, too?"

I thought about last night's conversation. "Sure, she does."

"I know you wouldn't lead her on on purpose, but it would be a terrible thing to do to her, to make her think you were serious when you aren't."

"Well, she doesn't think so." Mom was just being Mom; no reason to get angry. But I was.

"And it would break your father's heart if you got her in trouble."

"I'm not up to any hanky-panky with Sara Gutierrez, and I'm not going to be. Are you satisfied?"

"Watch your tone, young man. You may be grown up, but I'm still your mother."

I apologized, and did my best to be the perfect son for the rest of the trip. But the suggestion that anyone might think Sara and I would be doing things we'd be ashamed to let other people know about—it hung around like a bad smell, and made me queasy whenever I remembered it.

Did people see me with Sara and think I was sneaking off with her to—My God, even the words, ones I'd used about friends and classmates and strangers, were revolting. Somewhere in Hollier, someone could be saying, "Jimmy Ryan with the youngest Gutierrez girl! Why, he probably dazzled her into letting him do whatever he wanted. And you know he won't think about her for five minutes after he goes back to college."

When Mom and I got back from Tucson, I rang up Sam Koslowsky, who I knew from high school, and proposed a little camping and fishing in the Chiricahuas. He had a week's vacation coming at the garage, so he liked the notion.

For a week, I didn't see Sara, or mention her name, or even think about her, particularly. I hoped she'd gotten used to not seeing me, so when I came back, she wouldn't mind that I stopped asking her out or meeting her for lunch.

It would have been a fine plan, if Mom hadn't wanted me to go down to the library and pick up the Edna Ferber novel she had on reserve. When I saw that the girl at the desk wasn't Sara, I let my breath out in a whoosh, I was so relieved. Maybe relief made me cocky. Whatever it was, I thought it was safe to go upstairs and find a book for myself.

Sara was sitting cross-legged on the floor in front of the geography section, her skirt pulled tight down over her knees to make a hammock for the big book in her lap. She looked up just as I spotted her. "Jimmy, come look at this."

It was as if she hadn't noticed I'd been gone—as if she

hadn't noticed I wasn't there five minutes earlier. She had a wired-up look to her, as if she had things on her mind that didn't leave room for much else, including me. Wasn't that what I'd wanted? Then why was I feeling peeved?

I looked over her shoulder at the book. At the top of the page was a smudgy photograph of Mount Fuji, in Japan. Sara jabbed at the paragraphs below the photo as if she wanted to poke them into some other shape. "Mount Fuji," I said, as if I saw it every day.

"But that's not just the name of the mountain. The mountain's a goddess, or *has* a goddess, I'm not sure which. And her name is Fuji. And look—" Sara flipped pages wildly until she got to one with a turned-down corner (I was shocked—a library assistant folding corners) and another photo. The mountain in this one was sending up blurry dark smoke. "Here, Itza—Itzaccihuatl in Mexico. Itza is sort of a goddess, too. Or anyway, she's a woman who killed herself when she heard her lover died in battle, and became a volcano. And there's a volcano goddess in Hawaii, Pele."

"Sure. All right," I said, since she seemed to want me to say something.

"And there's more than that. Volcanoes seem extra likely to have goddesses, all over the world."

I laughed. "I guess men all over the world have seen women blow their tops."

Instead of laughing, or pretending to be offended, she frowned and shook her head. "There's so much I need to know. Did you want to go to lunch? Because I'm awfully sorry, I just don't have time."

That reminded me that I was annoyed. "I just came to get a book. People do that in libraries." I pulled one down from the shelf above her head and walked off with it. The girl at the desk giggled when she checked it out, and it wasn't until I was outside that I found I was about to read *A Lady's Travels in Burma*. Between that and Mom's Edna Ferber, I figured I was punished enough for being short with Sara.

I waited a week before I stopped by the library again. Again she was too busy for lunch, but as I moved to turn from the desk, she said, "I really am sorry, Jimmy." She didn't look like a girl giving a fellow the brush-off. In fact, something about her eyebrows, the tightness of her lips, made her look a little desperate.

I could be busy, too, I decided, and with better reason. I wrote to the Colorado School of Mines to ask what a transfer required in the way of credits, courses, and tuition. I wrote to some of the company's managers, in town and at the central office, inquiring about scholarship programs for children of employees who wanted to study mining and engineering. I gathered letters of recommendation from teachers, professors, any Pillar of the Community who knew me. Pop helped, and bragged, and monitored my progress as if he'd never had visions of a son following him into medicine.

In mid-August, I got a letter from the School of Mines, conditionally accepting me for the engineering program. All I had to do was complete a couple of courses in the fall term, and I could transfer in January. I took it down to Pop's office as soon as it came, because he was almost as eager as I was.

He was with a patient. I sat in the waiting room for a

few minutes, but I felt silly; waiting rooms are for patients. I ducked into the little room that held Pop's desk and books and smelled like pipe tobacco. The transom over the door between it and the examining room was open, and the first words I heard were from Sara. I should have left, but I didn't think of it.

"See, Margarita? Just a sprain. But don't you go near the tailings again."

"*You* do," said a little voice with a hint of a whine.

"I'm grown up."

"When I'm grown up, can I?"

"Maybe," said Sara, something distant in her voice. "Maybe by then."

"Tailings dumps shift and settle for a while," Pop agreed on the other side of the door. "They're not safe at first for anybody. *Including* grown-ups."

"Have . . . have many people been hurt, in South Hollier?" Sara sounded as if she wanted Pop to think it was a casual question. But I knew her better.

"Some sprains and bruises. Probably some scrapes that I never see, but only minor things. Folks just can't seem to stay off a hill or a high building, whatever you tell 'em. Especially the little ones," Pop added in a new, dopey voice. Margie squealed, as if maybe Pop had tweaked her ear.

I was mostly packed and ready to head back to college when Lucas Petterboro, three years old, wandered away from his yard in South Hollier and out to the new tailings dump. From what could be told after the fact, it seemed he'd caused a little slide clambering up the slope, which had dislodged a much larger rock, which had produced a still larger slide. Searchers found his shoe at the bottom of the raw place in the dump, which gave them an idea where to start digging.

Pop and Mom and I went to the funeral. Pop had delivered Luke. Everyone in South Hollier was there, and so were a lot of other people, mining families, since the Petterboros had been hard-rock miners down the Princess shaft for thirty years. Mom sat beside Mrs. Petterboro at the cemetery and held her hand; Pop talked to Joe Petterboro, and now and then touched him lightly on the shoulder. The pallbearers were South Hollier men: Mr. Dubnik, who'd won the hard-rock drilling contest three years running; Mr. Slater, who ran a little grocery out of the front of his house; Fred Koch, who'd been in my class and who was clerking in a lawyer's office downtown; and Luis Sandoval, the cage operator for the Dimas shaft. It was a small coffin; there was only room for the four of them. The children of South Hollier stood close to their parents, in their Sunday clothes, confused and frightened. Their mothers and fathers held their hands and wore the expression folks get when something that only happens to other people happens to one of their own.

And me? There wasn't a damned thing for me to do.

So when Sara came up to me, her eyes red in a white face, and slipped her hand into mine, I wanted to turn and bawl like a baby on her shoulder. If she'd spoken right away, I would have.

"So," I said at last, harsher than I'd meant to. "Guess that mountain's still unhappy, huh?"

She let go of my hand. "Yes. It is." She pulled her sweater

close around her, though the sun was warm. "It keeps me awake at night. The engineers say the ridge ought to be stable, but there was a slide last week that came within three feet of the Schuellers' back door."

"Too much rain this summer." That made her shrug, which made me look closer at her. "What do you mean, it keeps you awake? Worrying won't help."

Her eyes were big and haunted and shadowed underneath. "I can hear the mountain, Jimmy."

Her mom called Sara's name. Sara shot me a last frightened look and went to her.

I went back to college the day after the funeral. I sat on the train still seeing that look, still hearing Sara say, "I can hear the mountain." I told myself it was poetry again, and banished her voice. But it always came back.

I shut it out with work. By the time the term ended and I packed all my worldly goods on the train for home, I'd gotten top grades in my classes, a scholarship from the company, and an invitation to visit my fraternity's house on the School of Mines campus at my earliest convenience.

I walked in the back door of the house on Collar Hill and smelled pipe tobacco, ginger snaps, and baking potatoes. I saw the kitchen linoleum with the pattern wearing away in the trafficked spots, saw Mom's faded flowered apron and felt her kiss on my cheek. Suddenly I felt safe. That was the first I knew that I hadn't felt safe for a long time, and that the feeling building in me as the train approached Hollier wasn't anticipation, but dread.

"You'll have to go find us a Christmas tree," Mom said to

me over dinner. "Your father's been so busy lately that it's full dark before he gets home."

"And your mom won't let me buy a Christmas tree in the dark anymore," Pop added.

"Oh, the poor spavined thing you brought home that year! You remember, Jimmy?"

It was as if I'd been away for years. I shivered. "Why so busy, Pop?" If it was the tailings, if it was South Hollier . . .

"Mostly a bumper crop of babies—"

"Stephen!" Mom scolded.

"—along with winter colds and pneumonia and the usual accidents. Price of copper is up, the company's taken more men on for all the shifts, and that just naturally increases the number of damned fools who let ore cars run over their feet."

"Right before I left, the Petterboro baby—"

"Lord, yes. Nothing that bad since, thank God."

"Then the tailings are safe?"

Pop cocked his head and frowned. "Unless you run up to the top and jump off. It's true, though, that the South Hollier dump made more trouble in the beginning and less now than any others. I guess they know what they're doing, after all."

The tightness went out of my back. It was all right. Of course Sara hadn't meant it literally, what she'd suggested at the funeral. And now everything was fine.

When I saw Sara on Main Street the next afternoon, on her way to catch the trolley home, I knew that something wasn't fine at all. Her cheeks were hollow, her clothes hung loose on her, and the shadows around her eyes were darker than when I left.

EMMA BULL

"You've been sick again," I said, before I realized how rude it would sound.

"No. Ask your dad." She thumped her knuckles against her chest. "Lungs all clear."

"But—" I couldn't tell her she looked awful; what kind of thing was that to say? "Pop's car's down the block. Can I drive you someplace?"

"I'm just headed home."

"Why, I know right where that is!" I sounded too hearty, but she smiled.

"There's still room, with all that chemistry and geometry in there?"

"The brain swells as it fills up. My hat size gets bigger every year."

"Oh, so it's learning that does that."

When we got to the tailings, I saw that the culvert pipes were in place on the roadway, and the fill crested over them about six feet high. I steered the car into the right-hand pipe. I felt like a bug washed down a drain as the corrugated metal swallowed the car and the light. The engine noise rang back at us from the walls, higher and shrill. I wanted to crouch down, to put the Hudson in reverse, to floor it.

"Looks like they've moved a lot of stone since summer." I watched her out of the corner of my eye as I said it.

She nodded. It wasn't the old nervous silence she used to fall into near the tailings. She wasn't stiff or tense; but there was a settled quality to her silence, a firmness.

"Pop says the dump's quit shifting."

Sara looked at me as we came out of the pipe and into South

Hollier. "That's right." She made it sound like a question.

I didn't know what to answer, so instead I asked, "Is your dad back at work?"

"They brought him on as a mechanic at the pit. He likes it. And it means he'll get his full pension after all."

South Hollier was now enclosed in its bowl, a medieval walled town in the Arizona mountains. It looked constrained, like a fat woman in a girdle. But kids played in front yards, women took wash off their clotheslines, smoke rose from chimneys. Everything was all right.

Except it wasn't. Something was out of whack.

When I pulled up to Sara's front door, I said, "We're still friends?"

She thought about it. I realized I liked that better than if she'd been quick to answer. "We are."

"Then I'll say this, one friend to another. Something's eating you, and it's not good. Tell me. I'll help."

Sara smiled, a slow one that opened up like flower petals. We heard her screen door bang, and looked to see her mom on the front porch.

"Jimmy!" Mrs. Gutierrez called. "Jimmy Ryan, when did you get home? Come in for coffee!"

Sara gave a little laugh. "Don't argue with my mama."

I went in, and got coffee Mexican style, with a little cinnamon, and powdered-sugar-dusted cookies. Mrs. Gutierrez skimmed around her scoured red-and-yellow kitchen like a hummingbird. But here, too, something wasn't right.

Mrs. Gutierrez gave Sara a pile of magazines to take to a neighbor's house. When we heard the screen bang behind her, Mrs. Gutierrez turned to me. "You see how she is?"

"Has she been sick?"

Mrs. Gutierrez twisted the dishrag between her hands, and I was reminded of Sara twisting at her skirt, the first night I'd driven her home. "When . . . At night, late, she goes to bed. She says she's going to bed. But I lie awake in the dark and hear her go out again. It's hours before she comes back."

I felt so light-headed I almost couldn't see. "Is it some boy?" I was scared at how angry I sounded. "Is she—" Everything else stuck in my throat. I had no business being angry. I was furious.

But Mrs. Gutierrez shook her head. "Do you think I would let that go on? Almost I wish it were. Then we'd have shame or a wedding, but not this—this fading away."

It was true. Sara was fading away.

"What can I do?"

"Find out what's happening. Make her stop."

So I began to meet her for lunch. She wasn't too busy anymore, but she was always tired. Still, she smiled at me, the kind of weary, gentle smile that women who work too hard wear, and let me take her to the drugstore lunch counter. I made her eat, which she didn't mind doing, but didn't seem to care much about either.

"Are you going to tell me what's wrong?" I asked every time. And every time, she'd say, "Nothing," and make a joke or turn the subject.

One day—I know the date exactly, December 12—I badgered her again.

"There's nothing wrong, Jimmy. Everything's fine now."

"That sounds like things used to be wrong. What's changed?"

Sara gave a little frustrated shrug that made her collarbone show through her blouse. "You remember I told you we used to be happy? Well, we're happy again. That's all."

"Your mom's not happy."

"Yes, she is—she's just looking for something to be unhappy about. Is that why you're always nagging me? Because she told you to?"

"Well, why shouldn't she? You're skin and bones, she says you don't sleep, you sneak out of the house—"

Sara's face stopped me. It was like stone, except for her eyes, which seemed to scorch my face as she looked at me. "You know what you are, Jimmy Ryan? You're a busybody old woman. Keep your nose out of my business from now on!"

She spun around on her counter stool and plunged out of the drugstore.

By the time I got out to the sidewalk, she was gone. She wasn't at the library, or the high school.

That night I picked at my dinner, until Mom said, "Jimmy, are you sick?"

"I had a big lunch, I guess. Pop, can I borrow the car tonight?"

"Sure. What you got planned?"

I felt terrible as I said, "Supposed to be a meteor shower tonight. I thought I'd drive out past Don Emilio and watch."

This time he didn't give me a look across the table. I almost wished he had.

I drove out the road toward South Hollier at about 9 P.M. I didn't know when the Gutierrez family went to bed, but I didn't want to arrive much past that time, whatever it was. I parked the car off the road just before the culvert-pipe tunnels and walked the rest of the way.

The night was so clear that the starlight was enough to see by. I circled South Hollier, only waking up one dog in the process, until I found a perch where I could see the front and back doors of the Gutierrez house. That put me partway up the lower slopes of the tailings dump. I'd thought there was another house or two between theirs and the dump; had they been torn down to make room?

It got cold, and colder, as I waited. I wished I had a watch with a radium dial. Finally I saw movement; I had to blink and look away to make sure it wasn't just from staring for so long at one spot.

Sara was a pale smudge, standing in her backyard in a light-colored dress, her head tipped back to see the stars, or the ridgetop. She set out to climb the slope.

She wasn't looking for me, and I was wearing a dark wool coat. So I could follow her as she climbed, up and up until she reached the top of the ridge. I had the sense to stay down where I wouldn't show up against the sky.

Sara stood still for a moment, her head down. Then she lifted her face and her arms. She began a shuffling step, rhythmic, sure, as if the loose stones she danced over were a polished wood floor. About every five steps she gave a spring. Sometimes she'd turn in place, or sweep her arms over her head in a wide arc. I followed her as she moved along the ridge, until in one of her turns the starlight fell on her face. It was blank, entranced. Her eyes were open, but not seeing.

I couldn't stand it. "Sara!"

She came back to her own face; I don't know any other way to say it. She came back, stumbled, and stopped. I scrambled up the slope to her, and grabbed her shoulders as she swayed. They were thin as bird bones under my hands.

"Sara, what *is* this? What the hell are you doing out here?" My voice sounded hollow and thin, carried away by the air over the ridge.

"Jimmy? What are you doing here?"

I felt my face burn. The only true answer was "Spying." I felt guilty enough to be angry again. "Trying to find out what you wouldn't tell me. Friends don't lie to each other."

"I haven't . . . I haven't lied to you."

"You said everything was fine!"

She nodded slowly. "It is, now."

"You're sleepwalking on the tailings!"

Her face took on a new sharpness. "You think I'm sleepwalking?"

"What else?"

"Oh, God." She scrubbed at her face with both hands. "Don't you remember, when I told you about Fuji and the others?"

I let go of her shoulders. For the first time I felt, in my palms, the heat of her skin, that radiated through the material of her dress. "This isn't some bunk about the mountain?"

"I had to fix it. There wasn't anybody else who could."

"You're not fixing anything! This is just a pile of rocks that used to be a hill!"

"Jimmy. I *am* the mountain."

She stood so still before me, so straight and solid. And I was cold all the way through, watching the light of the stars waver through the halo of heat around her.

"Sara. Please, this is—Come down from here. Pop will help you—"

Her eyes narrowed, and her head cocked. "Can he dance?"

She was still there, still present in her crazy head. The rush of relief almost knocked me over. What would I have done if she'd been lost—if I'd lost her?

If I'd lost her. Before my eyes I saw two futures stretching out before me. One of them had Sara in it, every day, for every minute. The other . . . The other looked like bare, broken rock that nothing would grow on.

The shock pushed the words out of my mouth. "I love you, Sara."

She shook her head, wide-eyed. "Oh . . . "

"Marry me. I'm going to Colorado next month, you can go with me. You can finish school there—"

Sara was still shaking her head, and now her eyes were full of tears and reflected stars. She reached out a hand, stretching it out as if we were far, far apart. "Oh, Jimmy. I want—Oh, don't you see?"

"Don't you care for me, Sara?"

She gave a terrible wordless cry, as if she were being twisted in invisible hands. "I can't leave!"

"But for you and me—"

"There are more people than just us. They need me."

"Your folks? They've got your brothers. They don't need you the way I do."

"Jimmy, you're not listening. I *can't* leave. I'm the mountain."

Her face wasn't crazy. It was streaked with tears and a deep, adult sorrow, like the saints' statues in St. Patrick's Church. Sara reached out to me the way Mary's statue reached down from her niche over the altar, pity and yearning in the very fingerjoints. I saw the waving heat around her, and the stars in her eyes and her hair.

I stepped back a pace. I couldn't help it.

I saw her heart break. That's the only way I can describe what I watched in her face. But when it was done, what was left in her eyes and her mouth and the way she held her head was strong and certain and brave.

"Good-bye, Jimmy," she said. She turned, sure-footed, and ran like a deer along the tailings ridge into the night.

I think I shouted her name. I know that something set the dogs barking all over South Hollier, and eventually Enrique Gutierrez was shaking me by the shoulders.

When Sara hadn't come home by morning, we called the police. Mr. and Mrs. Gutierrez were afraid she'd broken her leg, or fallen and been knocked out. I couldn't talk about what I was afraid of, so I agreed with them, that that could have happened.

Every able-bodied person in South Hollier joined the search. Everyone thought it would be over in an hour or so. By afternoon the police had brought dogs in, and were looking for fresh slides. They didn't say they were looking for places where the rocks might have engulfed a body.

If she was out there, the dogs would have found her. Still, I had to go down to the station, because I was the last one to see her, because the girl at the lunch counter had heard our fight. And God knows, I must have seemed a little crazy. I told them what I'd seen and what we'd said. I just didn't tell them what I thought had happened.

I didn't transfer to the Colorado School of Mines. Leveling mountains didn't appeal to me anymore. I went back to premed, and started on medical school at the University of Arizona. When Pearl Harbor was bombed, I enlisted, and went to the Pacific as a medic.

After the war, I finished medical school and hired on as a company doctor at the hospital in Hollier. Pop had passed, and Mom was glad to have me nearby. I couldn't live in the house on Collar Hill, though, that looked down the canyon to where Guadalupe Hill had been. I found a little house in South Hollier, small enough for a bachelor to handle.

The Gutierrez house was gone. As the dump grew, it needed a bigger base, and the company bought the house and knocked it down to make room for more rock. Mr. and Mrs. Gutierrez bought a place down at the south end of Wilson, and while they were alive, I used to visit and tell them how their old neighbors were getting on.

I'd lived in South Hollier for a couple of months before I climbed the slope of the tailings one December night and sat in the starlight. I sat for maybe an hour before I felt her beside me. I didn't turn to look.

"The mountain's happy now," I said. My voice cracked a little.

"I'm happy," she said. "Be happy for me, Jimmy."

"Who's going to be happy for me?"

"I'll do that. Maybe someday you will, too."

I shook my head, but it seemed silly to argue with her.

"What used to be good still is," she said. "Remember that." And after a minute, "I take care of everybody, but you most of all."

"I'll die after a while and save you the trouble."

"Not for a long time." There was motion at the corner of my eye, and I felt warm lips against my cheek. "I love you, Jimmy."

Then there was nothing beside me but a gust of cold wind.

I'd watched the mining of Guadalupe Hill, and thought men could do anything, be anything, conquer anything. I'd thought we'd cure cancer any day.

Now Guadalupe Pit is as deep as Guadalupe Hill once was high, and next to it there's a second pit that would hold three Guadalupes. Both pits are shut down, played out. There's no cure for cancer, the AIDS quilt is so big that there's no place large enough to roll the whole thing out at once, and diabetes has gone from a rarity to an epidemic.

But in South Hollier there's a ridge that could have been nothing more than a heap of barren, cast-off rock; and a cluster of buildings that could have slowly emptied and died inside their wall. Instead there's a mountain with a goddess, and a neighborhood that rests safe and happy, as if in her warm cupped hands.

—*For Elise Matthesen, and the necklace of the same title*

EMMA BULL lives in Tucson, Arizona, in the twenty-first century, but is fond of road trips and time travel. She's the author of several fantasy novels, including *War for the Oaks*, *Finder*, *Bone Dance* (Finalist for the Hugo, Nebula, and World Fantasy Awards, and the second-place Philip K. Dick Award novel), and (with Steven Brust) *Freedom and Necessity*. With her husband, Will Shetterly, she edited the Liavek fantasy anthologies (see Pamela Dean's story, "Cousins," for a window into Liavek). She's been in several bands, most recently the Flash Girls. Her cat, Toby, is teaching her to play tag. Her latest novel, *Territory*, has recently been published by Tor Books.

For more information, visit **www.qwertyranch.com**.

AUTHOR'S NOTE

If I were writing a term paper, I'd have to say, "Landscape and history are one of the author's most dependable sources of inspiration." For this story, one inspiration was Bisbee, Arizona, which seems to me to have more story ideas per capita than is reasonable. Bisbee's full of weird magic.

Inspiration was also provided by Elise Matthesen's named necklace, "What Used to Be Good Still Is." For glimpses of Elise's awesome jewelry, check out **www.lioness.net**.

acknowledgments

Note: People have come and gone since this book was originally published in early 2006, but these acknowledgments stay the same. A book is a moment captured in time.

If a book can be compared to a theater production, a list of books like Firebird is basically a continuous repertory season. There are a lot of people behind the scenes who make it happen, and who are never thanked. Let me tell you who they are.

FIREBIRD

The editorial boards, both teen and other

Ginny Schneider was my 2005 summer intern and I wish she could've stayed

PUFFIN

(Note: Firebird is an imprint of Puffin)

Eileen Kreit: Vice President and Publisher

Gerard Mancini and Phil Airoldi: Associate Publisher and Utility Outfielder

Pat Shuldiner and Martin P. Karlow: Copy Editors

Deborah Kaplan, Linda McCarthy, Nick Vitiello, Kristina
Duewell, Jeanine Henderson, Tony Sahara, Jay Cooper
(in absentia), Sam Kim (who typeset this book and
made all of the exhaustive changes), and Christian
Fünfhausen: Art Directors and Designers
Lori Thorn: Creator of the Firebird logo, and designer of
this book's cover
Amy White and Jason Primm: Production
Nally Preseault: Almost everything else

VIKING
(Note: All of the other fantasy and sf books I edit are published
by Viking first)
Regina Hayes: President and Publisher
Gerard Mancini and Laurie Perl: Managing Editorial
Denise Cronin, Nancy Brennan, Kelley McIntyre, Jim
Hoover: Art Directors and Designers
Janet Pascal: Fellow Diana Wynne Jones fan and Executive
Production Editor
Nico Medina: Copyediting

PENGUIN GROUP (USA) INC.
Doug Whiteman: Head of the Children's Group
Mariann Donato: Director of Sales and Marketing
Jackie Engel, Jennifer O'Donohue, Nancy Feldman (in
absentia), Mary Raymond, Annie Naughton, Robyn
Fink, Allan Winebarger, Janet Krug: Sales
Our field and inside sales reps rock the house and
should be worshipped (a special acknowledgment here
to Dave Cudmore and Ron Smith)

Gina Maolucci (in absentia), Emily Romero, Gina Balsano, Katrina Weidknecht, Lucy Del Priore, Lauren Adler, Andrea Cruise, Jess Michaels, Ed Scully, Lara Phan, Kim Chocolaad, Courtney Wood: Marketing

George Schumacher and Camille DeLuca: Contracts

Susan Allison, Ginjer Buchanan, Anne Sowards: Ace Books

Betsy Wollheim, Sheila Gilbert, Debra Euler: DAW

Cindy Spiegel: Riverhead Books

OTHER NICE PEOPLE

Jude Feldman titled this book. She and Alan Beatts are the main people responsible for Borderlands Books in San Francisco (www.borderlands-books.com). Go there and buy things.

I remain amazed by the wholehearted support and friendship offered me by both fans and pros in the genre fiction field. Thanks to everyone who has e-mailed, come up to me at cons, and bought the books. And special thanks to Charles M. Brown and the staff at *Locus*, Ellen Datlow, John Douglas, Jo Fletcher and Simon Spanton, Diana Gill, Gavin Grant and Kelly Link, Anne Lesley Groell, Eileen Gunn, Greg Ketter and Lisa Freitag, Jaime Levine, Elise Matthesen, Shawna McCarthy, Farah Mendlesohn, Jim Minz, Patrick and Teresa Nielsen Hayden, Stella Paskins, Judith Ridge, Bill Schafer, Jonathan Strahan, Rodger Turner, Gordon Van Gelder, Jo and Sasha Walton, Jacob Weisman, and Terri Windling, among many others.

An honored thank you to the Minn-StF people for Minicon.

I want to again acknowledge all of the stellar authors in this book, and their agents.

Our cover artists are fantastic. Special thanks to Cliff Nielsen for another stunning piece of art for this book!

There are so many librarians, educators, and teachers who have gotten behind Firebird, and they all deserve applause.

And of course, I need to mention my father, Frederick November. Not only is he genetically responsible for my reading speed and somewhat bizarre sense of humor and dubious social skill, but he is one of the best people in the entire world. He even laughs at my jokes. Everyone should know someone like him; I get to be related to him!

ABOUT THE EDITOR

SHARYN NOVEMBER was born in New York City, and has stayed close by ever since. She received a B.A. from Sarah Lawrence College, where she studied and wrote poetry; her work has appeared in *Poetry, The North American Review,* and *Shenandoah,* among other magazines, and she received a scholarship to Bread Loaf. She has been editing books for children and teenagers for over fifteen years, and is currently Senior Editor for Viking Children's Books and the Editorial Director of Firebird. Her writing about her work with teenage readers (both online and in person) has been published in *The Horn Book* and *Voice of Youth Advocates.* She has been a board member of USBBY and ALAN, as well as being actively involved in ALA, NCTE, and SFWA. She was named a World Fantasy Award Finalist (Professional Category) in both 2004 and 2005—in 2004 specifically for Firebird, in 2005 for editing.

She has played in a variety of bands (songwriter, lead singer, rhythm guitar), and maintains an extensive personal Web site at **www.sharyn.org**. She is an unrepentant candy eater and caffeine consumer. She divides her time between New York and San Francisco.

The Firebird Web site is at **www.firebirdbooks.com**.